Ebook ISBN 978-1-80280-784-4

Kindle ISBN 978-1-80280-785-1

Audio CD ISBN 978-1-80280-776-9

MP3 CD ISBN 978-1-80280-777-6

Digital audio download ISBN 978-1-80280-779-0

Boldwood Books Ltd
23 Bowerdean Street
London SW6 3TN
www.boldwoodbooks.com

EAGLE OF MERCIA

BOOK 4 THE EAGLE OF MERCIA CHRONICLES

MJ PORTER

B

Boldw**o**od

First published in Great Britain in 2023 by Boldwood Books Ltd.

Copyright © MJ Porter, 2023

Cover Design by Head Design Ltd

Cover Photography: Shutterstock

The moral right of MJ Porter to be identified as the author of this work has been asserted in accordance with the Copyright, Designs and Patents Act 1988.

A CIP catalogue record for this book is available from the British Library.

Paperback ISBN 978-1-80280-782-0

Large Print ISBN 978-1-80280-783-7

Hardback ISBN 978-1-80280-781-3

For my Dad, MC. Thank you for the maps.

MAP OF EARLY ENGLAND

Designed by Flintlock Covers

CAST OF CHARACTERS

Icel, orphaned youth living in Tamworth, his mother was Ceolburh

Brute, Icel's horse

Edwin, Icel's childhood friend, although they have been separated

Cenfrith, Icel's uncle, brother of Ceolburh and one of the Mercian king's warriors, who dies in *Son of Mercia*

Wine, Cenfrith's horse, now Icel's alongside Brute

Wynflæd, an old herbwoman at the Mercian king's court at Tamworth

The Kings of Mercia

Coelwulf, king of Mercia r.821–825 (deposed)
Beornwulf, king of Mercia r.825–826 (killed)
Lady Cynehild, Beornwulf's wife
Wiglaf, king of Mercia r.827–829 (deposed) r.830–
Queen Cynethryth, Wiglaf's wife
Wigmund, Wiglaf's son
Ecgberht, king of Wessex r.802 onwards, r.829 in Mercia

The Ealdormen/Bishops of Mercia
Ælfstan, one of King Wiglaf's supporters, an ally
to Icel
Beornoth, one of King Wiglaf's ealdormen
Muca, one of King Wiglaf's ealdormen
Oswine, an ealdorman who died fighting the East
Anglian king
Sigered, a long-standing ealdorman, who's survived
the troubled years of the 820s
Sigegar, Sigered's grandson
Tidwulf, an old ally of King Wiglaf
Wynfrith, an ealdorman who died fighting the East
Anglian king
Coenwulf, the son of King Coelwulf
Ælflæd, Coenwulf's sister
Æthelweald, bishop of Lichfield
Ceolbeorht, bishop of Londonia

Rulers of other kingdoms
Athelstan, king of the East Angles
Ecgberht, king of Wessex
Lord Æthelwulf – Ecgberht's son, designated king of
Kent by his father after the battle of Ellendun

The Ealdormen of the East Angles
Herefrith
Godwulf, East Anglian warrior

Mercians
Ælfred, ally of Lord Wigmund
Æthelmod, Mercian warrior
Ælfthryth, servant in Tamworth
Berhthelm, Mercian warrior
Cenred, Mercian warrior
Cynath, was the commander of King Beornwulf's warriors
Cuthred, inhabitant of Tamworth
Eadgifu, a woman of Budworth
Eahric, commander of the king's household warriors
Egbert, Mercian warrior allied to Ealdorman Sigered
Eomer, the reeve of Budworth, Icel's inherited estate
Frithwine, young Mercian warrior
Garwulf, young Mercian warrior, now dead
Gaya, previously a slave woman with a talent for healing, now freed
Godeman, Mercian warrior
Heahstan, one of Lord Coenwulf's men
Hunberht, an ally of Lord Wigmund
Kyre, Mercian warrior
Landwine, Mercian warrior

Lyfing, Mercian offering shelter to Lady Ælflæd
and Icel
Maneca, Mercian warrior
Ordlaf, Mercian warrior
Osmod, Mercian warrior
Oswald, at Kingsholm
Oswy, one of Wiglaf's warriors
Theodore, previously a slave man with a talent for
healing, now freed
Uor, Mercian warrior
Waldhere, Mercian warrior
Wicga, ally of Lord Wigmund
Wulfgar, Mercian warrior
Wulfheard, a Mercian warrior, Ealdorman Ælfstan's
oath-sworn man
Bada, Wulfheard's horse

Places mentioned

Bardney, a Mercian royal site

Icknield Way, running from Thetford in the kingdom of the East Angles to Londonia

Kingsholm, associated with the ruling family of King Coelwulf, close to Gloucester, home to Lord Coenwulf

Isle of Sheppey, off the coast of Kent

Lichfield, close to Tamworth and one of the holy sites in Mercia

Londonia, combining the ruins of Roman Londinium and Saxon Lundenwic

Peterborough, the site of a monastery in Mercia

Tamworth, the capital of the Mercian kingdom

Kingdom of the East Angles, part of Mercia at the end of the 700s but reclaimed its freedom under King Athelstan of the East Angles, the king-slayer

Kingdom of Wessex, the area south of the River Thames, including Kent at this time, but not Dumnonia (Cornwall and Devon)

THE STORY SO FAR

The kingdoms of the East Angles and Mercia have forged an uneasy alliance to fight the Viking raiders harassing the waterways that run through that of the East Angles and into Mercia. In the meantime, the Wessex king is licking his wounds following the defeat outside Londonia. But troubled times are coming, and Icel, still unaware of his heritage, has been found by Godwulf, an East Anglian warrior who knew his uncle. Godwulf is determined that Icel should pursue his birthright, no matter the obstacles it will cause Icel with the Mercian ruling family and the men of King Wiglaf's household warriors. Icel is an acknowledged member of Lord Ælfstan's warrior band and is eager to remain there.

THE MERCIAN REGISTER

AD831

In this year, King Wiglaf and King Athelstan forged an alliance against the Viking raiders ravaging the kingdom of the East Angles and swore with oaths to always be allies. King Ecgberht of Wessex took to his own kingdom.

1

AD831

Budworth, the kingdom of Mercia

'I don't understand.' I feel my forehead furrow while Godwulf holds my eyes with his. I shiver. It's cold, the wind blowing more fiercely as darkness coats the land.

'Your uncle was foster brother to a king of Mercia. You then, my boy, are as entitled to claim kinship with the king as though it were a blood bond.'

I shake my head, even as Godwulf's voice thrums with conviction. I'm not happy that the East Anglian warrior has followed me all the way to my home in the heart of Mercia. Yes, he was once a Mercian, but he's long called himself East Anglian.

'King Beornwulf's long dead, Godwulf. His name's barely mentioned any more, and if it is, no one has a good thing to say about him.' As I speak, I appreciate that I think the same. Beornwulf was responsible for many of Mercia's problems in the last decade. My childhood fascination with him is long gone. Why he was kind to me, I'll never know, and sometimes I wish he hadn't been.

'It doesn't matter what they say of Beornwulf. It's how it relates to you that's important.'

But again, I shake my head. I don't know why he tells me this. I don't know why he's followed me here, and I want nothing more than to speak to Lady Ælflæd of matters now, not events that happened in the past. I look to where she's disappeared along the roadway, but can't see her. She's the sister of Lord Coenwulf, and she'll know how Lady Cynehild and her pregnancy fares. I'd much sooner be conversing with her than with Godwulf. I want to know Lady Ælflæd much better than I currently do. I want to thank her for ensuring her brother apologised to me having accused me of killing their father's horse.

I shiver again, and Wine lets out a soft whinny. She wants a warm stable as well.

'Come. It's cold. We'll go to the reeve's house,' I say, but Godwulf's face shadows, the smile leaving his face.

'No, we should return to Tamworth now. Lay this knowledge before King Wiglaf. There are clearly many who've forgotten your uncle's position or who think to keep this from you. They mean to prevent you from claiming your rightful place. But the king loves you. Your name drips from the lips of everyone. Even King Athelstan of the East Angles knows of you.'

'No, he doesn't.' I try and smirk, shrugging my shoulders, my thoughts turning once more to the king's son, Wigmund, and the king's wife, Queen Cynethryth, and what either of them would say to me announcing that I wished to become the commander of the king's household warriors.

'He does, young Icel. Your name is becoming as well known as your uncle's.'

I shudder once more, and not just with the chill. I don't want to know this. I really don't. I've fought as I was commanded to do for Mercia's protection. I can't deny that I'm becoming a good warrior, acknowledged by the king, and gifted wealthy items, but to think that other kings of other domains might know my name is both ludicrous and fills my belly with a strange feeling. Not hunger. Not fear. But certainly something in between.

I try again. 'We should eat.'

'No, we should return to Tamworth,' Godwulf urges. I look along the darkening roadway. I have no intention of going back to Tamworth tonight. I must show my face and speak with my reeve and generally reassure the people who look to me as their lord that I'll not be as faceless as my uncle was. That I never knew of this place during my life shows just how often my uncle was absent from here.

'No, I'll eat. And Lady Ælflæd is here. I'd speak to her of how Lady Cynehild fares.'

I turn to head back towards Wine, but Godwulf arrests me, a hand on my shoulder.

I swivel my head and meet his eyes uneasily. They burn with the heat of the sun.

'Don't shy away from what you are,' he urges me, his voice thrumming with intensity.

'I don't, but I'll take no hasty action. Now, come, I invite you to my hall, or you can depart for Tamworth.' His lips form a hard line beneath the thickness of his beard and moustache, and then he shrugs, a tight smile on a chiselled face.

'As you will. I'd gladly eat and see what your uncle built here. He was an astute man. He knew to keep his holdings in good order and those who owed him their oath in good humour. Reeve Eomer, I know, is a firm and fair man. He and your uncle were friends for many years before his injury.'

Godwulf's words rumble over my muddled thoughts. I only half listen, but then I furrow my forehead, stumbling as I walk in the semi-darkness.

'Eomer was once a warrior?'

'Aye, lad, he was. A firm supporter of King Coel-wulf until his injury. Surely, you're aware of the wound he carries?'

But I realise I'm not. I've only met the man twice, both of them brief encounters. I saw nothing on him to show he wasn't hale. I'd assumed he'd always aspired to be a reeve. But now, it seems not.

'He has only two toes on his right foot. It unbalances him. He lost them in a battle. Wynflæd, the healer at Tamworth, did what she could for him, but they became infected, and so they were sliced clean off. He struggled too much with his balance to continue fighting for the king.'

I reach for Wine and begin to lead her towards the reeve's hall. Well, I suppose it's really mine, but I can't think of it like that. Soft sounds reach me in the gathering dusk, the smell of pottage heavy in the air, the bite of the coming winter, conjuring images of a land locked in ice in my mind. Last winter, I was restless inside Tamworth. I imagine the same will happen this year. Unless, of course, I ask to return to my uncle's holding for the duration of the dark times.

The smell of burning wood mingles with that of cooking food, and my stomach gurgles once more. I decide I'm hungry rather than anything else.

Godwulf is quiet at my side, his horse walking head lowered. He's ridden the animal hard, and I don't approve. Neither do I know what all the fuss was about. Surely, Godwulf didn't truly expect me to demand Commander Eahric's position from the king just because he informed me that my uncle once held that status for King Beornwulf? I'm only just acknowledged by Ealdorman Ælfstan's men as one of their numbers. There are many Mercian warriors, for instance, Horsa, who would refuse to heed my words. Neither, I consider, do I wish to be accountable to the king for his fighting men and for ensuring Mercia's protection from her enemies.

A square of light creeps over the courtyard, and a youth rushes to me.

'My lord, I'll take the horse,' he offers brightly, only for his eyes to alight on Godwulf. 'Horses,' he quickly corrects, reaching out with both hands. Eagerly, I hand him Wine's reins, sliding my hand along her nose and shoulder in thanks, and hurry into the welcoming warmth.

I hear murmurs from behind me, but my eyes are keen to seek out Lady Ælflæd, which they do quickly. She's seated close to the central hearth, a bowl in her hand for the boards have long since been removed as the day's eating is done. I make to stride towards her, removing my cloak, and hoping I don't stink too much of horse, only for Reeve Eomer to walk towards me. I don't know him well, but his face is twisted, and I consider what I've done wrong. I look down at my boots but see only the usual touches of mud. Certainly, they're clear from the horseshit that so often follows me everywhere I go. I realise then how tall he is, taller even than me.

'My lord.' His tone's respectful, but his eyes dart towards Lady Ælflæd, and he bends close to me. 'The lady seems content with the pottage, but I had nothing more to offer her and the men who accompanied her.'

I realise then that all of them are huddled tightly together and that another woman has joined the group. I don't recognise her, and my eyes narrow.

'I asked Eadgifu to attend upon the lady. She is, as you know, a woman of standing in our settlement, and I thought it imperative to ensure nothing unfortunate befell the young woman. Eadgifu will act as her maid and sleep across the doorway to ensure no one enters the room while she sleeps.' Eomer's words are breathless, but my eyes stray to his boots, looking for a telltale sign of his injury. But, to my mind, he walks well enough. Whatever problem he once had with staying upright, he's long since mastered it.

'My lord, did I do the correct thing?' Eomer further presses me. For a moment, I'm confused, unsure of why he's so concerned. 'She's to marry the king's son. All know of it. I can't allow anything to happen to her here.'

'Yes, yes, my thanks, you've acted most honourably.' Eomer visibly relaxes when I offer the words, even though they strike at me. All know of her marriage to the king's son, and yet she's here, in my hall. Once more, I make to walk towards her, only for Eadgifu, an older woman I don't believe I've ever met before, to stand at a command from Lady Ælflæd, who joins her. The men who escorted her here stay sitting, eating quietly, and drinking ale.

I want to shout a greeting to Lady Ælflæd, but her eyes are downcast. I'd almost think she was purposefully ignoring me. She must have heard us enter the hall. The door certainly complained with a loud screech. As Eadgifu leads the way, I appreciate that the pair are leaving the main room of the hall for the night. I watch their passage. Lady Ælflæd, nimble-footed and swift; Eadgifu, somewhat slower but still brisk. Eadgifu walks with all the confidence of a woman used to being obeyed and respected. I don't believe she's the reeve's wife, but she's still well respected, as he said.

I swallow my disappointment that I won't have the chance to speak to Ælflæd this evening, as my belly rumbles again. I blame Godwulf for keeping me outside too long. I wish the man hadn't tracked me to Budworth.

'Come, my lord. Sit and eat. And your guest?' Eomer looks towards Godwulf, who's still removing his cloak.

'This is Godwulf. I assumed you knew one another,' I murmur absent-mindedly. I can't deny being disappointed that Lady Ælflæd has left. I should have liked to glean more information about Lady Cynehild, as well as just spend time with her. Somewhat sulkily, I seat myself before the hearth, exchanging glances with those who escorted Ælflæd to Budworth.

I recognise the men from Kingsholm and almost speak with them, only to have my attention caught by Godwulf and Eomer. Close to the door Eomer stands, his back towards me at an angle so that I can hardly see Godwulf at all. Neither man seems happy, even as one of the servants brings me a bowl of rich-smelling pottage with a curtsey.

'My thanks,' I offer, uncomfortable with the curtsey. I've done little to deserve such respect. Eomer and Lady Cynehild may speak to me as lord of Budworth, but I'm no lord, not really. Yes, I own the lands, thanks to my uncle, but I don't truly believe that makes me a lord. Budworth is not a huge place. It's well endowed with grain stores, a small river, and a blacksmith plying his trade to the north of the settlement, but it's nothing compared to the vastness of Tamworth.

Spooning the rich mixture into my mouth, a sharp, barked word has me glancing at the two men once more. But Godwulf strides toward me, his face shadowed so that I can't see his features. Eomer, still with his back to me, remains where he is. Godwulf scrapes a stool close to the hearth and sits heavily, sighing as he does so, his face difficult to see in the dancing flames of the fire.

I want to ask him about what they spoke, but Eomer's once more all deference as he rushes to follow Eadgifu and Lady Ælflæd. My eyes follow his every movement. The servant hands another bowl to

Godwulf, and removes the empty dishes clasped in the hands of Ælflæd's men.

'The journey was good?' I ask of them, the silence between us all uncomfortable, as I eat eagerly.

'Not bad,' one of the men murmurs. His eyes sweep from me to Godwulf, lips slightly open, forehead furrowed.

'You're lord here?' he queries, unsure.

'This was my uncle's land,' I confirm quickly. I can't recall his name and feel I should know it.

'Edwin speaks of you as though you were no more than the healer woman's apprentice. And yet, you own a hall?' I work hard to keep a grimace from my face at the reminder of Edwin. I still wish I knew why he'd punched me earlier in the year.

'Well, I was, but this is my land, now.'

'Aye, the lad should have more land as well,' Godwulf mumbles, his tone dark and forbidding. 'The king's warriors should be more warmly rewarded, especially one related to the previous king of Mercia.'

Now the other man's face twists in confusion.

'He's too old to be the son of that blighted Ludica. He's barely younger than Ludica was when he died.'

'Not him. King Beornwulf.'

At the mention of Beornwulf, all four faces twist in disgust, and two of the men stand, hands going to their weapons belts, which I'm pleased to see are devoid of their actual seaxes.

'Beornwulf didn't deserve the title of the king, not after what he did to the rightful ruler, Coelwulf.' The man's voice thrums with conviction, and the menace in the hall is bright and likely to spark into outright fire if they're not careful.

'King Beornwulf was accepted by the witan, as you well know,' Godwulf growls, his spoon hanging halfway between his bowl and his mouth. I watch the mixture, glimpses of green showing the beans and pulses that comprise so much of it. Not long, and there'll be little of that to add to the meal. Soon, when the winter storms ravage the land, the food will be seasoned with garlic and onion, even the odd mushroom a treat to flavour the meal.

'Beornwulf played everyone for a fool then,' the first man retorts. His features are twisted with fury, spittle accompanying his words, and I'm unsure what to do. If this were the king's hall at Tamworth, or Lichfield, or any of his other steadings, the king's commander, Eahric, would be quick to intervene, to send the men to some duty they wouldn't appreciate to work off their bile. But here, well, here there's only me and Eomer, and there are four of Lady Ælflæd's men, and also Godwulf, who's handy with a blade as well. I don't much want to fight the five of them to maintain peace in my hall.

'King Coelwulf was useless. He was happy to let our enemies overwhelm Mercia, and he rewarded only those most loyal to him,' Godwulf retorts. I think he's spoiling for a fight.

'King Coelwulf overwhelmed the Welsh, as you well know, and his only failure was not to reward Lord Beornwulf with the riches he deserved. There, my friend' – one of the Kingsholm warriors speaks, and the words are tinged with disgust – 'is the reason Beornwulf hungered to be king. And a fat lot of good it did him, anyway. He lost Kent to the bastard Wessex king, and he lost his life to the king-slayer of the East Angles. He left no heir, and we were forced to endure that useless turd, Ludica, as the next king. No, the line should have been returned to Coelwulf, and all know it.'

'It's the fault of King Coelwulf that Mercia was so overwhelmed. He lost standing in the eyes of our enemies,' Godwulf persists.

'He did no such thing, and all know it,' is the hot reply.

'Then why does his son not pursue the claim? Why is your Lord Coenwulf not the king of Mercia?' Godwulf taunts with the words, but it's a good question, and yet one that infuriates the four men even more. They look fit to fight, and I seek out Eomer whose eyes flash between the group of men and Godwulf. I need to intervene, but how? I'm not sure. 'If Lady Ælflæd is to marry the upstart's son, then all must acknowledge the prior claim? Surely?'

'And where have you been all these years?' one of the other men asks instead. 'I've not seen you at the Mercian witan? In fact, I believed you'd become a favourite of the very king-slayer that Heahstan spoke about.'

Godwulf has the decency to nod along with those words. I'm pleased to be reminded of Heahstan's name, even if he is free with his opinions on the kingship of Mercia. 'There was little point in fighting for my lands to be restored to me in the upheaval of the change of kingship. King Athelstan was the much better option for me.'

'Yet, now, you've returned to Mercia? Is that because the Viking raiders have taken your land and you fear fighting them?' The sneer's impossible to ignore, and I wince to hear it. While the men haven't fought yet, I fear it's only a matter of time. I don't want to be caught between them, and yet, four men against Godwulf will not end well. I'll have to do something.

A leer touches Godwulf's lips, and his head tilts from side to side, considering his response. And then his eyes alight on me, and he nods, just once. I don't want him to be reminded of why he's in Budworth, but I'm not to get my wish.

'I've come to ensure young Icel here knows of his rightful place in Mercia. He should be more than just an oath-sworn man of the king of Mercia. He should be riding at his right-hand side, leading warriors, and not just one of the warriors.'

A startled bark of laughter erupts from Heahstan's mouth, and I close my eyes, wishing Godwulf could keep his mouth shut until I better know how to respond to his claim.

'His uncle was foster brother to King Beornwulf. He should be honoured as such,' Godwulf continues. The bloody fool.

'What, you think this boy' – derision ripples through the words, making me sit even taller. I'm hardly a boy any more. I consider the bulk of my muscles, the battles that I've fought, the lives that I've saved, and the gifts that I've received from the king. I'm no boy. I'm a warrior of Mercia – 'should be king in place of Wiglaf?' The three other men chuckle at the words, and my heart beats too loudly in my chest.

'Not king, no, but certainly commander of the

king's household warriors.' Godwulf's persistent, his chin sticking out, as he hands his empty bowl to a cowering servant, who, eyes wide, doesn't wish to become involved in what might turn out to be a fight, at any moment.

Heahstan's eyes blaze, but the look of derision has left his face. For a moment, I think he might be considering Godwulf's words, but then he shakes his head, looks me up and down and turns back to Godwulf.

'This boy has nothing that the king needs in a commander of his household troops. I hear Horsa knocked him unconscious, as did young Edwin, a member of my lord's warrior troop. If this boy,' and he grins once more, 'thinks to be more than that, then he'll need to do more than call on his relationship to the very king that all of Mercia wishes to declaim and bury beneath the tallest hill, and never think of again. This boy, if he is, as you say, somehow connected to King Beornwulf, would do well to forget it. All will ridicule him, and blame him for Mercia's predicament, now that Beornwulf has done the bloody decent thing and got himself killed by the East Angles.'

Godwulf's on his feet in a flash, a howl of fury pouring from his mouth, hand clenched, and I can scarcely breathe. I came here to remember my uncle, not to witness a fight between men I don't know arguing about something that happened years ago. I stand as well, Heahstan and Godwulf glowering at one another, my eyes flashing, one to the other, wishing Wulfheard was here to sort the pair out as they menace one another, fists bunched.

For a moment, I think the two men are nothing more than hot air, and then Godwulf swings the first punch, and I duck low and scamper out of the way, all at the same time. Heahstan's fellow warriors rush to his defence as he teeters on his feet before recovering his balance and roaring, mouth open, words incoherent, as he rushes into Godwulf.

The stools tumble beneath their weight, the crash so loud that I think the entire village will have heard it. So loud is it, I miss the creak of a door opening, and I gasp in astonishment as Lady Ælflæd, hair neatly braided down her back, eyes white with fury, glowers at the men.

'Heahstan.' Her words aren't shouted, and yet I hear them all the same over the commotion. 'And the rest of my brother's men, you'll sleep in the stable and let this be an end to whatever matter it is that has you brawling like cows in the field.' And yet, a further slap of flesh on flesh echoes around the suddenly quiet hall, as Godwulf thuds to the floor, Heahstan wincing as he opens and closes his fist. It seems that while we were all looking to Lady Ælflæd, Heahstan wasn't yet done fighting. Heahstan's nose is bleeding, his hair in disarray, and his tunic half-ripped down the left-hand side, and yet, he remembers his courtesy to his lord's sister now that Godwulf has fallen to the floor.

'My lady, my apologies,' he heaves into his tight chest, lowering his head. 'Come, we'll do as the lady suggests. My lord.' And Heahstan rounds on me. Not even a flicker of interest in Godwulf's fate, he bows. 'My apologies for bringing such disrespect into your household. I will,' and he heaves in another breath, 'settle the cost of any damages, and pay the fine, as you set it, and as laid out in King Wiglaf's law.' With a smart bow and the same from his men, they march to the door, where the servant rushes to open it for them as it shrieks in defiance, before marching into the howling gale. I watch them go, confusion on my face, and then turn to glance at Godwulf, who at least is breathing, even if he's insensible to the world around him. Then I turn to thank Lady Ælflæd for her intervention, only she's gone, a flash of Eadgifu's broad back all I see as the door to the private room slams shut on the mess of the fight that erupted from nowhere.

I meet Reeve Eomer's astounded eyes as I sit heavily back on my stool, which still stands upright, unlike the one Godwulf was seated upon.

'My lord,' Eomer stumbles, eyes fearful.

'It's nothing,' I murmur, wishing I could be so sure that's all it was. Why must these men fight when Mercia is secure? Why must they speak of matters that are irrelevant to what's currently happening in Mercia, and why must Godwulf persist in asserting that I am more than I am? I wish he'd stayed in the kingdom of the East Angles, and then I'd have had time to speak to Lady Ælflæd about more than just the pair of us offering our respects at the grave of my uncle. Lady Cynehild might well have sent Lady Ælflæd to Budworth on her behalf, but perhaps she knew I'd be pleased to see her? Although, well, that would mean that Lady Cynehild knew my plans before I did. That doesn't seem possible.

As I assist Eomer and the servants in righting the room, I can't help but look at the closed door, willing it to open and for Lady Ælflæd to appear once more.

2

The sound of hooves wakes me groggily from my place close to the hearth. Daylight streams through the open doorway, and I shiver at the blast of cold air that permeates my cloak and fur. Beside me, Godwulf snores, lying on his back, and I groan, remembering the events of last night. Abruptly, I recollect more and leap to my feet, rushing towards the open doorway, only for Eomer to fill it.

He startles as we almost collide.

'My lord.' His words are stilted.

'Who's that?' I ask, thinking of the sound of horses' hooves that woke me.

'Lady Ælflæd is up early and away back to Kingsholm with her warriors. She was keen that I thank you for the hospitality you extended to her. She also apologised for leaving so early. Lady Cynehild is due her child soon, and she wished to be there.' Eomer's words ripple with Lady Ælflæd's genuine intent, and yet I know she's trying to avoid me. 'Here,' Eomer continues, 'Heahstan was as good as his word and has left the coin to recompense for the damage and the hostilities in your house.' He opens his hand to show me the shimmering coins carrying the image of King Wiglaf, but I'm not interested.

I nod, trying to peer through the slowly closing door, and then sigh heavily. I wished to speak to Lady Ælflæd and ask her how she was and to Heahstan about the events of last night, but it's evident neither wishes to talk to me, or they'd not have left so rapidly and without bidding me a good day.

Eomer proffers the small pouch of coins again, but I shake my head.

'No, not for me directly. Ensure that all is repaired, and add the rest to the church's tithe. I don't wish to have the coins.'

'My lord.' Eomer bows out of my way, but when I make no move to follow him, he pauses.

'Are you well, my lord?' he queries.

'Yes, yes, I am, thank you. And there's no need to name me as "my lord".'

'Ah, but my lord, there is. You're Budworth's lord. When your uncle died, God bless his soul, our oaths were transferred to you, whether you like it or not. You're our lord, and all here must show their respect towards you, as young as you are.' A touch of a smile on the older man's lips, as though in understanding of my predicament, and then he's away, making his way through a curtained-off area, limping slightly, where I hear him opening and closing a wooden chest. And still, I stand. The sound of Godwulf's snores fills the hall, and I realise I need to piss and then I really want to be gone from here.

Budworth isn't my home. No matter what Eomer might believe. I journeyed here to remember my uncle having missed the anniversary of his death, but others have come here too, and now I'm even more confused than I was before. Lady Cynehild's continual interest in my uncle surprises me, and Godwulf's determination to make me more than I am has frustrated me. And then there's Lady Ælflæd. I would have spoken to her, but she's gone, perhaps disgusted by the fighting she witnessed in my hall. What, I consider, must she think of me for not being able to contain the men?

Outside, the day is bright and bitter. From the stable, I hear the soft murmur of the stablehands speaking to either one another or the horses, as I make my way to the latrine ditch. The smell assaults me as I empty my stream into a bucket, no doubt needed for the cleaning of clothes or the tannery. Perhaps they even sell the piss on. I don't know. I realise there's much I don't know about how certain elements of the settlement work, or indeed, how they function inside Tamworth either. I know of blacksmithing, thanks to Edwin's stepfather, and I know of healing, thanks to Wynflæd, but more than that, I'm ignorant about. I don't even know a great deal about ruling and being a lord, despite my proximity to the king.

I consider returning to the warmth of the hall, but Godwulf's snores still ripple through the air, perceived even from outside the building, and so I make my way along the roadway that splits much of Budworth. My eyes take in all around me. The smell of food cooking over fires, the busy labouring of men and women preparing for the coming winter. There are no more than ten buildings on either side of the road, the sharp smell of ale assuring me that one of them is an alehouse as I move along the road. Beneath my feet, the ground is hard-packed earth, the indentations of horses' hooves easy to see, just as much as the more distinctive shape of sheep and cow hooves. But the distant fields hold no animals that I can see. Some-where, they've either been brought beneath roofs, or they've been slaughtered, ready for the dark times.

In no time at all, I've reached the end of the buildings, and I turn to walk back along the way I've come. In the near distance, the church beckons to me, and I consider returning to it to finally offer my prayers for my uncle and my mother, but I don't want to. That was yesterday and the days leading up to yes-terday. Now that I've visited the place and completed my task, I'm keen to return to Tamworth and my place in Ealdorman Ælfstan's warrior band. Abruptly, I hurry my steps, eager to be gone from the place, even if that means leaving Godwulf, and his stories of my uncle, behind me.

There's no reason why I should trust what he says. But there's someone who'll tell me the truth of his assertions, but she's not here. I bid an abrupt farewell to Eomer, who nods, and casts an uneasy eye at the still-sleeping form of Godwulf. I'm sure the man will wake, but I don't want him to accompany me to Tamworth. No, I want to go alone and speak with Wynflæd. I think it's finally time she told me all that she knows of my uncle, my mother, and perhaps, even my father.

* * *

The roadway is deserted as Wine moves easily beneath me. I don't push her onward. I don't want Godwulf to catch up with me, but I don't believe he will. When he wakes, his head will pound louder than a drum, and he'll need to wait a day or two before trying to ride. That'll give me all the time I need to reach Tamworth.

I huddle inside my cloak, my breath blooming before me. It feels too early in the winter for the wind to be so fierce, and yet it matches my mood well. It howls around my ears, my linen cap and hood of my cloak pulled fiercely over my dark hair. My hands are held firm in their gloves, and yet I can feel the trickle of cold over my eagle-scarred hand. The damn thing. It's faded, but only a little.

My thoughts run rampant. Lady Ælflæd is to be tied to the current ruling family through marriage. She's to bring legitimacy to King Wiglaf's rulership and, even more so, to that of his son, by uniting the families of Coelwulf and Wiglaf. Coelwulf was the rightful king, deposed by Beornwulf. His son, Lord Coenwulf, didn't want the kingship, and has never put himself forward as a successor to Mercia's string

of short-lived kings. King Coelwulf's daughter, Lady
Ælflæd, plainly doesn't share her brother's scruples.

It's evident that for the first time since King Offa
died thirty years ago and bequeathed the kingdom to
his short-lived son, that Mercia is to have a king who's
the son of the previous one. Or, at least, that's the intention of Queen Cynethryth and Ealdorman
Sigered. For a moment, I consider whether Lord Coenwulf has even contemplated that.

I would wish Lady Ælflæd a nobler marriage. She
deserves better than the snivelling Wigmund for a
husband, even if the union might, in time, make her
a queen. Lord Wigmund's too easily swayed by his
mother, but perhaps Lady Ælflæd is happy to know
she'll marry a man she can manipulate so well. I wish
I could understand her ambitions and those of Lord
Coenwulf.

And Lady Cynehild? Why has she sent Ælflæd to
offer prayers for my uncle? My head swirls. I think it
would be better to have stayed on the road, travelling
the waterways and roadway that demarcates the
kingdom of the East Angles and Mercia. There, with
nothing to worry about but the menace of the Viking
raiders, my thoughts were less complex and more
my own.

Abruptly, my gaze is drawn upwards, the harsh

shriek of an eagle clamouring for my attention. Mercia's emblem is an eagle, and here, while I think of kings and queens, is the very embodiment of that creature. I catch the dark plumage against the brightness of the bitterly cold day, as the bird screeches its defiance. I can hardly draw my eyes away from the creature. Unbidden, I find myself pulling my glove free and glancing at the scar on my hand. Critically, I examine it. Is it as easy to make out as I always believe it is? Does it even look like the creature high overhead? I shake my head. My thoughts are twisted and difficult to untangle. At a crossroads, I stop and look back the way I've come, onwards to where Tamworth lies and also westwards, to where, if I'm lucky, I might be able to catch Lady Ælflæd.

The eagle screeches once more, as I pull my glove back over my hand and turn Wine's head. I want to talk to Wynflæd, but more, I wish to speak to Lady Ælflæd. Encouraging Wine onwards, I bend low over her head, grimacing at the cold from speeding our journey. It might be a fool's errand, but if I can find Lady Ælflæd before darkness then I'll do so. If not, I decide, I'll simply give up the chase and resume my travels to Tamworth.

At the least, it will confuse Godwulf should he come looking for me.

The day passes too quickly, and without sight of Lady Ælflæd and Heahstan. Resigned, I think to find somewhere to shelter for the night, only to hear the nicker of horses ahead, as well as the scent of food cooking and the smell of wood burning.

Suddenly, as I come upon Lady Ælflæd and her escort, I consider what I'm doing, and what I can say to her. I shouldn't have come, and yet, before I can turn aside, a voice ripples through the air.

'My lord, why are you here?' I meet Heahstan's perplexed expression. He's still mounted, for now, but Lady Ælflæd is quickly arranging shelter for the night. She seems oblivious to my arrival.

'I wished to apologise for the events of last night,' I stutter, my eyes barely leaving the figure of Lady Ælflæd, as she tends to her horse in the gathering gloaming.

'It is we who should apologise.' Heahstan speaks with none of last night's contempt for me. 'The lady is most aggrieved. It seems I'll be on latrine duty for some time when I return to Kingsholm.' The tone is rueful, and silence falls between us.

I can't share in Heahstan's martyred amusement, because all I want to do is speak to Lady Ælflæd.

'Come, seek shelter with us this night,' the Kingsholm warrior offers. 'Lady Ælflæd arranged for us to stop here on our return. I'm sure there'll be room for another.'

'I...' I stammer, unsure whether I should just retrace my earlier steps. 'I...' I try again, only for Lady Ælflæd to turn and catch sight of me. A perplexed expression on her cold-reddened face and she appears before me. Clumsily, I dismount.

'Icel.' Her voice is sharp. 'Why are you here?' She looks behind me as though Godwulf might be lingering there.

'I wished to apologise for last night,' I hurriedly reply.

'There's no need. It was Heahstan and his addled wits that were at fault.' If anything, her tone is even sharper now.

'All the same.'

'It was that other man. Is he with you?'

'Godwulf, no. I left him at Budworth.'

'Good. He's a troublemaker, I'm sure of it. Come, it's too bitter to linger outside. We should warm ourselves besides the fire.'

Without further argument, I find myself obeying her words. I'm grateful to lead Wine to a warm stable filled with many horses as well as a bull and some cows, separated, of course. The breath of the animals steams and there's a distinct smell of shit. Lady

Ælflæd leaves me there, to enter the hall, while I ensure Wine is comfortable. All the while, my heart pounds too loudly in my chest and my mouth is too dry.

Inside the hall, I remove my cloak and pull my gloves free from my hand, and plunge them into a bowl of warmed water set for just such a task. The hall isn't the largest, far from it, but the man who presides there seems only too happy to share, as I introduce myself to him.

'I knew your uncle,' Lyfing informs me, a tinge of sadness to his voice. 'He was a good man, but you'll be a fine lord for Budworth in his place. You're beloved of the king.'

'Well, not quite beloved, I assure you. But we're allies not enemies,' I admit with embarrassment. I'd sooner be known as the healer woman's assistant, but that part of my life is long done with.

'What brings you here on such a day?' Lyfing asks, as we're served warmed wine and a bowl of onion-smelling pottage.

'An apology for Lady Ælflæd. There was a fight in my hall last night.'

'There's a fight in my hall every night,' Lyfing laughs, his rounded belly juddering with the movement. 'But,' he sobers quickly, 'you're right to make your apologies. Mercia's future queen will remember these things.' While his laughter is full of good cheer, I find my smile slipping at the unwelcome reminder.

'Indeed. And tomorrow, I'll return to Tamworth, and Ealdorman Ælfstan.'

'Tonight you must accept my hospitality and the comfort of my hearth,' Lyfing confirms, a gleam in his eye. Our conversation moves aside to other matters then, and I'm fearful that I still won't have the chance to speak to Lady Ælflæd before she retires for the night, only for Lyfing to be called away by one of his servants.

Silence falls between us, broken only when Lady Ælflæd speaks.

'Why did you come?' she queries.

'Yesterday,' I begin. Her eyes watch me intently. 'Yesterday something happened and I wondered what it was, in the churchyard.'

A hint of colour touches Lady Ælflæd's cheeks but she shakes her head. 'I was chilly, nothing more. There was certainly no need for you to follow me.' I'm not sure, but I think she lies to me, but of course, I can't accuse her of such.

'I also wished to send my good wishes to Lady Cynehild,' I quickly add.

'I think she knows that, Icel, I really do. You and

her, you have a special connection, because of your uncle.' 'Uncle' is muttered with a strange inflexion, at least to my ears.

'Yes,' I confirm quickly. 'I believe they were friends for a long time.'

'Yes, Icel,' she demurs. 'They were friends.' I open my mouth to say more, but she stands abruptly. 'I bid you goodnight, and when we leave here tomorrow morning, I hope you won't be following us. I wouldn't wish word to get back to my intended husband.' She smiles, but all the same, the threat seems real enough.

'Goodnight, my lady.' I bow my head, and watch as she moves away. It seems I still don't have my answers, and that confuses me even more.

Come the morning, she and her escort leave long before I wake from a tormented dream of an eagle pulling the flesh from Wine's lifeless body and, with her admonishment in my ears, head towards Tamworth. My thoughts are a whirl, circular, and without cease.

When it becomes too dark to continue my journey, Wine and I seek shelter amongst a thick scattering of Mercian oaks, allowing the brunt of the wind to be borne by the trees as they shiver and dance, their leaves almost all long-since tumbled to the ground.

It's dark, and I light a small fire, allowing the smell of the smoke to comfort me, and the dancing flames to warm me before I sleep, only to wake to a world turned crystalline. For a moment, I lie on my back, looking up into the cloudless, bright sky, before the cold of the air forces me upright to cough away the sharp bite from the back of my throat.

'Come on, girl.' I stamp out the remaining embers of the fire and hastily mount, keen for the warmth from my horse. Winter is coming, a time of ice and snow, of wind and fires, and I crave the camaraderie of my fellow warriors.

* * *

'You're back quickly,' Oswy calls to me, looking up from where he's grooming his mount in the stables. The place smells warm with the press of so many horses, and I shudder as I struggle to pull my gloves clear from my hands.

'I am, yes. I need to speak to Wynflæd,' I murmur, leading Wine to her stable next to Brute, who eyes me with disinterest as he pulls at the hay from the netting.

He looks comfortable, and I smirk to see him, despite my need to rush to Wynflæd. Suddenly, I'm reluctant to face her. What will I say? How will she react? We've only just truly reached an accord where I feel she respects me as much as I do her. I don't want that to end. She's one of the very few links to my past and my uncle.

'Well, you're out of luck then. She's been called away to Kingsholm.'

'Why, what's happened to Lady Cynehild?' I demand, surprised by the flicker of worry worming its way through my stomach. Clearly, they didn't think to send word to Lady Ælflæd in Budworth, I try and reassure myself.

'I don't know. I just know that Goda and Kyre escorted her on the orders of Ealdorman Ælfstan.'

'Arse,' I complain, wishing I didn't feel so inordinately relieved. Opening the door and allowing Wine into her stable, I realise I should be disappointed, but I'm not. Instead, my thoughts turn to Lady Cynehild. Lady Ælflæd said she was close to birthing her first child. I can only assume it's on her wishes that Wynflæd has hurried away. I can't imagine Wynflæd welcoming such a cold journey. I also can't see that she'll be eager to return, not when the weather's so unpleasant.

'Ah, you're back.' Wulfheard appears, his words

echoing Oswy's, his forehead wrinkled. 'A shame you went if you were going to be so quick. Wynflæd wanted you to take her to Kingsholm but had to make do with Goda and Kyre.' I think he might tell me more, but instead, he turns and looks me over, from head to foot. 'Did that East Anglian find you? He said he needed to speak with you, something to do with your uncle or some such.'

I sigh then, wishing Wulfheard hadn't reminded me of Godwulf. 'Did you used to know him?' I ask instead. 'He said he knew my uncle before he changed allegiance from the Mercian king to King Athelstan of the East Angles.'

'No, I can't say that I did, but I recognised him well enough. I take it he found you?'

'He did, yes. I left him at Budworth two mornings ago sleeping off an altercation with one of Lady Ælflæd's warriors.'

'Lady Ælflæd?' Oswy queries. I hadn't realised he'd heard all of our conversation, but then, it's not as though he's far away.

'Yes, Lady Cynehild bid her offer prayers over my uncle's burial place as she's too great with child to carry out the obeisance herself.'

'Ah, yes, of course. I'm sorry, Icel. I'd forgotten why you went. I should have commanded Godwulf to stay here and wait for your return.' Wulfheard almost looks contrite. But I'm focused on Oswy. His eyes are narrowed, and I can see he looks confused. Only then he shakes his head and looks at me.

'I remember Godwulf. Bloody arse that he was. So full of himself when Athelstan reclaimed the kingdom of the East Angles. Desperate he was to think of himself as a man of the East Angles. But once, he did know your uncle. I wouldn't have called them friends, though,' Oswy cautions me, and I nod. And then, taking a deep breath, I ask the question that plagues me.

'He said my uncle was foster brother to King Beornwulf.' Wulfheard shakes his head as though to deny the words, but Oswy nods slowly.

'Aye, he was at that. I'd forgotten that until now. They were friends for many long years before Beornwulf was king.'

'If you know that, then do you know who my mother was?' I challenge. But Oswy's already shaking his head.

'No, and I'm not alone in that. No one knows who your mother was wed to. In fact, until your uncle appeared at Tamworth with you in his arms, few knew of such a marriage or even that he had a sister. Your uncle's family were never at the court of King Coelwulf.'

I shake my head, frustrated once more. I only ever seem to receive half an answer. I find it perplexing that I could be born and no one knows anything about me.

'Don't let Godwulf upset you,' Oswy continues, running a brush down the back of his new horse. His old one is there as well, but that animal won't be going on the road again. She'll be left behind should we ride forth under the king's orders once more. Some young child will learn to ride on her or some such. The animal is too old to be a warrior's mount, but not too old to be beyond use. 'He has some strange ideas, so I hear it,' Oswy appraises me, and I swallow down my frustration and nod. I even manage to find a smirk on my lips.

'He says I should be the commander of the king's household troops.' Wulfheard looks astonished at the statement, but Oswy merely laughs, the sound loud but not derisive.

'He's a bloody fool. We should send him back to the kingdom of the East Angles and have done with him. He means only to cause trouble here. Although, well, young Icel.' He pauses and runs his eyes along my long frame. 'I take it you don't want to become the commander of the king's household troop?'

I'm already fiercely shaking my head as Oswy continues to chuckle.

But Wulfheard fixes me with a sharp look, and I'm not convinced that Oswy's ready dismissal of the topic will be followed by Wulfheard. I wouldn't be surprised if Ealdorman Ælfstan knows of this new development before I can make it to my bed and unpack my few possessions.

3

'Today, Icel, today.' Wulfheard's hand is rough on my shoulder as he shakes me awake. I moan.

'What's today?' I ask, my words thick with sleep.

'It's almost midday, and you need to wake. The others have been on the training ground since daybreak.'

The knowledge astounds me, and I sit abruptly, almost colliding with Wulfheard's head, where he bends low over my side.

'I've slept so long?'

'Aye, you have. Now, come on, or Oswy will bitch about favouritism, and I'll have no choice but to send you on a run to Lichfield and back.'

Hastily, I scamper from my bed, and tug on my

tunic and trews. It's cold, but not as cold as the day before. It was, I think, just a brief reminder of what true winter will be like, but that should be some weeks away. We've barely celebrated the feast of Michealmas, and it's not until after All Saints' Day that the true storms should come.

I think Wulfheard will leave, but instead he lingers, as I thrust my feet into my boots and reach for my weapons belt.

'I think you should know that Godwulf arrived this morning. He still means to seek you out. I've spoken to the ealdorman about his claims. Ealdorman Ælfstan bids you ignore whatever he tries to prevail upon you to do. The king won't take kindly, no matter his regard for you, to any demands that you be something other than a member of Ealdorman Ælfstan's warriors and lord of Budworth as your uncle's successor.'

'I've no intention of listening to him,' I confirm grumpily. Perhaps, after all, returning to Tamworth wasn't the best idea. It must have been obvious to Godwulf that this would be where I came. Not that I know where else I might have gone. Godwulf seems the persistent sort. He would have found me no matter where I was.

'I've further spoken to Oswy on the matter. He

has only very faint memories of the man and of your uncle and King Beornwulf as foster brothers, but is adamant that they were. Certainly, I don't believe that Beornwulf made much of it other than allowing your uncle to have the command of his warriors. I doubt anyone else will remember. So many men have fallen beneath the blades of the East Angles warriors that there are few, other than Ealdorman Sigered, who've lived for so long. Commander Eahric was named in his position by King Wiglaf. I doubt he'd appreciate you wanting his place.'

'I don't want his position,' I confirm hastily, thinking of how many of Eahric's duties are un-pleasant and how many of the men hate him. 'I just wanted to know the truth of what he said.'

'Well, Godwulf spoke the truth, but that doesn't help you. Wiglaf is king now, not Beornwulf.'

'Aye, Wulfheard, I know that,' I murmur, stepping outside into the bright daylight. Overhead, clouds scud across a pale blue sky, but I'm right, it's not as cold as yesterday, even if the day is so far advanced that, no doubt, the chill has been replaced by the gentle heat of the sun.

'Come on, a quick run down to the training ground, and then the men will think I've punished you for being a lay-abed.'

'Fine, but a piss first,' I caution and hasten away. Wulfheard waits for me at Tamworth's open gates as I rush to his side, keen not to encounter Godwulf. Together, we run down to the training ground, where the king's warriors sweat and strain, fighting one another with wooden blades or dulled metalled ones. Oswy fixes me with a piercing look when I arrive, but Wulfheard doesn't allow him to speak.

'And another around the training grounds, you lazy shit,' he calls, a glint to his eyes that has me sighing even as I amble to a quicker pace. Bastard. He had me run here but now means to punish me for real. He pretends to be my friend, but sometimes, he still likes to remind me that I answer to him, and then Ealdorman Ælfstan, at least in regards to being a member of this brotherhood of warriors.

As I follow the well-beaten path amongst the summer grass that's turned brown and ragged at the edges, I consider Wulfheard's words. I'm grateful that he asked Ealdorman Ælfstan for his opinion, but his caution about Ealdorman Sigered has me wondering if I should ask him about my uncle and mother. Would he, perhaps, be one of the only people, other than Wynflæd, who might know the truth? After all, Ealdorman Sigered, and indeed, Ealdorman Mucel, have survived the strife of the past few years. What do they remember? Does Sigered know something? Could that, perhaps, account for why he doesn't like me? Engrossed in my thoughts, I return to Wulfheard quickly, hardly even panting, and he eyes me in disbelief.

'Go again,' he murmurs, with no hint of apology. 'And, Icel, this time make it look like it was at least a bit of effort, or I'll have no choice but to have you face off against Horsa again. The men must see that you've been punished for your laziness.'

I shake my head, smirk at his rueful tone, and head off once more. This time, I drag my feet on return, and Wulfheard's the one shaking his head at my exaggerated exhaustion.

'Right, you can battle, Oswy,' Wulfheard orders, thrusting his practice weapon into my hand. 'And, Oswy, don't go easy on him.'

Oswy grins, and launches an attack upon me that makes me take three fast backward steps before I can even lift my blade.

'Bastard,' I murmur to both of them, and while they laugh, I make sharp attacks against Oswy, that soon have the smirk sliding from his cheeks. The familiar action soothes me, and in no time, I'm breathing heavily for real. Oswy is a phenomenal warrior. Now that he's fully recovered from the wound he took inside Londinium, I'm surprised that someone managed to get beyond his guard. His movements are always well timed and placed with care to ensure they hit with precision. His stance shows no sign of the wound he took fighting in the kingdom of the East Angles either. Once more, I'm reminded of how quickly he's healed and how he carries almost no scar, whereas I'm forever marked by trying to heal my uncle with my eagle-headed seax blade.

'Stop,' Wulfheard eventually calls to the pair of us. I'm breathing hard, and I'm bruised from some of Oswy's attacking moves, as he must be from some of mine, but neither of us is on our arses.

'Well done, lad.' Wulfheard offers his congratulations. 'It won't be long, and you'll truly be able to counter Horsa's weight and overpower him.'

'And what of me?' Oswy huffs, his tone rippling with frustration.

'Aye, well, you're not bad either. Getting old and a bit slow in places, but not bad.' Wulfheard cackles, the sound slightly menacing, and I grin as well, reaching out to offer Oswy my arm so that we can arm clasp as allies and not the enemies we were pretending to be. Oswy's grip is firm on my arm, too firm, a reminder that he's a strong and seasoned warrior, no matter Wulfheard's words.

'I went easy on you,' he murmurs, as though to account for why we both stand upright.

'I did on you, as well.'

Wulfheard overhears my remarks and laughs once more, while Oswy's lips twist in annoyance.

'I think we should go again,' Oswy menaces.

'I think you've done enough for one day.' Wulfheard is quick to put that idea to bed. 'Come on, we're the only fools left out here apart from Cenred, and there'll be nothing to eat if we're not quick.'

Recalled to the time of day, Oswy squints into the sun and then mock bows. 'Well, tomorrow then,' he offers, and I nod to confirm our agreement to battle once more.

'Tomorrow, I won't go easy on you,' I caution him.

'And I won't on you either,' Oswy growls, and now we're all laughing as we make our way back towards Tamworth itself, Cenred joining us. I admire the view as I recover my breath, reminded of all I've seen in the last few years. Tamworth is little different to other places I've seen in Mercia, aside from Londinium. Peterborough monastery was much smaller, Hereford a little smaller, Lundenwic dwarfed by the size of Londinium.

I consider then why such settlements are drawn to the rivers. I mean, I know why they are, but perhaps, if the Viking raiders should appear once more, everyone will realise what a bad decision that was.

My good cheer evaporates when I catch sight of Godwulf, complete with a bruised face and purple eye, deep in conversation with Commander Eadric. I curse softly, and Wulfheard must hear me because his next words follow my thoughts.

'The bloody fool. What does he think he's doing?' Wulfheard marches off, but I linger with Cenred. Cenred looks from me to Wulfheard to Godwulf, forehead furrowed.

'Is that the man from the kingdom of the East Angles?'

'Yes, it is.'

'Why is he here?'

'He knew my uncle and thinks to make me the commander of the king's troops.'

Cenred looks even more perplexed at the revelation. 'But your uncle was never the commander of the king's troops?' he murmurs.

'Not even for Beornwulf?' I question.

'Not that I remember. I mean, it was some time ago, but I don't recall it. I think the commander fell at the first battle against Athelstan the king-slayer.'

'Then why's he saying as much?'

'I've no idea.' Cenred shrugs his huge shoulders. 'There's much you don't know about your uncle, Icel. There's much that many of us don't know. He was a law unto himself, but he always acted in the best interest of the kingdom. I wouldn't trust Godwulf. He means to stir up trouble. Who knows, he might even have been sent here by the king-slayer to cause disruption to the king's warriors.'

I nod. I'd not considered that, and it worries me.

'Does anyone know more about my uncle?' I muse, and Cenred grunts softly.

'Only Wynflæd, and her lips are tighter than a clam's shell. She'll only tell you what you need to understand. Ealdorman Sigered might know more, but we all know he's a piece of shit, so he won't tell you anything either. No, Icel, I think it's safer not to ask questions, and not rouse people's interest in what, precisely, your uncle was doing. King Wiglaf has certainly allowed himself to forget Cenfrith's disobedience in leaving Tamworth with you and Edwin when King Ecgberht moved into Mercia. I suggest you do the same.'

So spoken, Cenred increases his stride to match Wulfheard's and I watch him with interest. Cenred' s hints suggest he does remember more than he's telling me, and I've long known that Wynflæd knows more than she ever tells me. Perhaps, despite my belief that I would like to understand more, I truly don't. I can't help feeling I'm safer comprehending less. After all, if I truly wished to know, there must be ways of finding out.

'Icel.' Wulfheard calls me over and, reluctantly, I hasten to his side. Commander Eahric's scowl tells me all I need to perceive Godwulf's conversation.

'Godwulf here says you should have my position,' Eahric announces, his words rippling with fury, as he jabs his finger towards Godwulf. I glance at God-wulf's purpled eye with a wince. That must hurt. Heahstan has mean fists.

'No, no, I never said.'

'Well, if you want my rank, you need to prove yourself to the king, and to the men, in more ways than just killing a Viking raider jarl on the banks of a river.' I imagine my title as jarl-killer must still ran-kle. I'm sure he'd have liked that name for himself.

'I never said,' I try once more, aware that God-wulf's face is wreathed in a smirk.

'And, the queen, you'll need her regard as well.' It seems that Eahric isn't to be swayed from his fury, and that it's directed at me and not Godwulf frus-trates me.

'I don't,' I try once more, wishing that Godwulf hadn't followed me from the kingdom of the East Angles, and then from Budworth. And equally, that Wulfheard would do more than just stand there, listening as Eahric's wrath makes itself known over his reddening face.

'And, then there's Lord Wigmund, the king's son, and the ealdormen as well.'

'Eahric,' Wulfheard finally speaks, interjecting loudly into the conversation. 'Let Icel speak.'

Now those fiery eyes burn me. I swallow and glower at Godwulf one more time.

'Eahric, I don't want to be the commander of the king's warriors. I assure you. Godwulf sought me out with knowledge of my uncle's relationship to one of the previous kings. I'm happy as one of Ealdorman Ælfstan's warriors.'

'And yet, you're not oath-bound to him,' Eahric growls.

'That's merely an oversight,' I counter quickly. 'And I am oath-sworn to the king. I made my vow kneeling in horseshit at Bardney, as you well know. You were there, and you witnessed it.'

'And so, you call on that duty now to claim more than is your due.' His cry is still furious.

I shake my head, wishing the man would see sense.

'Eahric, I don't want what's yours. I don't. I'm too young and foolish for any to abide by my orders. I'm one of the ealdorman's men, and I'll remain as such. Godwulf here seems to have some half-remembered memories from before he became a man of the East Anglian king. The king-slayer. Remember that. I'm a Mercian. What Godwulf is remains to be seen.' I finish in a rush. I don't want to have Godwulf furious at me as well, but right now, it's more important that Eahric knows my true thoughts and feelings.

For a moment, I think he's going to argue with me, but then he turns to Godwulf.

'Icel's right, and he makes a good point. You're oath-bound to your king of the East Angles, not the king of Mercia. I suggest you gather your belongings and get your shit out of here. We've no spare room for troublemakers.'

Godwulf's mouth opens and closes, revealing his yellowing teeth, his rage settling on him as he scours me with fierce eyes. I wish I knew why he was so de-termined to press these claims. It's not as though it'll give him greater wealth and security. If he's a man of the East Angles, then he should return there, to whatever position and affluence he claims.

'You, Icel, are doing yourself out of your birthright, your place at the Mercian court. This man has no such ties to the Mercian ruling family. He has no right to be the king's commander.'

'He, Godwulf, has every right because he's been appointed by my king, and I'll honour him by respecting that decision. Now, I suggest you get back to the kingdom of the East Angles. And remember this as you go, I'm as Mercian as my uncle. And I fight and protect my Mercian king. That's all I want.'

4

We stand there, all of us, while Godwulf collects his possessions and his horse, and with a backwards glance filled with fury as black as his eye, makes his way over the wooden bridge that covers the ditch, and only then do I breathe deeply.

As though from a distance, I hear Eahric speaking to his warriors on guard duty at Tamworth's gates.

'Don't allow that man entry into Tamworth or any of the king's settlements, not without coming to me first. He's to be deemed an enemy of Mercia.' Eahric's words remain tinged with his anger, and I realise that my hands are clenched at my sides. My fingers have dug into my scar there. Why did Godwulf think to stir up trouble? What's in it for him? Unless, of course, his only intention was to cause disgruntlement between the king's warriors. Perhaps he does mean to undermine the unity of the Mercia king's warriors. After all, our friendships and alliances have been forged in battles against the Wessex king. If King Athelstan wishes to extend his control over Mercia, that won't please him.

'Come on, Icel. You need to change and eat,' Wulfheard orders me. I spare a glance for Eahric, and he looks at me appraisingly. I consider what he sees. Does he acknowledge that I'm a warrior now or little more than a boy? Does he see my uncle in my face, in the way I walk? Does he notice my thick mop of black hair, the bristles on my cheeks and chin, the width of my shoulders and the muscles in my arms and legs? Or does he still see me as I once was? Small and wiry, eager to never be truly seen? Does he see my youth as an affront? Does he think I should be older and wiser before receiving the acclaim of the king and having my name immortalised in a scop song?

I don't know. I know how my uncle carried himself, but I've no idea if I do the same. I should, perhaps, ask Wynflæd, but maybe it's better if I don't know. I need to be my own man, not an image of another. I shake away my unease.

'Apologies, Eahric. I tried to leave him behind at Budworth but he followed me here.' And now something else crosses Eahric's face, and I realise that I've erred once more. One moment I'm saying I'm not my uncle, that I fight only for Mercia, and the next, I remind Eahric that I'm different to the other warriors. I have land to my name that I hold independently to the king. I am, at least in Budworth and to those for whom such matters are relevant, a lord. Eahric isn't and likely never will be. If he lives to give up his blade, he'll be gifted something from the king, a piece of land somewhere, but it'll revert to the king on his death. I wish I'd kept my mouth shut.

'I understand, Icel.' Eahric is gracious with his words. 'Men will always be tempted by the offer of something that they perceive to be better than that which they currently have.'

I feel my eyes narrow at that. I'm not quite sure that Eahric does understand, but I'm not going to stand here and argue with him further.

'Good day.' I turn and walk away, following where Cenred and Oswy already lead and where Wulfheard waits for me, his eyes bright.

'You do seem to tend to get into trouble without

much effort,' he murmurs to me. I open my mouth to reply that it wasn't my devising, but he continues. 'Not that I blame you. If I'd known the intention of Godwulf, I'd never have told him where you were. Now, I doubt there'll be anything left to eat, so hurry up and change, and then you can charm the servants to get us all some food.'

'Charm them?' I query.

'Aye, lad. Some of the lasses look at you with such longing. Luckily, you're entirely immune to their charms for now, and long may that continue. A man such as you should make a good marriage, and not with the servants, but, well, it's still a skill that has some use.' He chuckles as he speaks, and I consider what Wulfheard must have been like as a younger man. Perhaps he spent much of his time tangling be-tween the furs with the servant girls. I know it's al-most expected of the warriors and the servants.

And Wulfheard proves prescient with his words, for when we four finally enter the king's hall, there's nothing but the hounds licking stray finds from the floor as the servants clear away the boards.

'Is there anything left for us?' I'm nudged into asking by the growls of fury from Oswy's belly.

'No,' the king's seneschal calls from his place close to the hearth, but I see one of the servants' winks, and as the seneschal strides from the hall, muttering about 'ungrateful bloody warriors', four bowls of pottage appear, heaped high with mutton.

'I held some back,' the young woman confirms, and I notice how she appraises me but not the three older men. Wulfheard chuckles as I almost drop the bowl of food, forced to grab it with my left as well as my right hand. Her fingers linger on the bowl, and I feel the heat of her skin on mine. It burns almost as much as my branded hand.

'I'll find you some bread as well,' she continues. I watch her walk away, hips swaying, and swallow heavily. Now Oswy and Wulfheard both laugh at me, knowing eyes watching me as they sit, beside Cenred who doesn't seem to understand the laughter, but eats eagerly, and I stay standing.

'Aye, lad. You might have yourself a few problems to contend with of the female persuasion.'

'I...' I stutter, frustrated to once again find myself struggling to enunciate my thoughts.

'Just don't get caught with her alone, or she'll have a claim on you. That way, you should survive her attentions. She likes to ride all the youngest warriors, does Ælfthryth. And then she tells the others who's worth their efforts and who isn't.'

A half-strangled cry leaves my mouth, and then I

choke on my pottage so that by the time Ælfthryth returns with the bread, I'm red in the face and gasping for breath. She scours me with her eyes so that I feel naked and then winks once more as she hands over the warm bread and also a jug of ale before walking away, this time her hips swaying even more alarmingly. Oswy concentrates on his pottage, as does Wulfheard and Cenred, and I force my eyes away. I've never truly considered the women of the settlement in such a way. And now, I feel disconcerted and confused. Hastily, I concentrate on my food, looking down at my bowl, and only when I'm sure Ælfthryth has left do I lift my face and, damn it, Oswy and Wulfheard watch me with knowing eyes, and heat once more suffuses my face. Bastards, both of them.

* * *

Cuthred seeks me out later, as I tend to Wine and Brute. Brute requires a good stretch, but I determine to do that the following day.

'Icel?' he calls to me, and I turn to him as he peers through the gloom of the stable.

'Are you back?' I redundantly call to him, and he nods as I move aside and look at him.

'Yes, and Wynflæd wants to see you.'

I've not heard the noise of hooves over the hard-packed earth, and so I realise they must have returned while I was eating. Hastily, I close the door on Brute and follow the lad. He bounds along, and his enthusiasm assures me that all must be well with Lady Cynehild. That pleases me.

Ducking low beneath the door, which seems to be getting lower and lower every time I visit, so that I have to be careful not to knock my head, my eyes alight on Wynflæd. In a rare moment of unguardedness, she doesn't seem to hear Cuthred and me as we enter the workshop. She looks old and tired, little more than a bag of bones, and for the briefest moment, I realise that she's really quite frail. Her personality is fierce, and her actions are much the same, but she's old, probably the oldest person I've ever known. Before I open my mouth to speak, she turns, eyes sharp as she straightens. There's a smile on her lips as she bids me to sit beside her while Cuthred hurries to tend to the fire.

'You've returned,' I offer, once more, aware the words are unneeded.

'Yes, lad, I have, and good news as well. Lady Cynehild and her husband have a fine and lusty son, blond of hair and red of face, and with the lungs to wake the dead. He's to be named Coenwulf, of course.' She smiles, her pleasure genuine.

'The birth was easy on her, then?' I ask quickly, desperate to be reassured.

'Not easy, no, but done, and she can rest now, with Gaya and Theodore in constant attendance on her. She'll lack for nothing. But, I hear you encountered Lady Ælflæd when you travelled to Budworth, and that you sought her, afterwards.'

'I did, yes, most unexpectedly, in Budworth, and then, well, she left before I could properly apologise.' I feel the need to justify my actions. Wynflæd knows me too well.

'Yes, I hear that as well. What did you say to her?' I can't tell, from Wynflæd's tone, if I've erred or if she's just being nosy.

'Nothing, well, not much, really. We prayed over my uncle's grave, and I asked after Lady Cynehild, and then I didn't get to speak to her again. She left my hall just as I returned to it for the night, and in the morning, she was gone before I woke, and so I followed her, because, well, there was a fight in my hall that night, broken up only thanks to her words. I felt she'd think poorly of me if I left things as they were.'

'Hmmm.' Wynflæd nods along with my words.

'And yet, something happened in Budworth, other than a fight. I could detect it when I saw her. She seemed flustered and uneasy and desperate to speak to her brother, although he was only interested in his son and his wife. You say you met her in the churchyard.'

'Yes. I went to find Cenfrith's grave. And I saw his parents grave as well.'

Wynflæd nods along, still clearly waiting for me to say something else to explain Ælflæd's reaction. I pause. I can offer little else. Cuthred hands me a beaker of water infused with some of Wynflæd's herbs and spices. I welcome the sharp bite mixed with a pleasant sweetness in appreciation.

Silence falls between us, and then I do remember something.

'My uncle never told me my mother was buried at Budworth, and I confess, I never thought to ask.' Wynflæd's hands, I notice, suddenly seem to clasp her beaker more tightly.

'I've heard,' she murmurs, 'that the grave feature is quite elaborate.'

'It is, yes. Nothing like that which crests my uncle's or his parents'. Were they,' I decide to risk asking, 'people of the court?'

'They were allies of Beornwulf's family, yes, but

not beloved of King Coenwulf, although he was closer to King Coelwulf, who was king after his brother.'

'Godwulf told me that my uncle was the commander of Beornwulf's household warriors. Is that true?' I'm remembering everything I wished to ask. And, if Wynflæd is going to ask me questions, I'll demand answers to my own.

Wynflæd's head tips from side to side in consideration.

'Yes, but really no. Your uncle didn't want the position. He had other tasks he wished to accomplish. So, really, no. Most will only remember Cynath as Beornwulf's commander, and of course, he died fighting the East Angles. Who is this Godwulf?'

'One of the men who defected to Athelstan, the king-slayer.'

'Then he merely means to cause you trouble. Lady Ælflæd mentioned there was an unwelcome visitor.'

'Yes, he followed me to Tamworth as well, but Eahric, Wulfheard, Cenred and Oswy have sent him away.'

'Good, you attract trouble like wool does dust.' She shakes her head, a small smile on her lips.

'I don't mean to,' I counter.

'I know. It just happens that way sometimes. But, at least Godwulf's gone, for now. But don't be surprised if he returns. I imagine he thinks to find gain for himself by telling you of his connection to your uncle. All you need to know is that your uncle was beloved of Beornwulf and also a friend to King Coelwulf. He might have supported Beornwulf but it was with unease. King Coelwulf had lost much support long before then. After all, Coelwulf was never destined to be king. He spent his long life supporting his brother as king and his brother's son as the future king. It was a tragedy when King Coenwulf's son died, and King Coenwulf followed not long after. But still, we're no closer to determining the cause of Lady Ælflæd's evident upset,' she continues as we drink in companionable silence, Cuthred joining us with a cheeky smirk that has me thinking he shouldn't be. But we're all friends here.

'They say it's going to be a bad winter,' I eventually offer, deciding to think about something else.

'Well, it's been a good summer, so a bad winter must follow it. Winterfylleð is almost upon us, and it'll not be long then until Blotmonað and then Geola. Soon the bishop will be busy with his preparations for Christ's Mass, and we need worry only about keeping fed and warm.' Wynflæd speaks with the confidence of a woman who's lived through many such events in the past. Some think the winter a time to be fearful of, but the summer has been good, and I've seen the king's grain stores.

'Just keep your nose out of trouble,' Wynflæd finishes with a wry smile. 'And then we can all sleep well, no matter the terrible weather.'

5

AD 831–832

The winter is long and hard. The ground is so solid that it's impossible to practise on the training ground, and no one even considers risking their horse over the slippery surface. And then, snow falls as well, covering the land in a thick cloak of purest white. The weather makes it impossible for the royal court to move to one of its other holdings, and that means I'm locked up with Lord Wigmund, and his growing band of cronies, as the snow freezes, adding to the layers of ice already underfoot. The king's warriors are tasked with clearing the snow inside the settlement, but it's a thankless one. No sooner is it clear of snow and ice, than night falls and one or the other returns. The well has to be cracked clear every morning, and even the twin flowing rivers are almost brought to a standstill.

Worse, the arrangement for Wigmund's union with Lady Ælflæd gathers pace. Each evening I hear of new details for the coming union of the king's son and Lady Ælflæd, whispered amongst the servants, or even from Ealdorman Ælfstan. Each new stray piece of information unsettles me. I don't think myself in love with Lady Ælflæd, but I do know she deserves to be tied to a much better man than the king's son, Wigmund. Wigmund spends his time gambling and drinking, his friends and allies robust in their drunkenness each evening. More than once a handful of warriors are called from the warm hearth to find one or another of them, lost on the way to the latrine ditch, and in danger of freezing to death wherever they've wandered off to.

Queen Cynethryth and Ealdorman Sigered are as close as thieves in their discussions, the king more likely to be found drinking and gaming with his ealdormen. Ealdorman Ælfstan is prominent amongst them, his youthful face a reminder of all the ealdormen who've died in recent years fighting Mercia's enemies in Wessex and the kingdom of the East Angles. Mercia lacks men of a certain age, unless black-smiths, farmers or traders.

We warriors are left with little option but to play games, endlessly tend to byrnies and weapons, and then, when it's all too much, I find myself, as so often in the past, seeking the solace of Wynflæd's hut. Not that she minds. She's busy. The weather is so poor that people suffer from all ailments. I'm set to work time and time again, preparing poultices and lotions to ease the suffering of others, even when my nose streams without cease, and I'm left coughing and reaching time and time again for warm water, sweetened with precious honey and infused with dried summer berries.

'When we talked of a bad winter, I didn't expect it to be so bad,' I murmur to Wynflæd as she sits before me. Exhaustion weighs on her frame, and I confess, I'm fearful for her. Even the bite of her tongue has diminished. I've even caught Cuthred, his eyes furrowed in confusion, when he makes a mistake and she doesn't berate him for his lack.

'The summer was bountiful, as I said.' Her voice is rough from a sore throat, and Cuthred hurries to refill her beaker with more of the soothing mixture.

'So, we must be punished?' I query, but she shakes her head and smiles softly.

'It isn't punishment. These things happen from time to time. We'll live through it and welcome the warmer weather gleefully. Don't fret, young Icel. All will be well, no matter what the queen implies.'

Queen Cynethryth has determined to rule the settlement with an iron will. She's severely restricted the quantity of ale available for the household warriors, and she's determined that all must attend daily services of thanksgiving in the church, despite the fact the roof has more holes than thatch. During one service, I watched, unable to look away, as constant raindrops fell on the head of Ealdorman Ælfstan. How he bore it, I don't know. He didn't even move.

The king allows her to do as she wishes, too caught up in his own efforts to survive the tedium of winter, while Lord Wigmund and his allies are allowed to drink all they want. If the queen thought to win her son more allies by such a tactic, she's utterly failed. The unease building around Wigmund far outweighs any who support him. I would tell her myself, but I know she wouldn't listen.

The queen believes that Mercia is being chastised. I've not determined for what Mercia is being rebuked, but the bishop is content to allow the queen to say it is so. The bishop, while remaining enclosed inside his voluminous robes and cloak, has discovered how much he likes to preach to the men of war who have no choice but to listen to his sanctimonious words. We're caged by the weather as well as his words, and the bishop is determined to enjoy his moment.

I've spoken to Ealdorman Ælfstan about the king. He shares my concerns. Wiglaf thinks himself a warrior, like his men. He's fought so many battles and been so victorious in them that the nature of true kingship, of charters and laws, of justice and careful food management, are tedious to him. With his ealdormen, he can relive the glories of his successes. I imagine they're more welcoming than the cold queen.

I stay silent. I almost think that Wynflæd is in awe of Queen Cynethryth. I believe she finds her current actions, while a little too over the top, to at least be a means of keeping the settlement safe from the fights of men who like to brawl, while the reach of the church seems to grow with every mass preached by the bishop. Of course, Wynflæd is often excused from religious services. She has people who need her aid. Sometimes, she bids me stay with her, and I too escape the wailing of the bishop.

'At least,' Wynflæd continues, 'while we're forced to remain indoors, no other can make war against

Mercia. Be grateful for the peace,' she urges me, reaching for her beaker to swallow down the warm fluid and stop herself from coughing. I share a look with Cuthred. Both of us are concerned about Wynflæd.

'You can stop looking at one another like that. I'm fine. A cold, nothing more. It'll pass, as the winter will. Now, I have news of my own,' she continues, fixing me with a firm gaze. 'The queen intends the marriage to take place after Easter has been celebrated. She's setting arrangements in place, even as we speak.' I keep my face smooth, determined not to reveal my true thoughts. 'The queen doesn't want her son far from Tamworth but has determined that her son should have his own household once he's married.'

She offers this to reassure me that I need not see Lord Wigmund and his wife every day.

'Then I'll welcome the feast,' is all I can think to say.

Wynflæd's eyebrows rise, and she nods, perhaps satisfied with my lack of a heated response. But then she continues. 'He'll look to build his own household warriors. I suggest you ensure you're not included in that.'

'I owe my oath to the king,' I remind her. 'And I'm honoured by Ealdorman Ælfstan.'

'Yes, you are, but your reputation might be your undoing. I'd recommend you speak to the ealdorman.'

'I'm sure Lord Wigmund wouldn't want me anywhere near him.'

'Perhaps not, but then, he might enjoy having your oath. He's that sort of an individual.' Wynflæd's words have fallen to little more than a whisper, and I realise she's actually more concerned about this than my thoughts on the actual marriage.

'I'll do as you say,' I concede. I don't want to be anywhere near Lord Wigmund, not if there's the possibility he'll be gone from Tamworth. Perhaps, he and his wife will settle at Worcester or Gloucester, both settlements close to Lady Ælflæd's home.

'Good lad,' she offers before coughing once more. When she recovers her poise, her eyes are watering, and her nose is running, but there's a rush of cold air as the door is opened, and someone enters, coughing as well.

I look to meet the miserable face of my fellow warrior, Maneca.

Wynflæd rushes to her feet, eyeing him as he takes her place.

'My voice...' The warrior tries to speak, but little noise comes from his throat. Before Wynflæd can even ask, Cuthred is at the fire, adding more water to the mixture, while I pour from the jug and offer it to Maneca. He takes it eagerly, only to wince at the smell of the mixture.

'It tastes better than it smells,' I assure him with a sniff and then blow my nose noisily on a strip of cloth. There are few who haven't been struck down by the shivering and running nose or sore throat of the winter illness. It makes for a miserable settlement.

* * *

Easter comes only slowly, the religious festivities of Lencten adding to the tedium of waiting for the warmer weather to arrive. I don't think a single member of the settlement has managed to avoid catching a cold that has everyone sniffing and coughing, although no one has succumbed to the chill. We've not been forced to hack at the frozen ground to inter the dead.

Wynflæd fusses that she'll run out of honey to soothe aching throats, but as the first lambs are born, all traces of the cold and the wind of Hlyða leave

Tamworth. I'm grateful for that respite, even as I prepare to watch Lady Ælflæd marry Lord Wigmund as soon as the festivities of Easter have been observed. When he's not been wiping his snotty nose, Wigmund has been busy adding more and more to his group of followers as well as drinking and gambling. King Wiglaf doesn't seem to notice Wigmund's accumulation of allies, but it's proving to be a problem for those who never thought a king's son would notice them.

I've spent less time with Ealdorman Ælfstan than such a small settlement implies is possible throughout the winter months. And yet, I've spoken to him of my concerns about the king's son, and the creation of his household warriors.

'If Lord Wigmund means to make you his man, then he'll have to approach the king directly. And, whatever you think of the king, and his lack of attention towards his family, he holds you in high regard. He won't give you up,' the ealdorman reassured me when I was finally able to ask him for advice. I hope the ealdorman's confidence isn't misplaced.

'He asked me to join his household warriors,' Oswy muses angrily. 'As if I want to be anywhere near him these days.' Oswy's not the only one to grouch about Wigmund's attempts to tempt men away from

Ealdorman Ælfstan's side. By rights, Wigmund should either already have his own collection of warriors or have asked his father to take them from the household warriors who are loyal to him. To try and take Ealdorman Ælfstan's men goes against all precedent. Luckily, none have been tempted by his offer, but it's becoming increasingly awkward for all involved.

'Ealdorman Ælfstan said he'd speak to the king,' Wulfheard consoles as we finish our run around the training ground. Sweat drips freely down my shoulder blades, but I welcome the slight edge of the biting morning on my throat. It's nice to take a deep breath and not worry about coughing afterwards.

'There'll be no point soon enough unless he means to ask Icel.' Oswy chuckles maliciously at his words, and I throw him a scowl that only makes him laugh even more.

'The sooner he's married and gone from here, the better,' Cenred adds. We come to a halt, all of us bending low to catch our breaths. Unlike previous years, when we might all have suffered from a little too much extra girth around our waists, I note that all of the men are as thin as ever. What we lack are the muscles we might need to fight our enemy.

'It's not long now, no more than seven days, and

Lord Wigmund and his poor wife will be far from Tamworth.' I turn to Wulfheard in surprise, it seems I'm not the only one to realise that Lady Ælflæd is definitely getting the poorer side of the bargain with this union.

'And how long until Queen Cynethryth thinks of an excuse to join her son?' Cenred murmurs. That startles me as well, but the queen has become over-demanding of late. She and Ealdorman Sigered are too often in one another's company. Even the king has finally made note of it, although, as Ealdorman Ælfstan tells it, he did try to make light of it, saying that Ealdorman Sigered was welcome to spend his time in conversation with his difficult wife. Aside from that, we're all aware that it's the servants who bear the brunt of Queen Cynethryth's tongue.

'As soon as there's a child, I would suspect.' Oswy confirms what we're all thinking about how long the king and queen will live side by side. The king and queen are no more distant to one another than any other married couple, but everyone can see that the queen has grown short in her temper towards her king. Equally, the king has become an expert at ig-noring his wife. The company of his warriors is what cheers him, not the complaints of his wife.

'The sooner there's another battle, the better.

Maybe King Athelstan of the East Angles will send word of more Viking raiders along the waterways,' Kyre glowers. We're all fed up with being stuck at Tamworth while the queen plays politics.

'We'll ride out this summer, as always,' Wulfheard assures us. He's quickly dividing us up into pairs so that we can fight one another. I turn to face Frithwine, and he arches an eyebrow at me. We're not the best fitted of the fighting men. Frithwine isn't the seax wielder that I am, and likewise, he's much better with his sword than me. We'll both end this with bruises.

There are few fighting men within Tamworth after the long winter months. I've heard the tale of Beowulf so many times I can recite it as well as the poor scop who's been stuck in Tamworth since Geola. I am, however, grateful that he's forgone his doom-laden tales of the Viking raiders. Now that we've fought them and beaten them, he can't truly terrify us with tales of their Gods and their strange religious beliefs. Equally, there have only been so many occasions that Uor has been asked to regurgitate the scop's words with his own interpretation of how they apply to King Wiglaf's warriors, as he did outside Peterborough.

Ealdorman Tidwulf has spent the winter at his

properties, whereas Ealdorman Beornoth has returned to Londinium. The king has only his household warriors and, of course, those who comprise Ealdorman Ælfstan's force at his command. For a while, we thought we might be sent to Londinium, but we weren't. Equally, we thought we might be sent to Peterborough as well, but that command was never given. And to the west, there's been no request from Hereford or Gloucester that they might need assistance from King Wiglaf. Yet, I'm not alone in thinking it's altogether too quiet.

'Now, you're just to spar,' Wulfheard calls to us. 'I don't want you with black eyes and bloody noses when the marriage goes ahead.' His words are greeted with the thud of iron on wood as we all begin to eye up our opponents. Frithwine seems particularly lacklustre as I manage to get close enough to him to really wound, and yet, just as I think I can count myself the victor, I feel his blade tip at my throat.

'Overconfidence will be the death of you,' Wulfheard hollers to me from where he's keeping a careful watch over us all. 'You've not won until your opponent is mewing on the ground like a baby or entirely silent. Well done, Frithwine.'

I glower at Frithwine, but he shrugs his shoulders

in a 'what can I do' way, and I resolve not to take out my frustrations against him. I could lash out angrily, but that will be no good. Instead, I step back and take my time bringing the pair of us back to a similar moment, only to step aside from Frithwine and place my seax at his throat.

'Better,' Wulfheard hollers, but I'm feeling the effects of so much activity after my days coughing and sniffing throughout the long winter, and for the third bout, Frithwine easily gains the advantage on me. I step aside from his attack, aware I'll have some bruises but none on my face. Reaching for my cloak, I turn to make my way back inside Tamworth. But Frithwine loiters, and I turn to him, eyebrows furrowed.

'Frithwine, are you well?'

Silence greets my words. He's staring out towards the rivers.

'Frithwine,' I try once more, but he still doesn't hear me, so I walk to him. I don't mask my steps, nor do I stamp my way to his side. I'm startled to find tears streaming down his face. He sobs but makes no noise. I stand beside him. I'll keep him company while he mourns for his brother. I know such things can take the best of us by surprise. No doubt he remembers their times on the training ground when they were young and foolish and believed they'd long outlive the attacks of Mercia's enemies. The truth has been horribly different.

Quickly, I realise that we're alone, but I don't urge him to hurry. Neither do I leave him unaccompanied. I know that in grieving my uncle, I've welcomed the understanding of others. Well, all apart from Wynflæd, who has no empathy where grief is concerned. I've decided that she's witnessed too much pain and suffering and that the only way to counter it is to pretend it doesn't happen.

Eventually, I'm forced to wrap my cloak more tightly around me, the chill of the day making itself known the longer I wait. My thoughts have gone to my uncle. I've tried not to think of the day I visited his grave, and Lady Ælflæd happened upon me. More importantly, I've tried not to think too much about her strange reaction and how she shied away from speaking to me again. I don't understand it even now. I wish I did, but I'm unlikely to ever ask her about it now. I had my chance, and I didn't take it. It would be far too awkward and, perhaps, far too personal to ask now, and as she's to be Lord Wigmund's wife, and the future queen of Mercia, it's truly none of my business. And yet? Well, I should like to know why all the same. Wynflæd was aware that something had happened in Budworth, and yet she didn't manage to get the truth either. I take some consolation from that.

'Does it get easier?' Frithwine's voice is distant, and I only just catch his words.

'Some days,' I counter, aware it's not very reassuring. 'Other days, it's as though it's just happened all over again.' I'm not going to lie to him. Frithwine has tried to contain his grief, but we all feel it for him.

'I'll kill all the bastards who took him from me.' Frithwine turns to glower at me, his furious face surprising me so that I take a backwards step, thinking he might hit me.

'I think we killed most of them,' I try to deflect.

'No, we killed some of them, and there'll be more, I'm sure of it. Whatever was happening in the kingdom of the East Angles is far from over. There'll be more, and I plan on meeting them and countering their attacks.'

'And I'll be there, fighting at your side,' I confirm. I miss Garwulf. I thought he was annoying when he lived, and he was, but that doesn't stop me from missing him.

'Then we'll vanquish his loss together,' Frithwine confirms, which seems to cheer him, for he strides away from me, back towards Tamworth, and I'm forced to run to catch up with him. So much for staying behind and keeping him company. He makes it across the wooden bridge and behind Tamworth's walls before I can join him. A fat lot of thanks for standing as his guard.

6

AD832

I try and catch the eye of Lady Ælflæd as she enters Tamworth mounted on her horse, Sewenna, but she either doesn't see me or doesn't want to. I'm not sure which it is. I suspect the second, but I hope it's the first. The area is filled with every single person who lives inside Tamworth standing to welcome the future wife of Lord Wigmund two days before her marriage is due to be celebrated. There's a feeling of intense joy all around me, and yet I don't share it.

Lord Wigmund has been strutting around Tamworth for the last few days as though getting married was something which only he was capable of achieving. That his cronies seem to agree with him isn't helping matters. The sooner Wigmund's wed and gone from Tamworth, the better for all of us. Especially for me.

Lady Ælflæd arrives in a convoy alongside her brother and her sister by marriage. I see Edwin, Heahstan and Oswald amongst those who've served as a guard on the journey from Kingsholm. The queen also sent Ealdorman Sigered and his grandson to serve in the escort alongside half of the king's household warriors. Luckily, none of Ealdorman Ælfstan's warriors were required.

I can't imagine it's been a pleasant journey for Lady Cynehild, surrounded by so many people she dislikes, and all bringing them memories of when she was queen of Mercia. The weather has been far from kind, which will have only added to the misery. Winter is slow to give up its hold on the land.

There's a great deal of fanfare as the king and queen meet their guests, Lord Wigmund striking some pose that he must think makes him appear manly and worthy of his bride. I do detect a slight smirk on Lady Ælflæd's face as she stands beside her future husband in a thick fur cloak, but I might be mistaken. Perhaps she's pleased to be wed into the family of the ruling king as opposed to thinking Lord Wigmund is an arse. I've not spoken to her since our meeting after Budworth. I've thought about her a great deal, however.

There's also another face amongst the group, bearing a similar look. With far fewer winters to her name than Ælflæd, I realise it's Lord Coenwulf and Lady Ælflæd's youngest sister. I can't remember her name, and I'm not actually sure I ever knew it when I was at Kingsholm. She's much younger than her brother and sister. She must have been born after her father was deposed from the kingship of Mercia.

And, of course, somewhere further back in the group must be Cynehild's son, Coenwulf, no doubt under the watchful gaze of women tasked to tend to him.

I also try and catch the eye of Lady Cynehild, but she's too busy with her tasks of dismounting and showing some friendliness towards the queen and the king. I know that Lady Ælflæd is only her sister by marriage, but I can't imagine she truly wishes the ineffectual Lord Wigmund on Lady Ælflæd. Pleased when the welcoming party is eventually concluded after numerous speeches and cheers of acclamation, all made in the chill day, I take myself to Wynflæd's workshop, and she eyes me with a knowing look. I can tell she's taken no part in the celebrations. Her cheeks are pink, and not from cold, but from the heat of the hearth.

'Here, I need these chopping, and Cuthred always does it wrong,' she orders me, her lips set in a line as she shoves a chopping board and a collection of early nettles towards me. I catch the glower of fury on Cuthred's face and his mouth opening to protest at her unfair words, and then he snaps it shut. I can imagine he's been given a look by Wynflæd from beside us. I appreciate her giving me something to do. Short of fighting against my fellow warriors, my only options are to drink excessively, which I don't like to do, or brood about what's happening. Briefly, I consider seeking out one of the servants who looks on me kindly, but one thing I'm sure about: I don't wish to become a father at the young age of seventeen winters.

I don't like Lord Wigmund. I'm aware that colours my view of him. Conversely, I do like Lady Ælflæd, and I don't think she deserves a husband such as Lord Wigmund. Not, I admit, that this union is a love match, but rather one of politics. And indeed, I don't know if I have feelings for Lady Ælflæd or merely look at her as an ally. I'm conflicted about my thoughts for her. I shouldn't be. She's to be queen of Mercia one day. No doubt, that's what she wants.

After all, her father was Mercia's king. She must have had expectations that one day she'd play an important part in the governance of her father's kingdom, even if she wasn't to be Mercia's queen. If this is the only way she can achieve that aim, and become queen in the process, then she's welcome to it.

From outside, the passing conversation of others can be heard, as can horses' hooves over the hard-packed ground and also the occasional whack of iron on iron from the blacksmiths. No doubt Edwin's mother is pleased to see her son. I can't say the same. Maybe I'll be able to avoid him. My nose has long since healed, but not my displeasure towards him for what happened between us.

And then, and perhaps as expected, Lady Cyne-hild calls for admittance into Wynflæd's workshop. Cynehild shows no surprise at seeing me as she settles herself before the hearth fire. It's good that Wyn-flæd has no patients to tend to, as there'd be no room for her otherwise.

'Wynflæd, Icel, Cuthred.' Lady Cynehild's cheeks are flushed, no doubt with the coolness of the day, the bite as winter bleeds away into spring. The warmer weather of the summer will be welcomed when it arrives. I lift my head and run my eyes over Cynehild. It seems that she's recovered well from the birth of her son. There's a glow about her. I think she must be happy.

'My lady,' Wynflæd offers, not bothering to curtsey or show any other form of respect. Cuthred surges to his feet, but Cynehild shakes her head.

'Here, we're all the same.' She waves him back to his seat. Now, all four of us sit, and there's a comfortable silence between us. I almost feel my tight shoulders relax, and my cutting action responds to the lessening of tension. The nettles, now I slice them, are more evenly spaced, and I manage to avoid stinging myself by holding them correctly as I work.

'How fares the child?' Wynflæd breaks the companionable silence, and Cynehild's face softens into one of love and devotion. I've seen it before on women who've become mothers for the first time.

'He's a delight and well formed. Gaya and Theodore assure me he's progressing well for his age.'

'Then you're content?' I almost gasp to hear Wynflæd's question, but Cynehild merely smiles even wider.

'It's wonderful to be a mother, but I came to see how you all were. Not to talk non-stop about Coenwulf, which, apparently, I'm quite likely to do. The

queen has already tired of my motherhood
babblings.'

Wynflæd chuckles darkly at those words while
Lady Cynehild's voice is filled with slightly wounded
pride. 'The queen has no maternal feelings at all. All
she sees is her son as an object that she can manipulate to achieve her own ends.'

'Yes, I realised that, and yet Ælflæd doesn't seem
to object to him as a husband. I fear she's as ambi-
tious as the queen. The two will, no doubt, butt
heads at some point.' Lady Cynehild's words are
mildly spoken, all the same I detect some malice behind them. I determine that she's not happy about
the marriage. Maybe I could speak to her about my
own fears for Ælflæd? I know it was a part of an
agreement between Lord Coenwulf and the king, but
should it really have involved Ælflæd?

I feel my shoulders tighten as my thoughts
tumble once more. I determine to distract myself.
'How are Gaya and Theodore?' I manage to ask,
looking up from my careful slicing.

'They were well when I last saw them, but Ealdorman Tidwulf had them summoned to his side,
and so it's been a month since they were last in attendance upon me.'

'I hear the ealdorman is collecting quite a variety

of healers to him,' Wynflæd mutters. She's pleased that Gaya and Theodore don't live at Tamworth, and yet I believe she's also envious. No matter the coin I gave to her to spend on herbs and remedies, I know there's much that she could still learn from the formerly enslaved duo.

'It seems so, yes. He's fascinated by all that they know and believes that if he finds the right people, he'll be able to cure any ailment.' Lady Cynehild speaks lightly, no doubt aware that if she says too much, Wynflæd will grow angry. And yet Wynflæd surprises me with her response.

'It's time that the art of healing was in more than the hands of the monks. I wish the ealdorman well with his task. I hope he has everything written down in our language, as opposed to in Latin or even Greek. We need to be able to understand the remedies if they're known.'

I'm not alone in looking shocked at Wynflæd's words. And she's not finished yet. She smirks as she meets our eyes. 'If I die before young Cuthred learns how to cure the sleeping sickness, then half of Mercia will always be asleep, and we can't have that, can we?'

* * *

I don't get to speak to Lady Ælflæd before her marriage to Lord Wigmund is celebrated in the church of St Chad's at Tamworth. I watch from afar, conflicted about the whole thing. Certainly, she shows no hesitation as the bishop binds them before God and all those assembled. Neither does she look unhappy as she presides over a lavish feast to which all the ealdormen of Mercia and their wives have been invited. There's no room for Ealdorman Ælfstan's household warriors, and while I might be accorded a place, as the lord of Budworth, I prefer to join the more raucous and badly behaved feast that spills into the roadway. We shelter within our cloaks against the sharpness of the wind until most men are too drunk to realise it's too cold to be sitting outside, even though a large outdoor fire has been lit to try and warm us all.

The food is good and plentiful. I ignore the ale and drink only a little mead. Frithwine drinks deep into his cups, and I feel some pity for him. While all celebrate, his brother is still dead, and no one truly seems to care any more. I know how he feels. It has been nearly two years since Cenfrith's death. Other than Wynflæd, I believe everyone has forgotten his existence.

'Will there be war with the kingdom of the East

Angles?' I hear some of the warriors asking on the bench behind me. I know the men there look to Commander Eahric, and I'm curious to see the response.

'The peace has been agreed, for now. I can't see that King Athelstan will think to strike those who aided him only last year, but we shall see,' one of Eahric's trusted men informs the others, only slightly stumbling over the words as he sways from side to side, holding a cup of ale before him. I think more falls to the floor than ends up being swallowed. The hounds who try their luck beneath the benches and stools will be as pissed as the men. They'll fight as much as the men do, as well.

'And Wessex?'

'Still licking their wounds,' the same man counters and a bark of laughter fills the air. I share their belief. I don't think we'll ride to war this coming summer, not unless the pestilent Welsh determines to attack Mercia on the western borders. And if that's the case, then I don't know how I'll be spending my summer months. Hopefully, it'll be far from Lord Wigmund and his bevvy of cronies. Once more, I find my eyes seeking out Lady Ælflæd in the crowd of people. She sits regally before the assembly, the stray words of the scop reaching me when there's a hush in the raucous cries of the drunk warriors and people of Tamworth. I realise then that I doubt we'll ever speak again.

There was a time when the thought of a peaceful summer was all I wanted, but now, the idea fills me with unease. I really need something to occupy my mind. Something other than Lady Ælflæd's union with Lord Wigmund. I don't suspect that I'll get my wish. I never seem to be that lucky.

7

AD833

'My lord king.' The man bows low before King Wiglaf, and I watch with only mild interest as the messenger is admitted to speak to Mercia's king. Another year has passed, and it's been altogether too peaceful. We spent last summer keeping a desultory watch on the eastern border, but there was no need. There were no Viking raiders, and the people of the East Angles, when we saw them, hailed us as friends, not foes. It's possible that there'll finally be peace between our two kingdoms. Neither did the Welsh kingdoms think to rise up against Mercia. After so many years of near-constant warfare, the summer months were tedious and uncomfortably hot. A spot of wind would have been welcomed. As would having something to do other than brood on the union of Lady Ælflæd and Lord Wigmund.

The winter has once more been cold and filled with the coughs and sneezes of those suffering its ravages. Wynflæd has tasked me with helping her keep a record of her cures, employing the services of one of Ealdorman Ælfstan's scribes who was unhappy at the task but who now seems to be as keen as Wynflæd to join in this great effort to write a leech book that others will be able to access to find Wynflæd's cures. I've watched her surreptitiously. She's slowing down, but with Cuthred and me helping her so far, I don't believe anyone else has noticed.

But once more, the promise of summer has brought a spring to the step of everyone. There's hope that the summer will be long and plentiful, if perhaps less hot than last year's. Fed up of my thoughts about Lady Ælflæd, I can't help thinking I'd welcome war more than peace. And if not war, then some sort of treachery afoot that requires my attention.

'Tell me your news,' the king orders his messenger. King Wiglaf is as firm in command of his warriors and any war effort as ever. I note that his wife is often not to be seen in his presence. In fact, she spends much of her time with her son and his wife,

Lady Ælflæd, where they keep themselves in one of the royal centres of Gloucester, Worcester or Lichfield. Tamworth is much more settled without Queen Cynethryth. I think King Wiglaf is as well.

I believe the messenger has come from Londinium, where Ealdorman Tidwulf is currently responsible for its defences. I'm not alone in entirely suspecting the Wessex king of being complicit in events in the kingdom of the East Angles two summers ago, and yet no proof has been forthcoming. Relations between Mercia and Wessex remain unsettled, but there has been no declaration of war, and the two sides have firmly kept to their borders.

'Ealdorman Tidwulf wishes you to know that a fleet of Viking raiders' ships has been spotted along the River Thames. He requests that you send more men to keep Mercia's borders safe.' I suddenly sit taller at these words. I glance around the king's hall and meet the eyes of the others. We're all keen to have an enemy to face. Warriors without an enemy to fight are merely bored men with little to occupy their thoughts.

'How many ships?' the king queries, sitting forward, his interest piqued. His voice betrays no fear.

'At least ten, perhaps as many as fifteen. The ealdorman believes they intend to attack Wessex, but all the same, in some places, the River Thames isn't that wide. They could easily assault Mercia instead.'

King Wiglaf nods and turns to his ealdormen. Ælfstan is there, alongside Beornoth and Mucel. They'd planned on some hunting in the nearby woodlands, but it seems they have bigger prey.

'Well, it appears we might finally learn the truth of events in the kingdom of the East Angles, and at Peterborough, two years ago, and whether King Ecgberht set the Viking raiders on us, or if they decided to come under their own sail. Mucel, you and your men will ensure the border area with that kingdom is secure. Beornoth and Ælfstan, take your men to Londonia and, in discussion with Tidwulf, determine the best course of action. I'll follow on more slowly. I must attend the bishop's consecration at Lichfield in ten days' time.'

I nudge Frithwine, who keeps me company, but his head is slumped on his chest, soft snores emanating from his nose. He drinks himself into a stupor earlier and earlier these days. It's become the task of one of us to ensure he's always watched. Frithwine has given himself, and a few others, some nasty scars in the last two years. I still pity him, but my sympathy is edged with frustration, and I too have a scar on my chin that he dealt me. He needs to sort himself out. What point was there in his brother dying to defend Mercia if Frithwine is merely to drink himself to sleep each and every day? I've tried to talk to him, to offer him the wisdom of what I've learned since my uncle's death, but Frithwine won't listen to me, and certainly not to Wynflæd. Even Edwin's mother has tried to console Frithwine, with her experiences of losing her first husband in battle. It didn't end well.

'My lord king,' the men all chorus. I realise that I'll have to inform Wynflæd and Cuthred of my absence. Hopefully, Cuthred has learned enough now to be able to help the scribe with his work on the leech book. Despite what Wynflæd says, Cuthred has a keen mind.

Eagerly, I stand and make my way to Wynflæd's workshop. From outside, I can hear her berating Cuthred for some new mistake. I wince at her tone and enter quickly in an effort to prevent her from flaying him alive. Only then I gasp, for Wynflæd isn't shouting at Cuthred. Instead, she's speaking, quite heatedly, with Gaya and Theodore. I didn't know the two were visiting Tamworth.

I meet their eyes from behind Wynflæd's back, where she continues to speak with passion, but as I listen to her words, I appreciate that she's not

shouting at them but rather sharing her rather forcefully given opinions.

'What is it?' She eventually rounds on me, her
words a snap of anger. Theodore winks at me from
behind her head, his distinctive green eyes flashing
in the firelight.

'We'll be leaving for Londonia tomorrow morning. I came to ensure you'd be able to continue with
your leech book in my absence.'

'Of course I will. Cuthred knows the remedies
better than you do now.'

Her response quite disheartens me.

'When you determined to become a warrior, you
left behind your old life.'

I want to reply, stung by her words, but now
Theodore shakes his head, and so I hold my angry
retort. It was hardly my choice to become a warrior.

'Then I'll take my leave of you.' I'm about to turn
when she reaches out and lays her hand on my
forearm.

'Take what you require first. If there are to be
battle injuries, then you must have everything you
need to tend to the wounds of your friends and allies. I've been storing supplies since last year when
they were only needed for the odd bump and
scratch taken falling from a horse.' Her grip is fierce,

and I'm reminded of her words to me when I returned from the kingdom of the East Angles. She
does look at me as her grandson. Perhaps I should
be grateful that I'm not actually her grandson, for I
fear she'd have whipped me with her tongue long
before now.

'You'll need vinegar, moss, linens, sliced nettles,
garlic, honey, betony, agrimony, woodruff, lily and
brooklime.' She lists them quickly, and I spy Cuthred
hastily running his hands along the vast collection of
jars and pots into which all of these herbs and treatments are carefully stored. I watch with fascination
as he lifts lids and sniffs them or grips them with the
long-practised ease of someone who merely knows
where they'll be in Wynflæd's particular order.

With the aid of the scribe, we've been making labels with scraps of old vellum for some of the jars,
especially the ones with the little-used ingredients
inside. It works well, provided we always replace the
jars and pots in the same position. Cuthred and I
have been trying to learn how to read all the labels,
but it's hard going. In the past, Wynflæd relied only
on her nose and her memory for each of the herbs
and spices. It's just another way that she's preparing
for the day she'll no longer be the one handing out
the potions and ointments.

'Are you well?' I manage to ask Gaya and Theodore while all this is happening.

'Yes, we've come from Londonia, with the messenger, to seek out Wynflæd. We have much to discuss with her, especially concerning a book of healing in the Greek tongue that's come into the hands of the bishop of Londonia.' At those words, spoken by Gaya, Wynflæd's face shows a flicker of annoyance, but she quickly recovers herself. I think it takes a very wise person to appreciate that they perhaps, and despite all the evidence to the contrary, don't actually know all there is to know about something which others think they're experts on.

'Then I look forward to hearing about it on my return,' I respond. I've enjoyed becoming reacquainted with the supplies Wynflæd keeps, but it has highlighted that I'm forgetting many of the more intricate cures she has. In time, I think I'll only be able to remember how to tend to war wounds. It doesn't take a great deal of skill to stitch torn flesh or apply bandages soaked with honey, or keep a supply of the correct type of moss for those wounds that are likely to bleed for a long time.

'Pig's gut,' I call to Cuthred, remembering how often I have to draw severed flesh together. 'And a few strong needles.'

'You'll need to get those from the blacksmith,' Wynflæd announces grumpily. 'He's been promising me them for weeks, and now he's run out of time to get them to me.' Her tone drips with annoyance.

'Don't forget corncockle,' Cuthred calls to me, his hand hovering over the jars still.

'And dandelion leaves,' Wynflæd adds. 'It'll do you no good if you forget the most simple of remedies.' Her words ring with a snap, but I detect a tremor of unease in them. Without thinking, I embrace her, feeling the wiry strength in her body. She doesn't batter me aside, and I smile to see the astounded look on Cuthred's face before I pull back, ensuring her footing is sound.

'I'll be back soon enough,' I assure her before she can get a word in, reaching over to take the bulging sack of supplies offered by Cuthred. 'And you'll be back to naming me a fool before you know it,' I conclude, hastening from her side as though she might slap my backside for the cheek.

* * *

Oswy leads us. The rest of the men ride in a loose formation. I'm at the rear, watching them, with Frithwine beside me. He's there, not because he's been sent to that position, but because he lolls in his saddle, barely conscious, and he's fallen back through the group of warriors to my side.

I believe the ealdorman would have been wiser to leave Frithwine behind in Tamworth, but what he'd have done in our absence, I'm unsure. Perhaps someone would have put him to work at an unpleasant task, and so it might have been better, as the ealdorman has done, to just keep him with us. At least we know him, or so I muse. We understand why he's so changed in the last few years. I fear for any enemy who thinks to face Frithwine.

Ealdormen Beornoth and Ælfstan ride together, their men mingling and sharing jokes and stories as we make our way southwards. While news of the Viking raiders is unwelcome, I confess, it doesn't feel urgent. If they really mean to attack Wessex, then Mercia need have no concern. King Ecgberht should be fearful, as should his son in the formally Mercian held Kent, but for Mercia, hopefully, all will be well.

I still consider the implications of why the Viking raiders seek out Wessex. Ealdorman Ælfstan has shared that it might be because they're an old enemy of the West Franks, thinking of taking out their revenge on one of the acknowledged allies of the West Franks king, as King Ecgberht is. Equally, the rest of us muse it could be because the Wessex king sent a collection of Viking raiders to attack the kingdom of the East Angles and Mercia two years ago. And that didn't go well. At all. But that's if King Ecgberht was responsible.

Equally, they might be bloodthirsty scum, determined to attack somewhere, take slaves and make coin for themselves. We'll know soon enough, I realise, as we continue on our way.

The road towards Londonia throngs with people about their business. No one speaks with fear or worry, and it's a far cry from when we followed the border between the East Angles and Mercia on that fateful journey two summers ago. Then we saw almost no one other than the refugees.

The harsh shriek of an eagle cuts through the still air, and I'm not alone in looking upwards, and sighting the magnificent creature, wings spread wide, riding the air above our heads. I am alone in running my fingers over the eagle scar on my hand. Perhaps the eagle's arrival is a sign that there'll be war.

'Wake up.' I reach across and slap Frithwine's arm, where it hangs low. It's a good thing that his horse is placid and happy to follow the rest of the horses.

'What?' Frithwine blinks his eyes, a thin line of drool pooling into his untidy beard as he awakens.

'Wake up, you bloody fool, before the ealdorman sees you.'

'Oh, Icel, we're merely riding. What does it matter if I sleep or am awake? The horse follows everyone else.'

'You should be alert and ready to ride to battle at any given moment,' I argue, half an eye still on the eagle as it banks and flies further north.

'I shouldn't be. I need to numb the pain of my brother's loss.'

'I thought you meant to take your vengeance for his death,' I goad him. I need to know that, one day, his drinking will end once he feels that vengeance has been gained.

'And I will if there's ever an enemy to kill. But they've been in surprisingly short supply of late. I'd happily kill someone.' Frithwine's words end with a growl.

'I don't know how you can drink as much as you do.' I decide to change tact.

'That, Icel, is because we're not all bloody do-gooders, as you are. I suggest you learn to drink and drown your sorrows as well. It would make you much easier-going. The other men might even like you more.' Those words sting, and I'm considering my response when I see the smile on his face. He's a cantankerous bugger these days.

'We'll all welcome some of the Viking raiders to kill,' I murmur instead. 'And perhaps, some of the Wessex warriors as well.' Our blades have been clear of blood for too long. Frithwine's not alone in decrying the lack of a bloody good fight.

* * *

We arrive in Londonia the following day. I'm unsurprised to once more see Mercia's eagle banner flying from the top of the fort of Londinium. I'm also impressed to find the defences around Lundenwic more substantial than the last time we were here. I knew the king had ordered defences to be built and reinforced. I hadn't appreciated quite how big a task that was. As my gaze is drawn higher, I see something else as well. Not only does Mercia's eagle banner fly from the top of the fort in Londonia, so too does an actual eagle. I consider if it's the one from yesterday, but dismiss the notion. Mercia has many eagles. This will be a different one. Once more, I take it as an omen. I'm not alone. Others mark its flight as well.

Riding through those defences, when the household warriors of Ealdorman Tidwulf allow us entry, I take a good look at the place. It seems to be a bustling hive of activity. The foreshore is littered with boats and ships of all shapes and sizes, and the houses extend further back onto dry land than the last time I was here. There are men, women and children of all shapes and sizes busy with their tasks. The tongues of many different kingdoms mingle together. The smell of woodsmoke and food being cooked fills the air, and it has the atmosphere of a feast-day celebration, not a place worried about the potential attack of the Viking raiders.

We're directed towards the main hall, and there, Ealdorman Tidwulf meets us with a wide smile on his face.

'Ealdorman Ælfstan and Beornoth, welcome to Londonia,' he calls. He wears his byrnie and weapons belt, and I realise that while all seem to be going about their day-to-day business, he's fearful of what the Viking raiders plan. His cheerful words are filled with relief at knowing he doesn't need to face the enemy alone.

The ealdormen converge inside the hall while we're left to tend to horses and seek food and drink from the many servants who hasten to assist us.

'Don't get too comfortable,' Wulfheard says, on

joining us. 'We're not staying here. We've instructions to travel east along the foreshore of the River Thames.' The news is unsurprising. There seems little point in protecting somewhere that already has much better ramparts than other locations.

Wulfheard stops before me and encourages a confidence.

'Frithwine?' he queries. I startle and realise he wants to know my opinion of him.

'He just needs to kill someone, and it should make him forget his ale and wine.'

'He's becoming an embarrassment,' Wulfheard growls. That amuses me. I've long known that Frith-wine was an embarrassment, but it seems that Wulf-heard has only just realised that. Perhaps, inside Tamworth, Wulfheard has been too preoccupied with other tasks to appreciate how far Frithwine has fallen in his grief.

'He can fight with the best of us, now,' I counter. 'But his sorrow is a heavy weight for him. I don't make excuses for him,' I quickly clarify. 'It's how he thinks to keep his demons at bay.'

'Then you must keep a close eye on him. I don't want him falling off his horse or wounding someone who's not actually one of the bloody Viking raiders. The ealdorman won't appreciate having to pay the wergild for any such fights.' I sigh at this.

'Couldn't Oswy or even Cenred?' I know the two like the young warrior.

'No, they couldn't. You can. Surely it comes under your healing duties or some such.' Wulfheard shows no sympathy for lumbering me with the drunk warrior. I turn and catch sight of Frithwine. Somehow, he already has jug and cup before him and is happily drinking himself insensible.

'I don't even drink ale.' I realise I'm whining, and Wulfheard knows it too.

'And that's why you're the perfect minder for him. At least we can trust you not to get yourself in the same state.' I have a mind to do just that, but I bite back my angry reply and instead lead Brute to the water trough and then remove his saddle. Oswy joins me as I make my way towards Frithwine. He already has a roast chicken leg in his hand, and juice drips down his bearded chin.

'Where did you get that?' I demand to know while my belly rumbles angrily.

'I made sure I had food before my horse.' He smirks. Only then a servant bearing food stops in front of me, and it's my turn to grin. Oswy might have a chicken leg, but I eagerly scoop a bowl of pottage, glistening with cuts of beef, and spoon it into my mouth.

'Wait.' I claim another bowl. 'For him, there.' And I point with my chin towards Frithwine. He's already swaying. It's going to take more than one bowl of pottage to absorb all that he's drunk.

'My lord.' The servant bows, and I open my mouth to tell him I'm not lord, only, of course, I am. I glance down at my byrnie and weapons belt, wondering what gave me away to the servant. I'm sure I look like the other warriors. I no longer have the arm rings the king gave me at Peterborough. Wynflæd had them melted down and turned into coins and then spent months moaning because the silver content was much lower than she'd hoped. Her ingratitude astounded me.

'Here, eat this.' I shove the bowl into Frithwine's cup-less hand, and then hold it until I'm sure he's got a good grip. 'Eat it all, and then you can drink more.' I hold the cup and take it from him, passing it and then the jug to Oswy. We've found barrels to sit on, while before us, all is chaos. The horses have been corralled into a corner of the open space before the main hall, and now the warriors of Ealdormen Ælfstan and Beornoth look for somewhere to rest while they eat.

Already, some of the men are playing games of chance, and I see an intense game of tafl taking place between Kyre and one of Beornoth's warriors.

'Kyre will win,' Oswy offers with his mouth open. 'He always does.'

Frithwine eats hungrily and thrusts the bowl back at me. 'My ale,' he demands, his words slurred.

'I think you've had more than enough,' Oswy counters, licking his lips before drinking deeply from Frithwine's cup. Frithwine leaps to his feet, almost knocking me flying to the ground, as he lurches to retrieve his ale.

'Wonderful.' I scramble to my feet and quickly get between the two men.

'Frithwine, you need to eat, not drink. Oswy, stop being a bloody arse and give the man his cup back.' Only Frithwine, with more speed than I suspected he'd be capable of when he's drunk so much, dashes around me, and now he does connect with Oswy, and the pair go down in a shriek of fists and shattering wood as the barrel upon which Oswy perched cracks under the weight of the two.

'Bloody hell,' I glower, aware that we've caught the attention of everyone now.

I wade between the two of them, a glancing blow

from Frithwine hitting my chin and knocking me off balance.

'Stop it,' I urge the two of them, but they're fighting, fists clenched, and the thump of the blows assures me that neither of them is playing at this. And all over some bloody spilt ale. Wonderful. I can hear my fellow warriors and those of Beornoth's placing wagers on who'll be the victor, the game of tafl forgotten, as I try and grab hold of one of them to pull them apart. But they're rolling and punching, and no sooner have I got a brief hold on one of them than my hands slip off their byrnie. I just hope they both forget they have much sharper blades to hand. The fists are doing enough damage.

'You bastard,' Frithwine huffs.

'You snivelling turd,' Oswy counters, as I once more just avoid a glancing blow to my right ear.

'Stop it.' Wulfheard is suddenly beside me, his eyes blazing with fury. He bends and manages to grab hold of Frithwine and pulls him away, leaving me with Oswy, with his bloodied nose and grinning face. I pull him to his feet while Kyre and Cenred finally get involved and step between the two opposing forces although the fight is long over.

'What the hell was that about?' Wulfheard roars.

We're not known for fighting amongst ourselves, as some of the other household warriors do.

'He stole my ale,' Frithwine sulks, and I'm not expecting Wulfheard's next words.

'Then he's done you a bloody favour. Now, get yourselves cleaned up. We're leaving,' and Wulfheard marches from the fight as I watch coins exchange hands around us. Someone has determined on the victor. Oswy spits a slather of blood from his mouth.

'You better watch out, Frithwine. You bloody arsehole. You'll pay for that.'

8

I'd sooner be nowhere near either Frithwine or Oswy, but somehow, I end up riding behind the one and in front of the other. I sigh heavily, aware this is deemed as punishment by Wulfheard. Damn him. It's not my fault the pair of fools decided to exchange fists in a very public way.

I keep my eyes on the fortress of Londinium as we cross the bridge that crests the River Fleet. I remember the fighting here. I recall holding the bridge almost single-handedly against the advance of the Viking raiders. We don't make our way inside the fort and its huge wooden gates. There's little point. It's not as though we can escape through another gate and save time on our journey east. Those other gates remain firmly blocked up. They were kept blockaded to keep the Wessex warriors from reclaiming Londinium, but it'll also keep the Viking raiders away.

'Who holds the garrison?' I ask of no one, and I get no response. It's too high and too bright to see those who watch from such a vantage point. I hope they have good eyes and can see almost to the far distant coastline where the River Thames meets the sea, according to Uor.

'Have the Viking raiders actually been seen recently?' Oswy grumbles. I can see where he has a blackening eye, and the end of his nose is crusted with blood. It's not broken. That's a small mercy.

'Yesterday,' is Wulfheard's immediate response. 'Three ships in the middle of the river.' His words are clipped. He's not happy. I would have thought it was because of the fight, but it might not be. He's not the only one to cast suspicious looks towards the river. He's also not the only one to search the skyline for clouds of smoke that might show where the Viking raiders have already begun their attacks. I feel a shiver of unease down my back and just manage to stop myself from reaching for my seax.

The lands to the far eastern side of Londinium are unknown to me. I look out across them, noting the dips and crests of hills and the woodlands, but the ealdorman and Wulfheard quickly direct us back towards the bank of the wide river. It's been a long day, and I can't see it ending anytime soon. Yet, we see no sign of any enemy incursion. There's no hint that a battle has occurred anywhere close by, and there's little sound other than the familiar hooves over the earth and the slurping and surging of the nearby river.

Despite my initial worry, I begin to relax, and when we're finally allowed to dismount for the day, I have no objection to being called to keep the first watch over our men and horses. If anything, as darkness covers the land, it's an effort to keep awake. We've been on the road for a few days, and it's always difficult to get used to activity after a winter behind the safety of Tamworth's walls. I remember the same from last year. More than once, I'm forced to blink grit from my eyes, stand to attention and then pace around the sleeping bodies of my fellow warriors. Even the horses sleep soundly, and it's a relief to wake Maneca for his watch duty and curl in my cloak and furs.

I'm woken early the next morning by the sound of rain drumming on the ground, and I scramble to my feet. We slept in the open last night, and now the fire sizzles with the rainfall, and I hurry to pull my cloak around my body or risk a day of being cold and damp.

'Anything during the night?' Wulfheard calls to Maneca, me and Cenred, the three with the onerous duty. At least we won't have to do the same tonight.

'Nothing,' I reply, hurrying to add more wood to the fire. If it doesn't catch, it'll be a cold meal to begin the day.

Maneca choruses the same response, but Cenred doesn't speak, and slowly, I turn to face him, aware that Wulfheard's tapping his foot with impatience. Cenred's shaking his head from side to side, his lips pursed in a line.

'I don't know what I heard,' he finally admits. 'But it was definitely something out on the river.' The news is far from reassuring as I turn to glower through the day's dampness at the river. I almost expect to see our enemy rushing up the incline of the bank, but of course, they don't.

'They'll probably be scouting the area,' the ealdorman informs us all, striding to the fire and holding out his hands towards it, no doubt hoping for some warmth. 'They'll be trying to decide where they can attack if they do decide to attack, and I can't see that they'd come all this way and not try their luck.' His voice is filled with suppressed fury. Eal-

dorman Ælfstan is unhappy, and I take it to be with
the Viking raiders and not with Frithwine and Oswy,
although he does sweep the pair of them with his
eyes. His face gives nothing away, but his fists clench.
Perhaps he wishes he'd had a chance with them.
After a winter of drinking with the king, maybe even
Ealdorman Ælfstan needs to vent some of his ag-
gression.

'Today,' he continues, 'we travel in our byrnies,
despite the bloody rain, and with our weapons close
at hand. If we come across any of our enemies, then
we'll fight them first and ask questions later.' Now it's
my turn to glance at my fellow warriors. They all
look fierce and determined, despite the mizzly rain
that clearly means to make everything as wet as possible. It would be better if the rain fell heavily and
cleared quickly, but I don't think that'll happen. It's
going to remain miserable as we seek out our enemy.
And no doubt, the low-hanging cloud will make it
much easier for our foemen to hide.

The remains of last night's pottage is barely
warm, but we eat it quickly and hurry to the horses.
Brute is uncharacteristically subdued, and quickly, I
run my hand along his legs and check his hooves for
any sign of injury. But there's nothing. I hold my head
to his neck, where his breathing also seems even.

'Don't like the rain?' I query as I mount up. He nickers softly in response. I remember previous rides where the rain was heavy, but at the end of it, we came across Viking raiders. Maybe he shares my trepidation about that.

'Oswy and Icel, you're to the rear,' Wulfheard orders us. 'Frithwine and Cenred, you're to the front. The rest of you, don't fall asleep and keep your eyes firmly open.' Wulfheard's as out of sorts as Brute. No one is particularly happy with our current orders.

'Nice day for it,' Oswy growls at me as we make our way to the end of our small line of warriors. There's not a huge number of us, but that's the idea. We need to be highly mobile, able to counter any small attacks, but more importantly, quick to return to Londonia and report any sightings of our enemy.

'Marvellous,' I counter, ensuring my cloak covers as much of my body and Brute's as possible. The scent of damp horse already pervades the air. We ride in silence, with Frithwine and Cenred leading the way. We don't move above a trot, and even then, the grasses are slick, and I fear for Brute. He doesn't seem to favour any of his legs, but he remains docile. That fills me with more worry than it should. Most, I imagine, would be pleased that their horse had calmed down. I'm not convinced of that. We've been rider and horse for several years now, but he remains un-predictable.

'I don't like this,' Oswy grumbles much later. No one talks as we continue eastwards. His words startle me, although I wasn't asleep. Instead, my ears strain at every slight sound. I've seen others peel off from the group and examine something they've seen or heard, but so far, there's been no cry that the Viking raiders have been found, and yet the slurping of the river can't be denied. We're close to it, and it's possible that one of their deadly ships could emerge from out of the rain-darkened gloom and surprise us all. One thing's sure. We can't see into Wessex from here. Our view only takes us some way over the River Thames.

'You don't like anything,' Landwine calls to Oswy, only making him mumble under his breath even more. I don't like it either, but I don't feel like we're about to be attacked. I don't sense we're being watched. After all, how could our enemy see us when we can't see them?

We ride on, eating hard bread and cheese in our saddles, allowing the horses to drink from a deep stream, and generally, trying our best to keep dry. The mizzle doesn't lift, and I'm grateful when our dull journey is called to a halt. Wulfheard has found us a stable to shelter in for the night, in a small, ditch-encircled settlement within sight of the River Thames, but far enough away that for the first time all day, I can't hear the surge of the water.

'We sleep here tonight,' Wulfheard informs us, twirling his cloak from his shoulders and using one of the harness nails to hold it against the wall, where it drips onto the straw and hay. There's only one other horse in the building, and it seems to offer a soft nicker of welcome before returning to nibble at its hay.

'The estate is a small one. The lord's away, ironically in Londonia for trading purposes. And so, we get to use his stable. The lady says she'll provide us with warm food in the hall. In the meantime, tend to your horses and then try and get dry inside the main hall. There's a fire, at least.' Wulfheard looks almost white with cold, and he hastens to the hall where the ealdorman will spend the night.

'It's all right for some,' Maneca grouses, but it's so much better inside than outside that I wouldn't mind if it were a hovel. At least I'll sleep without being woken by the rain.

Oswy and I walk to the main hall together, dodging puddles on the ground, Frithwine doing his best to stay away from the older man. A warrior stands on guard duty, and although he glowers at us, he opens the door and allows us inside quickly enough. There was also a guard at the gate who stood aside to allow us entry. It seems then that the lord and lady of this settlement are taking precautions against the Viking raider sightings as well.

A blast of heat touches my face on entry to the small wooden hall, and I feel warmer than I have all day. We join the rest of our warriors, sitting quietly close to the fire. The day has taken its toll on us all, and we stifle yawns in the heat and eagerly eat the offered food, which is a rich and flavoursome pottage. Wulfheard and the ealdorman talk to the lady of the settlement. She's an older woman, her hair entirely white, her face pinched, as though from the cold, which is impossible because it's so warm inside the hall, sweat beads down my back, almost as uncomfortable as the earlier rain.

Every so often, I turn to look at her. She doesn't make me uneasy, but her conversation with Wulfheard and Ealdorman Ælfstan seems more intense than just a pleasant discussion about how the estate fares. Not that anyone else seems to notice. And nothing is said, even the next day, which dawns bright and clear, for all the ground is damp underfoot. Now, we can see across the River Thames, and I squint into the brightness of the dawn because it's clear to see that on the far side of the river, a settlement burns, smoke rising high into the air, and that can mean only one thing. We've found the Viking raiders. We need to hope they stay on the Wessex side of the river.

'Can you see their ships?' the ealdorman calls, his head turning to face towards Londonia and then back, towards where the open sea lies.

'Not yet.' Wulfheard's response is immediate.

'So, they're not drawn up on the far riverbank?' The ealdorman seeks clarification.

'No, my lord, they're not.' It's Cenred who offers that, but my gaze is fixed on Frithwine. He and his mount are slightly apart from the group. As he and Cenred were leading, he's further away.

'Frithwine, what do you see?' I call to him. Brute's back to his robust self this morning. He bit my ear as I saddled him, and now he dances beneath me. I have to turn my neck sharply to keep Frithwine in sight.

'Have you seen the enemy?' Ealdorman Ælfstan bellows with more authority.

'I don't know, but look.' Frithwine points towards the open river, and for a moment, as I fight with Brute, I can't see what he means. By the time I have Brute pointing in the right direction once more, I can hear my fellow warriors pulling their weapons from their weapons belts.

'What?' I begin, but then I see it too. From the early morning haze, something moves across the water directly towards Mercia. How we've not seen it before, I'm unsure, but no doubt, the blazing flames, leaping along its length, have confused us. We were looking for a ship and sail, not a burning wreck, and that's surely what comes this way.

'Hurry,' the ealdorman calls, encouraging his horse along the side of the river. The ship is more than halfway over the River Thames and being dragged by the water towards the open sea, but there's the possibility that it will grind to a halt on the muddy foreshore of Mercia.

Brute eagerly surges to a gallop, even as I try and force him to no more than a canter. The ground is slick from all the rain yesterday, and I'm fearful that he might slip and really hurt himself. I realise now that it was little more than spite at the weather that made him so docile the day before. Today, with the smell of the river ripe in the air, the scent of smoke only wafting towards us occasionally, my horse is much keener.

'Icel.' Wulfheard shouts my name, and I wish I could tell him it's not my decision to go haring off as

Brute does. My eyes focused only on where we're going, I try and bring Brute under control.

'Wow, boy, wow, come on, slower,' I urge him, pulling so hard on the reins that my elbows end up behind my back, and Brute's head is forced lower and lower so that his vision must be impaired, yet still he thunders onwards. I spare a glance at the River Thames. The ship is still there. It continues to burn, and I realise that despite my initial thoughts that it might be empty, it's not. There are men on the ship, at least two of them, working with buckets to douse the flames, while outside the boat, others are holding on while they swim alongside it. It's evident they mean to save it if they can. One of the men catches sight of me, and he calls urgently to another, but there, on the river, they can do little to protect themselves. Likewise, we can only attack them when they're on Mercian land.

'Brute.' I roar his name as we surge over a narrow brook dispensing into the River Thames, and his hooves only just scrabble to the far side. Finally, he heeds my attempts to stop him and comes to an abrupt stop, almost forcing me over his shoulders.

'Bloody hell,' I glower, reaching down to slap him on the shoulder. His coat is thick with sweat, and he's panting heavily, as am I. 'Be careful,' I call to the others when they eventually catch me, for all they haven't jumped the brook. Wulfheard leads the charge, his face set like thunder for Brute's latest antics.

'Of what? Your bloody horse?'

'No, the brook. It's too wide. Go inland a little where the gap isn't so wide.' He does as I suggest, but I know he'll have words to say to me when we're re-united about how I shouldn't allow Brute to have his head.

The others follow on, Oswy smirking at me while Frithwine's eyes don't leave the river. It's a good job that his horse can direct itself.

'What was all that about?' Wulfheard eventually huffs, coming towards me.

'No idea, you know what Brute's like, sorry, but look, there are men on that ship and in the water, swimming.'

'So, they mean to come ashore then, to repair their ship if nothing else,' the ealdorman surmises, his face set in an unhappy grimace. 'Make sure you're armed and have your helms securely fastened,' Ælf-stan instructs us all, and I reach for my helm on my saddle and slide both the linen cap and the metal of my helm over my head. Immediately, I can hear much less. 'It's not as though they won't know they're being chased,' he further offers, and everyone looks to Brute, whose gallop has undoubtedly reached their ears.

I shrug my shoulders. 'We were going to fight them anyway.' It's far from an apology, but it is the truth.

'If they make it ashore, then our priority is to kill them all. Be careful. They might swim for it at different times.'

'Or they might stay on the river,' Cenred counters.

'They might, yes, but there's almost no ship left for them. They need to come ashore somewhere.'

I consider then how they've ended up in such a predicament. Is this related to the cloud of smoke on the far shore of the River Thames, or have they managed to set fire to their own ship in the night?

'Frithwine, ride beside me,' the ealdorman orders the young man, much to my surprise.

'Oswy and Cenred, you're at the front. Waldhere and Osmod, take the back.' I share a glance with Frithwine, who seethes at being denied the first opportunity to kill some of the Viking raiders. It appears that neither of us can be trusted to fight the enemy as we might want. Perhaps the ealdorman fears I'll try and save the men with my healing skills. I can assure him I'll do no such thing. And Frithwine? Well, he'll try to kill them all. I can't see how that's a problem.

We ride more cautiously now. I can't help realising that the ground is becoming boggier and less easy for the horses to ride over. It reminds me of our time in the kingdom of the East Angles.

Ahead, Oswy and Cenred ride no more than five horse lengths in front, while Waldhere and Osmod are even closer to the rear of our small group of warriors. The day begins to warm, or I'm just sweating more and more, unable to take my eyes off the burning ship. How much easier would it be if it just sank now, and we never had to fight the enemy? But, I'm not to get my wish. Just ahead, the land curves inwards, and I'm sure I'm not the only one to watch the burning ship and the sodden men as they disappear from our sight.

'Hurry,' Oswy calls from the front, and we all urge the horses onwards. Rounding the corner, I quickly realise that our worst hopes have been realised. Their ship has almost reached Mercia's shore, and it's not the only one. Already, Viking raiders have begun to set up a small camp. These men have had the easier task of reaching the shore in a ship that's entirely whole. Our only advantage is that they've set no guards. The arrogant sods.

I try and count how many enemies there are.
There's one ship, complete, and the burned ship,
which still sits on the water and not in it, but it's evident to my eyes that there are men enough to crew
both ships adequately. That puts their number at
least double ours. Yes, some of the men are wet and
bedraggled, but they're not, as I thought, fully
dressed in their warriors' equipment. I have the distinct impression that they've chosen to swim with the
ship to ensure it reaches this side of the river. Only
then do I become aware of the rhythmic sound of an
axe on wood, and I look up, trying to find what I've
missed. The bastard Viking raiders mean to use Mercian wood to repair their bloody ship.

9

We have one advantage, and it won't last long. As of yet, the enemy that's landed doesn't know they've been discovered. While they're busy at tasks, preparing food, tending to wounds, and even counting their collection of stolen goods, they're unaware the Mercians have discovered them. It speaks of arrogance. Or foolishness.

'We do this, and we do this quickly,' the ealdorman instructs us. 'We ride as close as possible to their camp, then dismount and attack them. Fight together, and ensure your fellow warriors aren't left stranded against our foemen.' His words thrum with conviction. I lick my lips, taste the salt of my sweat and nod along with his orders. There's no point in holding back the attack. When the swimmers make it to shore, they'll tell them of our arrival. We need to do this now.

'As one,' the ealdorman calls, and he, Oswy and Cenred spur their horses on. Brute is quick to follow, as is Frithwine's horse. Not that Wulfheard and the others are far behind.

The sound of the thundering hooves gives away our intention, but we're close enough by then that our advantage is hardly lost. Indeed, the cries of those on the burning ship, and those in the water, are loud, and I must assume they're trying to inform their allies of what's about to happen to them.

Ahead, Ælfstan, Oswy and Cenred quickly dismount, sending their animals back the way they've come, reins tied out of reach of legs that might tangle with them. I do the same, reaching for my shield as I do so.

'Go,' I urge Brute. Striding onwards, I can already hear that Oswy has encountered one of the enemies. The shriek of the Viking raider is loud and piercing, more like the cry of a vixen than a man. Oswy bloodies his blade, and the man falls to the ground, maroon flooding from his body. For a moment, his eyes watch me, chin resting on the ground, but as I pass him, I realise he's already dead, his gaze seeing nothing. I eye the camp before me. Viking raiders are struggling to their feet, reaching for any weapon they can find. The rhythmic sound of the axe chopping wood has stopped.

Ealdorman Ælfstan meets the next foeman, who rushes up the steep incline to face his enemy. He wears his battle gear, head covered with a black warrior's helm. He looks like a mean bastard, but he's not alone. More of his fellow warriors surge up the bank, and I thrust my shield before me to counter a wild axe strike from a small and wiry man who thinks to creep up on me. Only the squelching noise of his boots being released from the mud of the riverbank saves me as I follow up with a swipe of my seax. It goes nowhere near him, but he staggers backwards all the same, losing his balance on the lip of the slope. I rush him, one step, then two, and watch, astounded, as his arms windmill in the air. He thuds down the bank, rolling with a crack of bone.

'Bloody hell,' I exhale in relief. He's dead, and I've barely done anything but aid him in losing his balance. But there are plenty more of our enemies. More and more of them rush to meet the attack of the Mercians, and some of the stronger swimmers have also made it to dry land, carving a path through the water. I can see them running around, seeking weapons and byrnies before they join the fight. Perhaps, I consider, we should have attacked them before they could find the means to defend themselves.

But, a spear thuds into the ground at my feet. Belatedly, I jump out of the way, catching sight of a leering face from the spear thrower. Not that he seems to have another weapon to hand. I think to attack him, but another warrior gets between us, and he has blond hair flashing beneath the sun and a wicked-looking blade in each hand.

He stabs out at me, the point of the blade almost touching my nose before I can veer backwards and swing my shield to protect myself. The weapon clatters away harmlessly, but there's still another in his hand. He moves quickly, his eyes flashing with delight as trinkets jangle in his ginger-coloured beard. I lash out at him with my seax, but again, he moves out of my way. I should dearly like to force him down the slope, gain the advantage of the higher ground, but he must realise that, turning slightly, so that we face it side on. I'm aware of my fellow warriors fighting all around me, the smell of the burning wood from the ship is getting stronger, as is the dank scent of the river, but I focus only on the man trying to kill me.

For such a tall man, he's light-footed and sprightly and, more importantly, filled with the belief that he's better than me. I can tell by how some of his strikes are desultory, almost inviting me to impale myself on his blade. But I don't bloody think so.

I dash forwards, closing him down quickly, my shield before me to protect my body while my seax seeks to get past the guard of his blade. I punch with my shield and stab with my seax, but he avoids both blows, bending low and almost entirely backwards to expose his neck. I can't take advantage of the action, though, because somehow he turns sideways, showing me his backside, not his neck, and before I can get a boot on his arse, he's facing me again. He still grins but stands further back this time. Perhaps he realises I'm not going to be quite as easy to kill as those at the Wessex settlement he must have attacked yesterday and whose smoke alerted us to the Viking raiders in the first place.

I lick my lips and rush at him again, only this time I pivot to the side so that my shield offers protection from his right-handed blade but also forces his arm out and to the side of his body. I stab into his lack of guard, and my blade glances off his byrnie but little else. Quickly, I flick my blade upwards, and finally, blood shows on his chin. I'd wanted his neck, but again, he evades me. Now, we're almost back in our original position, with his back facing down the slope.

I glower and advance once more, one step, two steps, shield before me, seax ready to stab or slash as soon as possible. My enemy shows no fear, even though the shrieks and cries of his comrades fill the air. I might have killed a man by chance and now be stuck with only one foeman against whom I must battle, but the rest of the Mercians are doing much better.

My opponent understands what's happening and rushes towards me, his blade still busy in his hand, but I've had about enough of this. I meet him instead of trying to avoid him, my shield stabbing upwards so that it hits his chin where I've just cut him. I follow up with another slicing cut across his body, but his byrnie is too well made.

Again, my blade has no impact, so I reset my grip and, this time, jab toward his neck. His blade clashes against mine, a sharp shriek of metal on metal. The strength in his arm is immense. No matter what I do, I can't get my seax any closer. We are, it seems, locked in a struggle. But I have my shield. Only he has his fist. He hits me hard at the base of my stomach, and for a moment, I can't breathe. But that doesn't matter. He thinks to have won. For a moment, I believe he's triumphed as well, but then I swell upwards with my shield and seax simultaneously. My shield hits him under the chin once more, and my seax is at his exposed throat, his head flung back, and blood rises in a wave from the deep gash.

I stagger backwards, trying to suck in a much-needed breath, and determine how the rest of my allies fare, but still, no air reaches me. Stars dance before my eyes, my vision dimming, only for something to collide with my arse. I fall forwards, hands splayed, and at the same time, finally manage to grab a breath. Gathering my shield and seax to me, I heave back to my feet, turning to clout the foeman who pushed me with my shield rim across his face. His eyes already lack focus, but now he sags to the floor, and Frithwine, a threatening lour above his blood-stained chin, stabs down and kills the man.

'Watch what you're doing,' he intimidates, striding down the slope to find his next enemy. I gasp, pleased to be able to breathe more evenly, and realise that much of the fight is now taking place on the muddy foreshore. And yet there's one of our enemies, even now, running towards the horses. What does he expect to do? Steal a horse and disappear into the vastness of Mercia? I don't bloody think so. I amble to a run, coughing and choking as I do so, following him and avoiding the splayed bodies of those who've already died. Of course, the bastard makes a beeline for Brute, who stands, more interested than all the other mounts, watching what's happening, his lips open as though waiting for me to feed him a treat.

'Get out of the way,' I call to him, but Brute does no such thing. Should the man manage to mount my horse, it'll be all but impossible to catch him. Brute is the quickest of all the horses. I can't lose Brute in such a way. I'd expect him to lash out at the Viking raider should he try to steal him, but knowing my luck, Brute would actually be pliable for once.

I urge myself to run faster, to think more clearly, and then, just as the man reaches Brute's side and has to pause to mount, I fling myself at him, stretching my body as far as I can, and just manage to yank the man's raised booted foot, so that we tumble to the ground together, in a clatter of metal and iron.

He kicks out, his boot aiming for my face, while I both try to avoid his blows and attempt to pull myself along his body, even while we turn, over and over. I manage to grip both of his legs but no sooner have I done so than he kicks free once more, and I get a mouthful of mud and muck and have to cough it aside. Still, I try and grip him, and then, when my hands once more slide from his legs, I punch out. I'm hoping to get him in the stones, but I have no such luck.

I'm aware of noises from the horses, as though they're disturbed by what's happening, but none of them come to aid me, not even Brute. My foeman's hand pulls my helm free, although not my linen cap, and then he tugs on the parts of my long black hair that spring free while we continue to squirm on the ground.

Quickly, I change tactic, slashing up with my seax blade to slice my hair free, not his hand. As he loses his grip on me, I abandon my attack on him, focusing only on pitching upwards so that I'm standing and he's not.

Using his elbows, he tries to crawl backwards, feet scrabbling on the ground. I follow him, able to move far more quickly than him. His left leg trails behind the other, and I slice across his shin. He howls in pain and snatches his left leg away from me but leaves his right. I slice his right, and blood flashes bright red.

He shrieks, trying to pitch upright, but in doing so, slows even more. I stab down this time, aiming for his stones, but instead tear through the fabric covering his upper thigh and leave a ragged cut that only widens as he again struggles to move his body away from me.

My foeman yells incoherent words, his face sheeted in sweat, the scent of his piss and blood adding to the general filth from the riverbank. My seax runs with his blood, but he's still far from dead. Almost languid, I score my blade across his exposed belly, where his byrnie's caught beneath his body, and then dart upwards, meeting his eyes as I spear where I know his heart must beat.

His eyes close, and his chest stills as I stand, watching him, my chest heaving, and only then do I appreciate he didn't die in vain. A sudden wetness and I glance down, startled to find I bleed from my arm, a cut running almost from my hand to my elbow.

'Bugger,' I exclaim, bending to rip some of the dead man's tunic from him and hastily, using my teeth as well, tie off the bleeding cut above my wound. It stings, but not too badly, for all it bleeds heavily. I need to stop the bleeding and cover it, but first, well, I have to ensure my fellow warriors have prevailed against the bloody Viking raiders.

A brief glance to the horses, Brute watching me with his keen eyes, and I turn. Quickly, I stagger back towards the rest of Ealdorman Ælfstan's men.

Coming to the slope down to the river, I'm greeted by many bodies and men who still live but won't for long, huge wounds seeping into the sodden ground.

I make my way past them, my eyes on where the fighting continues. Frithwine still battles with a new-found ferocity since his brother's death, his movements concise and well-aimed. I'm mesmerised by the way he fights now. He's almost as lethal as Oswy, only without all the huffing and roaring. He'll have his vengeance, at last, for what the Viking raiders in the kingdom of the East Angles did to his brother.

Wulfheard and Oswy also face foes. Ealdorman Ælfstan has made his way to the ship, and I can see his intentions. At the same time, Cenred and Maneca have waded out into the river and menace those even now swimming ashore. I watch one man hastily swim away, back into the river's flow, hanging on to a wooden plank for buoyancy. Maneca grabs another, pulling him bodily from the water as the man gasps and squirms, wet and drenched, no weapons in sight, to slice his throat open so that pink water pools down his front. A man who must have swum underwater rears up before Cenred and comes at him, both fists swinging. Cenred stumbles beneath the water while his opponent rains down more and more blows on where his head must be. I stumble towards the water, down the slope, thinking to intervene, but by the time I'm at the water's edge, the enemy is being held beneath the water. Cenred with his hands on his head, holding him there until the turbulence of the water stops.

I turn again, surveying the scene before me, feeling the thrum of the fight throughout my body. It's been two years since our last fight. I'm pleased my skills remain. I'm also relieved that killing our enemy fills me with a sense of righteousness. I should like to know the identity of these Viking raiders. Who led them to Wessex and then Mercia? But I doubt we'll ever know, not now they're all dead.

On the foreshore, fire leaps along the wooden slats of the ship pulled ashore for repairs. The other craft, which was originally burning, is now a glowing blaze on the tidemark of the River Thames, the smell of damp smoke drifting towards us.

The enemy is dead. All of them, and now I need to assist those who bleed. But first, I have to tend to my arm, and as much as I don't want to, the welcome flames of the burning ship provide me with the best opportunity to fully heal.

10

'Just do it,' I glower at Oswy. He winces away from me, his lopsided grimace attesting to the blood pouring from his split lip. He's pulled his helm clear from his mess of hair, and his sweaty forehead is running with pink. He's taken a head wound as well, but not a bad one. The head always bleeds too much. Combined with his purple eye from the fight with Frithwine, Oswy looks like a mess.

'Do it,' I urge him again, holding out my arm towards him. My seax is in the flames of the burning ship, and I need him to put the seax blade along my cut. A thin scab is trying to form over it, but there's too much blood for it to hold, and in three places, narrow streams of maroon gurgle free and drip to the ground.

'Stitch it,' he grunts at me, feeling his head with his left hand.

'I can't, you bloody arse,' I retort. 'Just bloody do it.' But he shakes his head once more. I turn to meet the eyes of my fellow warriors. They all sit or stand, most of them with one bruise or wound, four of them needing my assistance, and I can't give it until they fix me.

'Wulfheard, you do it,' I plead. His face is pale. I'm sure he's hurt, but I can't see where. Not at the moment. He nods, swallowing heavily, and I think it must be a head wound as well, for he's fighting nausea.

'I'm coming, I'm coming,' he counters, only to land heavily on his arse as he tries to stand. I sigh heavily.

'One of you needs to do this. I can't do it myself. Well, I can, but I'll cause myself more problems if I do.'

I'm surprised when Frithwine marches towards me. Of us all, he's the least injured by what's just happened, as he vibrates with the after-effects of his first fight since his brother's death. I offer him the pile of wadded linens to stop his hand from burning, and he takes them eagerly and then pulls the seax from the flames.

'Don't look,' he warns me, his words hard and sharp, placing the superheated blade over my bleeding arm, and I shriek in agony. I'm glad I'm sitting down, or I'd fall. I feel Frithwine's shocked response to my scream in how the blade judders on my skin.

'Leave it where it is,' I urge him through gritted teeth, when I feel him trying to lift the blade clear. 'Better that this is done in one go.' Sweat beads my forehead now, and I want to vomit as much as Wulfheard seems to need to, but still, I hold my arm in place. It hurts like no other pain I've encountered before. Worse than when I scorched myself on the handle of my seax helping my uncle, and when I did the same assisting Oswy.

Only when I feel my pain start to dim, even as the smell of roasting blood and meat fills the air, do I allow him to remove the blade and move my arm aside. I glance at the pink flesh, slightly singed where the skin that didn't need searing has been burned.

'Thank you.' I swallow my nausea as Frithwine returns the blade to the flames, some steps away from me. I think I want to back away from the heat, but I don't. The sucking sound of the water is a counterpart to the heavy beating of my heart in my ears. I gaze around at the scene of destruction. It's very calm on the River Thames. The same can't be said for my fellow warriors.

We might have killed the enemy, but it's taken a heavy toll on us all. Not, I believe, that anyone is dead.

Hastily, I scrabble around in my sack of supplies retrieved from Brute's back, finding the vinegar, moss and bandages, as well as the honey. With a shaky hand, my right arm still throbbing with the agony of the cut and the burn, I somehow, making use of my knees, manage just about to get the wound tended to as I want to. Frithwine, once more, is the one to offer me assistance.

'Thank you,' I murmur, and he nods, satisfied, and then turns around and makes his way back to the dead enemy. He kicks them and sometimes bends low to steal their valuables. None of the others begrudges him that. None of them seems to want to join him. Perhaps it'll help Frithwine to confirm to himself that all these men are dead and far beyond my assistance.

Hastily, I swill water into my mouth, spit it aside so that the fire sizzles, and then drink more deeply. The horses have been brought closer by those able to move around easily, but they've not been brought down onto the lower bank.

'Wulfheard, what's the matter with you?' I call to him first. His face remains pale, and his hand holds his head.

'My head,' he mumbles, hastily turning aside to vomit onto the ground. I wrinkle my nose at the stream of cream-coloured fluid, too reminiscent of this morning's meal, but bend before him anyway, wincing at a sharp stab from my wounded arm.

'Here, I'll have a look.' I run my left hand, the one that's not wounded, over his head and quickly feel a huge bump.

'Didn't you wear your helm?' I pull back and glance at him.

'Aye, the arsehole hit me with his war axe.' I see that he holds his iron helm, and it's got a massive dent in it that matches up to where he has a wound now.

'You should be okay, but don't sleep. Keep yourself busy, and then when the nausea passes, you can sleep. Here, you can help me,' I suggest, but as he tries to stand, I push him back down. 'You're no use to me when you can't stand up straight. Stay here, and look after yourself.'

I make my way to Maneca, who's slumped close to the horses. He's helped collect them, but that seems to be all he can do.

'What have you done to yourself?' I murmur. He still wears his helm, but a bloom of blood shows on the left side of his byrnie.

'A cut, it's not too bad,' he counters, but I lift his byrnie clear and wince at the jagged cut along his chest.

'It's small but deep. I need to stitch that,' I inform him.

'You can, but I think the ealdorman needs you first.' I startle at that, not realising Ealdorman Ælfstan's wounded. I hasten to his side. He's sitting, slumped against the fallen tree trunk the Viking raiders were trying to rob to repair their ship. He looks well enough, and he even smiles on seeing me, but I quickly see the darkened patch near his ankle on his trews.

'What happened to you?'

'I was stabbed by someone I thought was dead.' With a wince, he pulls the fabric of his trews upwards, and I'm presented with a deep gouge that's taken much of the skin from his lower right leg.

'Nasty,' I confirm. I don't think I need to stitch it, and a fine scab has already formed, so it shouldn't bleed more. I consider why Maneca thinks the ealdorman is more badly wounded than him.

With occasional hisses of pain induced by my cut arm, I go about tending to his injury. Frithwine brings me a bowl of hot water, thanks to the fire, and I use it to clean the wound and then pack it with moss and a touch of honey before bandaging it tight.

'Is there anything else?' I query, looking to Maneca again. He holds me with his gaze. He thinks there is, even if the ealdorman doesn't.

'No.' Ælfstan huffs, his face running with sweat. I want to check him and ensure he's not lying to me, but there are others who need me. I stand and think to stride towards Landwine, only for the ealdorman to speak.

'My chest,' he says to me, and I realise he's breathless.

'Show me,' I demand, and painfully, he tries to lift his byrnie free. I watch him and then shake my head.

'I'll do it.' I bend to grip his protective byrnie, but it's bloody heavy, and it hurts my wounded arm as well.

'Frithwine, help me,' I urge him. Frithwine stands

from his pilfering and hastens to my side with his complaint dying on his lips.

'I need to remove his byrnie,' I inform him.

'Let me do it,' Frithwine demands. 'It'll be easier if it's just one of us.' I stand back and allow him to pull the byrnie free from the ealdorman's head. Beneath the heavy vest, I can see the ealdorman's sweat and also a tiny pinprick of blood.

'My thanks,' I offer Frithwine, but my eyes are already focused on the ealdorman's wound. It seems to be little and nothing, and yet it's clearly causing him a great deal of pain and discomfort. Frithwine hastily returns to his pillaging, and I focus on the ealdorman's other injury.

I pull his tunic upwards, releasing the odour of his body as I do so. There's only a small wound on his chest, but already a bruise is forming.

'A rib?' I suggest, feeling the tenderness of the wound. 'Yes, a broken rib. That's going to hurt, but it'll heal quickly. You probably won't want to ride,' I caution him, already reaching for a strip of linen to tie around the wound. I can't see that the ealdorman will give it the time it needs to heal, but I can at least try and offer some support for it.

'My breathing?' he huffs.

'Lie down,' I order him. I can see that he's strug-

gling to suck in the air he needs. I offer a swift prayer
that he's not done himself more damage than I can
fix, but once he's lying down, his chest begins to rise
and fall more easily, and the blue tinge of his lips
quickly fades.

'You need to keep supine,' I advise him. 'Give it
time to start to knit together.'

'I can't do that,' the ealdorman complains, his
hand running over his chest.

'I don't see you have many choices,' I counter,
shaking my head at his stubbornness. 'You can't ride
like that or fight.'

I think the ealdorman will argue with me, but he
surprises me by accepting what I say.

'We must send word to Ealdorman Tidwulf of
what we've found.'

I look around at my fellow warriors. Wulfheard is
almost green with his nausea. Maneca still needs his
wound stitching, and I've yet to even look at Osmod,
who requires my ministrations.

'We can send Oswy or Frithwine,' I decide.
They're the only two who aren't tending to some
ailment.

'Send both of them,' the ealdorman demands.
'And tell the pair of them that if they bloody fight,
they'll have to face me when I can stand once more.'

The ealdorman's words spit with fury, but I can't see him being as angry as the two warriors when I tell them of the ealdorman's requirements.

'Do you want them to go now?' I ask, my mind already on Maneca, and his cut that needs stitching.

'No, in a week,' the ealdorman coughs, and I almost take some delight in the wince on his face.

'I'll send them now.' I stand and shout for the two warriors to join me. The remaining men watch on with interest, as Frithwine once more complains at being pulled from searching the bodies of the dead men.

'You're both to return to Ealdorman Tidwulf at Londonia and tell him of what we found here.'

'It doesn't take two of us,' Oswy grunts.

'It does if one of you falls from your horse,' I argue, and dismiss them. I'm not about to debate the ealdorman's orders. Uor and Waldhere have made their way to the horses. Uor limps, and Waldhere holds his one arm with the other.

'What's happened to you two?' I query.

'I stubbed my toe,' Uor mumbles.

'It's just a muscle,' Waldhere counters.

'Good, then you can see to the fire and food. I don't know what we're going to do about the dead.' I wrinkle my nose at the thought of having to move so many corpses.

'Burn them,' the ealdorman calls feebly, and I appreciate that it'll be a good way of bringing our allies to our side as well, and potentially, long before Frithwine and Oswy could make it to Londonia. I look at the men. Waldhere's wincing. Uor's limping.

'Æthelmod and Godeman, can you manage to do that?' I don't mean it to sound as condescending as it sounds. Sharp eyes meet mine, and I shrug an apology while either Wulfheard or Ælfstan's loud retching can be heard.

'Aye,' Æthelmod hastens to answer as though worried I might ask him to tend to the two men. Godeman pauses for a moment longer but then follows his comrade.

I consider who else is largely in one piece. Osmod has decided to take Frithwine's place, and he picks through the possessions of the dead, being careful to stay away from Æthelmod and Godeman. Cenred is shivering from being in the water and needs to remove his clothes or wait for the fire to grow in intensity, which might not take that long, as the first of the bodies is unceremoniously dumped onto the burning ship. Ordlaf is moving amongst the horses, ensuring their reins won't tangle in their legs while Wulfgar has put himself in charge of cooking pottage. Berhthelm fills water bags from a stream that bleeds into the River Thames to the far side. There aren't that many of us. However, we've managed to kill all of the enemies, and we're just about all still intact. I take myself to Maneca's side, and carefully begin to stitch his wound together even as the smell of roasting flesh rises high into the sky. If the blaze doesn't get the attention of the rest of Mercia's fighting men, then nothing will.

* * *

We're too few to take watch duty that night, but we manage it all the same. The flames from the funeral pyre continue to soar skywards, but we move aside from the smell of roasting flesh and instead settle upwind from the stink.

The ealdorman is in a bad way, as is Maneca, but no one's fatally wounded, and I'm grateful when I'm ordered to sleep all night, allowing the others to take watch duty. When I wake, the world's bright and filled with birdsong, the horrors of the day before so far removed that if it weren't for the smell of burning that infects my senses, I'd think I might have dreamt it all.

Quickly, I check on the wounded, and I'm pleased to see all of them, even the ealdorman, struggling to their feet and getting on with their daily tasks. Ealdorman Ælfstan limps, as he ambles to the stream to piss, and when he returns to his place, I appreciate how pale his face is.

'You need to stay lying down,' I urge him. 'Give it a few days, a week at most, and you'll be able to move around much more easily. But, if you don't listen to me, it could take months.' I can hear Ælfstan muttering to himself as he seeks some means of being comfortable. I speak to scare him into compliance, but I doubt it'll work.

Wulfheard meets my gaze, bleary-eyed.

'Still sick?' I ask him.

'Yes.' His voice is thick from lack of use.

'You need to drink and eat,' I order him, hoping that someone, perhaps Wulfgar, is already busying himself with the task.

'What did you do to your hair?' he manages, and only then do I remember that I cut it when the Viking raider fought me.

'It got the bastard of me,' I counter, offering nothing further.

Frithwine and then Osmod, after Frithwine was ordered back to Londonia, have gathered together an enticingly high pile of valuables from the dead. I bend and sieve through the random collection of coins, silver arm rings, both wide strips of silver and ones that have been rounded for comfort, random beads, some amber and other precious stones, and only then turn my attention to the weapons the enemy had with them.

Here, there's a lot more on offer. I sift through the war axes, seaxes and the odd spear. The weapons are all sharp, well made, and tempered in the heat of a competent blacksmith's fire. Some of the blades flash as though the fire is trapped inside the metals. Others are so dark as to be almost black. The hilts are an equally diverse collection of plain wood and worked metal. And then I turn to the byrnies. Here, I can see that not all of the men wore the items, or at least that they didn't survive the sinking of the holed ship. The smell of the dead men's sweat turns my stomach, and I jump to my feet and make myself useful with the horses who all need leading to a brook and then feeding. Brute seems keen to be gone from the place. I'm not surprised. Even I can scent the spilt blood from yesterday, and the fire has yet to gutter and die. It smells of the charnel house.

And I'm uneasy as well. The fire was far from small, and it burnt all night. If there are any Viking raiders out on the River Thames, or on the Wessex side of the river, they're sure to come and investigate what's happened. They might even suspect that their allies have triumphed over Mercia and come to join in. And, I realise, if there are any Viking raiders in the kingdom of the East Angles, they might have seen the fire as well and raced down Icknield Way which runs from the top of that kingdom, all the way to Londonia.

Unease shudders through me, and I wish there were more of us and that nearly half of those there are weren't wounded. If it comes to a fight, we'll have to rely on the horses to get us to safety.

The day passes uneasily. The smell of burning flesh gradually dissipates, but my apprehension only grows as the injured spend most of the day sleeping, leaving so few of us to guard the rest. I think I'd feel more settled if Frithwine and Oswy returned, but it'll take a few days yet.

'Should we return to the settlement of a few nights ago?' Ordlaf asks me when I check on Brute and the other horses in the early evening.

'It'll be too painful to move most of the injured,' I counter quickly. It's not that I've not been considering it. I believe it's impossible. What we need are more men to come and aid us, not for us to leave this place.

He grumbles discontentedly, and I offer to take guard duty so that those who stayed up all the previous night can get some sleep. The night's cold and silent, and more than once, I jolt awake, convinced I've heard something out on the river, but come the morning, there's nothing to see. I eye the pile of treasure, certain it's been moved around. Only then, I do hear something on the river, and I turn, hand on my seax, to squint at the greyness of the watery expanse of the River Thames. There's something coming, of that I'm sure. I swallow down my worry, reach for my seax, wincing as I grip it and it pulls the wound on my arm tight.

If this is more of the bastard enemy, then we're in trouble. Few of the men can stand, let alone fight. Indecision wars inside me. We should get the horses. We should ride from here. But I don't think there's time.

'Wulfgar, Uor, here,' I call to them. The men rush as much as they can to stand beside me as a flash of daylight brings the ship into clear view. I sag with relief. It's not the Viking raiders, but rather Ealdorman Tidwulf, and more of his men, taking advantage of one of many ships that ply their trade along the waterfront at Londonia.

'What you trying to do?' the ealdorman calls jovially, stepping from the ship, as the hale men gather round to exchange greetings. 'Send all the bastard Viking raiders this way?' Despite his words, I detect unease in his movements, and I'm grateful when he and his warriors manage to gather together the injured and place them on the ship to return them to Londonia. Not that we all fit on the ship. The horses also need taking back to Londonia, and so a few of us find ourselves corralling our mounts back via the land route, Uor most keen of them all. He's no longer limping, but looks green just at the thought of getting on a ship. I can't say we've won a great victory, not with so many of us carrying cuts and lacerations, but we know one thing. The Viking raiders are just as prepared to attack Mercia as they are Wessex. They don't see the boundary between the two kingdoms as Mercians and the people of Wessex do. They only see the potential to make war, kill, steal our treasures, and sell our people as slaves.

On the journey back to Londonia, I consider all that. We need to ensure the River Thames is heavily guarded. We need Mercians along its length, not sheltering at Londonia. I can't see we'll be recalled for long, not when the summer is only just beginning. No doubt, as soon as King Wiglaf arrives after the consecration of the new bishop of Lichfield, and the ealdorman is hale once more, we'll be sent on our way towards the east again, for that's from where the Viking raiders will come. Our enemies in Wessex are threatened just as we are. There's no comfort in such knowledge.

11

'Icel.' My name rouses me from my thoughts, and I turn, startled to find Edwin before me. I didn't hear him approach, and that worries me. I should be paying more attention to what's happening around me as I keep a desultory watch not far from where we killed the Viking raiders close to the River Thames no more than two months ago.

'What do you want?' I growl angrily. Why is he here? Now? How did he even find me? I want nothing more than to roll in my cloak and sleep as soon as my watch is done. It's early morning, and the hint of the coming day is on the bruised horizon.

'I need your help,' Edwin hurries, his tone showing his fear and worry as he looks behind me as though chased. And yet, he's nothing to me. And he hasn't been for a long time. Our childhood friendship evaporated long ago. I don't blame him for it. Neither do I blame myself. It's simply one of those things.

'I've nothing to say to you, Edwin. Nothing.' I stand and stretch, from where I've been leaning against a handy wooden stump from some tree that was either felled many years ago or fell in a storm, trying to drive the ache from my back, but Edwin reaches over and grips my forearm, the urgency in his action astounding me. We came here thinking to fight off the Viking raiders, but other than our action against those Viking raiders two months ago, nothing else has happened. The men are bored, and I count myself amongst them, and also tired of the constant feeling of dread, which amounts to nothing.

I don't know what Lord Coenwulf has been up to, Edwin's oath-sworn lord. Certainly, Edwin being here, now, is unexpected, unwanted and frustrating.

'You must. I promised that you would.' Edwin's words are insistent, throbbing with conviction. For the briefest of moments, I consider punching him in the nose as a final payment for what he did to me. But although my right hand clenches, the touch of my raised scar recalls me to the here and now. I won't give in to my darkest wishes.

'It's not for you to be making promises on my behalf,' I murmur gruffly, stepping aside from his grip. I don't know who he's promised or why he's promised. I don't care. His hand falls uselessly to his side. I look at him, truly seeing him for the first time in the growing daylight. His clothing is dishevelled, his lips swollen, and his eye carries the vestiges of being blackened.

Where has he been? What has he been doing? I didn't think that he'd been involved in any battle with the Viking raiders along the River Thames. I don't believe he's had anything to do with ensuring the Viking raiders kept to the Isle of Sheppey, close to the sea and part of Wessex, and if not to Sheppey, then turned their attention to Wessex, and not Mercia. The Viking raiders are King Ecgberht's problem, not King Wiglaf's.

'But for Lady Cynehild,' he gasps. This startles me. Why is he mentioning her to me? He knows my loyalty to her.

'What of Lady Cynehild? She's well?' I demand, almost wanting to shake him for only giving me half of the story. Why didn't he begin with that? We've wasted time. Now I would know what she wants. I'll do what she commands me. I already know that.

'Lord Coenwulf. He's missing, taken by the Viking raiders. She begged me to seek you out. She's great with child once more. She doesn't want that child born to no father.'

'The Viking raiders have Lord Coenwulf?' I demand. I can feel my eyebrows furrowing. Why didn't the king know of this? Why didn't Ealdorman Ælfstan? Why has Lady Cynehild sent Edwin to me and not to her husband's warriors? What's been happening while Ealdorman Ælfstan and his men, with me included, have been keeping guard? It would appear we've not been doing a very good job of it, unless, of course, the Viking raiders have travelled overland from the southern tip of Wessex and then into Mercia, and not along the River Thames at all. If that's the case, then King Wiglaf should certainly be aware of this new development.

'Where are the rest of your men?' I demand angrily. A touch of sorrow on Edwin's lips, and I already have my answer. 'Bloody hell,' I exclaim, running my hand over my scar. The thought of all those men, dead, is unsettling. Heahstan might have had a mouth on him, but I still wouldn't want him to be sleeping eternally.

None of the other men has woken, despite our conversation, and now I look at them in their slumbers. We've been holding the same position for a few weeks now, and we do have tents to sleep beneath, but we often don't. Inside the tents, we might feel safer and be protected from the rain, but it's merely an illusion. It's much better to be out beneath the sky, alert to every sound and splash of a fish jumping free from the River Thames, only to enter it once more.

Who'll come with me to rescue Lord Coenwulf, wherever he is? Who'll break their bond to the ealdorman and to the king to ensure that Lord Coenwulf is rescued? Oswy? Perhaps Wulfheard. No, not Wulfheard. I lift my hand and find myself gnawing on my fingers. And then shake my head. How quickly I've determined to rescue Cynehild's husband. I didn't even give it any thought that I wouldn't.

I know these men, all of them. And I know Ealdorman Ælfstan. Now isn't the time to forget that we're warrior brothers.

'Does she know he still lives?' This is my next question as I scramble upright, clearing my head and thinking for the first time since Edwin's unexpected appearance. How, I consider, does he know to find me here? Surely, he must have sought our location in Londonia, and if he has done so, then the king must know of what's befallen Lord Coenwulf and his warriors. Why then has Lady Cynehild sent Edwin to me?

'Yes, I was forced to carry a message to her by his captors on the Isle of Sheppey. They sent me back to Mercia in a leaky boat, but it made its way across the River Thames, and then I rode to Kingsholm. The Viking raiders demand a huge payment, and then they'll release Lord Coenwulf once it's paid.'

'Do they now?' The growl of fury comes from Wulfheard. Here, in the glow of the campfire, I can see how rage touches his cheeks. His eyes are narrowed. If he weren't my friend and ally, I'd be bloody terrified.

'They do, yes.' Edwin stands taller before Ealdorman Ælfstan's commander. Absent-mindedly, I consider who'll take the position of commander for Lady Cynehild now. She has a small child already, Coenwulf. One day, he'll rule their family's lands in his father's name, but that day can't be now. He might not even be able to toddle yet, let alone hold a sword aloft. Not, of course, that Lord Coenwulf is a fighting man.

'And you were, what, captured alongside your lord?' Now Edwin looks abashed, his chin dropping to his chest.

'Yes, I was. They killed all of the other men.' Edwin stands erect, his body shuddering. I shake my head. Suddenly, I want to reach out and embrace him, drive back the years of our estrangement, but I don't want to break him either, and I think it will if I offer such sympathy. I think of Heahstan and Oswald, men I didn't particularly like, but no one deserves to die on the edge of a Viking raider blade. And certainly, no decent warrior of Mercia.

'Bastards,' Oswy grumbles. For a moment, I'm not sure if he means us for waking him or the Viking raiders.

'So, you can take us to them?' It's Wulfheard who asks the question.

'Yes, my lord, I can.' Wulfheard growls. 'Remember, I'm no lord,' he continues.

'But I am.' And Ælfstan's there. I sigh softly. I can't see that we'll be able to do anything now that the ealdorman's involved. He won't want to do anything without the agreement of the king. Since he recovered from his broken rib, he's been difficult and filled with bile, not at all the easy-going individual I first met at Bardney.

'My lord,' Edwin mumbles. His shoulders sag as well, and I think he too realises his only chance is lost.

'Men.' Ealdorman Ælfstan turns to face his warriors, and I appreciate that we're all awake now, even Frithwine, drunk once more, the sorrow for his lost brother never leaving his face. I can't denounce him for such actions. If I liked ale and wine, then I'd probably be no better. He claimed many of the kills against our enemy, but it wasn't enough. I fear it'll never be enough. 'You heard Edwin. He knows how to get to the bastard enemy on the Isle of Sheppey. And so, we'll go with him as quietly as we can. We must rescue Lord Coenwulf, and if, in the meantime, we kill all the Viking raiders, then our king will, one day, forgive us for our actions and for appearing to desert him. But, if you prefer not to, I'll not order you. In this, I'm not your commander.'

I can't believe what I'm hearing, and yet I'm grateful all the same. I must do all I can for Lady Cynehild and her children, but there's no need for these men to follow where I'll go. There's even less requirement for them to believe Edwin and his words. And yet we're all frustrated by King Wiglaf's decision that we need do little but stand and watch the enemy. His point is well made. The Viking raiders are on the Isle of Sheppey, a part of Kent, and so are the problem of the king of Wessex and his son, who rules Kent in his name. And yet the Viking raiders have taken a Mercian. I don't consider how it happened, or even why it happened. I've long known that Lord Coenwulf is no warrior. His capture is unsettling.

'I'll go,' Maneca confirms quickly.

'Me too,' from Uor.

'Aye, I'm bored sitting on my arse here each and every day, waiting for the Viking raiders when they've bloody disappeared.' Landwine adds his voice to the others, and slowly, I comprehend that all of these men will fight with me, and I don't know how to feel about that. I don't want to put their lives at risk any more than normal.

But Cenred nods along, as do Goðeman and Æthelmod. I meet the gaze of all of them, even Berhthelm, who, it seems, means to come with us as well.

'But how?' I question. The Isle of Sheppey is exactly that, an island. I don't have a boat. None of us has a boat, and we're going to bloody need one.

'I have an idea,' the ealdorman confirms, and I watch him, his face shadowed by the dancing flames and the growing daylight. I nod, realising, as I should have done some time ago, that the ealdorman has long had a plan to counteract the scourge of our deadly enemy. He just needed a reason to implement it, and one which even the king would be unable to deny him, provided all goes well. No doubt it's that which has made him grumpy while healing. Ealdorman Ælfstan wanted to take the fight to the Viking raiders and not sit on his arse, as Landwine states, waiting for them to decide to either attack, or not to attack.

'We leave, now,' the ealdorman confirms, looking at his men in turn, mirroring my earlier actions. Luckily, we're the most distant of the king's warriors from where he keeps command in Londonia. We can make our departure, and none should know of it, provided there's no assault in our absence. Only then I pause and look at Edwin, forehead furrowed once more.

'What of the Lord Wigmund? And his wife?' I've forgotten of Lady Ælflæd and her union with the king's son. How, I don't know, but it again makes me question why Edwin is here, seeking my aid, instead of the king determining to rescue his missing ally. Edwin's face clouds, the darkness of a storm in his eyes.

'He'll do nothing. He is, as we've long suspected, a coward. He'll let his brother by marriage die at the hands of the Viking raiders and blame none but Lord Coenwulf for what happens to him.'

'Coward,' Oswy growls, and from him, that means a great deal, with his old allegiance to the queen and her son. Oswy's come a long way since the days when he'd do her bidding without questioning it.

'Then Lord Wigmund's aware of Lord Coenwulf's fate?'

'He is, yes, but he won't even send word to the king.' Of course, Wigmund is in Tamworth, or Gloucester, or even Worcester or Winchcombe, with his wife and his mother, I should imagine. He'll not bestir himself. The king has ordered his family to stay safe, in the hinterlands of Mercia. Still, it only adds to my feelings of antipathy towards Lord Wigmund. He'll never fight for Mercia. I don't see, then, how he can ever be king.

'And Lady Ælflæd accepted this?' I further probe.

'He wouldn't even tell her.' Now I snarl, angrily reaching for my seax, although who I'm going to war against, I don't know. Wigmund is less than horseshit on my boot, and I'd kill him given half the chance. He doesn't deserve to be wed to a woman of such firm resolve as Lady Ælflæd.

'Then we should inform the king, after all?' I query, but Ealdorman Ælfstan shakes his head. Their alliance is strained. Ealdorman Ælfstan wishes to do more than just wait for the Viking raiders to strike. The king doesn't. The king delights in knowing that the problem of the Viking raiders is King Ecgberht's to contend with. He feels it is his dubious reward for the reaches of previous years, when Ecgberht claimed Mercia as his own. The ealdorman thinks that rather than enjoying the Wessex king's misfortune, Mercia should be protecting itself. I know he's called for more defences along the River Thames. All well and good, I've heard him rant, having Londinium and its high stone walls, but what of other places? I know he's right. The ditch and ramparts that protect the smaller steadings within striking distance of the river will be quickly overwhelmed should an attack come.

'No, we go anyway, now come, make ready and mount up. We need to steal our way into Kent, and I hope I have just the means.'

'Do you have a horse?' I question Edwin, looking behind him. I heard no horse approach. I didn't hear Edwin either, I remind myself.

'Yes, I do,' he confirms. 'But she's old and slow.'

'She just needs to get you there,' Ealdorman Ælfstan consoles, and now I turn to him.

'To the Isle of Sheppey?' I ask him, considering the width of the River Thames at my side, and how we're going to cross it to get anywhere near the Isle of Sheppey.

'Of course,' the ealdorman confirms, but there's something about the obstinate cast of his lips that makes me think it's not going to be anywhere near as easy as he implies.

* * *

We're crouched low in the undergrowth, the River Thames in front of us. Not for the first time, I consider how wide the River Thames is to the east of Londonia. I don't fancy swimming in the fast current that brought the Viking raiders to us earlier in the year, and I fear that's exactly what the ealdorman has planned.

I've never been to Kent. I don't truly think I want to go there now, but to get to the captured Lord Coenwulf, there's no choice. Daybreak isn't far off. We've ridden through much of the night, grateful for the full moon to guide our horses' hooves. I've nodded off in the saddle more than once. And now I stifle yet another yawn. We've ridden all day and through much of the night. I'd have welcomed Edwin arriving when I'd had more sleep. Equally, it would have been good if Ealdorman Ælfstan hadn't forced us onwards.

Edwin's stayed close to me throughout the ride, but he's not spoken. I've heard him wince more than once, and I think he must be in pain, the bruises to his face only the most obvious of the wounds he's taken. I want to ask him how Lord Coenwulf was captured. And what he was doing facing off against the Viking raiders, but I fear it'll be cruel to make him replay those events. I consider Oswald and the other men of Coenwulf's household warriors. They must all be dead, and I mourn for men who were, on occasion, kind to me when I sought shelter behind the walls of Kingsholm.

'We go as soon as the water level drops,' the ealdorman confirms.

'Go where?' I'm glad it's Wulfheard who asks the question and not me.

'Across the river. When the tide's low, it'll be easier.'

'But my lord, the currents will be strong,' Uor questions, reminding me that he spent his childhood in Lundenwic.

'Aye, but the horses are strong, and we can all swim? Can't we?' The ealdorman dares any of us to admit that we can't. I snap down my argument.

'Can we not use a boat or a bridge?' Wulfheard

counters quickly. I'm with him on this one. There must be a ford close by? Surely?

'Where?' The ealdorman shrugs his shoulders, his eyes looking at his warriors as though testing our mettle. 'Have we ridden past one?'

'Well, we can find one?' If we hadn't burned those ships at the start of the summer then we could have used them. But of course, we did burn them.

'No, we can't, and we need the horses.'

'The risk is too great,' Wulfheard attempts, but the ealdorman's face lifts in a smirk of triumph.

'If we can beat the men of Wessex, and the Viking raiders in the kingdom of the East Angles, I assure you, we can beat the River Thames as well. Haven't you heard of the tales of Roman warriors? They often used to swim rivers with their mounts. That, they say, is how they overcame the rebellions from the Britons to secure this island as part of their empire.' I've not heard this story, but it seems that others have, as they nod along or offer grunts of agreement. Uor looks the most unhappy as he does so. But it seems he can't deny the truth of it.

'My lord, those are just dry words, spoken about a time long ago. A bridge or a boat is required. A ford at the very least.'

'Then, my warriors, you're welcome to find one,

although where, I don't know, but I'm trusting my horse and my legs to get me across the river. It'll be quicker and attract no attention from our enemy or from the Wessex warriors.'

I eye the sludge of the River Thames from our vantage point. The water is dark and menacing, and yet I can also see that it should be possible to swim across it. The Viking raiders did it beside their burning ship. Still, I turn to Uor.

'Currents?' I question.

'The water pushes and pulls in different ways,' he offers, his lips pursed unhappily. 'And it's powerful. The horses will probably be fine. It's us who'll suffer.'

I don't much like the sound of that, and I turn, shocked at the noise of metal hitting the ground. The ealdorman has returned to his mount and now removes his weapons belt, byrnie, and anything else he fears will weigh him down. I watch him as he bundles his items and secures them on his horse's saddle. I look from Ælfstan to the rest of the men, considering what they'll do. I know I have no choice but to follow where he leads, even if I'd sooner not.

'Bloody hell,' I moan, obeying the ealdorman's example, aware that no one else has done the same, not even Edwin. Perhaps, I consider, as I stow my possessions into various saddlebags and work to ensure Brute's reins are secure while he watches me, breathing heavily, as though he knows what's about to happen, Edwin needn't come with us. He's clearly wounded. He might even, I consider, have damage that needs repairing beneath the skin.

But, no sooner have I thought it, than he joins me in removing the heaviest items from his body.

'Bloody hell,' he echoes. Only when we're standing, with little more than tunics and trews, not even boots on our feet, do I appreciate that others are beginning to prepare themselves. My heart thuds loudly in my chest, and I know this is folly. We should find a boat. We really should. Or a bridge. Or a ford. There must be one somewhere. After all, Uor has told me that the water levels on the River Thames can be lower during the summer months. That's why so much of Lundenwic's trading takes place during the winter months. Only then can the water be trusted to remain deep enough to allow crafts to wallow up and down the River Thames to that marketplace in both directions.

It's evident that Uor agrees with me that swimming isn't the right means of transportation. He's the last to finally turn to his horse, shoulders tense, and begin to prepare himself. Ealdorman Ælfstan watches on, impatient, and even I'm feeling the bite of the chill air over my skin. I think about how cold the water will be. I also consider when I last went for a swim. I'm sure it was long before my uncle died, in the Tame, on a hot summer's day when all who could took to the water as the only means of keeping cool. This is going to be an entirely different experience.

'Come on, men,' the ealdorman encourages us. 'Or the tide will turn, and then we'll be in the shit.'

'We'll be in the shit anyway,' Uor offers unhappily. I can see where he shivers.

'If you think like that,' Wulfheard huffs angrily, 'then you need to remain behind. Thinking we can do this is half of the battle, isn't it, Icel?' I wish he didn't indicate me, but he's right. I didn't think I'd survive inside Londinium, and yet I had to. I certainly didn't think I'd slip in and out of Londinium so many times under the watchful eye of the Wessex warriors. But I had to, and my thoughts no doubt convinced me that there was no choice.

'Aye, we can do this,' I confirm, wishing my voice was free of a wobble of fear.

'Well done, young Icel, well done, for filling us all with such reassurance,' Wulfheard mutters ominously, rousing a few chuckles from the other men, who stand in a variety of poses, most of them with hands in armpits in an effort to keep warm.

'No time like the present,' the ealdorman reaf-
firms, but pauses before he turns aside. 'If this goes
wrong, remember to find a footing on the Mercian
side of the River Thames.' His words are dark, filled
with command. He's right. If we end up on the
Wessex side of the river, it might be all they need to
launch a further strike on Mercia. After all, they're
already under attack from the Viking raiders. The
Wessex king will be overly alert to the possibility that
Mercia might think to take advantage of their preoc-
cupation. The presence of the Mercian warriors
stretched along the banks of the River Thames is
hardly a reassurance that King Wiglaf doesn't plan as
much, and yet we're there to protect Mercia from the
Viking raiders, not to launch an attack on Wessex.

With that, the ealdorman rushes down the slope
and straight into the water, taking his horse with him.
The animal doesn't even shy at the expectation of a
swim, and in no time at all, the two have waded out
as far as they can, and I see both heads bobbing, the
ealdorman holding tight to the reins of his horse.

'Come on then,' I urge myself with no enthusiasm, and I'm the first to follow Ælfstan. With my first
foot into the dark mud that clings to the riverbank, I
shiver. It's too early in the day for the sun to have
made much impression, and the air is brisk but not

as cold as the water. Gasping and urging Brute on-wards, I make it up to my knees, and only the sight of the ealdorman, already almost in the centre of the river, forces me onwards. Compared to me, Ælfstan is an old man. I have to show him that I can swim just as well and that Brute is as powerful in the water as he is on land.

I'm swimming before Brute, my legs stretched be-hind me, but Brute quickly joins me, and I feel the force of the water around me as I frantically attempt to correct my course to follow that of the ealdorman. I can just see his head in the far distance as the gurgle of the water absorbs my senses. I grip tightly to Brute, reassured by my horse's firm kicks, as he keeps his head above the surface while I spit the foul-tasting water from my mouth.

'It's so cold,' I say to no one in particular. I want to turn back towards Mercia, but I don't allow myself to. Lady Cynehild has bid me rescue her husband, and if this is the only way I can do so, then I will.

For a moment, Brute seems to sink, and I grip him tightly, urging him to kick his legs more quickly to force his head clear from the water, and he does so, only to push a wave of water over my head. I choke, hacking and spluttering as my head resurfaces. I can hear the sound of others in the water now, and holding tightly to Brute's saddle, I risk looking back the way I've come.

Edwin isn't far behind me, Wulfheard next to him, Uor as well, but there are still some who remain in the lee of the copse of trees, and I wonder if they'll come. Oswy's voice reaches me from the riverbank, his back to me as he urges the others on. And another wave of water pools into my mouth, forcing me to face the way I'm going, gripping even more tightly to Brute, as my legs kick ferociously. At least, I consider, the water is clear from my mouth, and I'm starting to warm up.

'Come on, Icel.' Ealdorman Ælfstan's cry has me redoubling my efforts. He's out of the river now and jumping from one leg to another, no doubt to fight off the cold. I feel Brute rear out of the water, his hooves hitting the muddy banks of Wessex, and I surge to my feet as soon as I can touch the slippery ground as well. I'm trembling and shaking, unable to believe what we've just done, as I hastily turn and watch the rest of the men, Maneca only just entering the water on the far side.

'Well done.' The ealdorman pulls my blue feet clear from the river, and I join him, shivering, while Brute shakes as much of the water clear as possible. He doesn't have the same means to do so as a dog, but he makes a good effort of it. Water pools down my trews, making the solid ground I stand on sodden. The ealdorman has wrapped himself in his cloak, and I move to do the same, fingers fumbling with the rope around the sack that keeps it secure. I'm so cold, so very, very cold, but I persist, and the welcome smell and warmth of my cloak finally rests around my shoulders.

Edwin joins us, and then Wulfheard and slowly, slowly, all of the men appear, and none of them struggles with the current, even as I appreciate it's pushed us further east than I might have thought possible.

I turn to aid Edwin, who trembles so violently he can't get his hands to his own sacks.

'You have a cloak?' I ask, hurrying to his side. I don't want to give him mine, but his face is so pale, he looks half-dead.

'Yes, yes.' His teeth chatter, and he indicates where he means. As swiftly as I can, the feeling returning to my chilled hands, I find his cloak and hand it to him. It stinks of the damp already, and yet Edwin's eyes close as though I've gifted him the thickest fur cloak of the finest bearskin as the weight settles around his shoulders.

'Come on, Icel.' The ealdorman's filled with commands today, and I growl low in my throat before understanding his intention. He wants me to move Brute from where the horse blocks the easy passage of others out of the water.

'Come on, Brute,' I urge my horse, tugging on his rein to get his attention. 'Come on.' Slowly, Brute moves up the steep slope, his hooves leaving huge mud imprints in the ground. Anyone who comes to this place will easily be able to see that something has happened here.

'Will the river rise and cover our tracks?' I ask the ealdorman, wishing my words didn't shiver with my body.

'Yes, but still, we should try and obliterate them.' I nod and turn to find some wind-torn branches which we can drag through the mud. I don't relish walking through the mud again, but at least this time I have my boots on. I'm still shivering, though, and the last of the men and horses are only just making their way up the bank. Their faces are pale, and water pools down their legs.

'Get up there and pull your cloaks on from your sacks,' I urge them.

I just hope the ealdorman knows the rest of the way so that we can move quickly and evade the reach of the Wessex warriors. If they find us, I believe we'll be overwhelmed.

If the Wessex king or his son has ordered a troop of their warriors to scout this place, they'll see the hoof prints and know to follow them. And I know how important it is that no one discerns what we're doing. Not the Mercians. Not the Wessex warriors. And certainly not the Viking raider bastards.

'Well done, men,' the ealdorman calls when we're all seeping water on the side of the River Thames, our feet thrust back into resisting boots, cloaks around our shoulders. 'That, men, was the easy part. Now, we ride on. Stay alert. Who knows who we might encounter from now on?'

The words are the least reassuring I've ever heard, and my gaze lingers on the far shore of the River Thames. I'd welcome being back in Mercia at this moment. I could curse Lady Cynehild for laying such a command at my feet, but despite all that happened in my childhood when she gave the distinct impression of hating me for no good reason, I'd give my life for her now. And she certainly knows it.

12
_____

The going is easy once the sun has warmed the air a little. My shivering finally stops and, sniffing deeply, I realise that the extended bathe has done wonders for Brute's stink. And Ealdorman Ælfstan seems to know where we're going.

'Have you been this way before?' I eventually ask him, as we make our way inland. The ealdorman does seem to know which tracks to pick, and ahead I'm sure there's something that might well be a road. I can't imagine we'll be using it, but perhaps it will keep our path true.

'Yes, many times. Remember, Icel, Kent was once part of Mercia. Those older than you will know their way around Kent.'

'Then is there not a bridge?' I ask. I might be dry and grateful for the bath, but it was still cold and unpleasant.

'Yes, a bridge, fords and boats, but it was better that we crossed without anyone knowing of our intentions. Not even the king, and certainly not the Wessex king.' I'm more than aware that King Wiglaf would have forbidden our actions. I don't need reminding of that. But still, a dry crossing would have been appreciated.

When we first started our journey, I could hardly direct Brute, my eyes scouring the surrounding landscape for any sign of our enemy as we surged upwards from the low-lying river. But now, with my weapons belt back in place around my waist, I feel more reassured. As long as we're not hugely outnumbered, we can kill the enemy should they come against us. And I fear they will. If King Ecgberht and his warriors are as alert as the Mercian king and his, then I just can't see how we'll manage to escape detection.

'How will we get on to the Isle of Sheppey?' I query. I don't much fancy another swim, and the name implies there's water between it and the mainland of Kent.

'There's a way,' the ealdorman confirms. 'We just

have to find one of the locals who can direct our path.'

'Ah,' I don't much like the sound of that. 'And if we don't?'

'We won't consider that until it becomes a problem,' the ealdorman confirms with a wry grin. The mad bugger seems to be enjoying this. His face has worn a smirk of satisfaction ever since we emerged, dripping and shivering, from the River Thames. In contrast, Wulfheard's has become ever bleaker. I'm with Wulfheard on this one. This is the first time, other than when we ventured along the River Nene, that I've truly known myself to be out of my birth kingdom of Mercia. I know the men and women who live here were once part of Mercia and that they won't be strangers to me, and yet I'm fearful all the same.

And I don't wish to encounter the Viking raiders. Not until I'm wearing my byrnie once more, and we don't ride armoured. Close to me, Edwin's silent. Most of the men are. We're in enemy territory, not just once, but twice over. If we're unfortunate to encounter the Wessex warriors and then the Viking raiders, we'll be forced to defeat them both and only then make our attempt to rescue Lord Coenwulf.

'Tell me. What was Coenwulf doing in Wessex?' I

finally think to ask Edwin. I realise that I don't know how Lord Coenwulf was captured.

'He wasn't in Wessex. He was in Mercia, but we were caught and taken by ship to the main encampment on the Isle of Sheppey.'

'Then what was he doing close to the River Thames and not with the king's forces?' I could be wrong, but I don't believe that King Wiglaf called upon Lord Coenwulf to join the main body of warriors patrolling the line of the river. Edwin doesn't immediately answer. Indeed, he waits so long to answer that I turn to look at him. His face, no longer as white as when we first left the River Thames, is filled with mutiny. Whatever Coenwulf was doing, he doesn't wish to tell me. And then he does, the words wrenched from him as though a physical pain. It seems that Edwin needs to tell me the truth, even if it makes him disloyal to Coenwulf, and puts our rescue attempt at jeopardy.

'The Wessex king.'

'The Wessex king?' I feel my forehead furrow. 'What does any of this have to do with the Wessex king?'

'King Ecgberht made overtures of friendship to Lord Coenwulf. He asked to meet him at a location close to the River Thames. Lady Cynehild begged him not to go, but Coenwulf has become stubborn since his sister married Lord Wigmund. I think he's finally come to realise just how much he's lost since his father was deposed, and King Beornwulf's subsequent death. After all, he could have been king after Beornwulf, and that's certainly the incentive that made him seek our King Ecgberht.' I don't really need Edwin to elaborate. I suddenly understand all too well.

'And then what happened?' This still doesn't explain how Lord Coenwulf was apprehended by Viking raiders.

'Either King Ecgberht didn't send the message and it was a trap, or he was just unlucky. There were Viking raiders there at the meeting place, far down the River Thames. They were marooned, the water level being particularly low for their ship. But they weren't going to let that stop them from taking a lord of Mercia. They quickly overpowered us all because we were so outnumbered.'

'So, there were Viking raiders west of Londonia?' This fills me with renewed worry. King Wiglaf has his warriors patrolling from just west of Londonia all the way to where the river meets the sea in the east.

'Yes.' Edwin is unhappy about admitting that as well.

'Ealdorman Ælfstan.' I urge Brute onwards to catch the ealdorman, where he remains at the front of our line of men, although Oswy and Wulfheard now escort him. 'Did you hear what Edwin said? There have been Viking raiders to the west of Londonia.'

'Aye, lad. I'm aware. So is King Wiglaf, but there are only so many places that can be protected.'

'Perhaps,' I murmur, but the knowledge sits uneasily with me. King Wiglaf's focus is on Londonia, but maybe it shouldn't be. There's much of Mercia that could still be threatened.

'We can only do one thing at once,' the ealdorman informs me. 'Would you sooner go back to Mercia, now? Leave Lord Coenwulf in the hands of the Viking raiders.'

'No, no, my lord. I just thought you should know.' Despite the fact that Lord Coenwulf might well have been about to ally with Mercia's enemy, we're set on our path now. Whatever his loyalty, mine is to Lady Cynehild.

'Then you have my thanks. Now, we'll soon be free from these trees, and we'll have to exercise more caution. I'll call the men to a halt. We need to wear our byrnies and ride with our shields and seaxes to hand.'

So spoken, Ealdorman Ælfstan reins in, and his warriors do the same. We all take the opportunity to piss and drink, to offer the horses what oats we have while leading them to a small brook, making its merry way towards the River Thames. I can't get a true feeling for the landscape around us; not as hedged in as we are by the trees far overhead. I expect to see the expanse of the sea at any moment and realise I've never truly seen it. I've heard stories of it, and we almost came close when we were in the kingdom of the East Angles, but it'll be my first sighting of it. I consider what I'll feel when I see so much water and not a trace of land in sight.

'Hurry up, men,' the ealdorman urges us. I'm not the only one to stifle a yawn. We've been awake far more than we've been asleep in the last few days. Shrugging into my byrnie, wincing as it rubs against my still-damp tunic, I open my mouth to suggest we get some sleep, but Wulfheard's already shaking his head.

'I know where we are, lad. We'll get some rest, but not yet. I understand what the ealdorman is thinking.'

'And what is that?' I question, but he shakes his head once more, a smirk on his lined face.

'I think I'll leave it so that it's a surprise for you,'

he counters. I realise then that his good humour has returned as well. Indeed, aside from me and Uor, the majority of the men are in high spirits. Whatever the ealdorman intends to try, the others have grasped it, and they're happy to go along with it. I consider then that perhaps it involves a boat? Might that account for Uor's unease?

I turn to Edwin, realising we've not finished our conversation from earlier. He's struggling to lift his byrnie over his head, and I go to help him. He's wincing as he does so, and with his tunic caught on the byrnie, I finally see the extent of his wounds. His back is sliced with two cuts, starting to scab over, but red and inflamed all the same, while his chest is a welter of blue and purple bruises. I wince, reminded of how Ealdorman Ælfstan carried similar wounds earlier in the year. Ælfstan can ride now without discomfort, but it's taken a while.

'Should you be here?' I ask Edwin, meaning it considerately. He must be in agony. But he rounds on me, anger on his pale face.

'You're not the only one to win the acclaim of your lord, you know, Icel. The rest of us can take wounds and still fight on as well.' He spits those words into my face, shoving me aside for all it makes him hiss with pain, and I wipe his spittle from my cheeks and glower at him.

'I meant it to be kind, not to cast doubt on your skills. Edwin, you really are a bloody arse sometimes,' I retort, stung by his words. He came to me, after all, and yet it's evident that he's far from happy about that.

'Well, you can piss off,' he finishes, mounting his horse as though it's not just taken him twice as long as everyone else to shrug into his byrnie. If this comes to a fight, or rather, when it comes to a fight, I'm far from convinced that he'll be any good to anyone. I share a glance with Oswy, and the wisdom on his face assures me that he sees it too. Edwin is here with us, but he's like a wounded hare, trying to escape the snapping jaws of a hunting hound. He'll need guarding even while we attempt to find and win free Lord Coenwulf. I sigh softly. Not for the first time in my life, I wish I could turn back two days and have none of this be my problem to contend with.

But when did wishes ever become a reality?

* * *

'Stay here,' Ælfstan calls back over his shoulder. The day is once more nearing its end, and I can see the glow of fires and lights in the distance, coming from a settlement that looks to be far from prosperous.

We've long ago left the noise of the River Thames behind, and somehow, and I don't know how, our presence has yet to be spotted. I rein in Brute and bend to run my hand down his shoulder. Brute's steps have flagged as the day's worn on, but of course, I can't carry him while he sleeps. Hopefully, we'll be able to stop soon, and everyone can get some rest.

Wulfheard hurries Bada forward to join the ealdorman while the rest of us sag in our saddles. I'm not the only one to be exhausted. Frithwine snores in his sleep, and I consider nudging him so that he falls from his saddle, but Frithwine struggles to sleep at the best of times, haunted by the memories of that final battle with his brother. I'll not wake him. I hope no one else does.

Edwin is another one who's more asleep than awake. I want to stop and make him a healing drink or infuse his next meal with something that will make him stronger, but I don't have that option. Not yet.

My mind turns to what he alluded to about Lord Coenwulf. King Ecgberht of Wessex has proven himself to be wily in the art of undermining King Wiglaf. We believe he sent Viking raiders into the kingdom of the East Angles with the express purpose of having them attack Mercians. And now, it appears, he's tried to bring Lord Coenwulf to his side. If Edwin's correct, and Coenwulf resents his sister's marriage to Lord Wigmund, then perhaps he would betray the Mercians to the Wessex king in order to be named as their king. But Coenwulf has no local support. I know that. Few even mention his name at court these days. Ironically, no one has forgotten Lady Ælflæd's royal blood, but most seem to have mislaid the fact that the same also extends to her brother, and her brother now has a son who could inherit from him one day. I imagine that can make a man reconsider many previous decisions.

'Icel.' Oswy brings his mount close, his words softly spoken. 'I'll keep an eye on Edwin, I assure you.'

I wonder why he's telling me this, but actually it does make me feel better to know he's aware of Edwin's current condition.

'My thanks.' I find a tight smile for my wind-roughened cheeks, threading my fingers through my thick beard. I've been considering shaving all my facial hair away, keen to run my fingers over the skin, not a beard, but I appreciate that the damn thing will just grow back. Perhaps it's easier when I can just snip away at the hairs that grow too long around my mouth.

'Lord Coenwulf has taken a great risk,' Oswy continues. 'His wife, his sister, and his king will be furious when we rescue him.' I nod. I've realised this as well.

'Well, they're welcome to be furious with him, provided we retrieve him alive,' I murmur. Oswy stills for a moment and then looks at me keenly in the growing dusk.

'You've stopped thinking that anything is possible and realised there are some limitations, even to what we can do!' He nods in approval. I open my mouth to retort, but Wulfheard has returned.

'Come into the village unmounted. We're going straight into the barn, where half of us will sleep for the night, and half will keep guard, and then we'll exchange roles. In the morning, we'll make our way to the Isle of Sheppey.' Quickly, I slide from Brute's back and then reach over and place a hand on Edwin's leg, for he still snores. He startles awake, his seax coming within a finger's width of severing my hand and gouging his own leg.

'Dismount,' I urge him. Confusion in his eyes, but with no word of apology for his earlier outburst, Edwin does as he's instructed. Together, we make our way past the ditch and rampart that surrounds the small collection of buildings, all of the lights doused now, even the candlelight no longer visible. The barn we're led into by Wulfheard is large and smells of fresh hay. It's also devoid of all animals apart from one ox, held behind a collection of carts in the far corner. The animal lows at us but then returns to eating its food. It seems we're going to have no problems with the animal.

I remove Brute's saddle and run my hand down his limbs. All seem well, and there's a barrel of water from which the horses can drink. Only then are they allowed their freedom, separated from the ox by the wooden carts.

I reach for my saddlebags, but Wulfheard thrusts a platter into my hand, and I'm surprised to find warm bread on it.

'Divide it up. There's some pottage as well and some cheese,' Wulfheard informs me. He doesn't speak in his normal tone, and I lower my voice as well. It seems we've been invited into the settlement, and yet it must all be done so that others don't suspect our presence. What sort of relationship does the ealdorman have with the men and women who live in this place? Not that I give it much thought. Instead, I offer the bread around and find a clean space to lean against the barn's walls and sit on my arse. I can almost feel my eyes rolling in my head, even as I try to eat. A bowl of pottage is passed to me, but I'm nearly asleep. It takes all of my effort to spoon the meaty mixture into my mouth, and I'm snoring before Wulfheard can determine who'll stand guard and who'll sleep. As such, when I'm woken by Oswy's huge hand on my shoulder, my wooden bowl is still in my hand, and I startle, squinting into the gloom. Grit in my eyes makes it hard to focus, but Oswy's yawn assures me I need to wake up.

Slowly, I stand, aware I need to piss. It's almost too dark to see, but I just make out where others are standing, in the open doorway, hands on weapons belts. I venture to join Æthelmod as he stifles a yawn.

'Over there.' He points, and I can hear the drum of someone else's stream hitting the ground. I scamper outside, the relief of pissing almost bringing a gasp of joy to my lips.

Only then do I peer into the near distance, trying to make out more of where we are, but it's impossible. The moon, so bright the night before, is shadowed by thick clouds, the scent of dampness ripe in the air.

I return to Æthelmod's side, and notice Uor, Landwine and Maneca as well. That's not quite a quarter of us. I wonder where the others are, only for a movement in my peripheral vision to startle me.

'Good to see you're alert,' Ealdorman Ælfstan comments, his voice lacking all humour.

'Sorry, my lord,' I feel compelled to apologise. Ælfstan offers nothing further but moves into the barn, and after a few moments, his movements cease, and all I can hear is the rhythmic snoring of the warriors. I'm curious about where he came from, but I don't ask. It appears we're to be as silent as possible.

Yawning widely, I determine to stay alert, breathing deeply to slow my pounding heart and then settle to a stance I know I can hold for as long as needed. There's next to no sound other than the snoring of men, the farting of the horses, and the occasional huff from the ox. I almost relax, but I don't. We're in enemy land, and enemies could surround us.

Wulfheard appears from out of nowhere as the very first faintness of a new day can be seen over the horizon. Æthelmod was clearly aware of where he was, for he didn't seem alarmed, and then we're all urged to make ourselves ready. With hasty bites of the leftover food, we're once more mounted and headed eastwards long before any sort of daylight illuminates the path. The horses follow closely, nose to tail, and while those who've slept throughout the second part of the night suppress their yawning, those who've been awake for that part of the night, including me, yawn even wider. It's going to be a long and difficult day.

I stay away from Edwin, content to follow Oswy's horse, with Uor's behind me. The track we follow isn't wide. If I didn't know better, I'd say it was little more than a sheep or goat track, one perhaps used by the shepherds herding their flocks between summer meadows and winter quarters. Ealdorman Ælfstan leads the way. I consider how he even knows of this place. He must have been here before when he wasn't an ealdorman of Mercia. Or perhaps he was involved in the fight for Kent when the Wessex king claimed it from Mercia after King Beornwulf's defeat by Wessex eight years ago.

Not for the first time, I genuinely wish I knew more about the past and even events that have oc-curred in my lifetime. I need to be more vigilant and ask more questions of those who lived through such happenings. Unbidden, my thoughts turn to God-wulf. I've heard nothing from him since he was forced to leave Tamworth. Has he, I muse, returned to the kingdom of the East Angles? And there's some-thing else to be wary of: did he think to tilt the past to

his own interpretation to gain something at my ex-
pense? There's much for me to consider.

The day advances, and all of us are just about
silent, the landscape coming into focus. In the distance, I can see a cut through the view and take it to
be where the River Thames lies, but then, slowly but
surely, I begin to realise that there's an even bigger
expanse before me, and for the first time in my life, I
witness the sea.

The blueness of the water astounds me,
stretching away into the far distance to merge with
the sky, where the scattered white clouds scud overhead. I can hardly tell where the water ends and the
sky begins, and I know my mouth hangs open in
shock.

Oswy turns to grin at me.

'It never gets old,' he assures me, lacking all signs
of teasing. I respect him for that. Behind me, Uor
chuckles darkly.

'Try being out there on a ship and then tell me
about it never getting old.' I remember then that Uor
told me of his seasickness, and that was how he became a warrior, not a shipman. I think of the roll of
Brute beneath me and know a moment of sympathy.
At least I know, when mounted, that I can dismount
if I feel sick. The same can't be said of the sea.

All the same, it fascinates me. I should like to try sailing. I want to experience it for myself. Only then my delight in the spectacle disappears. The scent of cook fires that I've been smelling for some time impacts my thought, and I turn my eyes away from the expanse of the sea and understand that, while the sea is there, the vastness inviting, it's not unending. In front of me, a thin layer of smoke clouds the horizon. It seems we've found the Viking raiders and their island hideaway, and all without being discovered by the warriors of Wessex. I'd like to think that's half the task completed, but I know better than that.

13

Ealdorman Ælfstan gathers us together just to the side of a small hill or perhaps an earthwork. The shape of it seems too regular for it to be natural, but I'm no expert.

'There, my brave warriors, is the Isle of Sheppey.' I don't think Ælfstan needs to tell us that, but he does so all the same. I want to shudder into my cloak and perhaps turn tail from that place, but I know I can't. Not if I'm to help Lady Cynehild, and somehow, doing so has become my primary purpose after ensuring Mercia is clear from enemy attacks.

'We'll leave the horses inside. There's someone there who'll care for them while we're gone.'

'Gone?' I almost squeak. 'Where are we going

without the horses?' I gasp, unsure what he even means by inside.

'To rescue Lord Coenwulf,' Wulfheard grunts. I want to say he sounds fearful, but he doesn't. In fact, none of the men do. I wish I knew more about what we were about to do.

'Our force will be divided between four ships,' the ealdorman continues. 'All of them will be going to the island. We do as we're told by the ship's commanders, local fishermen and women. They'll do this for us, and in return, we must do all we can to both save Lord Coenwulf, and to kill all the bastard Viking raiders.'

I gasp at the audacity of the plan, wishing not for the first time that I couldn't count to seventeen, not including Edwin, so that I wouldn't know how few of us there were.

'What do we do when we get to the Isle of Sheppey?' I query.

'It's to be hoped that the Viking raiders don't notice we're not the usual fisher people. I'm assured that the enemy thinks themselves safe on their island. They don't expect the Wessex king's son to attack them. There's some alliance, as I understand it, the bloody cowards,' Ealdorman Ælfstan continues. Whatever he was doing last night while I slept, Ælfstan seems to be remarkably well informed of local events.

'The fisher people are taking a huge risk, but one they're prepared to honour. So, keep alert, and bloody stay alive, and we'll meet up on the island it-self and plan from there. These people have seen no further than the small quayside on Sheppey to the southern tip. They don't truly know how many ene-mies there are because some of the ships are moored on the far side of the island. But they hate them. The enemy made the island their home and killed everyone who lived there. Now they want them dead. And we must ensure that for them.'

I want to argue and decry the recklessness of such an act, but no one else speaks, and I appreciate these men think they're perfectly capable of bringing this about. Just as in Londinium, we must infiltrate our enemy to rescue our allies. I swallow, tasting my fear and wishing I didn't, as I begin removing Brute's saddle. I spare a thought for Lady Cynehild, her son, Coenwulf, and her unborn child, and also for Wyn-flæd and Cuthred, but if I thought I had a choice about whether to continue with this rescue attempt, I'm aware that I never actually did.

If the Viking raiders think to take a man of Mercia as their pawn, no matter his intentions with the Wessex king, then we Mercian warriors must do all we can to retrieve him. And I suppose, at least, I'll get to sit in a ship and feel the waves beneath me. Then, I'll know whether Uor was right to decide not to be a shipman.

I notice then that a wizened old man is talking to Ælfstan. I consider who the man might be as he flashes an almost toothless grin, but whomever he is, Ælfstan is comfortable leaving our mounts in his care as he leads us inside a rough-hewn doorway. I didn't even realise it was there.

Brute eyes me ruefully as I finish removing his saddle, laying it over a handy barrel, before turning to pull hay from a net. This isn't a stable or a barn. I don't really think I can call it anything other than a cave, but it's evidently been put to such use before, and there are troughs gouged through the rock and water pools through them. It's a handy location, and from not far away, the whiff of the sea is ripe in the air.

I spare a thought for Edwin as he labours down from his saddle with his terrible wounds hidden beneath his tunic, but I don't offer to help. I'm never going to offer to help him again.

'Wulfheard, you'll go first and take the more experienced warriors with you: Uor, Kyre, Cenred and Osmod.' The ealdorman points to those warriors. They nod and prepare themselves. I realise that Wulfheard is busy taking off his byrnie, and I can't think why. Only then he bundles it into a sack, and I begin to understand. He keeps his belt in place but removes all of his weapons other than a seax. The other men do the same, all of them adding their protection and weapons to the sack.

'This way.' Wulfheard leads his warriors through to the cave's rear, opposite to that which we came into, and out into brightness, which I suddenly realise is visible. This then is a structure with two entrances. I think it a risky move to be so blatant, but none of the others seems to think it strange.

'Oswy, you'll take Icel, as you and he get on so well together, and Frithwine as well. You'll be on a smaller fishing ship, so there's only room for the three of you.' As he speaks, Ælfstan hands me a sack, and I comprehend I'm to follow Wulfheard and the others in removing my byrnie and weapons. I don't like doing away with my byrnie. It feels as though I've only just donned it again. Neither do I like not having the weight of my weapons around my waist. Oswy grumbles as well, which makes me feel better.

'Æthelmod, Edwin, Ordlaf, Maneca, Waldhere and Wulfgar, you'll be in the third ship. It's a bigger craft, and you'll need to row because the sail is missing.' The men all groan at that, but I'm being urged to leave by Oswy, and so I don't hear the ealdorman's final instruction, but it's easy enough to work out who'll be escorting him: Berhthelm, Goðeman and Landwine.

I follow Oswy with Frithwine behind me, and we emerge on a sharp incline that leads down to the sea. I drink in the view before me, that of the sea, and the island, and small buildings, homes I assume, which nestle almost into the cliff face. I can also see a small harbour, boats bobbing on the water, and already Wulfheard and his men are scrambling into a fishing craft.

'The tide is just right for fishing,' Oswy informs me conversationally.

'Are we going fishing?' I gasp with surprise, the sack in my hands, heavy with the three byrnies and our weapons.

'For a while, yes. We have to make sure we look the part.'

I'm not sure I like the sound of that. Do I really want to try my hand at fishing?

'Don't worry. The fisherman knows what he's doing. Just follow his orders, and we'll be fine.'

'How has all this been arranged?' I huff, feeling my knees twinge at the steepness of the path.

'Ealdorman Ælfstan knows people hereabouts. He was able to arrange it all during the night.'

In no time at all, we're level with the harbour, and a man comes towards us. He has the same look about him as the toothless old man watching our horses, and his eyes light up on seeing Oswy.

'You're a big bugger,' he exclaims, his words gently rolling, only to catch sight of me. 'And you're an even bigger bugger,' he echoes, a smirk on his lined face. He doesn't refer to Frithwine, and that's because Frithwine has grown thin with his grief. He's lost his bulky muscles, but he's replaced them with speed and some grace. 'Ever been on a ship before?' the man asks, not telling us his name.

'Only one on the side of a river,' I retort, and his eyes twinkle.

'Well, lads, you're in for a treat then. Now, come on. In you get and whatever you do, don't fall overboard. You'll look a right arse if you do, and anyone watching from that island there will know you're not who you pretend to be.' Those words give me no comfort at all, and as I watch Oswy lower himself into the cramped space of a vessel that stinks of fish and seems to be all hempen net and little room, I really wish myself elsewhere.

Stepping onto the craft, I'm reminded of the way the Viking raider ship beside Peterborough monastery wobbled and twisted with the water beneath it and my steps over it. I bend my knees, hoping to slide in on my arse, but the craft lurches away from the quayside so that I almost dip my foot into the water. The water's filled with small silvery fish and some strange creatures that seem to bob on its surface, and I don't want to touch them.

The man hauls on one of the ropes, and the craft moves closer to the wall, and this time I'm able to step into it and quickly sit down, not wanting to risk falling in.

'Elegantly done,' the man cackles, and I feel a glower of fury on my cheeks that only worsens when Frithwine skips onto the ship as though he's been doing it all his life.

'Wonderful,' I exclaim.

'Right, take an oar each, and row when I tell you to. Dip it in behind you, and pull it forwards. And try and make it look like you know what you're doing. And for now, you can call me Cap. And I'll call you big lad, bigger lad, and wee lad. Now, do we know what we're doing?' I'm astounded that Oswy not only doesn't clatter the man over the head but even chuckles.

'Aye, Cap, we're yours to command for now.'

I grip the oar, aware it's much smaller than the ones I threw into the water outside Peterborough, and dip it into the water, then try and pull it forward. I grit my teeth. I've always known this was harder than it looked, but still, the movement sparks an angry response from my shoulder blades.

'At the same time, you damn fools,' Cap complains to us with a shake of his head. He's sat beside Oswy, at the front or rear of the ship, I truly don't know, and I watch his back and the angle of the oar and try and mirror the movement. For about four strokes, we seem to have it. Only then we don't.

'Right, I'll count, you bloody fools,' Cap complains, the humour gone from his voice.

As we're still facing the quayside, I watch as Ælfstan leads his men to their ship and realise they have a much firmer grasp on what they're supposed to be doing as they effortlessly glide past us and out into the expanse of the sea in their larger craft.

'You do know, don't you' – Cap turns to glower at Frithwine and I – 'that the bastards over there know how to row a ship, and they'll know that you don't if you don't do as you're bloody told?' I can detect the hint of fear in Cap's voice.

'I'm trying,' Frithwine counters, huffing heavily.

'I am too,' I feel stung into saying.

'Now, on one,' Cap murmurs, turning back to face land.

And on one, we move, with a sure stroke, and on two, we do the same, and finally, before the last of the other three fishing vessels can move out into the sea, we manage to make a half-decent job of what we're supposed to be doing. But Cap continues to count, a steady rhythm that allows me to keep in time with my fellow warriors, and while the ship rocks a little, I don't feel any swell of nausea, which pleases me. So focused on what I'm doing, I don't realise how far we've come from the mainland until the ship bucks up and down on a wave, unsettling my oar so that I miss the count from Cap, and water slaps onto my face, which is salty when I lick it.

'Keep it steady,' he urges, clearly expecting this, even as I look at where we've come from. From here, the hill we climbed down seems less steep, and although I squint, I can't determine the entrance to the hidden passageway we used to get here. I can see smoke pooling into the air from steadings, but the sharp bite of the ocean and the firm breeze ensure I can't smell it.

'In a few moments,' Cap says, 'we'll stop and throw the nets out. Then you can take your ease for a while before we move on to the next spot.'

'So, we're actually going to be fishing?' Frithwine queries beneath gritted teeth. Sweat beads his forehead, and I can see that while he might have made it into the ship without any problems, he's not enjoying the motion of the waves.

'Yes, that's the plan,' Oswy confirms. 'The four vessels are each going to scout a different location, and then, later, we'll converge on the small harbour, offer up our catch, and steal our way onto the island.'

'Can't go there with nothing to offer the foemen,' Cap confirms as he stops rowing and stands. I notice his stance is wide as he hauls on a net and flings it over the ship's side. I want to watch it, but I don't want to stand, so I hold my place, oar still held out into the water, although it's not moving. Every so often, a wave bashes it, and the oar hits my knee. I watch as the fisherman secures the net to the boat.

'Is there anything to drink?' Frithwine whines. I can see that he's started to swallow convulsively, and I fear he might spew his guts into the fishing net.

'Here.' Cap passes a water skin to him as my belly

rumbles. 'I have bread as well.' He smirks, bending to pull two loaves from a sack at his feet. He offers the first to me, and I rip it in two and offer half to Frithwine. He grips it tightly, having swilled a lot of water into his mouth.

I eat ravenously, eyes busy all around me. Cap has angled the ship so that we can see the island. There's a band of smoke above it, but I can't see the enemy encampment or even any ships.

'We've got the end of the island where not much happens,' he offers conversationally. 'Mind, that field there used to be filled with sheep, but the scum have eaten their way through all the lamb and mutton, and now they demand fish from us. I would have expected them to fish, but they seem to think too much of themselves to have learned how to harvest the sea.'

'How many people lived on the island?' I think to ask, chewing rhythmically as I muse on the location. The sea breeze gently ruffles my hair. If we weren't trying to sneak our way onto the Isle of Sheppey and hopefully kill all the Viking raiders at the same time, I might almost be enjoying myself.

'No more than fifty. Mostly just three families, and the monks, of course. I knew them well. But they're all gone. All of them.' Cap's voice thrums with fury. I shake my head at his words. It fills me with anger for what's happened here. Why, I think and not for the first time, have the Viking raiders come to our shores? There are some, I know, who think that this, too, is the work of King Ecgberht of Wessex. And yet, I don't quite see it. After all, these men are killing men and women of Wessex and, some say, taking those they allow to live as slaves to be sold along the trading routes leading to the land of the Rus, exchanging people for the silver coins they call dirhams.

'Right, we'll give it a while longer and haul in the net. We might not have many little fishes, but we just need a few. When they come on deck, we put them in those buckets there.' Cap points to some empty buckets, which I confess, I'd thought were to piss in, but of course, no doubt, we do that over the side of the ship.

'What sort of fish do you get here?' Oswy questions.

'It doesn't matter as long as you eat 'em,' Cap choruses and then turns to me and Oswy. 'The pair of you can pull the net in. It'll be heavy. Whatever you do, don't overbalance the damn ship.'

Warily, I stand and try and force a wide stance, as I've seen Cap do, but the ship's so narrow it's hard to do. When we were rowing, Frithwine and I almost bashed elbows more than once.

'Get a firm grip on it, or you'll lose the bloody lot, and I'll be sending you in to retrieve it,' Cap offers by way of encouragement.

Feeling the strain on my shoulders from all the rowing, I bend and tug on the net. I gasp. When Cap threw it overboard, he made it look easy, and now, as I haul it onto the boat, silvery fish caught in its grasp, I just can't see how one man could have handled the net alone.

'Come on, hurry up. We need to get these all in the buckets.' Behind me, I can sense Cap grabbing for the fish, trying to escape as seawater pools into the bottom of the ship. Fishes leap into the bilge while Cap attempts to catch them and place them in the bucket. And still, the net keeps appearing from the depths of the sea. I didn't realise how big the thing was.

'Catch 'em, you damn fool,' Cap shouts to Frith-wine, the ship rocking unsteadily beneath my feet. And finally, the end of the net emerges from the water.

Only then do I turn, seeing the quantity of fish in the bucket.

Cap's grinning. 'It seems to me,' he offers, 'that the Norse God of the sea is keen to feed them today, and that'll only make it easier to get on that island and kill all of the bastards.'

* * *

What feels like half the day later, my shoulders in agony from all the rowing, because despite the ealdorman's words, this ship has no sail either, Cap directs us to the quayside. I've been watching the rest of the warriors for much of the day as the ships crisscrossed in no set pattern, although Cap murmured something about tides and schools of fish. Even one of the Viking raider ships had left the island at one point, coming perilously close to us but not seeming to notice that we were anything but fishermen as they slid past. I watched them through narrowed eyes, but the ship headed towards the open expanse of the sea.

'They'll be off to Frankia or some such,' Cap assured me. 'They've got what they came for, and now they're going to sell the poor buggers.' And that had caught my attention the most. While the ship had a far from bleached white sail overhead, there'd been few, if anyone, rowing. Instead, the vessel's hold had been filled with the frightened eyes of men and women, children as well, and my heart had sunk.

'We can do nothing for 'em now,' Oswy had muttered darkly. 'King Ecgberht of Wessex has just another crime to answer for, letting the good people of Kent be sold as slaves.'

As much as I'd wanted to chase that ship, despite the impossible odds, I'd realised the wisdom of Oswy's words. Our fight was for Lord Coenwulf. I needed to remember that.

'We're the first to make landfall,' Cap informs us. 'Keep your heads down, and obey my commands. Don't look any of them in the eye if they even come to examine what we've got. They think themselves invincible on this island.'

Slowly, the ship glides into the quayside, bumping against the wooden struts held above the waterline. With quick grace, Cap springs onto the slippery wooden planks and ties the craft firm. He winks as he does so, perhaps anticipating our feelings on the matter.

Quickly, he ties another rope to the quay as well, securing the rear of the ship.

'Come on then, lads. Get those fish up here. I need the coin to live another day,' he urges loudly.

I reach for one of the baskets, ensuring my oar's safely stowed. Cap's adamant that we shouldn't lose an oar. By now, we've aroused the attention of some of the Viking raiders, and although I don't look up, I can feel the wood of the quay quivering as I heave the bucket onto it. Cap's already turned to face those walking towards him.

A gabble of words is exchanged, and I realise that Cap speaks the Viking raider language, even if it's halting.

'Hurry up,' Oswy murmurs to me, bending to retrieve another of the buckets. There is, indeed, a lot of fish for Cap to sell.

Once the ship's free from its catch, we bend and pick up one of the buckets, making our way towards where Cap's already haggling with the Viking raiders. Only now do I lift my eyes to look at my enemy.

There's a collection of them, standing further back than the man haggling for the fish, and they're armed but relaxed. The arrogant sods seem content that none will dare attack them here on this island.

The men, for I'm sure they're all men, are a variety of shapes and sizes, but they look mean. Not one of them, I note, has a straight nose. This, then, isn't their first fight, but it might well be their last. I swallow deeply and concentrate on what I'm doing instead of sizing up my enemy. That will come, but not yet.

The gabble of words continues. It's some sort of complaint, but I only hear half of the conversation.

'Blame these useless buggers,' Cap argues using our language, and I consider if the Viking raiders are hungry and wish the fish had been brought to them sooner. I can't imagine they've yet eaten their way through every single sheep, as Cap mentioned, but it's possible they have. Perhaps, I think, bending and dropping the bucket close to Cap's feet so that one of the fish slithers free and lands on the foot of the man Cap's haggling with, they should have thought a little bit more about that before they ate all the bloody food.

The man kicks the fish contemptuously aside, and I bend and hastily return it to the other pale flesh from our day's catch. Hastily, not truly wishing to turn my back on my enemy, I return for the next bucket, passing Frithwine as I go. His eyes are dark and shadowed, his arms straining at the great weight.

'I'll take it,' I offer quickly. I can see that Frithwine might just be the man to give away our intention. He hates the Viking raiders for murdering his brother. I know he hungers to slice his blade through the neck, waists and eyeballs of every one of our enemies. And I want to give him that chance, but not yet.

For a moment, as I place my hands on the handle

of the bucket, I think he'll argue with me, but he gives it up eventually, biting his lip so that his flesh turns even whiter. Only then does he turn and make his way back to the ship. We need to be both quick and slow with unloading our supplies. We want the sky to darken further so that we can sneak onto the island and stay there, attacking the enemy when all is in darkness. The tide has done us a favour, but the sun is still bright overhead. We've taken our time, but I think not quite enough.

With the next bucket on the ground, I slowly return to the ship, trying to get a feeling for the landscape of the island, for where the Viking raiders might be sheltering, and also for where the remainder of Ealdorman Ælfstan's men are hiding. Or not hiding, waiting to come ashore as well.

I hear Cap's voice thrum with amusement and hope that means he's reached an accord with our enemy. And yet, I still don't know where we can hide, and I have a feeling that the Viking raiders will stand there, forming a line across the beaten track that leads into the heart of Sheppey. There's the smell of woodsmoke in the air, but it's not coming from the ramshackle collection of buildings close to the quayside. I decide these must be huts for the fisher people to store their nets and other equipment when the weather's bad or in need of repair. Where, then, are the Viking raiders making their home?

I hear the unmistakable bray of a donkey and the clatter of a wheeled cart making its way towards the quayside. A bowed-headed man leads the animal. I wince to see the marks on his body from where his tunic has been ripped away. He's not been well used by our enemy. The donkey looks healthy but angry as the man bends to begin adding the containers of fish to the small wooden cart.

Without thought, I hurry to aid the man, lowering my head to match his. The Viking raiders part to let me pass, one of them belatedly leaving his foot in my way so that I trip and land heavily on my hands and knees. I breathe deeply, take a moment to recover my composure, and for my hands to unclench. I hear a tut from Cap and immediately realise I've no doubt erred in doing so, but it's too late now. I've made my intention clear. While Oswy and Frithwine are back at the ship, I lift the buckets, trying to catch the eyes of the man, and see if he can tell me more. His hands are bloodied, and he stinks of fish and donkey, an odd combination and one that makes me veer away from him.

'Good day,' I murmur softly. I see him startle at the words, and he looks at me. Only then do I notice

he has only one eye. The other cavern is a gaping
ruin. I wince at the sight of the seeping mass,
thinking of how the man could keep it cleaner and
help it to heal. The loss of an eye need not lead to his
death, but unless he treats it, it will, and soon.

'That looks nasty,' I continue, rearranging the
buckets so that I can fit another one onto the back of
the cart.

'Aye, well, the devil's plucked my eyeball,' he
replies, in a voice scratchy from lack of use.

'You need to bathe the wound with boiled water
and add salt or douse it with vinegar,' I offer.

'No point. Sooner I'm dead, the better,' he retorts.
But his actions have slowed. He doesn't rush back for
the next bucket. I think he wants to talk to me.

'I would tend to it and hope for rescue or release
from your enemy,' I say even more softly.

I feel the heat of his gaze but realise we've lin-
gered too long and hastily return for another bucket
of fish. Cap is doing his best to chat with the enemy,
covering whatever I'm doing, and so I feel nothing
more than a passive interest in my actions. At the cart
once more, the other man is busying himself on rearranging something that doesn't need moving, but it
gives us more time to talk, and the scrape of wood on
wood covers much of our conversation.

'You're not the usual ones,' he offers, looking at me with his single, keen brown eye.

'No, we're not,' I admit.

'I'll do as you say,' he confirms, sucking on his lower lip in thought. 'You can find them in the monastery,' the man offers. 'Where they pollute God's church with their stink and shit, and where my brother monks lie unburied and festering.' I grimace at the thought of that but nod.

'My thanks. Stay well,' and I press my hand over his shoulder, offering him my strength, if only for a moment.

Head bowed, I hasten back to the ship, where Frithwine and Oswy are preparing it to make the short journey back towards the mainland. Not that we'll be going that far. But as of yet, the light is still too bright for us to try and make our way onto the island undetected. We'll have to return when the next ship lands.

Cap jumps down into the ship, winking at me as he does so. I can hear the jingle of coins in a pouch in his hand. I consider whether they're silver dirhams, or coins carrying the head of King Ecgberht of Wessex. I don't suppose it truly matters.

'A bit too early,' he mutters. 'But the next ship should have it, and then it'll be dark, and we can return.' I settle myself and we begin to pull away from the small quayside. This time, I keep my eyes on where I've been, watching the stubborn old donkey begin his slow progress back towards the monastery as the Viking raiders break off their desultory guard, some of them returning with the cart, others settling to wait for the next ship to dock on the quayside. It's all far too easy and natural for them. They walk around the Isle of Sheppey as though they own it, and that makes my blood sizzle with anger. Bloody King Ecgberht claimed Kent for his son, but lacks the ability to repel the Viking raiders from his own kingdom. Just like in the kingdom of the East Angles, I consider what makes men reach for more land to control when they can't defend it.

14

'Don't go too far,' Cap instructs us as the ship wallows in the thin channel between the mainland and the island. 'When it's dark, it'll be difficult to see. Just take the craft around this corner, and we'll shelter beneath the rocks.'

I don't much like the idea of that, the pale rocks menacing overhead, but neither do I want to be too far from where we mean to disembark later. As we leave the more sheltered bay, Wulfheard and his warriors pass us, making their way to the quayside. I meet his eyes, and he grimaces. I can well imagine there are going to be complaints about sore backs and blistered hands when this is all over. Already, I can feel calluses forming on my hands from rowing. I thought my skin was quite toughened from all my training and fighting, but the wooden oars are another matter entirely.

'He said they were at the monastery,' I finally speak, confident we're far enough away from the quayside that I can talk at my usual volume.

'They killed all the monks, I've heard, apart from the one with the donkey,' Cap informs, his words mournful. 'Good men, all of them. They cared only for praying and eating.'

'Yes, he said they've not buried them.' This causes a frown from Oswy and Frithwine.

'Bloody fools, inviting rats, maggots and flies into their homes.' Oswy shudders at the thought.

'What were you talking to them about?' I ask Cap, curious to know if it was about more than fish and the sea.

'They were asking about the winds and the tides. They mean to remain there, but I think they've set their sights on attacking the mainland of Kent as well. Of course, they added a few threats to keep my mouth shut and to ensure I keep bringing the fish. They paid me, yes, but it's a poor amount. The coins don't feel the correct weight for my liking. They say they'll pay no more, for we fisher people are buying the safety of our people as well as providing food for our enemy.'

'Did they attack your settlement?' I ask.

'They burned some of the fisher people's huts just to make a scene. And they stole our damn donkey as well. Bloody fools killed their own for pissing on their jarl's foot.' Disbelief clouds Cap's voice at that news. An ox might be needed in the fields, but a donkey is just as good when the only requirement is to carry a greater weight than a man or woman can easily manage.

'How long have they been there?'

'Near enough six weeks, not quite two months. They came just after the Easter festivities,' Cap muses. Around us, I'm aware that the sun is finally starting to sink. It's almost midsummer, the days are long and filled with brightness, and it's not really the correct time to be trying to sneak anywhere, and yet we must. The island, as I've seen that day, is larger than I thought, and yet the Viking raiders are only in one place. They seem to guard the quayside when they expect trouble but nowhere else. I consider why we don't try and alight on the island elsewhere. But Ealdorman Ælfstan seems to know what he's doing. I decide not to ask the question for fear of being ridiculed.

'They come and go. They went along the River Thames, and we thought to never see them again, but they returned far too quickly, with more men, but they've remained on the island since then.' I nod. This must be when they captured Lord Coenwulf. While his intentions might not have been favourable to Mercia, in this he appears to have been unlucky.

'Here, eat before you go,' Cap offers, pulling more bread from a sack and a slab of cheese as well. Oswy takes the bread and divides it between us all, offering some back to Cap.

'No, thanks, lads. I'll eat while you're fighting.'

Eagerly, I tear into the bread and cheese, aware that Frithwine, as so often the case, is less mindful of his need to eat.

'Frithwine. Eat your fill,' I urge him, but he still chews absent-mindedly.

'Eat it, lad, or you'll have no strength to kill all the bastards,' Oswy growls. At that, Frithwine begins to chomp with more relish, and Cap glances at me.

'He has revenge on his mind,' I offer with a tight smile, recalling Garwulf far more fondly than I thought of him at the time. He helped secure Londinium for King Wiglaf, but Garwulf is little more than bones now. I can't help wishing he was remembered by more than just his brother.

Wulfheard's ship appears from out of the growing gloom, an unhappy expression on his face. The two ships rest, almost side by side, against the swell and fall of the sea.

'Ealdorman Ælfstan's turn next,' Wulfheard calls over to us. 'And then, I think it'll be time for all of us to disembark.' I catch sight of Uor, Cenred, and Osmod as well, and I see the fires of fury in their eyes. They wanted to go first, to be the ones to risk their lives, not the ealdorman, but here the planning of this encounter has gone slightly awry. I hope it's just an oversight and not a sign of things to come.

'Glad you found time to eat,' Wulfheard resumes. His words are almost drowned out by the smack of the seawater against the side of the ship, but I shrug.

'I always thought it best to eat when you had the opportunity.' I chuckle to hear Wulfheard's growl of fury and bend to lift a drinking bottle to my lips. When I'm upright once more, the other ship has almost disappeared, the darkness of night finally covering us.

'Time to take you back,' Cap confirms. 'Take to your oars,' he commands us, and I leap to it, keen to get this long and tedious day over with.

But it's strange rowing in the dark over the constantly moving sea. There's firelight from the settlement we borrowed the ships from, but there's no illumination coming from the Isle of Sheppey. I'm grateful that Cap knows where he's going. Even sound is strange in the darkness. I can just detect the slap of oars from one of the other ships, but I don't quite know where it's coming from. I try not to conjure up enemy ships in my mind. Surely, after all this time and all this waiting, we'd have seen if there was a Viking raider ship making its way back to the Isle of Sheppey.

'Stow your oars,' Cap calls in the gloom.

I can barely make him out, it's become so dark, and then the ship bounces away from something, and I realise we're already back at the quayside. Again, there's no light coming from the land. Wherever the monastery is, it's hidden enough that I can't see any glow from fires or candles that the enemy must be using to beat back the advance of night.

'Off you go, and good luck, my friends. And remember, if you ever have need of a new profession, you'll all make passable fisher people.' Cap chuckles as he grips my hand and aids me onto the quayside. It's strange to be on dry land suddenly. I feel my legs give beneath me, and he steadies me with his strength. 'Kill one for me. Offer my name over his dying body, for I've not the skill to kill 'em myself.'

'I will, and my thanks.'

'You can tell me all about it when you get back.' Cap releases me, and I squint down, trying to differentiate the water from the wooden quayside. Ahead, I can make out the sound of men murmuring to one another, and I follow the sound more than knowing where I'm going. 'Don't forget this,' Cap calls as I begin to walk away. He hands me the sack containing our byrnies and weapons. I can't believe we almost forgot it.

'Watch the bodies,' Goðeman calls to me as I make my way towards where I think the rest of the men are. I veer aside from the sharp stench of spilt blood. 'They were just sitting around, minding their own business, but we gutted them,' he offers, and I can determine he's smiling, although I can't see him.

'Are we all here?' Ealdorman Ælfstan calls. I hear the sound of someone retching noisily, but I can't decipher who hated our time in the boat.

'Even the sick ones,' Wulfheard confirms, so at least I know it's not him. If I had to wager on it, I'd say it was Uor. The poor sod. He became a warrior rather than living a life on the seas. I imagine he's regretting our current predicament.

'Now, does anyone know where the buggers are?'

'The monastery,' I offer, keen to make use of the knowledge I've gained.

'And does anyone know where that is?' Wulfheard asks with a hint of frustration. Silence greets those words. I realise then that this plan is actually much less well planned than I thought it would be.

'I can take you.' The familiar voice of the man I spoke to, with the donkey, fills the silence.

The rustle and clank of hands on weapons, and I step to protect the man where I think he is in the dusk. 'He helped me earlier,' I confirm quickly. 'He was the one with the donkey.' Again, silence follows those words, but at least no one has a blade to his throat.

'I stole away,' the man offers. 'All I ask is that you help me escape from here and kill all the heathen scum at the same time.'

'He's a monk,' I explain, and slowly the tension eases from our small group of warriors, the rustle of hands leaving weapons audible. 'We need to don our byrnies,' I call, hoping that Oswy and Frithwine will be able to find me. I'm not sure if the others have already thought to do this.

'Where are you?' Oswy hisses, and I grin, even as I run my hands over the sack's contents. How we're to know what belongs to whom is just about impossible.

'Over here,' I hiss back. I can feel another's hands sorting through the weapons and take it to be Frithwine.

'This is yours.' He thrusts the heavy byrnie towards me. I grip it, trying to determine which way round it goes. But, just as I'm about to shrug it on, someone collides with me, and I tumble to the hard ground.

'Bloody hell,' I explode, my knees and hands throbbing from my earlier trip, even my healed wound along my right hand pulsing with the unexpected impact.

'Sorry.' But Oswy's voice shows no contrition. I hear a huff of annoyance as I reclaim my feet and know that the ealdorman is far from impressed. Still, better to prepare ourselves now than forget and end up skewered for want of our byrnies.

'Lead on then, good man,' the ealdorman eventually calls to the monk when I'm suitably prepared. 'And I assure you, we plan on killing all of these men, and you're most welcome to escape with us. I'm sure we can find you a new position in a monastery in Mercia.'

'It's this way. I'll lead you via the secret entrance

that the Viking raiders haven't discovered,' the man quickly replies. It's clear he's been considering how best to take the enemy by surprise. He might have put more thought into this than Ealdorman Ælfstan.

'What's your name?' Wulfheard demands.

'Brother Eadgar,' the man replies evenly. 'I've been a monk here for over thirty years.' He sounds proud, although sorrow wavers on the word 'years'.

'Thank you for helping us,' the ealdorman affirms. 'How many of them are there?'

'I've not truly counted, but at least fifty.' The news is far from reassuring. But Ælfstan takes it in his stride.

'Now, men, follow carefully. The ships will wait for us out at sea. We don't need to fear that the Viking raiders will attack our fisher-people friends, and there's no need to leave a guard here. We go together, and we stay together. Our purpose is to kill as many as possible and, of course, to rescue Lord Coenwulf.'

'Then you'll need to carry him,' Eadgar offers sadly, evidently aware of whom we speak. 'They broke his leg, and it won't heal correctly.'

'We'll contend with that when we get there,' the ealdorman asserts confidently. 'Now, lead on, if you will, and my thanks for your assistance.'

'I'll help anyone provided they kill the bastards,' Brother Eadgar murmurs. 'And all the better if they're good Mercians.'

With that, Brother Eadgar must begin to move off, for I'm jostled into position by whoever's behind me as we start to follow the road I think the donkey took earlier. A hand on my shoulder, and I peer behind me, just about staying upright, to catch sight of Oswy.

'Not afraid of the dark, are we?' he taunts.

'No, but I'm afraid of the light,' I counter, cutting off any further comment as we all hurry. It's the wrong time of the year to be praying for the darkness to cover our passage. It might be dark now, but dawn won't be far off. It never is at the height of summer, and I don't know how far we need to travel.

For a long time, we walk in almost silence, veering away from the trackway into the undergrowth, although a thin path seems to run through it. We move quickly, the jangle of our weapons muffled by hands on blades. We have no shields. They would have been too hard to hide in the ships and might well have slowed down our progress on dry land. Depending on what we find when we meet the enemy, I'll decide whether I think it was a good decision or not.

Brother Eadgar guides our group, and I'm un-sure how the rest of us line up. However, Godeman is to the rear. He has one of the shields the Viking raiders who were killed held. I'm not sure whom he's going to fight off with it. There's no sheep, and it's unnaturally silent above the soft shush of the waves as they collide with the mass of the island we're on. I look towards the settlement on the main-land, seeing a few sparks of light, but soon even that's lost to our sight, as the path twists and turns, and I do worry that Brother Eadgar could be leading us anywhere, and we'd not know until we got there. This could all be a trap which could end with our death. What if he's told our enemies who we are? What if they've threatened him unless he leads us to our death? After all, he is the only monk still living on the island. He's offered no explanation as to why.

I breathe shallowly, the exertion after the day of rowing, and the previous night of riding, draining me. It doesn't help that my knees hurt from my two falls. I run my hands one over the other, feeling the new welter of calluses caused by the rowing, as well as the imprint of my seax on my right hand. I flex my fingers as well. They're threatening to stiffen now that they're free from the oars, and I want to know they'll obey my commands when we have to fight our enemy.

Slowly, we begin to move higher, and I can feel it in the back of my legs and hear the huff of Oswy from behind me. In front, Frithwine moves as silently as a wraith. I can't even hear him breathing heavily. Perhaps the promise of killing some of the enemy is driving him onward. He seeks vengeance, and I know how powerful a motive that can be.

'Get down.' The whisper echoes back through the line of men, and I crouch quickly, wincing but making no noise as I do so. I peer around Frithwine, but we're low, and whatever has given rise to the caution, it's further up the slope than I can see.

'Advance, but keep down,' is the next order passed to me by Frithwine, his words only just audible. I inform Oswy, and then we begin to move onwards. We're almost so low to the ground it might be better to crawl our way through the remnants of sheep shit and the straggling pieces of fleece that mark the incline. I can still see nothing ahead, but every so often I touch Frithwine's foot with my hand, as Oswy does me from behind, and so I know that we're staying close together. I'm both grateful for the thick cloud cover that masks the moon and stars and curse it. I feel as though I move through the thickness of night, and although my eyes burn with exhaustion, I keep them wide open, straining to see anything.

Ahead, Frithwine stops, and I almost shove my head up his arse, as there's no warning. I just hope the bugger doesn't fart to add to the very sheepy smells I'm already enduring. Who would have thought so many sheep, all in one place, could leave behind such a stink?

Finally, a shimmer of light ahead catches my attention. I narrow my eyes, keen not to be blinded by it, and only then try and take a reckoning of where we are and what we're doing. We're still lower than where the light is, but the sound of men's voices can be easily heard, and the smell of roasting fish is strong in the light breeze. It seems we've found our enemy. Now we just need to determine a way of overpowering them and fleeing from this place before they can kill us.

15

'Keep to your ship crews,' Ealdorman Ælfstan informs us in a harsh whisper. We've managed to gather together. We're not yet inside the extent of the monastery. A thick stone wall blocks our passage, but Brother Eadgar assures us the wall is broken down in one place and we'll be able to scramble over it once the ealdorman has determined how we'll attack our enemy.

'The sheep used it all the time.' There's sorrow in his voice. I take it that the Viking raiders have truly killed all of the island's sheep as Cap believed. Mind, it can't have been long ago, for the smell of sheep is all around us.

'And how many buildings are there?'

'Six,' Brother Eadgar offers immediately. 'The stables are where the Mercian lord's being kept, with no
one but the donkey for company. The enemy is inside
the great hall and the church. Foul heathens that
they are. I've seen them, in there, conducting their
blood rites to their Gods.' Brother Eadgar spits at the
words. I don't so much see it as hear it.

'And tell me the placement of the buildings,' Ealdorman Ælfstan continues.

Oswy is next to me now, Frithwine to my right. I
can see the pair of them by the whites of their eyes
but little else. I can, however, hear the heavy
breathing of every single man, all of them trying to
recover from the steep upward climb. I can see why
the enemy might not know of this entrance.

'The stables are closest, directly ahead from here.
The church is to the westward side, the great hall further south from there. The sleeping quarters are as
far as it's possible to get from the stables, along with
the grain store.'

'So, we need to get to the stables and the church
and hall?' Ælfstan surmises quickly.

'Yes, my lord. That's where you'll find the enemy.
The Mercian lord is in the stables, as I said. Although
I confess, they sometimes take him out of there to
have some sport with him.' I shudder at the thought

of what that sport might be. Lord Coenwulf's not the most robust man I've ever met. I don't want to think about his pain and torture, and yet I do all the same.

'Oswy, Icel and Frithwine, you go to the stables. Wulfheard, lead your men to the church. My group, and that led by Æthelmod, are going to take the hall.' Ælfstan gives the commands easily. 'We kill everyone. I want no prisoners. If you trouble befalls you, get back to the quayside by any means possible. Oswy, Frithwine and Icel, you must rescue Lord Coenwulf. If you don't, they'll kill him.' The words are far from reassuring. But I nod, despite the fact Ælfstan can't see the action. 'Brother Eadgar, stay here. I don't wish to risk you further. You've done enough.'

'My thanks for that, ealdorman, but I've no intention of standing to one side. They killed all my brother monks. I'll also have my revenge on them, and then I'll beg God to have mercy on my soul.' At that, I see a glint of iron and realise that the monk carries almost as much weaponry as I do. I consider where he got it from.

'We'll go first,' Ealdorman Ælfstan confirms, 'but we'll only attack once we know you have Lord Coenwulf. If he's not there, come to us at the hall. If they know of our arrival before that, I fear they'll kill him anyway. Stay alive, my fine warriors. Stay alive.'

A shush of men moving is the next sound, and I hasten to keep pace with wherever the ealdorman is being led by Brother Eadgar. I'm not alone in that, and Oswy stumbles behind me. I wait for him to recover his footing. Should I lose him now, I don't think I'll find him before daybreak.

Brother Eadgar is as good as his word. I'm soon scrambling over a pile of rubble where the stone wall once stood proud. It's rough and difficult with no natural light, but I can quickly determine why the route is unknown to our foemen. The slope here is even steeper. By the time I've crested it, I'm breathing even harder, and my heart thuds loudly in my ears. There are more lights now, and it's easy to determine which building is which. The hall and church have light leaking through the wooden planks of the walls where the daub has either come free or never been smeared. The stable, in contrast, is entirely dark, as are the storehouses and sleeping hall. All the same, it feels too easy. I think the Viking raiders can't be such fools as to have no guards on duty. Surely, they can't be so complacent in an enemy land? Don't they expect someone to try and rescue Lord Coenwulf?

I feel Ealdorman Ælfstan and the rest of the men striding onwards to their destinations. I even catch sight of some of them as shadows against the brightness of fire and candle, but my focus is on the stable. From inside, I hear a soft murmur, perhaps hooves over the wooden floor or a man crying in pain.

'Come on,' Oswy urges and, hand on my seax, I follow in his footsteps, Frithwine behind me. Only then do I realise the one thing that Brother Eadgar didn't tell us. While there's light enough to see by from the hall and church, the entrance to the stables is to the far side of the building, looking out towards the fields and not towards the other buildings. Quickly, the dark covers us once more, and after the glow from the fire, it's even more difficult to see. There are clumps of grasses and nettles, weeds as tall as my shins, for, without the sheep that cut them back, the summer weather has given them the opportunity to grow far beyond a manageable level.

'Arse,' Oswy exclaims, as I hear him tumble to the ground. I go to help him up, only to fall myself. That leaves only Frithwine still standing, but I can't hear him.

'Bugger,' I exclaim, rolling back to my feet, mindful of the pain of my knees as they've been banged once more. But I can't see Frithwine, or even detect his movements. 'I think Frithwine's gone,' I murmur to Oswy, keen not to speak too loudly for fear the noise will somehow reach our enemy.

'Well, it's just us then. Come on, stop bloody falling over all the time.' My mouth drops open in shock at the complaint, and resolve touches my cheeks. It was Oswy who fell first, not me. The bloody arse.

I haul him to his feet, silently making the point that he stumbled first. We continue, aiming for where there's a darker shadow in the already black night and also the occasional noise from the donkey. All the same, I almost collide with the wall of the building, only just saving my face from another knock as my foot touches the foundations of the building first.

'Stop,' I urge Oswy, who's fallen behind me, my hand reaching out to halt him, where he trails closely behind. Now, we just need to find the way in. First, I pause, listening to see if there's any noise caused by the rest of the men, my allies or my enemies, but there's nothing. Neither is there any sound coming from inside the stable. Even the donkey has fallen silent.

I run my hand along the structure, but the scraping sound is too loud. The walls are built of rough tree trunks and covered with patchy daub to fill the bigger gaps. After all, it's just the stable for the animals. It needs holes for fresh air to circulate. Instead, I walk as close to the building as I dare, hoping there's nothing to trip me, such as jutting-out supports, as we try and find the door.

And then I sense it. Here, the air is different, scented with the ripeness of animals, and I know we've found the entrance. I reach out, hoping to find the lock that keeps it shut, fearful that now, at the last possible moment, our presence could be detected, and it could all go wrong.

But the door is barely shut, and I push it open with the smallest creak, hand on my seax, into an area that somehow is even darker than outside. I blink and blink, and then I open my eyes wide, but still, I can see nothing. I wrinkle my nose, the smell of the donkey strong, as is the scent of sheep, for all there can be none inside because everything is stillness and silence. And then, I hear a very human noise, a soft snore, that could only come from someone deeply asleep. I step further inside the stables, reaching out to ensure Oswy follows where I go. Whatever's been done to Lord Coenwulf in the past, I sense the Viking raiders have always been noisy about it. Either that, or he's so badly wounded that he sleeps in a sweat-drenched fever. I hope he's just exhausted.

I wince at the noise of our boots over the wooden floor. I fear that, any moment, we'll elicit a squeak or creak from an old piece of wood. My breathing is hard and fast, my heart pounding as I step ever further into the dark space. I feel blind and uneven on my feet, as though the waves continue to rise and fall beneath them. The snoring continues, sometimes soft and sometimes loud. I try and angle myself towards the noise, but Oswy reaches out and grips my arm, taking me along a different route. I want to argue with him, but it's impossible. If I open my mouth and speak, I might wake any guard set over Lord Coenwulf. I follow him, but I'm not happy about it.

Abruptly, the sound of the snoring stops. I cease my steps, aware that whoever slept is now awake. I can hear them moving on the ground, the chink of iron, and I think the Viking raiders haven't been fool enough to leave Coenwulf unprotected. I try not to breathe, or rather breathe very shallowly. If the enemy, like Oswy and I, are straining to hear, to determine where we are in the room, then I want to give them as little opportunity to find us as possible.

Only then, there's a cry of outrage from outside the stables, and I know the Viking raiders realise they're under attack. An unintelligible shout echoes through the still air, and I sense the very thing I didn't want to feel, the cold iron of a blade at my neck.

'Who are you?' The words are flecked with fury and carry the thick accent of someone for whom my tongue isn't their usual one.

I'm horribly reminded of when the Viking raider apprehended me in the kingdom of the East Angles. Then, my enemy was weak and didn't have long to live. But this man stands tall behind me, the heat of his breath in my ear. And I believe there's no chance I'll be able to overwhelm him as the cries from the rest of the settlement intensify. I feel my foeman stiffen, listening carefully, but I believe he's alone, and more, I don't think he knows there are two of us here.

'Who are you?' I retort. I have my seax in hand, but I don't know whether to take the chance that I'll be able to strike him before he slits my throat. His grip is tight, and I can't move my head from side to side for fear that he'll gouge open my neck and I'll die here and now.

I feel the quiver in the man's hand as he does crane his neck, as though doing so will make it easier for him to hear what's happening outside. The sharp smell of smoke assures me that someone, some-where, has the light to see by, but we don't.

And then, from nowhere, I detect a rush of air and gasp as the donkey careers into the pair of us. I'm knocked to the ground, a stab of pain assuring me that I've not escaped unscathed, but my enemy is down, his blade no longer at my neck. My hand ricochets off the floor, but I still grip my seax. I reach out, left-handed, to scrabble across the floor to find my enemy. I must kill him while the donkey has given me the chance I need to escape. The animal continues his path to the open doorway, his hooves loud enough to cover the sound of my enemy. I'm unsure where Oswy is, but it must be him who released the donkey and somehow directed its steps.

But my foeman has recovered as well. His hands audibly grope around on the ground, but my hand encounters his lost blade first. I grab it quickly. I doubt it's his only blade, but while he searches for it, I can seek him instead. Round and round I go, surging to my hands and knees in my search, and then I grip his foot. He kicks my hand aside, and his boot strikes my chin, but I quickly reclaim my hold on him, putting all my weight into my hand to hold him down long enough to stab at him.

He bucks and twists, his hands coming into play as he rounds on me, both legs trying to kick me. His free leg knocks against my stomach, and an *ouff* of pain pours from my mouth. I thrust my body forward, determined not to let him go. I clamp his feet beneath my legs to stop them moving, and use my hand to stab at him. Time and time again, my blade hits flesh and, over and over, he twists and turns, trying to win free.

His fist hits my chin, but the blow is weaker than it should be. Although tears spring from my eyes at the force of the punch, I don't stop stabbing, jabbing and hacking until, eventually, the body beneath me stills, the last breath erupting from his throat in a soft gurgle. I roll free from him, and just to be sure, stab down with my blade into where his heart must have once beaten.

'Took your bloody time,' Oswy calls as I slowly clamber upwards. I'm beaten and bruised. I can feel a tear on my neck, but not a hot gush of blood. I'm wounded but still very much alive.

'My thanks,' I offer, coughing around the tightness of my throat. 'For sending the donkey to aid me,' I continue.

'I'd like to say it was planned,' Oswy murmurs, 'but I startled the creature as much as it did me.'

'Are we alone?' I ask, aware of what's happening outside, with the increasing stink of smoke and blazing light flooding through the gaping holes in the walls. We were sent to rescue Coenwulf, but I don't know if he's here. I wince to hear the cries, especially as I don't know who prevails. Certainly, any hope of secrecy has long since evaporated.

'I can't find anyone else,' Oswy announces.

'Lord Coenwulf, are you here?' I call, hoping we haven't messed this up.

A scrabble of something assures me that we're not alone.

'Find him,' I urge Oswy. 'You have a much better sense than I do of where the sounds are coming from.' Oswy makes no response, but I hear his steps as he moves carefully around the barn. I wish I could see more. Ideally, I'd like to find the wall and move around its extremities, but just doing that, I trip and collide with equipment, a clatter of metal and wood startling me, for all it's only a handful of shovels and other farming implements.

'Nice and quiet, eh?' Oswy calls to me. I growl. I'm bruised all over, I can feel my skin tingling in places, and the dead man's blood has coated my byrnie so that I stink of him, which is far from pleasant. I pull my glove clear and touch my neck. There's a definite wound there, but it's impossible to determine its extent. It doesn't seem to bleed too fiercely, so I don't think it's serious, but I might never know.

'Ah, Lord Coenwulf.' Oswy's voice comes from the farthest edges of the stables. I couldn't be any further from where I need to be.

A rough voice coughs and then coughs some more. A strangled word comes from the man, and only then do I recognise his voice.

'Who are you?' His tone is as imperious as ever, a flicker of fear evident, all the same.

'Your wife sent us to release you,' I offer. I doubt he'll recognise me.

'Icel?' Lord Coenwulf surprises me by saying. 'Is that you?'

'Aye, my lord, and Edwin is here as well, well, not here, but fighting with Ealdorman Ælfstan's men. Can you walk? The old monk said your leg was in a bad way.'

'No, I can't walk,' Coenwulf confirms, frustration in his voice.

'Then we'll carry you,' I announce, still trying to find my way to where Oswy and Coenwulf must be.

'Over here,' Oswy offers, far from helpfully. 'Bloody hell, you really can't determine where we are, can you?' he continues when my foot hits something heavy that tumbles across the ground with a metallic twang.

'No, thank you, I bloody can't,' I growl. Oswy's

found Coenwulf, but now I can't find either of them. It's so frustrating.

'Head towards the door,' Oswy announces. 'I'll meet you there, and remind yourself never to go hunting for a friend or an enemy in the dark. You'll bloody fall over your own feet.'

I snarl angrily, wanting to deny Oswy the chance to ridicule me, but it's much easier to find the open doorway. There's a faint breeze, bringing with it the salty scent of the sea. I turn that way, only to kick something else. My balance falters, and my arms wave in the air, the grip on my seax tightening as I fall to the floor, someone holding on to my foot.

I shriek and stab and slash, and only then do I realise I'm fighting someone who's already dead.

I collapse to the ground, breathing heavily, my heart thudding. Oswy's words reach me from close by. He must have already encountered the body.

'Fighting the dead. What will we do with young Icel and his imaginary foes?'

Once more, I lumber to my feet, but this time Oswy is beside me, and he's dragging Coenwulf. I can tell from the sound over the wood that Coenwulf isn't walking. Using my hands, I determine that his one leg stretches out far behind him, scraping on the floor. I manage to get my shoulder under Coenwulf's arm, a hiss from the other man's lips assuring me that he's in considerable pain.

I wrinkle my nose at his smell. He stinks of donkey, shit and piss, and I almost gag on the too-ripe scents, but Oswy directs us towards the door, and as the night air once more washes over us, we manoeuvre our way towards where we entered the compound of the monastery, and as we turn the corner to head back down the slope we're greeted by such a sight.

16

The monastery burns, casting bright, dancing flames high into the blackness of the night. The shrieks and cries of wounded men echo in the air. I want to stop, and ensure Ealdorman Ælfstan is well, as it's impossible to tell who's winning, but Oswy presses on.

'We need to get him out of here,' Oswy urges, when he feels my steps falter. Lord Coenwulf's head is also twisted, looking back, as opposed to forwards. 'Concentrate on the task,' Oswy huffs and, in the flame light, I can see how much he's sweating from his exertion.

'Sorry,' I murmur, looking where we're going instead of where we've been, as I focus on trying to find the tumbled-down wall so we can escape over it. The slope is even steeper on the way down. It's difficult to keep my own footing even without Coenwulf strapped across my shoulders.

'Where are we going?' Coenwulf finally notices that we're not heading towards the main entrance of the monastery, or at least, where I assume it must be.

'There's another way,' I huff. 'Brother Eadgar showed it to us.'

'Who's he?'

'The man with the donkey,' I offer, but it's getting too hard to talk. The strain in the back of my legs is making my knees shake, and I can feel whatever wound I carry around my neck pulsing.

Oswy's breath is so loud I can hear it above all of the commotion taking place behind us. Voices are both clear and indistinct, and to my hearing, at least, it seems as though all I can detect are the cries of the Viking raiders, and then I hear a thundering noise coming towards us.

I reach for my seax, aware we're about to be attacked. They must be able to see us in the glow from the flames, but I still think we've been bloody unlucky.

Down and down we go. I swear the wall is just about in sight, but the rumble of approaching steps is getting ever closer.

'Arse,' I cry. 'Take Coenwulf, and I'll defeat our foe,' I urge Oswy, only for Brother Eadgar to veer up from this side of the wall.

'It's the donkey, you fool,' Brother Eadgar cries and, with a swirl of air, the donkey comes to a panting halt just in front of him. 'Good lad,' the old man praises the donkey.

I realise if we can just get Coenwulf mounted, then we can go back and aid Ealdorman Ælfstan. It doesn't feel right to have them fighting while we try to escape.

'Come on, boy,' the old monk reassures the donkey, and together, with me barely wanting to look for fear one of the animal's legs will become wedged in the pile of stone and rock, the two of them make it over the ruin of the wall, the monk offering reassurances to the donkey every time it falters. From here, the actual monastery buildings can't be seen, but the blazing lights from the fire illuminate the sky. We certainly don't need a moon for illumination.

But, if we can get the donkey over the tumbled-down wall, I'm not sure how we can get Coenwulf over. I can see where sweat beads on his face, and he's trembling even though we're carrying him more than he's walking. I'd like to attend to his leg, but there are other matters that need my attention.

'Help me,' Oswy urges. We've lowered Lord Coenwulf to the ground, and he's attempting to crawl over the wall, but isn't making any progress.

'You go over and pull him, and I'll push him from here.' I wince. This is really going to hurt the poor man, but I can't think of a better solution.

Between us, and with Brother Eadgar helping as well, somehow, we manage to manoeuvre Coenwulf to the side where the donkey now waits, eyes wild as it watches the fiery sky.

'Can you take him back?' I gasp to Brother Eadgar. 'To the ships.'

'Alone?' The monk doesn't like the idea.

'We need to return and ensure the rest of the men are okay.'

'What if we're attacked?' Lord Coenwulf gasps as well.

'I think all of our enemies are engaged in fighting at the hall,' Oswy confirms. He stands on the other side of the wall, just waiting to make his way back up the hill.

'Do you have a weapon?' I think to ask both men.

'I do, yes,' the monk reassures, and I remember he was well-armed, although seemingly, unable to use the weapons himself. I know Coenwulf will have had his taken from him during his captivity.

'Here,' I thrust a blade towards Coenwulf, and he takes it, gripping it tightly, for all he shakes and is sweating profusely, even mounted on the donkey. It can't be comfortable, but it's the only way we'll get him to the ships. 'Go,' I urge them both, and with many misgivings, I scramble back to Oswy's side, and we begin to retrace our steps. This time, it's harder going. Knowing how steep the hill is makes it more of a test of will. And not even the dancing flames make it easy. Instead, there are shadows and hollows that we need to avoid as we make our way upward. Oswy pauses, hands on his knees as he breathes deeply.

'Where are they?' he glowers, and this is my thought as well. Where are Ealdorman Ælfstan, Wulfheard, Edwin and the rest of the warriors? They weren't supposed to attack until they knew we had Lord Coenwulf. Even so, they should have retreated by now with the time it's taken us to find Lord Coenwulf and get him to the donkey. The enemy should all be dead, no matter when the fighting started. We ought to be returning to the ships with Coenwulf, but there's no sign of our missing men, or of Frithwine. I hear some shrieks and cries, and once more, I realise that the majority of them are in the Viking raider tongue and not mine.

Urgently, I grip Oswy's shoulder, where he powers away before me.

'What?' he growls. He's furious. I can tell his thoughts follow mine. Have our allies been overcome?

'We need to be careful,' I urge him through a tight chest, my upwards pace too quick for me. 'It sounds as though Ealdorman Ælfstan and Wulfheard have been overpowered.'

'No, I won't accept it,' Oswy retorts.

'If they have, we need to rescue them,' I urge him. 'We're their only chance. No one knows we're here. No one else will come and aid us. Think, think.' My words thrum with intensity. If there's only us two, against so many of the Viking raiders that they've managed to overawe Ælfstan, Wulfheard and the rest of the warriors, then I don't know how just the two of us will be able to free them, but we must try, all the same.

Slowly, Oswy turns to me, his eyes dark in the blaze from the fire.

'Then what do you suggest?' he queries as though taunting me.

'We need to go carefully and stay together. Who knows where Frithwine is, but it would be a lot easier if there were three of us instead of just two.'

'No shit,' is his less than helpful response.

'We can't just head towards the fire,' I caution, wanting to smack him in the face for his tone and fury but knowing that if we fight each other, we won't be helping anyone. I run my hand around my neck, feeling the wound once more, and try to clear my thoughts.

'Then where shall we go?' Oswy actually looks as though he's perplexed by the idea.

'We should go back towards the stable and then try and make our way from there. We need to find our men first of all. We don't want to blunder into whatever's happened and get caught ourselves.'

'Fine, you lead on,' Oswy grudgingly accepts.

I strike out slightly across the steep slope as opposed to directly up it. It's both easier and more difficult. But we're quickly at the stable again. We don't walk around it to the main door but stand with our backs to it, trying to determine what's happening. The church and main hall are fully ablaze, and figures cavort before the flames, or at least, that's what they seem to be doing. I wish I could tell if they were Viking raiders or men I've come to think of as my friends, but it's impossible. And I realise being able to see what's happening and feel the heat from the flames isn't helping us at all. I still don't know what to do.

'We should go that way,' Oswy announces. 'See, that building there isn't on fire.'

I squint against the combined threat of the brightness and the darkness and determine what he means. In front of the hall, there's a small building and no smoke billows from its walls or rafters.

'From there, we should be able to see more,' Oswy confirms. He sounds more assured.

'But we stay together, no running off on your own,' I advise him. 'We do this together, or we'll both fail.'

'Fine, have it your way,' he confirms, and just to prove me wrong, strides off without me. I hasten to catch him, yearning to shout at him to stop being such a bloody arse. But I don't want to garner any unwelcome attention. The smell of burning and the thick smoke from the fires is choking me. I can hear others coughing as well. All the same, I try not to give myself away by joining them. The smoke is as bad as when thick fog curls in the autumn, and it's not easy to see far or make out where the sound is coming from. My eyes swimming, we reach the unscathed building. I'm not quite sure what it is. Perhaps a grain store or some such. It's small and narrow but provides a much-needed solid wall at our back.

Barely breathing, we stand shoulder to shoulder, trying to understand what's happening before us. It's a mess, whatever it is, but I see heads bobbing, men tied together, just far enough away from the burning hall that the fire won't burn them but will sporadically cover them in the gusting smoke from the fire. The sound of coughing is loud, sometimes joined by choking and cries of pain. And then, more figures emerge from somewhere ahead, and the glint of weapons is impossible to ignore, as is the harsh bark of their language.

17

'They have our men,' I murmur to Oswy, straining to keep hold of my fury and fear.

'Aye, the bastards do have them,' he confirms, his voice heavy at having our fears confirmed.

'We need to get them back.'

'No shit,' he rumbles once more, but only loud enough that I can hear.

'How?' is my question. I sense rather than see Oswy taking a deep, soothing breath.

'I don't bloody know,' he eventually says, his words surprisingly calm. 'But there'll be a way.'

'We need to do it before daybreak,' I continue. It's bright, yes, but the shadows still allow us to hide. If it were fully daybreak, then we wouldn't have the same options that we do now.

'Yes, thank you, Icel. Are we going to spend our time saying the bleeding obvious, or are you actually going to shut your mouth and think of a solution?'

I glower into the darkness, closing my mouth shut with an audible snap.

I think back to my time in Londinium, trapped behind enemy walls. And I turn to Oswy.

'We have to pretend to be one of them,' I urge him.

'How? We don't speak their tongue, and we don't know any of those men there.'

I shake my head. It is a bad suggestion.

A man with an unsheathed blade walks between the lines of bound men, the sound of his voice reaching us for all I don't understand the words. I see him stop, and a flash of shimmering metal catches my eye, accompanied by a shriek of pain.

I move to step forward, but Oswy's hand on my arm stops me.

'Think, Icel, as you keep telling me. Think, and we'll find a way.'

'Arse,' I exclaim, heart hammering in my chest again. I don't know who lives and who's dead, but I'm sure that we won't all leave this island alive. Mutiny stirs inside me. We shouldn't have come here. Or rather, I shouldn't have allowed Ealdorman Ælfstan to accompany me. I should have journeyed alone and not risked the lives of my allies and friends. Lady Cynehild wouldn't have expected men to die to save her husband. Would she?

'Look.' Oswy's thoughts are other to mine, and I try and see what he means, following the line of his outstretched hand.

I squint and then shake my head, attempting to clear the splotches of light from my eyes, and then look once more.

'So, not everyone is captured?' I murmur. To the right of the blaze, there's another figure crouched low to the ground, hovering. His movements are so furtive that he must be one of my fellow Mercians. 'Who is it?' I muse.

'Who knows, but we should go and meet him. Then they'll be three of us.' I hold out half a hope that it's Frithwine. He left us, yes, but I know he's driven purely by revenge for the death of his brother. I can well understand that desire.

Another shriek of agony has me turning back to where the bladed man walks amongst those he holds captive, and a growl rumbles from my throat.

'Wait,' Oswy cautions me, his eyes elsewhere.

'Look,' and he directs my gaze once more to where the warrior's now crawling towards the top of the slope by turning my head where he wants me to see.

'Whoever it is, they're not standing around bloody talking about it,' I grumble.

'No, you're right there, but it was you who told us to be cautious.'

I shrug, although Oswy can't see the action. He's right.

As we watch, the figure disappears from sight, swallowed up by the night and with no illumination from the fire. Whatever they're planning, it looks like they're about to do it.

'Come on. We'll do the same. Get closer, and then assess what we can do. Standing here is just wasting time, as you say. It'll be light soon enough. Follow me.' Oswy crouches low, keeping his weapons sheathed so that firelight flickering on them can't give us away.

I follow him. It's much flatter here. This is evidently the top of the hill. The closer we get, the hotter we become. I can feel sweat pooling down my nose. I dab it aside with frustration, blinking the stinging moisture from my eyes. And then Oswy crouches even lower, his movements surprising me, distracted by my sweat. I move to mirror him but instead remain immobile. I can hear it as well, the heavy breathing of someone close by. They're not doing a good job of keeping themselves hidden, but perhaps they're not trying to do so. Once more, I glower into the night, attempting to pick out some small movements so that I can see who flanks our movements.

A great gust of superheated air erupts from the collapsing timbers of the building, the crack so loud, I jump, but so too does whomever it is out there, and I touch Oswy's arm.

'Over there.' I direct with my hand, showing him what I mean.

'Go that way,' Oswy directs me, and I do, squatting as low as possible so that I can keep my eyes on the movement. I don't move on hands and knees, and luckily, the ground here is much smoother than along the steep slope. Whether we crest grass kept short by sheep, or an area that's devoid of much growth, I don't know, but I welcome it all the same.

And then we're close enough to the other figure to touch them.

Hand extended, I grip a boot, aware I don't want to be kicked in the face again, and Frithwine turns to greet me.

'You took your time,' he glowers as I sag with relief.

'What's been happening?' Oswy demands to know, almost as though he knew it was Frithwine. The git could have told me.

'There were fifty of the bastards. They caught Ealdorman Ælfstan, and it's all gone to shit since then. I've been waiting for you. Where have you been?' Frithwine whispers frantically.

'Getting Lord Coenwulf out of here.'

'Ah.' That one sounds assures me that Frithwine had forgotten our purpose. 'They have them tied up over there. I think Æthelmod's dead.' The news chills me. I know I thought someone would die, but to know it's a fact is devastating. This is all my fault.

'They have the ealdorman?' Oswy queries, just to be sure.

'Yes, and Wulfheard, Cenred and Waldhere. I've seen those anyway. I'm sure they must have others.'

'Arse,' Oswy exclaims, but it's a word to mask his fears.

'We need to get behind the bastards and pick them off, one by one,' Frithwine announces. 'They're not looking for more of us. They think they've captured everyone. They've not even thought to check on Lord Coenwulf. Arrogant sods.'

'Where were you going?' Oswy whispers.

'Behind the flames. They won't see us coming.'

'We'll follow you,' Oswy confirms. 'And then we'll slice the buggers open and leave their innards for the carrion crows.' His words thrum with menace, and I'd shiver at the implied threat, but my plans for them are even more violent. I won't just slice them. I'll do much worse than that.

Still crawling, we follow Frithwine. He's clearly been watching what's happening for much longer than we have. He knows the location of the enemy. We just need to get there without being seen. Fifty Viking raiders. It's a lot of men for three warriors to kill. But we can't fail. Otherwise, it'll only be a matter of time before Lord Coenwulf is recaptured, Brother Eadgar killed, and all of this, including Æthelmod's death, will have been for nothing.

The noise of the fire covers our movements, or so I hope. The ground under my hands is rough and smooth, filled with tufts of grass, and also, less pleasant sensations that stink as we crawl through them. I keep my eyes only on where I'm going, not risking looking at the fire and trying to ignore the cries of pain that come from men I've known for a good few years now. I don't wish death on any of them, and yet it seems impossible that we'll all escape from here without more loss of life.

Ahead, Frithwine stops, and I almost collide with him, as does Oswy with me from behind. I'd cry out, but it seems intentional as Frithwine turns to face where our warriors are being held captive. Head down, attempting to ensure that the dazzling flames of the fire don't mark my vision, I follow him. Oswy mirrors my movements.

I can't see Frithwine's expression in the darkness, but his harsh whisper just about reaches me. I consider when he became such a seasoned warrior. Has it happened, and I've not noticed or is this a case of a man taking advantage of an opportunity presented to him? I wish I knew.

Slowly, we stand, although I keep my head lowered, and then, we move forward, coming closer and closer to our enemy. I still don't look at the fire, but in the reflected dancing firelight, I'm able to pick out the enemy. My allies and friends are closest to the fire. I can just about see feet where they've been forced to kneel, awaiting whatever fate the Viking raiders want to deal out to them. But behind them, either standing still or cavorting with delight at the seeming ease with which they've apprehended our men, are many of the Viking raiders.

I don't count them. I merely focus on the first I mean to kill, aware that Frithwine and Oswy have determined on their victims as well.

It's simple. We kill as many as we can before they truly realise what's happening. It would help if they were sloping off to piss, but they're not. I breathe deeply, ensure my grip is right on my seax. Then I reach out, left hand cupping my enemy's hairy chin before he can realise I'm even there.

I yank him backwards, feeling his body tense as I do so, but it's too late.

I slide my blade beneath his shoulder blade, deep into his body, my hand moving upwards to cover his mouth so that he can't cry out. The fire roars with the crack of more falling wood, masking my actions, as a strangled cry seems to ring loudly in the smoke-gazed air. My enemy falls to the ground, hands frantically reaching for weapons, but I move my seax and slice across his throat, silencing him before grabbing his arms and pulling him away from the rest of the men who still live.

I can't truly see Frithwine or Oswy, but I can sense they're as busy at their work as I am.

When I'm happy the dead man is out of sight down the slope, I abandon him and move back, once more sighting my intended victim. These men think they're so clever, but from the rear, they're lit up brighter than daylight. I manage to stand so close to the next man, just a few steps behind the rest of his comrades, that I can slice my blade straight across his throat without him hearing my steps or perceiving my intentions, thanks to the roaring of the fire. He bucks as he goes down, a gasp of air that I hear too loudly but which no one else seems to notice.

This is too easy, I think as I deposit his body out of the way and decide on my next kill. My eyes are starting to get used to the brightness of the fire, but I still dare not look directly at it. I'm aware that the Viking raiders are beginning to work their own mischief down the line of my apprehended fellow warriors. And as much as I want to hurry and ensure I save as many of them as possible, there are still too many of our enemies to do so.

Patience wars inside me as I again determine who'll be the next to die. I decide on a man who stands a little aloof from the others, his head raised, hound-like, as though he senses that all is not right. If he's about to give us away, he needs to be the next to die.

I hear the slither of a body on the rough ground and understand that Oswy or Frithwine have killed another. But this one warrior concerns me even more so I watch his body turn, his outline thinning as he must look behind him. I pause but quickly resume my movements as I observe him reach out as though to summon one of his allies to his side. Perhaps, I consider, he's realised one of the others is missing.

I change my movements slightly, advancing at an angle to him so that he shouldn't be able to perceive any noticeable disturbances in the blackness of night. My blade's slick in my hand, the scent of blood unmistakable. I feel sure that's what my foeman can smell, but I can't hear him. The Viking raiders cheer as I hear the thud of another lifeless body hitting the ground. I use it to mask any sounds I might make, sneaking behind him, wanting to do nothing but slit his throat, but instead, I stab through his back, driving my blade with all the force I can manage so that he tumbles to the ground.

'Bugger,' I murmur to myself, for as the man dies, his leg kicks out, and it alerts the warrior standing next to him that all isn't right. For a long moment, I feel unable to move. The dead man is still, but the foeman has his hand on his weapons belt, a menacing growl coming from him, audible even over the fire, his head turning from side to side.

'Sigrid,' he calls, his words slurred with ale or mead. I can smell him from here. 'Sigrid,' he calls once more. I should do something, but the man's looking directly at me, for all he can't see me, and I dare not breathe or move. This is only my third kill. We must take out at least half of them before attempting to rescue my fellow warriors. 'Sigrid,' the man calls again. I know I need to do something. But what, I'm unsure.

I open my mouth to answer him, considering what I might say, only to sense movement behind the foeman. I'm so close, I hear Oswy's words.

'Sigrid's dead, you arsehole,' and the man shudders to the ground himself. I want to thank Oswy for saving the situation, but he bends and immediately begins to pull the body clear. I hasten to do the same with Sigrid before someone else realises what's happening.

We must move the bodies so that none of the others trip over them. But it's hard work. These men are built as warriors. They have byrnies and weapons around their waists, and my hands are slick from the blood that's sheeted over them.

With a heave of effort, I pull the man free, hoping I leave him where the others are, but with sweat in my eyes and the light from the fire, it's becoming even more difficult to see, not easier. I want to cough away the stink of the swirling fire from my clogged throat, but even that risks exposure should I do so.

I can also sense that the Viking raiders are becoming wary. None of them actually shouts out, but the cavorting has stopped, the string of men has drawn closer together, and I think we might just have to risk the next part of our rescue operation. We can't afford to get caught, especially not with so many of our enemy still to kill.

The heat from the fire is intense as I once more turn to seek out my next target. The legs of the men, some thin, some fat, some nondescript and in the middle, are easy to see against the flames, as are the bent heads of my allies. I bite my lip and turn to scamper towards the end of the line, where the blackness of night prevails as opposed to the dancing orange flames of the fire.

The man here seems wider than others, his stance is broad, his legs far apart. But he also sways, one foot back and then another, as he wobbles on the spot. If the other man stunk of mead and ale, this Viking raider smells as though he's bathed in the stuff.

I grip my seax, aiming to slice this one's throat as the easiest way of silencing him, but he surprises me, turning to meet my attack, little more than a white line of his teeth visible. He snarls angrily but doesn't raise the alarm, and the next man to him, at least two horse lengths away, has no idea of what's happening.

A weapon surges up at me, an axe, I think. I veer away from it, ducking beneath his wildly swinging arm, the scent of his sweat and the stink of his drinking enveloping me. He might be the only one to know I'm here, but he can barely stand up. Another giant swing from his axe and I step outside his reach. The axe lands on the ground, his body entirely un-balanced by his arm crossing his chest. I kick him in the arse. He falls, crumbling to his hands and knees, and I leap onto his back, stabbing into it, hoping to spear his heart. His byrnie is thick and well-padded, and he battles to buck me as though he's the horse and I'm the rider.

Frustrated and fearful that such a fight will be-come too intense and visible, I reach behind. With more luck than skill, I manage to slice open the back of his right leg. His body shudders with the pain of it, and still, he doesn't cry out. I feel sure he should let others know what's happening, but he doesn't. I don't have time to consider why not, as I once more stab through his byrnie, one hand grip-ping his shoulder, my thighs tight around the breadth of his back. But still, he fights. Leaning forwards now, I pull back his long, dirty hair, the whiff of his sweat even more rank, to saw through the back of his neck. His hand comes up, wanting to grab my blade, but somehow I keep a firm hold, and this time I jab into his neck. The resistance is great, but finally, I hear his choking breath and leap clear. I don't want to be stuck beneath him in his death throes.

I'm sweating, my heart pounding. I feel sure that our actions must have been seen. I spin, blade raised, determined to fight off my next foe, but there's no one there. In fact, the Viking raider line is no longer dancing before the fire. Instead, they've pulled together in a circle, some unconscious feeling assuring them that while they think they're alone, they really aren't. Voices call out from the group, names of their friends, I'm sure, but my eyes are on something else. My fight has brought me closer and closer to where my allies are corralled, bound, and on their knees. I recognise those men, the first being Wulfheard, head low, his eyes glinting at me in the bright light as though urging me to see him.

Without thought for anything but freeing him, I dart forward, wishing my hand didn't hurt so much, that my thighs weren't complaining about what I've just been forced to do to stay alive. I slice my blade through the hemp rope, stinking of the sea, that binds Wulfheard's hands.

'About bloody time,' he coughs as I also release a strip of rope that's been tied around his mouth. 'Get the others,' he urges me, staggering to his feet.

Beside him, Cenred watches me, his eyes wide with shock and delight. I move behind him, do the same, and he springs upright. I can't see where Oswy and Frithwine have gone, but I hope they're trying to mirror my actions.

Cenred merges into the darkness, Wulfheard gone as well, and I appreciate that they must be looking for weapons. They have none, their weapons belts taken from them.

The heat of the fire blazes against my face as I slice through the bonds that bind Uor. He gives a hacking cough as he tries to stand and then sways alarmingly. I leap to help him, trying not to focus on the pleading eyes of Osmod next to him.

As I offer Uor my shoulder, my hand encounters the slickness of his byrnie, close to his shoulder, and I realise he's wounded, perhaps mortally so.

'Go down to the wall where we came in,' I urge him. I don't think he has the capacity to assist us, but he shakes his head.

'I'll kill 'em all,' he mouths instead. He smells

sour and dry. Hastily, I turn to Osmod, and cut through his bindings as well, but that's the last one of the men I get to help with ease. For, while I've been freeing our men in secrecy, avoiding the gaze of our enemy, Frithwine has done the exact opposite.

With a sharp cry, I turn and melt back into the shadows as Frithwine's pushed into the firelight by a man with teeth glinting as though made of blades so that I can see little of him but his gaping maw and the shimmer of his iron.

Frithwine sags forward, and I wince to know he's wounded. Yet I can still detect the sound of men dying, caught unawares, and know that Oswy must be busy, perhaps joined by those I've freed, provided they've found weapons with which to attack.

For a moment, I'm not sure what to do. I need to rescue the rest of our men and also Frithwine, and while the number of Viking raiders has been substantially reduced, we're still outnumbered.

Frantically, I glance down the row of kneeling Mercians, hopeful of finding Ealdorman Ælfstan amongst their number, of seeing Oswy, Wulfheard and Osmod cutting through the bindings of the other captives.

But I don't. Instead, I feel the cold, biting edge of iron at my throat for the second time that night.

18

I've become a captive once more, and that wasn't my intention.

I try not to swallow, or move, or feel the rough grate of another man's beard on my neck, as words I don't understand are whispered into my ear by my captor who smells as though he's been bedding down with the king's hunting hounds.

Abruptly, he moves me forward, his feet kicking the backs of my legs as a means of making me obey his commands. The shimmer of heat flashes over my face, the dazzling brightness of the yellow and red flames impossible to ignore. I'm blinded and stumble forwards, fearing that, any moment now, the blade will slice deeper into my skin. I've killed men with such a move tonight. I don't, in turn, wish to be killed in the same way.

But I have one advantage. Whoever has apprehended me has his hand at my neck and his other hand on my shoulder, but I have free rein of my hands, and in my hand is my seax. The fool hasn't taken it from me. Perhaps he doesn't realise I have it. Maybe he thinks I'll have dropped it in fright. But it's about impossible to employ it. It dangles in my right hand, and the blade at my neck is a frightening reminder of the dying man on the banks of the river in the kingdom of the East Angles. I beat him then, but only because he was fading anyway. Now, I don't have the same option.

As the man nears his comrades, he barks harsh words, and suddenly, everyone turns, hands on blades, peering into the gloom at their backs. Some of them, I can just about tell from the corner of my eye, also move to ensure their prisoners are secure. I curse myself for a bloody fool. I shouldn't have rescued my fellow warriors as now I've put everyone in even more danger, as has Frithwine.

There were only three of us, and now two of us are captive once more. I only managed to free four of my fellow warriors, and one of them won't be able to do much fighting. And, as far as I know, all of them are weaponless.

I'm flung to the floor, my neck released from its tight constriction so that I cough and spit onto the ground. I can smell burning flesh, mixed with the sharp rust smell of blood and too much ale. These men are drunk and deadly. Trying to blink the brightness from my eyes, I focus on Frithwine. He's crumpled to the floor as though dead already, and I hope he's not. I need him to help me.

I'm kicked and kicked some more. I'm only grateful that my face remains unscathed, and as of yet, I don't carry a terrible wound, unlike Frithwine and Uor. I also still have my blade. Carefully, I try and hide it beneath the folds of my tunic. If I place it back on my weapons belt, the Viking raiders will see it and take it from me, and I need it. I just don't know what for yet.

'Where are you hurt?' I murmur to Frithwine, but he's slumped, his head resting on his chest. His breathing is laboured and watery. I fear I know exactly where he's hurt. I don't believe I'll be able to save him, either. This has all gone very wrong. I want to curse my stupidity for allowing Ealdorman Ælfstan and his men to come when I should have done this alone for Lady Cynehild. But I'll have time to berate myself when we're out of this cock-up.

I try and determine what's happening. I haven't been tied up, and neither has Frithwine, but that's because some unholy argument is taking place around us. The men who caught Frithwine and me linger for some time while the heated words grow louder and louder, becoming more filled with fury and venom. I can't see where some still fight, their actions blocked by the legs of four people in front of us. But soon, and I can't quite believe it, the man who kicked me, and held the blade to my throat, kicks me one more time and marches away, in front of those four sets of legs. I look up and think I see him lean closer to one of the Viking raiders as though to urge them to caution, but none of them turns to scrutinise Frithwine or me.

I look behind me, but we've been moved aside from the rest of our allies, who are along the length of the burning hall. Frithwine and I are at its farthest end, actually closer, if I'm correct in my orientation, to the stable where they had Lord Coenwulf captive. That also means that not far from here should be a means of escaping through the tumbled-down wall.

But that would mean leaving the rest of my allies and friends, and perhaps also Frithwine.

'Come on.' I scamper to my knees, hoping to get Frithwine on his feet.

'What?' His single word is edged with pain and barely coherent.

'Come on. Get up. Stand, we can still escape from here.'

'No.' This word is much easier to understand, and Frithwine's gaze has found its focus, as he watches me with hollow eyes.

'These bastards, or some like them, killed my brother. I'm not leaving here until they're all dead. All of them.' There's calm fury in Frithwine's words. I know he dreams of revenge and vengeance, but it seems he's prepared to pursue it even if it means his death and perhaps the deaths of others.

'No, we need to get you out of here, and then I'll come back and find the others.'

'No, Icel, no.' Frithwine's head wobbles, but he concentrates on me. With a start, I realise I can see him much more clearly. Dawn can't be far off now. I can't believe we've been doing this all night long. 'I have to do this. You don't, though,' he continues, his eyes blazing.

I've almost forgotten about the Viking raiders standing less than a horse's length in front of me.

'You go,' Frithwine urges me fervently. 'I'm wounded. Not even you and your herbs can heal me. But before I go, I can kill more of these bastards.' Before I can tell him no, Frithwine surges to his feet, with only a slight stumble, and launches himself forward, a seax blade in both hands flashing wetly as he jabs and slashes. Two of the men before me collapse to the floor as though the tide has taken their legs from them. The end two, turning to see what's happened, are both mortally wounded as well, one through the chest, the other, a slash across his neck.

A slap of warm, wet, sticky blood covers my face. I gag on the richness of it all as Frithwine moves onwards.

'Come on, you bloody fool.' I'm already surging to my feet, even without the reminder from Wulfheard, who's appeared beside me. I hurry to join him, aware that there are more than just four others with him. While I've been apprehended, Oswy and Wulfheard have completed the task of freeing almost all of our allies. Now there's only one who remains in captivity, and through the seething fury of the Viking raiders who argue in front of the smouldering remains of the hall, I can see Ealdorman Ælfstan, bound, gagged, forced to his knees, head hanging low. One of our enemies grips Ælfstan's hair tightly, an axe in his other hand, just waiting to sever Ælfstan's neck, while another figure gesticulates wildly. I don't understand the words, but I do the intent.

The war axe comes lower, the blade seemingly illuminated by the burning colours of a new dawn, and I fear to look away, even to blink, for if I do, I know that blade will be cutting through Ealdorman Ælfstan's neck.

Only then it doesn't. Instead, it flies through the air, landing heavily, buried not just in the ground but in the foot of the man who just held it, a howl of pain erupting from his open mouth. I can't believe what I'm seeing as Frithwine lurches against the man who threatened Ælfstan, where he wobbles, foot wedged as he careers into the other who argued for the ealdorman's life. That man is pushed into the fire with a crash of the few remaining skeletal timbers of the building's blackened frame.

A gout of fire bursts forth, Frithwine's hair catching the flames, briefly surrounding him as though a saintly figure in a priceless book, his head picked out in a golden halo. Then the flames are gone, the lengths of his hair taken in a moment, the rest of him burning less quickly as he tumbles into the flames without even a cry.

'Leave him,' Wulfheard urges me roughly, his gaze seeing what I do, as I make to move forwards. I can't allow Frithwine to burn to death, but the flames are too hot, even from here. I close my eyes, and offer a prayer that his death is swift. But Wulfheard pushes forwards to get to Ælfstan. 'Help me,' Wulfheard commands, and although I fear I'll never forget the image of Frithwine's burning hair, or the outline of his face, edged in the monochrome heat of the flames, I try to think about rescuing the ealdorman.

If we can leave here having lost only two men, I'll think it a miracle, but first, we must retrieve Ælfstan, who, while still alive, remains bound, gagged and on his knees.

Wulfheard and Oswy are the first to act, menacing with blades at the collection of remaining Viking raiders. There aren't fifty of them any more. There aren't even half that number, but there are still more of them than there are us, and they look furious and terrified in equal measure. Not a good combination.

I hasten to catch Wulfheard and Oswy, desperate to avoid the kicking remnants of the dying men; one Frithwine, a man who was determined to kill all of our enemy even if it cost him his life, which it has, and one an unknown Viking raider. I swallow down my nausea at the smell of roasting flesh.

Wulfheard's found weapons, perhaps from the dead foemen, and now he threatens our enemy. I do the same, wishing I had more than a seax in my hand. I'd welcome a shield. This was meant to be a quick strike to retrieve Lord Coenwulf, not an extended fight.

I look around and notice Edwin is beside me. I'd almost forgotten about him, but it's good to see him, despite the welter of bruises forming on his face and the fact his left arm hangs almost limp at his side.

The Viking raiders, while they might outnumber us, are not in a good state either. Two of the men before us have deep cuts on their faces, the one running left to right, the other right to left. I swear I can almost see bones through the lacerations. Behind them are more of our enemies. They carry war axes and also shields, but few have helms, and fewer yet seem able to stand upright. Whatever happened for my allies to be apprehended, they put up a bloody fight first. I wouldn't be surprised to know there are a pile of dead Viking raiders already.

'Come on, you craven arseholes,' Wulfheard roars, Oswy at his side, as they launch themselves at the two lead men. I mean to do the same, joining the fray and adding yet more blood to this fight, but Edwin stops me.

'Get the ealdorman,' he urges me, and I realise the two of us are close to Ealdorman Ælfstan. He's no longer being guarded, although the flames flick closely to him.

'Come on then,' I willingly agree and we scamper over the dead and dying.

I bend to cut through the rope that binds the ealdorman. Swiftly, the rope gag is removed from his mouth, and he stands on unsteady legs and spits into the fire, his eyes alighting on the burning body of Frithwine with a shudder.

'He was grievously wounded,' I huff, as though that makes it better, which it doesn't, and slide a stolen seax into the ealdorman's hand, taken from the man whose body no longer twitches. Edwin is no longer beside me, and I turn to find him facing a huge man, perhaps twice as wide as Edwin, who carries a sword almost as tall as Edwin.

Who is this man, and where has he come from? I feel sure I would have noted him before. In fact, it's bloody impossible to miss him.

'Don't,' I urge Edwin. 'Take the ealdorman,' and I push Ælfstan towards my childhood friend. It's growing lighter and lighter now; the promise of daylight welcome after our night of fighting in the darkness. The path to the secret entrance will be becoming visible to all, and I need to ensure Ælfstan escapes from here before our foemen spy it.

'Go, take him out the way we came in. The others are already going to the quayside, Lord Coenwulf included. Catch them, and get away from here.'

Ælfstan opens his mouth to argue with me, but I can see the collection of wounds he carries. Our men have been sorely tested. He limps. Blood mars his tunic, and one eye is almost closed where he's been headbutted or some such. I can't see he'll be able to do much with a seax. Even his right arm is thick with blood below the elbow.

'Go.' I push them both and turn to face our enemy.

He's a big bastard, yes, perhaps similar to Horsa. I just hope that, like Horsa, he only knows one way to fight and is particularly slow with it.

'Come on then,' I urge him as soon as I'm sure his eyes are on me and not on the staggering figures of Edwin and Ælfstan as they disappear down the slope. 'Come on then,' I roar again. The flames have almost done with licking at the flammable elements of the hall, and the two dead men. Now there's a more gentle dance of light, and in it, I see the face of my enemy. He looks determined.

The swing of his sword almost has me tripping over my own feet and into the embers of the fire as well. It passes me with an audible shush of cold air. I appreciate that this man is nothing like Horsa. This man is a warrior, almost godlike in his stance and skills.

I rush him, hoping to force him into losing his balance, but he doesn't even seem to notice the movement, too focused on his next strike with the sword. It comes at me, two-handed, aiming for my helm and to batter the sense from me. I jerk my head aside, but the blow lands on the padded fabric of my byrnie, even knocking my head so that my teeth seem to rattle in my mouth. I don't manage to get anywhere near him with my seax. His reach is huge. I wish I'd picked a smaller combatant. I can't see how I can beat him.

Another blow aims for my helm, and I skip backwards, preferring to risk burnt feet than a severed head. A spark of heat erupts up my left leg. I wince at it, knowing it'll hurt but less than having no head.

The man I face growls at my evasion. I realise that the only way to survive this is to do the unexpected.

He didn't anticipate me risking the fire, so I'll endanger something else as well.

I skip from the flames, even as the sword once more catches the glimmer of the early morning sunlight as it arcs towards me. To the side of him, just for half a breath, I hurry my feet, desperate to succeed in this.

I'm inside the reach of his sword, his arm extended, and I grip it tightly, using his own body weight against him. My feet scrabble against his knees and find purchase. I'm climbing higher and higher. I feel his swordless hand on my back, but his grip is surprisingly weak as I crest him, and swing my legs around, even as I'm ripping the helm free from his head. I look down, seeing nothing but the smooth pate of a man with no hair. I stab down, aware there are parts on a man's head where the blade will merely slip aside and others where, if I get it right, I can kill him by piercing the greyness of his innards.

A big meaty fist rears up towards me, my legs encircling his neck, the sword point coming towards me, reversed and ready to pierce me from his back like an annoying gnat. I flick my own blade, ensuring I can stab, not slash. With a brief glance at the rising sun, I stab down, and down and down. It takes all of my skill to jump clear from the man as he thunders to his knees and then rolls to his side, lifeless.

I'm panting, more heavily than if I'd run from Tamworth to Lichfield, but I don't have time to recover myself.

'Come on,' Wulfheard huffs into my ears. 'Come on. We need to escape from here before they regroup.' And with that, I'm running, my feet struggling for purchase on the slick grass, some of it covered in the ash of the fire, and towards where I know we gained entry into the monastery complex. I almost lose my balance, running so quickly down the slope that's given me so many problems, but somehow, and with the aid of Wulfheard, I just manage to keep myself upright.

And then we scramble over the tumbled-down stones, the howling fury of our enemy coming ever closer. It's evident they had no idea of this place. I don't understand their words, but their rage is easy to hear.

I don't even know who runs beside us because I can't risk looking, my eyes focused on where I need to place my feet. I'm grateful for the daylight. Without it, I'd fall or even trip on the piles of sheep shit. I hope that Ealdorman Ælfstan and Edwin have already scurried this way, that Lord Coenwulf is at the quayside, and that we have the time we need to get to the ships as well because, as the Viking raiders howl with frenzy and fury, I know they're not going to give up their chase. They mean to kill us all, and the only thing that will save us from such wrath is to make it to the ships. And even then, or so I've heard about their skill in a ship, it might not be enough to ensure we survive.

19

It seems to take half the morning to reach the quayside, sweat beading down my face and back, my knees throbbing from where I was tripped and then fell, my neck wound aching with each thud of my boots on the track we follow. And yet, for all the time we run, I can see where we're going. It's just that it never seems to come closer. No matter how quickly I think I'm running, I can still hear the slap of other feet chasing us down. I should be grateful they had no horse amongst them, or we'd have been overrun. I should be pleased we took the donkey, or one of them might have come after us on the gentle animal.

And yet, while I can see the sea, I can't spy the

quayside or any of the ships we brought here. I don't know if Cap will be there waiting for us or if the Viking raider ship we saw running towards the open sea might have returned. I just don't know, and my unease grows and grows.

We came here to free Lord Coenwulf, and yet, despite the enemy being unaware of our intentions, they've roundly defeated us. We leave Frithwine behind, and that doesn't sit well with me. I don't care that he willingly gave his life. He should be beside me, running as Wulfheard is doing. And so too should Æthelmod, if it's true that he's dead as well.

'Hurry,' is about all Wulfheard can gasp. I can't even manage that. It's strange to run this way when we've only travelled it in the darkness. I see buildings and trackways leading to other places, but we only beat the one path, that which will take us to the quayside if we're lucky.

Wulfheard, Oswy and I aren't the last of our men to run, but the others are quicker. I don't turn to look, but I'm strangely unsurprised when it's Kyre and Maneca who join our retreat. Kyre looks at me, almost with a smile on his face. Maneca is puffing hard, and I can see a patch of dark fluid on his byrnie. He must have taken a wound. I think we all probably have.

And then, ahead, I see what I've been hoping for: the quayside, with at least two of the ships making their way towards it and another which seems to be leaving. More importantly, there are no enemy craft in the sheltered bay, not yet, anyway. I don't allow myself to get carried away. Getting to the ships is just part of our escape plan.

I glance at the fleeing ship, and then I almost trip as I realise what I've seen that's so surprised me. Even the bloody donkey is being taken away from this place. It's a dead place now. I've seen no sheep and no people. The Viking raiders have killed everyone, and we've done our best to kill as many of them as possible.

Seeing the donkey cheers me. Surely that must mean that Lord Coenwulf and Brother Eadgar are safe. The closer I get to the quayside, the further away the ship gets, but I'm sure I see the sagging body of Uor on board. I hope he yet lives as well.

And then we thunder onto the wood of the quayside. There are seven of us. Added to our number are Landwine and Godeman. Godeman encourages the ships closer, and I catch sight of Cap. Landwine puffs heavily.

'Where's Æthelmod and Frithwine?' Landwine demands.

'Not coming,' I confirm, and immediate understanding covers his face.

'Then we make sure we get out of here alive, hurry,' and he turns to force me onto the wobbling sanctuary of Cap's ship. Cap winces to see me, and I'd say something, but I almost overbalance getting into the ship, and his hand is there, steadying me. I'm grateful for him as I sag with exhaustion, just taking my seat before Wulfheard seems to launch himself beside me, threatening its stability once more. Oswy is next, and then Godeman. I look to Landwine, realising the ship is full, and he grins, using his weight to force the ship away from the quayside.

'How?' I call to him, but still he grins, and then as footsteps resound off the quayside, I fear he'll do something stupid. My eyes flash from him to the approaching Viking raiders, and my heart almost stops, only for him to wink at me, turn his back on the enemy, and run along the length of the quay, where, still too far away to be close enough for Landwine to board, is the other ship.

My warning dies in my throat as the insistent oar batters against my palms, and I bend to it with a will, hoping the distance between the quayside and the enemy will grow so much more quickly than it does. I can't look to Landwine and row at the same time. One of the Viking raiders throws a seax towards the ship, a fruitless exercise, that ends with a splash as the blade drops below the level of the sea, and the next sound I hear is a loud thud.

'The daft fool made it,' Cap murmurs, his voice filled with disdain. 'Damn fool. He could have sunk the ship.' I'm just glad that Landwine's on a ship. Now we need to row and row. I don't know if the Viking raiders have ships they can chase us with. I must assume they do, and yet I can see nothing. My forehead furrows and Cap notices my attention wavering. He barks out instructions, counting as we row, the movement exhausting me in only a moment. Yet we're almost out at sea, almost far enough away that nothing can reach us from where the land curves around the bay, perhaps hinting that once the land was joined together before the sea forged a path between the two land masses.

'We filled their ships with stones and sank them all,' Cap chuckles, clearly content we're far enough away now for him to stop forcing us to row as quickly. 'They're stuck on there until one of their jarls arrives with another ship. Bloody arseholes.'

I suck in a much-needed breath, allowing the oar

to dig more shallowly into the sea. Wulfheard, sat beside me, does the same. He's bruised and bleeding, his beard streaked with blood, his hair in disarray, and his helm entirely missing.

Oswy looks no better. In fact, as I glance at him, where he sits behind me, I realise he's breathing shallowly, as though it's too painful to suck in a deep breath.

'Bloody hell,' Kyre exclaims, and I turn to look at him, but he's laughing and pointing. I look where he indicates, and there's Landwine, dripping wet, his ship's captain chuckling to himself, as Landwine shows his bare arse to our enemy.

'And that's how we show the bastards what we think of them,' Wulfheard murmurs, his voice light with humour, for all he looks well and truly broken.

* * *

It's an effort to get back to the small settlement from where we took the ships. We've seen no sign of the Viking raiders at sea, and the current is gentle with us, depositing us back with next to no effort on our part, which is good because we're all drained. Cap braces himself in the ship and helps us all to clamber ashore.

'My thanks,' I offer him, and he nods.

'A pity they're not all dead, but a good effort all the same,' he confirms, nodding back towards the Isle of Sheppey. 'Let's hope when they do get rescued, they sod off back to their own kingdoms.' I nod, trying to stay upright, for all the crossing was smooth.

I'm trying to work out how many of our warriors there are. I've caught sight of Edwin, and also Lord Coenwulf, once more mounted on the donkey and making his way up the steep slope. Even from here I can tell that his tunic is drenched in sweat. He must be in agony, but there's no other way to move him, not with the state of his injuries.

I've also seen Ealdorman Ælfstan, standing tall but swaying all the same. It would have been better for him if he'd accepted the help offered by Cenred. Brother Eadgar is there too, encouraging the donkey onwards. And yet I'm aware that men are missing from the party who left this shore only yesterday. I know of Frithwine. I've been told about Æthelmod, but I can't determine if that's the sum of our casualties. I hope it is. Two men is two men too many.

I gaze at the island before me, noting the spiral of smoke which must still burn at the ruins of the monastery. It's thick and black, and I'm reminded that Frithwine is part of that building's funeral pyre. I wish we'd not left him, but then, we'd never have managed to get a mostly burned corpse back to the ship. And why would we have wanted to? Where would we have buried him then? Perhaps it's best that he met his death as he wanted. He can be content that he killed a great number of our enemies. I hope he believed vengeance was gained before he died.

'Come on, Icel, stop lingering. We need to get away.' Wulfheard's voice rings with conviction, and I bow my head and do as he asks. My lips are thick with blood and salt. I'd like nothing more than to collapse here and tend to my wounds and those of others, but, of course, we're still in Wessex, and not Mercia. Should the Wessex king become aware of what we've done, he might come for us as well. I've no inclination to fight two battles in the space of one day. I can't imagine he'll thank us for dealing with the problem of these Viking raiders for him. He's more likely to kill us and claim the victory for himself. The smoke from the fire will certainly bring someone to look and see what's happened. Whatever arrangement, if indeed there was an arrangement, between King Ecgberht's son and these Viking raiders, it'll surely be at an end. No matter that it was the Mercians who finally had the stones to counter the Viking raiders.

With exhaustion dragging at my heels, I gaze at the steep path we must take to retrieve our horses. I'm sure I'll never make it. It's an effort just to stand upright without swaying, let alone walk up such a sharp incline. Yet Brute is there, at the top, and I must get to him.

With little enthusiasm for the task, I turn and head down, take my first steps. Every part of my body aches or throbs with some unlooked-for pain. A sheen of sweat quickly slides down my face, and I pause, wanting to stop.

'Come on,' Wulfheard growls at me, prodding me in the back, and I realise that he's not going to let me falter. Not now.

'What if the Viking raiders come back?' I query, wanting to do something to take my mind off my exhaustion and pain.

'The people of this place know how to defend themselves,' Wulfheard murmurs. He sounds tired as well.

'Yes, but the Viking raiders still had them working for them.'

'Yes, they did, but they had to pay them. I think, should they return, that they'll be welcome to the deserted island and little else. Not that I think the enemy will reappear. Whatever they agreed with the bastard king of Wessex, if anything, must surely be forgotten about now. After all, they didn't know we were from Mercia. They'll just think we were Saxons. They might even believe that the good king of Wessex played them for fools and killed many of their comrades.'

Such thoughts keep me going, even when I feel myself faltering as the climb seems to go on and on. My breath rasps sharply in and out of my dry mouth, and more than once, I lick my lips, forgetting the salt there, and almost choke on the dryness of my mouth. I keep my head down, looking only at my feet and the path disappearing beneath them. I know that if I look upward, the distance still to go will seem unbearable, and I won't make it.

The climb is interminable. How much easier, I consider, it was to make our way down the slope. And then, when I'm warring with myself, my knees aching and my shins crying out in pain, I finally realise I've made it. Panting more than breathing, I turn to view the Isle of Sheppey. Smoke continues to bloom into the sky, so black I wonder what we burned that gives off such foul fumes. Still, we're back inside the small cave with two entrances, and that means that we're

one step closer to Mercia and returning Lord Coenwulf to Lady Cynehild. That thought keeps me going
until I can stagger over to a waiting Brute, mount up
and, once more, be heading towards Mercia, and
home.

20

It's dark when Ealdorman Ælfstan calls a stop to our headlong dash back towards the River Thames, and I'm far from surprised. I'm just about hanging on to Brute, my thighs aching as much as my calves, but others are doing less well.

'Icel, get here.' Wulfheard's strident cry has me off Brute's back and hastening towards where a spark of fire assures me that we'll be warm throughout the night.

'What?' I gasp, passing others of the warriors who more fall than dismount from the backs of their horses. But my eyes are quicker than my movements, and quickly, I realise the problem.

'Why didn't we stop sooner?' I demand, my fear making my words whip-sharp, for even in what little light there is, I can tell we have a big problem. Lord Coenwulf's badly wounded, his eyes fluttering shut in a daze while perspiration sheets his face. He looks more fluid than solid, perched on top of one of the horses, it must be Æthelmod's, for I know it's not Frithwine's. How, I consider, did they manage to get Lord Coenwulf mounted? I know how hard it was to get him on the donkey, and that animal was half the height.

I stumble to my knees and quickly begin determining what wounds he carries as he falls forward and slumps to the ground, my arms only just catching him and stopping him from hitting his face on the hard-packed earth. But other than the wound to his leg that makes it impossible for him to walk, I can find nothing else. I look to Ealdorman Ælfstan and Wulfheard for confirmation, as they help me lie him flat on his back. 'Is it just his leg?' I demand to know. 'He took no other injuries?'

'Not as far as we know, no.' It's Ælfstan who speaks, his words thick with worry.

'We should have stopped sooner,' I glower once more. I catch sight of Brother Eadgar. He and the donkey are keeping pace with us, but he's exhausted, barely aware of what's happening around him. I can't think he'll be any use to me. Just because he was a monk doesn't mean he knows how to heal.

'We couldn't risk it,' the ealdorman counters, and I realise that I can have this argument once we're back over the River Thames. For now, I need to concentrate on Lord Coenwulf, or Frithwine and Æthelmod's deaths will have been for nothing.

'I need something to hold his leg straight, a splint, and we must find a way of getting him on a horse that doesn't make him pass out with the pain.' Eyebrows high, I direct this at Wulfheard. He always thinks he has the answers to everything. He can bloody think of a solution now.

'I'll find something.' Edwin hovers close by, no doubt worried about his oath-sworn lord, even as I notice he holds his left arm with his right.

'I've put water on the fire,' Oswy informs me, his voice tired but showing pride at accomplishing the task. He looks better, able to breathe properly now. I really want to round on Oswy, but perhaps he's done me a favour despite the fact that I just don't see that warm water and bandages are going to help me this time.

'My thanks,' I mutter, turning, only for Godeman

to appear with my sack containing all of my healing supplies. It seems my requests are getting to be well known among my fellow warriors. I just wish I knew how to treat such an injury. Ideally, Coenwulf should be somewhere that I could lie him immobile and dose him with every herb I carry in my sack that will relieve his pain, but that's not going to happen. How we're going to get him over the River Thames, I just don't know. Perhaps we would have been better served to keep him on the fishing ship, although maybe they can't survive in the currents of the River Thames. But I shake my head, my worry gnawing at me. I need to concentrate on the task at hand and not think about what comes next. There won't be a next if I don't help him.

I can't feed him pottage while he's asleep. I can set his leg, but that'll wake him. I can prepare something to help him heal, but first, I need to give him something to soothe the pain and set his leg. Hands shaking, I reach for my sack of supplies. But I know what it contains. Vinegar, moss, some fresh linens, and of course, tightly packed containers with the most commonly used herbs. But garlic will be useless. I don't need Coenwulf to purge himself. Honey won't aid him, not until his broken bone begins to knit together. Horehound, which Wynflæd gave me to stop the men from coughing when they suffer from a cold or sore throat, will be as ineffectual as garlic. Coenwulf doesn't have a cold or a sore throat, not yet. Removing his pain is what's required.

And yet, for all Coenwulf's asleep, or rather in so much pain that he's passed out, he's clammy to the touch.

'Come on, Icel.' Wulfheard hovers behind me. I want to turn and scowl at him, but I'm trying to still my rapidly beating heart. I'm thinking of what I can do and not what's beyond me. Coenwulf was in pain but wasn't insensible when we found him. It's the travelling that's made him like this, so I tell myself. So, I consider it must just be the pain that's causing the immediate problems.

'Will this do?' Edwin erupts before me, panting heavily, his face white with the strain of the last few days where it's not green and black with bruises, as he glances fearfully at Lord Coenwulf. I eye the collection of sticks he's found for me, and which he holds awkwardly in his right arm. I nod, tongue licking my lips only to taste the salt of my exertions once more.

'I need some water,' I announce, aware that everyone is watching me as though I can summon some strange magic to heal Coenwulf in the blink of an eye.

'It's not boiled yet,' Oswy comments, worry in his voice. And I find a smile on my tight lips.

'I need a drink, for me,' I explain. 'I'm bloody thirsty. I imagine we could all do with a drink and something to eat.' I aim this at Wulfheard. 'It'll give me the time I need to make Coenwulf more comfortable.' I don't add that I'm unsure how to do that. Now isn't the time to show any fear. If I can fight the bastard Viking raiders, then I can bloody well help Lord Coenwulf.

'Here you go.' The ealdorman thrusts his water bottle at me, and eagerly I tip the too-warm mixture into my mouth, having first swilled the worst of the salt from my throat.

'My thanks,' I murmur. 'But we need more and fresher than that.'

'There's a brook close by. I'll take the horses and the water bottles,' Osmod offers quickly.

'And some pottage,' I continue. It feels strange to be giving orders to my fellow warriors, and yet they scamper to do as I ask, as though I'm the lord here and not Ælfstan. In the end, only Edwin, Wulfheard, Brother Eadgar and the ealdorman remain to watch me at work. The monk is murmuring softly, I imagine prayers, but I don't believe they'll help me or Lord Coenwulf at the moment.

'I'm going to cut through his trews,' I confirm, deciding I really need to get a good look at his leg before I determine what to do next. Quickly, I remove my seax and slice through the material of Lord Coenwulf's trews. I realise my blade is filthy, but at the moment, I just need it to cut. Even in the fire light, I can see livid marks all over Coenwulf's leg, and worse, I determine where the skin has begun to knit back together on his lower shin but that his bone isn't yet straight. It's not what I was hoping to discover.

Running my hand up and down his leg, I wince at the tilt of the bone, even as I bend to sniff the wound. It's not good. The skin is red and inflamed. I can feel the misalignment of the bone. It wouldn't take much to reveal his white bones and shimmering muscle. I hear the wincing of those who watch me, and I turn to meet Ealdorman Ælfstan's concerned face, noting that his one eye is swollen so much he can't see out of it. He does seem to have done something to staunch the blood flow from the cut on his right arm. I'm pleased about that.

'I need to make sure his leg is set straight, which it isn't at the moment. I'll have to undo some of the healing that's begun, and it'll have to start all over again. I don't know if I should do it now.' Feeling ex-posed, even with my warrior allies surrounding me, I peer into the growing darkness of night. We're far from home. Very far from home. There might be Viking raiders or bloody Wessex warriors close by. Perhaps we shouldn't have a fire. But we need to eat and I need clean water. I shake my head, dislodge those thoughts once more, and focus on Lord Coenwulf.

'You know best, Icel. Would it not be better for the healing to start afresh though? He's in a bad way, already. It seems cruel to leave it as it is and then undo it all when we're back in Mercia.'

I nod at Ælfstan's wise words, and chew on my lip, before running my hand through my scruffy beard. I'm thinking the same, but still, it worries me. There's much to do. Should I begin the task, and we be attacked, then Coenwulf won't be able to protect himself, and he'll be in even more danger than he is now.

'I'm going to do it. But I'll need help.'

'The water's ready,' Oswy calls suddenly, and I crack a smile once more.

'Thank you,' I rejoin. 'I'll need more. Lots more.' Hastily, I begin to pull items from my sack, laying them out around me. And then I turn and really look at my seax. I wince to see it covered in the muck and filth of the slaughter I carried out to retrieve Lord Coenwulf from the Viking raiders. Now I'm going to have to put it to another use.

Without thought, I thrust it into the leaping flames of the fire. Heat will cleanse it better than vinegar and water, and for what I need to do, it must be devoid of our enemy's stink.

I turn then to look at Wulfheard and Ealdorman Ælfstan. Edwin hovers close as well, his eyes more white than colour, his one arm still held tight to his body by the other. Brother Eadgar continues to pray, the occasional soft 'Amen' assuring me that's what he does.

'I'll cut through the healing flesh and manipulate the bone back into position. Then, we'll secure the leg against the splint that Edwin's found. All of this will rouse Lord Coenwulf. Two of you must keep him as still as possible, and one of you will do what I demand and when I demand it. No questions. It'll look bad, and then, hopefully, it'll look a little better.'

I've never attempted anything like this before, but I've watched Wynflæd try to straighten broken bones. I understand that bone can knit back together, provided it has the right conditions. Keeping the leg immobile is one of those conditions. But so is trying to keep Coenwulf still and calm while I prod and poke at his wound. It won't be easy. It might be better to leave it as it is, but if I do that, Coenwulf will be in constant pain, and more, he'll never walk without a limp again.

'Are you sure about this?' Wulfheard asks me sympathetically.

'We can hardly take him back in the state he's in,' I huff softly.

'I'll keep him immobile,' Wulfheard confirms. 'With the aid of Oswy. Edwin, you aid Icel, and if there's anything else that needs doing, then Ealdorman Ælfstan will be on hand to do it, as will the monk.' Wulfheard's words are filled with command. I'm grateful for that.

'Whatever happens, don't disregard my instructions.' I meet their eyes, daring them to doubt those words, and slowly, all of my helpers nod, Ealdorman Ælfstan last of all.

'Bloody get on with it then,' Oswy glowers, breaking the tension, and as a tendril of sweat drips down my nose from being so close to the fire, I reach for my seax in the flames, swallowing against my doubts and fears. I have to do this. There's no choice.

He and Wulfheard have taken up position on either side of Coenwulf's prone body, their backs to me. I wish I had the luxury of not looking.

With a wad of linens to stop my hand from burning once more, I feel the blast of heat on the flashing blade, lit up blue as the superheated parts of the fire are. I sever the skin, knocking the scab aside so that blood flows freshly once more. The stink of the sizzling blood turns my stomach as Lord Coenwulf moans in his sleep. Edwin is at Coenwulf's foot, ready to hold his leg steady should he fight me. I offer a swift prayer that Coenwulf will simply stay asleep, adding my words to those of Brother Eadgar. The pain of what I'm about to do will be immense.

I return my seax to the fire. I'll have need of it again.

With blood flowing once more from the wound, I shuffle down Coenwulf's leg, one of my legs to either side of his, as I place my hands on his injury. A wince, and I'm reminded that I placed my foot in the fire on the Isle of Sheppey. I'll need to do something about that. But, first, this will be the difficult bit. I hope I have the strength to do what needs to be done. This is the part I've never done before. Watching Wynflæd and doing it myself are two very different things.

The crackle of the fire is the only sound I can hear above my breathing. The knob of the broken bone is easy to detect, as is the bump where it's begun to heal at an angle to its original position. I breathe deeply through my nose.

'Ready,' I exhale, and then before I can think about it further, I force all of my weight against the broken bone. It doesn't want to give, that much is clear. It might have begun to heal incorrectly aligned, but the bone is still bloody strong. Coenwulf moans, his leg moving beneath my hands.

'Hold him,' I huff once more, sweat dripping into my eyes.

I try again, thinking about Wynflæd's actions when I watched her do the same. Beneath my hands, Coenwulf's beginning to stir again. I know my time is short. I need to do this now, or it'll be impossible.

'Ready,' I repeat, and this time I feel the crack of the bone beneath my hands as it slips once more. Lord Coenwulf shrieks in pain, and I'm grateful for Edwin's steady hand on his foot as I leap clear of his leg and grab the stick Edwin found. 'Help me,' I urge him. Thankfully, Coenwulf's lapsed back into a deep sleep, and I know the pain will have made him lose his awareness of what I'm doing. With hands that shake, I secure his leg against the stick, tying it all the way along its length, apart from close to his knee where the bone must have broken through. It's there that I need to be careful.

Edwin assists me as ably as he can with one arm while Ealdorman Ælfstan takes control of Coenwulf's foot. I want to sit back and admire the work of the straightened leg when I'm happy that we've done what we can, but blood oozes sluggishly from where I removed the scab. I would welcome the time to stitch the wound tightly, but the skin is already so reddened that I know I only have one option.

'I'm going to seal the wound,' I inform them all. No one comments. All five of my helpers are quiet and composed as I force what remains of the linens into my hand before taking the blade from the flames.

'I'll have to hold it for a while,' I confirm before quickly placing the blade against Coenwulf's skin. Once more, his body judders, and then he screams in agony before falling silent. I hold the seax for as long as I can, the edges of my flesh slowly growing hotter and hotter until I thrust it back into the fire, dropping the linens. I can't see if the skin's burned, not with the orange glow from the fire, and I dare not run my fingers over my old eagle scar either.

And it doesn't matter anyway. I had to do what was needed.

Hastily, I bind the wound, making use of my vinegar and moss to hold close to the seared wound. Tomorrow, when the wound is less hot, I'll apply a mix of honey to it as well. Only then do I sit back on my knees and meet the gaze of Wulfheard and Oswy, Edwin and Ælfstan, and Brother Eadgar.

'Well done, Icel.' The ealdorman is the first to recover his composure. 'Well done,' he repeats. And I slug more water from a refilled water bottle, aware that I've been busy for a long time. The horses have all returned to the impromptu campsite. Pottage has been cooked, and the men eat it just out of the light of the flames, their voices subdued. I still don't know if everyone yet lives, and I'm shaking as much as Lord Coenwulf was before he lost his senses.

'He needs to sleep.'

'We need to move on,' Wulfheard counters aggressively. 'We're not safe here.'

'No, we're not,' Ealdorman Ælfstan confirms. I open my mouth to argue, but already, the unease is returning. I felt it while we rode here. As I helped Coenwulf, it disappeared, but it's back now.

'Do you think they know where we are?' I demand, washing my hands in the warm water that Oswy prepared and wincing at the touch of the heat on my bloodied hands. I don't think it's from the work I've just carried out. No doubt, it's from the salt of the sea and the wounds of battle that I took as well.

'I think it's possible,' the ealdorman confirms. A bowl of food is thrust into my hands by Godeman, and I lift my eyes to thank him.

'Try it first,' Landwine murmurs, stopping me, and Godeman rounds on him.

'You could have bloody cooked it,' Godeman growls.

'Aye, I could, and I'd have done a better job than you.'

I think the two will argue, but Wulfheard's on his feet, yanking the two of them apart so that Godeman only just keeps his feet.

I taste the mixture. Not the best, but it's warm and oniony, and that'll do for now.

I shovel it into my mouth and then hand the bowl to Edwin, who has it refilled. In the meantime, I take a beaker full of hot water and hastily add some herbs to it. I can't see that they'll do much good as they're not steeped, but I can sense we won't be here for long, and Coenwulf needs something in his belly.

'Can we use this?' Uor demands, coming into view and pulling something behind him. I can't quite tell what it is. It looks to be little more than sticks for the fire. He drags it with one hand, and I'm reminded of the fact he's wounded, and I've not had time to tend to him.

'Yes, yes, we can. Come on, help me move him,' Wulfheard confirms, his voice filled with resolve. I've only just finished trickling the herb-filled water into Coenwulf's mouth. He moaned in his sleep, but he swallowed some of the mixture, for all his eyes never opened.

'What is it?' I ask.

'It's some sort of sled,' Wulfheard huffs, Uor to his other side.

'Keep his leg straight,' I urge them, only then noticing that Coenwulf's skin is even clammier than before. I need to give him something else, something stronger for the pain, but I don't have anything. Not here. I must get him somewhere safe, but at the same time, I realise as a spot of dark blood blooms on the linens that bind his wound, I also need to keep him still.

'Come on, help us,' Wulfheard calls to others of his men when Uor is unable to provide the help required. I watch as Ælfstan and Edwin aid the two in sliding Coenwulf onto the sled, both one-handed, and then tie him to it.

'How will we move it?' I suddenly think.

'The horses will pull it,' Uor informs me, as though it's the most obvious thing ever. I want to examine the dark stain on his shoulder, but for now, I have other concerns.

'It'll be no good over uneven ground,' I caution, wishing I could stop all this.

'Do you have a better bloody solution?' Wulfheard huffs, using whatever he can find to secure Lord Coenwulf: bits of hempen rope and even leather straps taken from the horses.

'We need to stop here, for a few days,' I caution, wincing as Coenwulf's head lolls from side to side, as though it might roll free from his neck.

'We can't,' Uor informs me, standing back to admire his work, his face pinched in pain.

'Why?' I counter, but it's Kyre who speaks, dashing back into the temporary campsite from where he must have been on guard duty.

'Because we're being hunted,' Kyre exclaims, rushing for his horse. 'And we need to leave here, now.'

I hasten to the side of the fire, but Edwin's beaten me to it as he thrusts all of my precious supplies back into my sack and hands it to me.

'My thanks,' I murmur.

He looks like he could do with some of the

healing potion I gave to Lord Coenwulf. I notice he also has a large cut on his face that needs stitching, but there's no time. The sense of being watched intensifies, and my hands fumble for my seax as soon as I've reclaimed my gloves. I grip it without thought, and the heat infuses my gloves. I drop it quickly, reach for my sack, and only then grip it again through the sack's material, scrunched together. It's still too hot.

I can hear my fellow warriors mounting up, the horses protesting at having no rest. I glance up, hoping to find Brute close by, as Wulfheard, with the sled trailing behind Bada, slowly moves forward while the ealdorman watches to ensure that Lord Coenwulf doesn't fall from it.

'Come on,' I urge myself, wishing I could move more quickly, but every action I take is so slow. I still need to make my way to Brute, and aside from Edwin, and Oswy, everyone else has already moved on, even Brother Eadgar.

I look from my seax to Brute, acutely aware that I can hear the rumble of something coming closer. I fear it's mounted warriors. But I can't leave my seax. It's been my blade for too long now and is so closely associated with my uncle that to leave it behind would be akin to losing him all over again.

Hastily, I wrap a stray piece of linen around my hand and reach to grip my blade once more. The palm of my hand tingles, but I think I can hold it, for now.

I rush to Brute's side. The horse watches me with impatience, pawing at the ground, while Oswy, mounted, glances back down the path we must have come along, as though, even in the darkness, he'll see our enemy. Whatever is coming this way, it's not moving slowly, and if these warriors are mounted then they're risking the horses stumbling in the darkness to get to us. They must really want to apprehend us.

One-handed, holding my still too hot blade away from Brute's shoulder, I mount up, while Edwin fumbles to tie my sack to the saddle. Only then does he find his own horse, and then finally, we're ready.

'Come on, boy,' I urge Brute. I know well enough that I shouldn't ride with my weapon unsheathed, but I fear that if I house my seax in its holder, it'll burn through the leather, and I'll lose it. Instead, I grip it tighter, holding the blade to the side so that the passage of the wind will cool it.

Brute skips forward, and I nudge him to encourage him to follow the other horses. Ahead, I can just about make out the rear of the final horses to leave. Edwin hastens to get in front of Brute, and only then does my animal realise what I want him to do. My head pounds, and my hand throbs, or it's the thunder of hooves coming ever closer.

'Hurry up,' Oswy urges me, coming alongside me.

I want to meet his gaze, nod in understanding, but I'm exhausted and hobbled by having to hold my blade. And Brute is being an absolute arse. He takes my orders for only so many steps and then tries to veer aside.

'Control your bloody horse,' Oswy growls at me.

'I would if I could.'

'And sheath your damn blade,' he instructs. 'We need to ride from here, not walk at slower than a man's pace.'

My hand's starting to throb once more, the heat coming through the linen and my glove, and I realise that I'm just going to have to sheath it or risk being caught by whoever is trying to pursue me. Edwin has already moved out of sight. I don't imagine that Oswy will be any more likely to wait for me.

'Wait,' I glower and move my body so that I can slide the blade into place. A welcome warmth comes from the blade, where it rests around my waist and down the top of my left leg, but I can't see it being pleasant for long. And it only works to remind me once more that my lower left leg is burnt.

'Come on then,' I urge Brute, gripping the reins tightly and directing his head so that he looks where I want to go. With the thunder of whoever is following us getting ever closer, Brute finally takes my command and streaks onwards, the sound of Oswy behind me, ensuring that Brute doesn't stop.

21

I dare not shout to those ahead, asking them to slow down, or to Oswy behind, asking him if we're being followed. The sound of the horses' hooves is more than enough to give away our position. And I don't want to know either.

The ground beneath the horses' hooves seems flat enough, but it's too dark to see. Brute could run into anything, and we wouldn't know until it was too late. But quickly, we catch up to Edwin's horse. I spare a thought for Lord Coenwulf, hoping he's remained tied to the sled, and also that he doesn't wake anytime soon. I can't imagine how terrifying it must be to be dragged somewhere at a good canter. But at least we're only cantering. A gallop would shake the sled loose, I'm sure of that.

I've no idea where we are. It's impossible to tell with the thick cloud cover obscuring the moon and most of the stars. We find a brook, which I hope means we're close to the River Thames, but then I shake my head. It took us two days to travel from the River Thames to the Isle of Sheppey. We can't be close to the river. Not yet. But, I realise, we can't hope to ride for two days without stopping either. I've barely slept, and neither have the rest of the warriors. The only one who sleeps is Lord Coenwulf, and that's because to be awake would be too painful to tolerate.

Brute is happier now he's caught the other horses. I release my grip on the reins and realise that the heat from my superheated seax blade has dissipated. Either that or I've become used to it, and when I finally check, I'll be scoured down my leg and hip as well. I hope that's not the case.

Riding in the dark is similar to being in a tunnel. At any moment trees and branches rear up at me, and I batter them aside, only just not shrieking when something silk-like touches my face. I snatch at it, assuming it's little more than the work of a spider, and pull away thin strands of gossamer web.

My eyes hurt from being so wide open. But when

I blink, I'm reminded of my fatigue and have to rub at my eyes. I hope Lady Cynehild is grateful for the risks we've taken in rescuing her husband, and then I reconsider. I hope Lord Coenwulf makes it back to Mercia alive. The Viking raiders might have treated him poorly, but we, his rescuers, are hardly handling him any better.

And on we ride. Somehow, I've lost the sound of anyone following behind us. I finally spare a look over my shoulder, holding tightly to Brute, and meet the gaze of Oswy.

'I think we've outridden them,' he huffs. Peering behind him, I realise I can see no sign of our pursuers, but there's a new problem for us to contend with. The sun is rising. Wherever and whomever our enemy is, they'll be able to find us easily; they need only follow the churned ground from where the horses have passed.

I grunt and turn back to ensure Brute stays on course. I appreciate it's been slowly getting lighter for a while now. I can make out Edwin and also some of the other horses. I still don't know if anyone other than Frithwine and Æthelmod died on the Isle of Sheppey. I still don't know if other wounds need treating other than those I've seen on Uor, Ælfstan, Maneca, Wulfheard and Edwin, and of course, my own burn. I should have taken the time to ask, but our onward progress has been too rushed, the threat of riders chasing us, too great to ignore.

I'm aware that Edwin's horse is starting to lurch. More than once, I've seen it lose its steady footing only to recover itself and continue chasing the other horses. Even Brute is starting to falter. While the horses might not have had as little rest as me and the rest of the men, it's still too much for them. We could do with finding somewhere to stop if only there were somewhere safe. We need to hide out so that we can get some rest, and only then make our way to the River Thames and try and determine a way across it. I can't spot Brother Eadgar and that worries me as well. We promised him safe haven in Mercia, but I can't see that his donkey will have managed to keep pace with the horses.

Brute's sweating, and once more, I feel as though I'm on a ship, swaying with the movement of the waves beneath the wooden struts of the craft. The next thing I know, I startle awake, my hands instinctively gripping Brute's reins as he comes to a halt.

I look around me. I've not been aware, but we're beneath the boughs of trees now, and the horses have all slowed to a careful walk. I finally spot Brother Eadgar and his stubborn donkey. I'm amazed the animal has made it this far. I turn. Oswy is there, a smirk on his lips. He must have known that I slept.

'We rest here,' the ealdorman informs me, dismounted now, as he moves amongst his men and their horses, offering soft words, and slaps of acclaim to the horses.

I more slide from my horse than dismount.

'When you've watered him, see to Lord Coenwulf. He still sleeps,' Ealdorman Ælfstan informs me, his one eye little more than a narrow slit. 'We'll rest but only to get something to eat, and then we must be on our way.' For all I thought the day was dawning, here, beneath the trees, it feels like dusk. I watch where the men are leading their horses, and I take Brute to the small stream, the water clear enough that I can see the stones that mark its path. He drinks eagerly, but like the rest of the men, I don't remove his saddle. I do bend and pull some of the rushes from the stream and use them to wipe the foaming sweat from his shoulder and neck. All the time, I speak to him. 'Good lad,' I inform him. 'Good lad.'

'Where are we?' I ask of no one.

'Wessex,' Kyre glowers at me, and I wince at the deep gash that runs along his nose. I think I can almost see the bone beneath it.

'That needs stitching,' I inform him.

'Not now,' he counters, lifting his hand to touch it but then stopping himself with a wry smile. 'Get some sleep. You look like you're dead on your feet.'

The words are hardly comforting, but I'm aware that without Brute at my back, I'd have fallen over as soon as I dismounted.

There's no fire this time. Instead, my fellow warriors reach for saddlebags and pull forth hard bread, lumps of cheese or strips of dried meat. They share with Brother Eadgar who has nothing but the filthy robe he wears. I leave Brute where he can crop at the thin grasses growing through the mulch of the woodland floor and make my way to Lord Coenwulf.

His sled has been removed from the back of Bada, but it's liberally splattered with the rich green of horseshit, and I wrinkle my nose at the sharp stink of piss as well. Bada didn't know not to relieve himself when he felt like it.

Lord Coenwulf doesn't notice, though, his face lifeless as I bend to run my hand over the splinted leg. Surprisingly, the contraption has held, but I can't say the same for the sled. The left-hand side has buckled and twisted. Coenwulf is only still attached to it thanks to the ropes and leather straps.

The colour of his skin worries me, but his breathing is even. I consider bending to examine the linens that cover where I cauterised his skin, but while there's blood there, it does seem to have stopped, the colour of the linen brown like dung as opposed to red like wine. I know it'll hurt him if I meddle with it, and it would be a kindness not to wake him. Shrugging my shoulders, I move aside and instead reach for whatever food I have in my saddle sacks.

Eagerly, I bite into a rich cheese, savouring its texture and grateful that it's not too salty. I feel dry enough as it is. I swig from my water bottle and then turn to return to the stream to refill it. As I do so, I finally get a good look at the rest of Ealdorman Ælfstan's warriors.

My immediate concern is for Uor. I know he took a bad wound on his shoulder, or close to his shoulder, and this is the first time I've truly looked at him. He's pale-faced, and sags to the ground. I need to aid him, as I do Maneca, who I recall also took a fearful injury that showed as a dark patch on his byrnie. But in my mind, I'm counting up the numbers. I know that Frithwine and Æthelmod are dead. I also know that Ælfstan, Wulfheard, Oswy, Brother Eadgar and Edwin are still alive, although Edwin and Ælfstan aren't unscathed. But the rest of the men?

My eyes stray to Waldhere. He's not dismounted

from his horse, and he sways from side to side. Hastily, I rush to him.

'What ails you?' I demand. His eyes flutter open, and he looks around in surprise.

'What?' he queries, and follows it with, 'Where are we?'

'Not in Mercia yet.' It's hardly comforting. 'Where are you wounded?'

'My head.' He winces, lifting his hand and holding it against the back of his head. I peer upwards, while his horse rests, head hanging low. It would be better if Waldhere dismounted.

'Get down and let me look at it.'

'I'd rather not,' he counters. 'We won't be here long, and I don't think I'll be able to get back on the horse. It's not just my head,' he confirms, his words elongated and filled with pain.

'Where else?' I glower at him, wishing the stubborn fool would just tell me. I'm as tired as he is.

'My foot.'

'Your foot?'

'Yes, my left foot.'

I reach for his foot and only then notice that it's wrapped in a dirty linen streaked with blood.

'Your foot?' I exclaim again. Despite it all, foot injuries are rare.

'Yes, the bastard stabbed me through the bloody foot as he lay dying.' I wince in sympathy and slowly begin to unwrap the linen. I want to see what it looks like. And, I realise, I need to remove his boot.

'You should have taken your boot off. It'll get the wound rot.'

'I know, but we've been in such a rush, I didn't want to.'

I nod, again, my eyes on what I'm revealing. The wound has clearly bled a lot, but it's going to bleed much more if I remove his boot. I look behind me and meet the concerned expression of Ealdorman Ælfstan. He nods at me, aware of what I'm doing, and that's all the acceptance I need.

'Wait here,' I urge Waldhere. 'I'm going to get my supplies.'

'I'm not going anywhere,' he reassures me with a faint smirk. I smile and scamper back to my sack of supplies, my trews rubbing against the twin burns on my left leg and foot. I'm thinking about what I can do without boiled water and with what I have left in my sack of supplies that Wynflæd gave me. I don't like to think it, but it'll have to be the vinegar to clean it, and that's going to hurt like a bitch.

I grab my supplies and return to Waldhere. True to his word, he hasn't moved, but Wulfheard has made his way to him and hands him up a water bot-tle. I might have been the last to know of Waldhere's wound. And I still need to check on Uor and Maneca. If Waldhere's done nothing to tend to his injury, then I doubt the other two have either. Certainly, Edwin and Ælfstan haven't. Wynflæd's always vocal about the lack of care the warriors show to their own health. She'd flay them with her tongue if she were here.

'I'm going to remove your boot,' I inform Wald-here, 'and clean and bandage the wound. Will your horse still take your commands?' A huge grey head turns to face me, and I rub my hand along the ani-mal's long nose as she whiffles as though in reas-surance.

'Aye, she's a good mare,' Waldhere assures me as I take hold of my seax and begin to saw at the leather of his boot. 'This is going to hurt,' he comments, and I nod, licking my lips and wishing I'd eaten and drunk more before becoming embroiled in this. I don't know how long it's going to take. The leather is surprisingly unyielding as I attempt to determine how I can detach the boot. I think it'd be cruel to re-move it the normal way. It's going to be better to cut the foot free, even if that'll leave Waldhere without a boot.

His wound is on the top of his foot, but blood pools to the bottom as well, and I quickly realise that the blade has bitten entirely through it. It's a wonder he's been able to walk up the steep hill, let alone ride since then. Poor sod.

Biting my lip, I manage to cut through the bottom of the boot, and the rest comes away far more easily. The steady drum of blood on the ground assures me that I've made it bleed once more, but Waldhere could hardly keep his boot on until his foot healed.

I move quickly then, cutting through his socks to reveal a surprisingly hairy foot. He's trying to keep still, as is his horse, but it's paining him.

'Sorry,' I murmur.

'Just get on with it,' he huffs through tight teeth, and I do.

'This is really going to hurt,' I inform him, my precious vinegar to hand once I've cleared away the worst of the clotted blood.

'I know,' he growls.

Quickly, I splash the salty mixture over his two wound sites, on the top and bottom of his foot, while his foot twitches and his leg drums against the side of his mount. The wound is deep but not long, and I don't think it needs stitches, not only because it'll be difficult to draw together enough skin on such a tight area.

'I'll wrap it,' I inform him, and quickly bind moss to the twin puncture sites, and then tie more linen tightly enough that it should stay in place, no matter what he does. But that leaves us with a problem. His boot is broken and useless, but without it, his foot is exposed. I don't know how to solve that because we don't take spare boots with us. I can't even take them from Lord Coenwulf because he doesn't have boots either, his feet filthy. If we're lucky, we have a decent enough pair. Only men such as the ealdorman will have more than one pair of boots.

'Here, use this.' Edwin hands me something using his good arm, and I wince at his cut face and then nod. It's not a lot of use, but it'll be better than nothing. It'll keep Waldhere's foot warm, at least. Between us, we work the tunic over his foot, the occasional grunt coming from Waldhere. Then me and Edwin secure it to Waldhere's foot using his leg bindings and extending them over the foot, hopefully, avoiding the site of the wounds.

I stand back and admire the work.

'You'll have to try and keep your weight off it,' I confirm, wishing I could do more. So many of these men carry wounds that are best treated by keeping them still.

'I'll have to perfect the way I piss from the back of a horse then,' Waldhere glowers, sweat on his dirty face from my ministrations.

'I wondered what the stink was,' Wulfheard mutters from the far side of the animal. I turn to survey the rest of the men. Everyone displays some sort of wound, even if it's just a blackening eye or a strike to the chin. I seek out Uor and Maneca, and find them huddled together, eyes closed. Eagerly, I gather together my supplies and strike out towards them, but Ealdorman Ælfstan interrupts me. I notice then that he has attempted to clean up his wounded right arm. He has a bandage around it. His eye is somehow even more swollen, however.

'They've survived this long. Get some sleep, or you'll be no good to anyone.'

'But—' I counter.

'Icel, we've been in many such fights before, and carried much more lethal wounds back to Tamworth. They'll be well for now, as will I, and you need some rest before we strike out for the River Thames. Now, go and sleep.'

Angrily, but still counting the men as I pass them, I find a space and force myself to lie down. I can't see that we've lost anyone but Frithwine and Æthelmod, but I'm concerned by the injuries I can't see as much as the ones that are blindingly obvious. I swill more water into my mouth and think I'll never sleep. Only then I do, to be woken by an urgent hand on my shoulder.

'Wake up, Icel, and bloody get moving. They've found us again.'

22

Once more, I feel as though I'm moving too slowly. It takes me forever to grab my sack, find Brute, and mount up. I'm sure everyone else is already mounted as Oswy directs his horse onwards, leading the rest of the men. I might have gotten some sleep, but my eyes remain gritty, and my mouth tastes as though I've swallowed a boar's arse.

But Brute is alert, and as soon as I'm almost in the saddle, my sack still in my hands, he eagerly follows the line of our men. I glance behind, nearly falling from my saddle, and see that while Oswy leads, Godeman and Landwine are at the group's rear. They're ready to ride out, eyes alert as they look behind us. From not too far away, I can hear the sound of pursuit.

'Arse,' I huff softly, bending low over Brute's shoulders so that we can make it through the low-hanging boughs without me being knocked off. I can't see how the sled that carries Lord Coenwulf will cope amongst the tightly packed trees, and yet it must, for it's not been left behind, and Wulfheard is ahead of me.

We move as quietly as we can, which isn't that quiet when we're mounted and moving through a woodland. Branches snap and crack beneath the heavy hooves of the horses, and the further we travel, the tighter and tighter the trees seem to be. I don't even bother sitting upright but hunker low over Brute's shoulder, offering him comfort as we move through the strange sepia of the boughs of the trees. I try not to jump at every sound, aware that the animals of the woodland will add their noises to those we make. I turn to glance behind me, but it's impossible to see much more than the horse directly following me, and that happens to be Waldhere's. He wears a sullen look and I appreciate that he's in substantial pain.

Abruptly, I'm aware of the rumble of moving water, and my heart leaps. Are we truly at the River

Thames already, only for my heart to sink once more? We made our way over the river when the tide was at a certain point. I just can't see that we'll be lucky enough to encounter the same conditions. And, if we're being hunted down, we won't have the time to wait. And how will we get Lord Coenwulf, and the other wounded men, across the river? They won't be able to swim. Coenwulf isn't even alert enough for us to consider it.

Worry has my heart beating too quickly, and yet the sound of the rushing water comes no closer, even as we continue on our way. Perhaps, then, it's not the River Thames I can hear.

Slowly, it grows darker and darker, and I must assume that overhead the end of the day is fast approaching. We'd do well to have some moonlight with which to see by. Equally, it would be good if it remained moonless. Then our enemy wouldn't be able to see us.

Whoever is pursuing hasn't found us yet. My back aches from being in such a strange position, but then I realise we must have moved from the trees and into the open air again. I sit upright, peering all around me. I can see some way forward and hear the murmur of my fellow warriors.

'Where are we?' I query, but no one answers as we

bunch together, the horses shaking their heads, no doubt as grateful to be free from the probing branches as we are. I shake my own head, hoping that there aren't too many insects inside my tunic. I pull small branches from my hair, dropping them to the ground. I wish it were brighter, but the sun has long since set, and the moon, despite the lack of clouds overhead, has yet to make an appearance. Our way is lit by a handful of stars, and that's just not going to be enough.

The last of the ealdorman's warriors erupts from beneath the trees, Godeman and Landwine still in that position. I hear a murmur of words but can't make out what they are.

'We go this way.' The whispered words reach me, and I startle. I hadn't realised Edwin was so close to me. 'Stay close, and follow the tail of my mount. Tell the man behind you.'

I turn and pick out the piercing eyes of Waldhere but little else.

'Stay close to Brute,' I whisper to him. 'Tell the man behind you.' A few moments later, Oswy, or whoever leads us, must be satisfied that we're all pre-pared as Edwin moves on, and I hasten to join him, turning to ensure I can see and hear Waldhere and his horse following on behind. While we might be clear from the woodland, it still feels as though we move in a tunnel because it's just so dark. But I think we must be following a path or a road. Certainly, the ground beneath Brute's feet appears to be compacted, from what I can tell, and he doesn't kick aside a stone or any other impediment. I'd like to know where we are. I'd like to know how Lord Coenwulf, Waldhere, Ælfstan, Maneca and Uor are doing, but clearly, that's not going to happen anytime soon.

When I feel we've moved far enough away from the woodlands, I risk looking backwards to determine if I can see where we've been, but it's impossible. I can't even see where I suspect Godeman and Landwine still keep to the rear of our group. I don't even know where the ealdorman or Wulfheard is. And it's so dark that it's an effort to keep awake. I've not had enough sleep for days now. If the enemy abruptly lurched out of the darkness, I'm not sure I'd be able to defend myself adequately. Everything I do seems to be too long-drawn-out.

And on we go. The night drags, the moon little more than a thin orange slither that does nothing to light up the road. I can't help but think we must be getting close to the River Thames by now. It took us less time to reach the Isle of Sheppey, even with the time we've been moving slowly beneath the trees, trying to keep out of sight. And yet whatever water source I heard earlier has long since faded away, and I can't make out the sound of water close by. Wherever we are, we're still deep in Wessex territory, with many of the men wounded and sleep-deprived. If we have to fight – either the Wessex warriors, who hate us, or the Viking raiders, who we bloody hate – I can't see that we'll be able to put up a good enough force to combat them.

When Brute comes to an abrupt stop, his lack of forward movement wakes me from a half-sleep, and I startle. It's still too dark to see, and I can't hear a river, but it does seem that the horses have been brought to a halt for a reason. I wait, able to hear the murmur of men talking, the occasional fart from the horses, not the men, and even the odd snore. Someone other than me was asleep in their saddle.

A hand on my leg, and I jump, reaching for my seax.

'Be calm,' Wulfheard grunts. 'We rest here for a while. You can dismount. There's a stream where you can water Brute. Do it quickly, and don't get lost.' His caution is much needed because, somehow, it's darker, not lighter. I shake my head. It's the summer. The nights should be short, but this one has lasted an eternity. Looking up, I can see why. A thick bank of cloud obscures everything, and the wind has risen. I think we're going to get wet long before we reach the River Thames.

I grip Wulfheard's hand before he can move on.

'Where are we?' I hiss at him.

'Somewhere in Wessex,' is his less than helpful reply as he walks away, and I dismount to lead Brute to the water, bumping into others of the men and horses, soft apologies exchanged between us all. No one speaks other than that. No one dares risk a conversation, although I can hear the mutters of men relieving themselves or rustling in sacks for water bottles and what food we have left. I shiver, despite the heat of the summer night, and once more feel as though we're being watched.

'Where are we?' Edwin hisses to me as we make our way back from the stream.

'I don't know. I've never been to bloody Wessex before,' I snap, and then regret it. 'Sorry, Edwin, I really don't know. I'm not convinced anyone knows.'

'Are we still being pursued?' he asks, a wobble to his words that shows his fear.

'It certainly feels like it,' I confirm, sliding to my arse in what I hope is an area free from horseshit and piss. I have my sack behind me and lean against it, feeling all the jars of herbs against my back and shifting uncomfortably as my burns rub against my trews. I wear my byrnie still, and I stink, of the battle, of smoke from the burning buildings, of sweat and my fear. I should like nothing more than to remove all of my clothes and jump into the river, wiping it all from my skin.

I'm aware of voices around me, rustling, of the soft sounds of horses finally being allowed some rest. Their chewing is so loud, I fear they'll be heard in Mercia, and the thought brings a smirk to my lips that's still there when I wake, to bright sunshine and the leering face of Cenred.

'Get up, and come with me.' His words are clipped. 'Bring your weapons,' he further advises, and I scramble to my feet.

The horses are restless, but many still sleep, curled on the ground, so that I have to skip my way through them to follow Cenred, wincing as my muscles ache. He slips through a gap between the horses, and I follow him, attempting to make sense of where we are and what we're doing. I spare a thought for Lord Coenwulf. I really need to take a good look at him while it's light enough, but now is clearly not the time.

'What do you see?' Cenred demands from me as

we find a hedgerow in our way, and he pulls some of the branches aside.

'Where?' I demand to know, but then I understand. On the other side of our position is a roadway. It seems as though no one is about this early in the day, but such thoughts are merely wishful thinking because there is someone there, crouched low to the hedgerow on the other side of the road, that borders the fields there. I dare not breathe, unsure why Cenred would need me to see this single person, but then realisation dawns. If there's one person, then there's bound to be more. I reach for my seax and feel my fingers close around the comfort of its familiar hilt.

'Wait,' Cenred exhales. I look to him, quizzically, and he indicates I should carry on observing before doing anything else. I do as he says, straining to hear more, to see more, to understand what it is he wants me to know, and then I comprehend, and I turn to him, shaking my head, but he nods confidently.

Somehow, and I have no idea how, our enemy, who I believe are Wessex warriors, have spent the night on the far side of that other hedgerow, and now someone, by the looks of them a stray Viking raider, means to sneak up on them and steal all they have.

But there's only one of him, and while he crouches, he must be thinking about overpowering our enemy. Unless he's scouting and waiting for others to support him. Belatedly, I hear the sound of many horses and many men and realise that they've lit a fire to cook some food as well. Our enemy, on the far side of that hedgerow, is within spitting distance of catching us.

Eyes wide, I turn to Cenred again.

'We need to kill the bastard,' he murmurs, 'and I need your help to do so. If we kill him, then he won't arouse the suspicion of the Wessex scum, and we'll escape from here.'

'Shouldn't we just leave him?' I query.

'No,' Cenred confirms, his words barely above the sound of a breath. Now really isn't the time to argue, but I can't determine how we're to get through the thick hedgerow, with all its summer growth of bloody spikes and thorns, without giving ourselves away. I think the same problem is staying the hand of whoever thinks to attack the Wessex warriors. I turn to Cenred, and he beckons me on, walking further and further away from where the rest of our warriors and horses sleep. A deep sense of unease fills me with every step further. I think Cenred would have done better to wake everyone and move them on. Surely, I consider, we can't be far from crossing the River Thames now.

Only then I understand that Cenred doesn't mean to take us far away from the rest of my allies. There's a part of the hedge that doesn't quite join, and someone as slim as me can get through it, but not Cenred.

'No,' I hiss angrily. How am I supposed to make my way to the Viking raider without being seen? What if there are more of them?

'It has to be you,' he counters quickly, in little more than a whisper. 'No one else will fit.'

'Edwin,' I mouth. I can't believe that, once more, I must be the one to place myself in danger just because I know not to eat and drink everything I can get my hands on.

'Do it,' Cenred urges me, and I shake my head again, knowing that I'll have to do as he orders me. I don't like it, not one bit, but if we can keep more of the enemy from attacking us by just killing one man, then I'll have to do so. 'Get through and crawl along the drainage ditch,' Cenred advises me.

'As if you'd bloody do that,' I glower, but I know he's right. I can't just walk down the roadway, whistling as I go. I wish it were bloody dark again. I think I'd stand more chance then of doing what he suggests.

'Fine,' I eventually sigh. 'But if I bloody die, I'll bloody kill you,' I huff into his face, turning myself sideways so that I can try and slip through the thin area where the thick bramble-filled hedge hasn't grown. There'll be some reason for that. I don't need to know what it is. Immediately, I feel thorns digging into my legs. I growl softly and force myself onwards, trying to do so as quietly as possible, which is just about impossible.

I yank my arms, struggle to lift my feet and finally erupt on the other side of the gap, my eyes scouring the area for a sign that I've been heard. But there's a sharp turn in the road just ahead of me and, whomever the person is, is further along than that. If they've heard me, they've not taken the time to seek out the source of the noise. With a glare at the stinking drainage ditch, I lower myself into it.

'Keep your head down,' Cenred hisses unhelpfully. I'll tell him where to put his sodding head if he's not careful. All the same, I do as he advises and lower myself onto all fours, and begin to advance. The smell of the ditch is disgusting. If I didn't already smell of five days in the same clothes, I'd think twice about what I was doing.

I move quickly. I feel exposed and isolated. The only way to clamp down on the fear is to get this over and done with as soon as possible. Only when I reach the bend do I pause, lift my head, while lowering my arse, and scout the area ahead. I can hear Cenred's steps mirroring me from the other side of the hedgerow, and I'd sooner he wasn't there. It makes it too difficult to determine if I've been spotted.

But the figure still stoops on the far side of the road, about four horse lengths away. Now I just need to get to them and silence them before the other enemy hears what's happening. I'm sure they must have scouts on duty, but so far, I've not seen them, and on the other side of the road, the hedgerow is thick and filled with twisting weeds and nettles, as well as the thorns of the berries that won't show for a few months yet. We have it easier with a thinner hedgerow. I can see why the figure remains stationary. They must be waiting for someone. The thought worries me, and I turn to peer back along the way I've just come, but I can't hear anyone approaching at a gallop, and anyway, the person faces the other way. They must think themselves safe. Or they're too scared to move.

'Get on with it,' comes the less than reassuring

whisper of Cenred. I climb to my feet and with my hand on my seax, run towards my enemy. I can't think of another way of doing it. Whatever I do might alert them to my presence. Better to just try and sneak up on them in one offensive.

Holding my breath, I'm just within closing distance when startled eyes turn to face me, the inkings of the Viking raiders evident on the man's face now that I can see him. He opens his mouth to shout, or shriek, or some such, but I merely use it as an excuse to plunge my seax into his open mouth so that it grates over his blackened teeth.

His hand snakes out, gripping my hand, holding it firm, and I release my grip, allowing him to hold the seax blade that kills him. I know it's the way of his people. He shudders in death. Quickly, I grab and lower him as soon as his body's stopped shaking. His death has been quick, and I can leave him here, in the drainage ditch, and hopefully, whatever force is on the other side of the hedgerow will never even know he was there.

Wincing at the noise of scraping teeth over the iron of my blade, I extract my seax, and move to peer through the gap in the hedgerow the man was using. Through it, I witness a large force of Wessex warriors, a fire with a few cookpots wedged into the side of it, and many horses corralled to the far side of the field. Whatever crops were being grown here, barley, I think, the stalks have all been trampled down, and I realise these men have been here for a lot longer than we've been in Wessex. Have we ridden past them, not once, but twice? These aren't the men who've chased us this far, that's for a certainty. Hastily, I step back, keen to return to the rest of the Mercians and ensure we leave here quickly. Only as I do so, I catch my weapons belt on a reaching thorn. I slice it with my blade, wincing as the sharp spikes try to embed themselves in my gloves. I turn to move aside, but before I do, I take one more quick look and then rear backwards. A hazel eye meets mine, and I gasp. I've been discovered.

In my fear, I tangle with the lifeless limbs of the man I've just killed and fall heavily in the drainage ditch. I bang my already bruised knee, ears listening for an alert from the man who saw me before springing to my feet and hurrying back to where I can force myself through the small gap in the hedgerow.

I erupt into the field beyond, where Cenred is waiting for me, his eyes wild. I'm sure he knows what's happened, but he shakes his head, grabs my arm, and pulls me down.

'They're not doing anything,' he informs me.

'What?'

'Whoever saw you isn't doing anything about it. They've not raised the alarm. Maybe they think you're just a child or a lone traveller. They didn't see you kill the man.'

I can hardly hear Cenred over the thundering of my heart, but I realise he's right. There's no sound of a war band being roused to a fight. If anything, it's even quieter than it was when I went to find the solitary figure of the Viking raider. I consider where the rest of the Viking raiders are. I can't imagine the man being alone.

'Come on, we'll get back to the others,' Cenred informs me when he's happy that nothing's going to happen. I shake my head. I can't believe that we're going to get away from this unscathed. But, then, we're probably not, for the war band are sure to hear us when we move on. How we've made it past them in the night is a miracle worthy of some saint's life. I can't see that we'll manage to continue our journey without being seen. Only then, something catches my eye in the distance. A bank of what I thought was the low-hanging grey cloud, but it's nothing of the sort. It's the River Thames, and we just need to reach it without being discovered.

23

'Where have you been?' Wulfheard's voice thrums with anger and, perhaps, fear as Cenred and I slip back into the camp. I hold a finger to my lips, and his eyebrows come together in a fury. 'What?'

'The enemy, just the other side of the bloody hedgerow,' I murmur at him. His eyes flash from me to Cenred, and he shakes his head in disbelief and drops his voice to a whisper, even though he's just about woken everyone else with his initial question.

'How many of them?'

'Impossible to tell, but enough. And they were already being hunted as well,' Cenred confirms. 'Icel killed the Viking raider who was stalking them, and now that man lies dead in the ditch, but we need to decide whether to leave here or wait for them to depart first. We risk the rest of the dead men's comrades finding him, should we linger.'

The ealdorman joins us, his head turning between the three of us, so that he can see out of his one eye, as Cenred repeats what we've told Wulfheard.

An unexpected flicker of fear flashes on his fatigued face. Like me, Ealdorman Ælfstan realises that our tenuous luck must end eventually.

'I can see the river,' I inform him, in case that makes a decision. I keep wincing at the noises the other men and horses are making as they wake and begin to move around. To my ears, it's as though they bang weapons against their shields in the way of our Viking raider enemy. Any moment now, I expect the Viking raiders, or the Wessex warriors billeted, perhaps like we were, on this side of the River Thames, just waiting for the enemy to arrive, to discover us.

'Yes, but the tide's wrong,' Wulfheard confirms. 'Landwine went out under cover of darkness to check. We must wait, he believes, until at least midday to be able to attempt the crossing. But,' and Wulfheard pauses, the attempt at a smile on his shaggy-bearded face, 'he did find a ship.'

That means we'll be able to get Lord Coenwulf across the river, provided some of us can use the oars.

'We'll have to wait,' the ealdorman confirms slowly, peering around as though our enemy is about to attack us, his eye wild, his movements jerky. 'We can't be exposed. Were they Viking raiders or Wessex warriors?'

'Wessex warriors, but the man I killed was a Viking raider.'

'Then they might be camped here to counter the Viking raiders. We're really not far from the river. We'll set up guards. Icel, you know where they are. Cenred can get some sleep, and you can keep watch on them.'

But Cenred shakes his head. 'No, I have a better idea.' He smirks, looking upwards at the overhanging trees, and I'm already shaking my head.

'I'm not going up there,' I growl, but Cenred smiles again.

'I didn't ask you to. I've always been good at climbing trees. If I can get above the main treeline, then I can keep a watch from there,' he determines.

'What? All the way up there?' I exclaim, only to clamp my hand over my mouth for being so loud. The majority of the trees must extend far above our heads, and there's one tree, I imagine it might have stood when the Romans held sway over this island, which is even taller.

But Cenred merely grins and makes his way over to the base of the tree trunk. He stands back and gazes at it for a moment, and then I watch, mouth open, as he pulls himself upwards, from limb to limb, until he's all but hidden behind some of the branches and leaves, and still, I can hear him rustling upwards.

'But how will he tell us?' I question. If he shouts to us, then the enemy will hear.

'He'll think of a way,' Wulfheard confirms, striding off to order some of the men to guard positions.

'I'll go back and keep an eye on them through the hedgerow,' I confirm to Ealdorman Ælfstan, not looking forward to it.

'If they're just moving on, then we don't need to know more than to keep quiet,' the ealdorman announces. How I'm supposed to determine that, I'm unsure. All the same, I bow my head and forge a path back through the branches to where Cenred first summoned me.

All seems quiet. I spare a thought for the man I killed. Perhaps he wasn't up to no good. Only I know he was. The morning stretches, the sun rising high in the sky, the heat intense behind the hedgerow despite the bank of clouds, and I find myself sweating and shifting uncomfortably. The voices of men shouting one to another are loud in the still air, but the Wessex warriors make no move. It seems they're to stay in position for a while longer or until the summer passes in its entirety. Certainly, their camp is substantial. I pass much of the time trying to catch sight of Cenred in the tall tree. But the sun is so bright it hurts my eyes to keep looking upward. Once more, I see an eagle, high overhead, its screeches strangely comforting. I consider what it can see and which I wish I could see.

And then I startle, the sound of mounted horses reaching my ears. I peer through the hedgerow, but it doesn't seem to be coming from over there. The Wessex men are oblivious, the smell of pottage and meat cooking assuring me that they're not breaking camp anytime soon. And yet the sound of hooves grows ever louder. I look back at the way we've come, standing back from the side of the tall hedgerow in the hope that I might be able to find an angle that allows me to see along the road towards the east, but it's impossible. I'm sure Cenred must have seen something, and yet no one beckons me back to Brute. Whatever's happening, the ealdorman has decided to let it happen.

The sound grows closer and closer, and I return to the hedgerow, my eye peering through a small gap where the twisting branches of the thorns aren't quite so tightly woven. I clutch my seax tightly as soon as I see the riders. I can't tell how many of them there are, but there are enough of them, and of course, they wear the wyvern of Wessex daubed on shields and byrnies. These men, then, I believe, are those that have been following us.

'Hail,' the leading man calls to those on the far side of the hedgerow. Just as I thought, they're all Wessex men.

'My lord,' a voice replies.

'How did you get in there?' is the quarrelsome reply.

'There's a gap, a little further along.'

'Then why make camp there?' I wish I knew who was speaking.

'We get a better view here, my lord, of traffic coming along the road.'

A disgruntled harrumph meets those words. 'And have you seen anyone?' he asks. I'm holding my breath, sure that someone will see the dead body. How, I consider, can they miss it? It must be directly between the two men who converse. The horses breathe heavily, recovering from their canter along the road. And the men dismount, relieve themselves in the ditches so that the smell of piss fills the air.

I look towards the tall tree, hoping that Cenred's hidden, even as I listen to the men, holding my breath, and when I must breathe, taking only shallow breaths.

'No, no one at all.'

'Truly? There have been reports of fighting on the Isle of Sheppey? And that the enemy came this way?'

'Then they've not passed us here, for we'd have heard them,' the voice responds, an edge of anger to it. Whoever speaks doesn't like being questioned. I wish I knew who spoke. I wish I knew who the man was leading the mounted group.

'Then we must turn around. We've evidently ridden past them, hiding no doubt somewhere along the road.'

'Who were they?' the voice from behind the hedgerow demands.

'Viking raiders,' the mounted warrior announces confidently.

'Then why was there fighting on the Isle of Sheppey?' I curse the man behind the hedge, who's clearly given more thought to this than the mounted warrior.

'What do you mean?'

'Why fight on the Isle of Sheppey and escape this way if they're Viking raiders?'

'They must be from another ship. Perhaps rivals?' the mounted warrior confirms, without even pausing for thought. 'Keep a good lookout. We can't allow them to get further inland. I'll take my warriors back the way we came. We're sure to find them, and then we can kill the arseholes.'

'Aye, my lord. I'll double the watch,' the voice confirms, and the sound of the horses being forced to turn reaches my ears. I still can't believe they haven't found the dead man. Surely, I can't have hidden him that well? Or, perhaps they're so used to finding abandoned bodies that no one has thought to mention it.

And then, just as I think we might weather this storm, I hear an outraged shriek.

'What's the matter?' the mounted warrior demands.

'There's a dead Viking raider here,' a startled man informs him. I can't see, but I imagine him pointing down at the body.

'What?' Two voices chorus at the same time, and I turn, catch sight of Edwin furiously beckoning me onwards from the shelter of the trees. While the two groups of warriors discuss what they've discovered with voices loud enough to wake the dead man, I turn and begin to make my way back towards the trees we've hidden beneath. I hope the sounds of the loud argument drown out my movements and that no one thinks to examine what's happening on this side of the hedgerow. Equally, I want no one to look towards the tall oak tree, for I can see the tree visibly shaking as Cenred must hasten to the ground.

'We're leaving,' Edwin huffs to me as soon as I'm close enough that he can tell me without shouting. 'Hurry up,' he urges. Once more, I try to move quickly but struggle to do so. Brute is waiting for me, my possessions affixed to the saddle, but the crush of horses and the small donkey make it difficult to get to his side. I spy Cenred moving swiftly towards his horse while Wulfheard leads those who are more prepared than us northwards. He must mean to take us directly to the river, along sheep paths, rather than risk the roadway, where our enemy searches for us.

I finally mount and bend low to follow the rest of the horses and men. I've not had time to check on Lord Coenwulf or Waldhere. I'll have to do so when we make it across the river – if we make it across the river.

Oswy is at the back of our small group as we emerge into the bright daylight. Ahead, I just see

Wulfheard leading the group on, but the river seems further away, not closer. I look over my shoulder, expecting to see we're being chased. The land dips lower as it reaches the river. I'm sure the Wessex warriors will see us soon. Certainly, I can see the line of the roadway more clearly, the two hedgerows demarcating it easily. Just because I can't see them doesn't mean they won't be able to see us.

'Eyes forward,' Oswy calls to me, his voice pitched so it just carries over the sound of the horses' hooves thudding over the hard earth. It's a very different sound to that of horses on the stone roads, but still, all will know what it is.

My hand sneaks towards my seax, but I return it to the reins. Brute is keen to go faster than the horses in front. I need him to keep his head, or he might be the one to give us away by upsetting the rest of the mounts. One of the horses in front is Frithwine's, riderless and likely to spook if Brute doesn't behave himself. Perhaps, I realise, I should have counted the horses rather than the men when trying to determine who was missing. My eyes snake down the line, looking for the easily identifiable marks of the horses. Edwin leads Frithwine's horse. Æthelmod's is ahead as well, but I can't determine who leads that horse. We're in such tight formation, but then we come to a sudden dip, and stretching ahead, I can see all of the men and horses, and I realise, as I should have done long ago, that someone else is gone. There are three riderless horses, not two.

Worry gnaws at me. Who else is missing? I hope it's not Waldhere. I'm sure his wound shouldn't have killed him yet. I also feel a burst of self-loathing. I ought to have done more to determine who still rode at my side, not less. Only then the sound I've been dreading can be clearly heard behind me. I glance over my shoulder to where Oswy is preparing to encourage his mount onwards.

The Wessex warriors have found us.

* * *

'Hurry up,' Oswy urges me, and his words spark a response from those ahead as well. Edwin's terrified eyes meet mine, and he encourages his two horses to greater speed. Brute is nipping at Frithwine's horse's tail, whereas Oswy almost overtakes me in his haste to get away from the thunder of advancing hooves. Brother Eadgar is at least far ahead with Wulfheard. His poor donkey won't be able to canter as fast as the remainder of the horses, but it's doing its best, spurred on by the horse with legs twice as long as it has.

We need to make it to the river, but what do we do once we're there? We can't just plunge into the water. What of Lord Coenwulf? What of the horses with their saddles and harnesses? What of us? I wish I'd been able to count how many might be chasing us. We beat the Viking raiders on the Isle of Sheppey, but it was dark, and they were at a disadvantage, for we knew where they were, although they didn't know we were there. Now, the enemy can see us and no doubt can count us as Wulfheard leads us on. The pace of the horses has increased, but I'm not sure by enough. Wulfheard has Lord Coenwulf behind him. The sled will slow Bada, and if Bada can't go faster, then neither can the rest of us. And Brother Eadgar is between the sled and the next rider. We should have given him a horse to ride, not the damn donkey.

I reach for my waist and check my seax is still there. I need to stop doubting my weapons, only I can see a problem up ahead, and we're going to have to stop and fight the enemy. Either that, or we risk leaving Lord Coenwulf behind when he's the very reason that we're here, deep in Wessex territory.

Oswy must realise our conundrum as well.

'Stay with me,' he urges, racing alongside me, for

all the strip of ground we ride over is only just wide enough for both horses. The fields have been harvested. The rich loam of the soil stretches brown in the distance. Perhaps it's for this reason that the Wessex warriors have been stationed by the woodland? Maybe King Ecgberht was determined that his people should feel safe to gather in the crops and sent warriors to protect them.

By rights, we should be able to allow the horses to run over it, but the soil is claggy, soft in some places and even softer in others. The horses won't be able to keep to their hooves over that, and neither will we should we dismount and try to run.

'I will,' I shout to him. Ealdorman Ælfstan's men will have to aid Wulfheard and Lord Coenwulf to escape through the rapidly approaching hedgerow. If it were just Wulfheard and Bada, they could risk jumping it. I can't truly tell how high the straggling hedge reaches, but they could try it. But not with the sled. Neither, I think, will the riderless horses be encouraged to escape that way. Ideally, we need another means to flee the field's confines before our enemy catches us. Just to the other side, or so I convince myself, is the river, and, hopefully, the ship that's been found so that Lord Coenwulf can escape. I do wonder why we were heading towards the hedge when one of our numbers went this way earlier. Surely, they should have known it was blocked?

I can hear the Wessex warriors now. Their shouted words are indecipherable, swept away with the speed of our passage, but they're advancing, getting closer and closer. And as of yet, there's no way to bolt.

Ahead, I see Ealdorman Ælfstan bring his mount to an abrupt stop, mud flying up from beneath its hooves. His intentions are clear. We need to face down the enemy while others make good their escape. Ælfstan allows some to pass, Edwin amongst them, but Wulfgar and Landwine settle beside him, turning their horses, and force me and Oswy to rein in our horses or face colliding with them.

'Five of us?' I question, wheeling Brute tightly so that Oswy can join the small grouping, blocking those who try to escape behind us.

'Cenred says there are no more than twenty-five,' Ealdorman Ælfstan informs me.

'So, five each,' I muse, my eyes on the men racing towards us. Their horses seem to be almost beyond control, the downward slope of the field making them speedy. Will they, I consider, stop or just barrel through us?

'We need to hold them until the others can get

the small gate opened, Coenwulf off the sled and then be on their way,' Ælfstan informs me, dismounting and reaching for his shield.

'We're getting down to fight them?' I almost squeak. I really don't like this idea.

'Yes. We're not going to fight mounted. There's not enough room.'

We're hemmed in now by more than just uneven soil. There's also a stream or a purpose-built drainage ditch running down the side of the field. Yet, Ælfstan, now that we've all dismounted, urges us backwards, the horses leading the way as they recover their breath.

'We only need to guard a small area, in the far corner,' he informs, his good eye flashing as he holds his shield defensively, his seax ready to stab and slash. 'There's no other way out of here. I've been assured of that. So, we hold them off and kill as many as we can. Just down there is the river.' I encourage Brute to move aside. I don't want him wounded in what's about to happen. Standing beside the ealdorman, I look up and face those coming towards us. There aren't that many of them, admittedly, but the horses seem huge, much larger than our own, and they're not slowing.

'And if they don't stop?' I query, wishing my voice didn't squeak on the final word.

'Then we'll kill them as they ride past,' Oswy growls.

'Easier said than done,' I counter, but then, there's no more time to talk.

The enemy is there. I see their eyes. I feel the ground thundering beneath my feet, and the first horse crashes between us. I dance aside, almost falling into the drainage ditch, but Ælfstan's even quicker. He jumps upwards, thrusting his shield against the rider. I watch the man as his grip on the reins falters, and he lurches towards me, where I'm trying to keep on my feet. I stab upwards with my shield and seax, more to keep him away from me than anything, and as he falls to the floor, limbs flying in the air, my seax somehow slices into his belly, my shield knocking against his face and ex-posing his neck. Not that I need to cut through it. He falls heavily to the floor, a sharp snap of broken bone assuring me that he won't be getting up anytime soon.

The next rider thinks to do the same, but his horse is far from as convinced. I risk stepping into its path, feet behind the dying man, and the animal rears upwards, almost as straight as a warrior with only two legs. The rider isn't prepared for such a move, his hands holding seax and war axe. He slides down the horse, and lands, arse first, on the ground. Ælfstan makes the killing stroke, the man's weapons falling from his hands with the force of his fall.

The next rider is quicker to react. He pulls his horse to one side, the animal leaving huge holes in the claggy soil in the wake of its passage, struggling to control its forward momentum. I leave him to Ælfstan, Wulfgar and Landwine, for that man has done the right thing in pulling aside, but others don't.

The two horseless riders mill around, unsure what to do, looking back the way they've come, so that by the time the next two riders are close enough to threaten us, I've slapped the one animal hard on its backside, and it runs at them, not away from them. The two men are forced to veer aside into the soggy, clarty soil. One of the horses is unable to collect its legs beneath it, and another of the enemy falls to the ground. Only his landing is softer, and I know he'll be coming at us.

'Dismount,' a Wessex warrior roars at those still coming towards us, but they either ignore his words or don't hear them. Despite the broken bodies of their comrades, and the riderless horses now racing up the slope, desperate to get away, the others remain mounted. They must think themselves better riders than the others. It's the way of some men not to admit to a lack, but to see it in others.

'Come on,' Ealdorman Ælfstan glowers at them, his words thrumming through his chest. I've bloodied my blade, but little else, while Wulfgar, the furthest away along our short line, is engaged with the man who fell to the ground. He's powered his way to Wulfgar's side, but his face glistens with sweat, and in some places, he sinks up to his calves in the mud. All the same, he swings his blade towards Wulfgar, while Wulfgar attacks him side-on, not wanting to allow the man to reach where the rest of our warriors are still stripping Coenwulf from the sled to get him through the thin gap in the hedge. Brother Eadgar and the donkey are already on the other side. I can't see that it's the usual way for people to access the field, but perhaps the warm summer has encouraged the twisting vines to knit more tightly together than usual.

Three horses gallop towards us, the riders clutching weapons and, no doubt, hoping to stab us with their spears. I'd sooner step aside from them, but Oswy holds firm beside me, as does Ealdorman Ælfstan. I can just about hear the angry voices of my fellow Mercians but I can't determine what they're saying. I take it as a bad sign. They clearly haven't managed to get Lord Coenwulf through the gap just yet. We need to fight on.

The first of the spears flies through the air, the rider choosing to launch it at us, as though we're fighting shield wall to shield wall. But his aim is appalling, and it thuds into the ground behind us with a resounding twang. Quickly, I force Oswy aside.

'What the—?' he exclaims, but then the horse runs on to the thrown spear, the crack of wood through the horse's chest shocking to hear. The animal's legs collapse beneath it, a soft sign escaping from its pink-rimmed gums. I rush to stab into the man, his legs trapped beneath that of his horse. The damn fool.

'Come on, we're through.' The welcome words reach me. I want to turn and dash to safety, but there are still too many of the enemy, and they've realised it's impossible to overpower us while remaining mounted when we're not.

The man Wulfgar fights goes down with a howl of pain and lies twitching on the ground, while eight of our enemies have dismounted, and come towards us, shields in hands. Those on the edges of the short line struggle not to fall in the drainage ditch or get stuck in the claggy soil, but they still outnumber us. They look fiery and very, very angry.

'Mercian scum,' the leading warrior spits. 'What are you doing here?' he glowers.

'Doing your bloody job for you,' Ealdorman Ælfstan retorts. 'Killing your enemy.'

'I doubt that,' the man counters. 'You've come to steal something of ours. Something you think should really be yours. Well, know this, the rest of our men will soon intersect yours. There's no way you're going to evade us.'

I spare a thought for those racing towards the River Thames. I hope they reach it. I hope they get Lord Coenwulf back to his wife. But I'm far from convinced that I will. The Wessex warriors look fierce, scars on chins and along exposed arms, assuring me that this isn't their first fight. These are seasoned men of Wessex, just as we're seasoned men of Mercia, and they outnumber us.

Wulfgar's slain his man. And I've finished off another two, but the Wessex warriors are filled with resolve. A pity they didn't take it to the Isle of Sheppey and kill the Viking raiders there. It seems we've done it for them, and now they want to fight us. Damn them all.

'We came to retrieve something, yes, but a man,

not a thing,' Ælfstan offers, and I'm unsure why he's telling him such secrets. What good can that do us? 'He was taken by our enemy to the Isle of Sheppey. We took him back.'

This does seem to give the man pause. Perhaps he's seen the smoke from the island. Maybe he realises we've done them all a favour. Only then his lips curl into laughter, and he looks along his line of men.

'Then, we thank you for killing those maggots. But, now, we'll kill you and have away with your man, after all. If you've gone this far to reclaim him, he must be worth a pretty coin to someone.' Greed lights his face, and I want to punch the smirk from it. But I don't. Not yet. Now isn't the time to let anger dictate the outcome of this fight. 'Kill 'em,' the man instructs his fellow warriors. They advance towards us, growling and leering. I swallow down my sweat and fear and prepare to meet the blades of men who think of stealing my life. Bastards.

The attack is quick. They don't delay, no doubt keen to get to Lord Coenwulf.

I lift my shield and meet the axe attack from the warrior before me. He's tall. Taller than me, and his reach means that he doesn't need to get close enough that I can use an offensive more likely to be found in a wrestling match. The blow sends a strange sensation down my shield hand, and before I can do anything more, he follows up the clout with another. The crash and clatter of wood and iron, the huff and grunts of men trying to stay alive, fills the summer day.

I finally manage to stab out over the top of my shield, but the man, closing on me because he thinks he can overcome me so easily, veers aside, and I don't so much manage a slice on his neck.

Beside me, Oswy is battling against another of our enemies. He's moved outwards, allowing a small gap to form between the two of us, and I use it to step slightly aside and then angle towards the right-hand side of my opponent, but my left. Only now does my seax blade get anywhere near him as I use my shield to knock his arm aside, his grip on the war axe not lessening, but his next swing goes wild. My seax leaves a trailing line of blood on his arm. He winces with the pain, eyes visible beneath his helm. I step back into position, Oswy forced to retreat a step or two, and the space seems even tighter now.

I can't determine how my allies fare, apart from Oswy and Landwine. Landwine is struggling against his enemy. The man's attack seems wild, and poorly timed, but there's a terrible rhythm to it as he attempts to tire Landwine. He crosses into my path, and although it leaves me temporarily unprotected, I use my shield to knock against one of his flailing arms, disrupting his plans to down Landwine.

I offer him a smirk, but the man I face takes advantage of my distraction, his blade slicing down my byrnie. I feel its heft, but luckily my byrnie holds. I'll be bruised, but I'm not bleeding.

'Mercian scum,' he growls at me, no doubt disappointed not to find me bleeding and on the ground.

'Wessex bastard,' I counter, thinking the pair of us are putting the lyrical verse of the scop songs we've heard to good effect.

I can feel my arms starting to tire. I've been awake for hours, and Mercia is just within sight. If we can just beat this enemy, and get back to the rest of the men before the remaining Wessex warriors overwhelm them.

I stab upwards, hoping to find his belly, but he jumps back, using his war axe to counter the blow. I tighten my grip and just manage to keep hold of my seax as my right arm swings out wide. Punching upwards with my shield, half of his body exposed, I finally manage to land a decent blow with my shield hitting his chin. I feel the bite of his teeth snapping as they're smashed together. And I use my seax arm to keep his war axe away from me, the two weapons slightly tangled. I jab again, shield into his chin, but this time he tries to move his head aside, exposing his throat. If only my seax weren't so far away, I'd take his life now.

I drop my shield, knowing it's hindering me not helping, and before it can land on the ground, I curl my fist and slam it into his throat. Wild eyes meet mine as he endeavours to suck in much-needed air, but it's impossible as I punch him again. And then again. His war axe spirals towards me, the last act of a desperate man, but he's dying, and he knows it.

His frantic eyes hold mine, and with my seax in hand, I slash it across his throat, ending his life a little more quickly before bending for my shield. I'm breathing heavily. The man was a beast to overcome.

'About time,' Oswy murmurs, and only then do I realise that while I've been fighting only one man, my allies have overcome all the others.

'Sorry,' I huff, but my thoughts are on the rest of our men. 'We need to get to the others.' I'm already turning to lurch to Brute and then continue our dash towards the river.

'We do, yes,' Ealdorman Ælfstan murmurs. His movements seem slow, his words dazed.

I turn back and glower at him.

'Where are you wounded?' I demand, running

my eyes up and down his body, looking for some sign of blood other than his swollen eye and wounded right arm from the fight on the Isle of Sheppey.

'It's nothing,' the ealdorman murmurs, but I've seen enough wounded men to know that he's lying. I move to him, avoiding the twitching limbs of the last of our enemies to die and run my hands up and down his body. The fact that Ælfstan doesn't stop me gives me even more cause to worry. He must be losing blood. A lot of it, but from where I don't know. All the way down his legs I pat, checking for blood at the top of his thighs, but it's only when I turn him around that I realise the problem. And I have no idea how he's managed to get such a wound.

Blood soaks the top of his byrnie, a seax blade still embedded to the left of his right shoulder blade.

'Arse,' I exclaim. It's not an easy place to staunch the bleeding from. Not when we need to be on our horses and hurrying towards the rest of our men. Neither is it simple for me just to rip the seax loose.

'What is it?' Ælfstan's voice is dreamy and seems to come from far away.

'Get his horse,' I urge. I need to get Ealdorman Ælfstan far from here, and quickly. 'Now,' I growl, fearful the ealdorman will stumble to his knees and that it'll take us too long to get him back on his feet.

I eye the seax uneasily. If we have to ride quickly, it won't stay in place. And if it comes loose without me having something to stop the blood, the ealdorman might even die.

'Bugger,' I exclaim. I'll have to remove the seax before we do anything else. 'Hold him,' I urge Landwine, rushing to reach Brute. My horse is wild-eyed, pawing at the ground, the smell of blood and the battle that happened just in front of him unsettling his already difficult nature.

I reach for my supplies, a calming hand on Brute's neck, which he completely ignores, moving his rear away from me so that I have to reach much further to get what I need.

'Stand still,' I urge him. 'Come on, lad, stand still.' My words are surprisingly soft considering my thoughts. They tumble, one over another, concern for the ealdorman making every future scenario form in my mind.

I shake my head, grab my supplies, and hasten back to the ealdorman. His horse is there, and Ealdorman Ælfstan uses the animal to stay upright. I'm pleased he's not yet mounted.

'Hurry up, Icel,' Oswy urges me. He's already astride his horse. I consider that he can see the rest of our group. Does he know they're under attack?

Wulfgar has collected the reins of our enemy's horses, and he mounts as well, having looped reins together so that only one of us need lead the animals.

'I need to do this,' I urge Oswy.

I don't have fire to close the wound. I'll have to pack it with linens and hope that we'll soon get time to stop so that I can stitch it tight. I'm sure it shouldn't be bleeding as much as it is. I fear the ealdorman has done himself worse damage than I can cure.

'This will hurt,' I caution, repeating my oft-spoken words, and with a handful of linen in one hand, I swiftly pull the seax free and drop it to the ground. In only a moment, the linens are sodden. I shake my head while the ealdorman bucks beneath my ministrations. 'Hold still, please,' I urge Ælfstan. I grip yet more linens and hold them over the wound, trying to get a better look at it. But it's only a small cut through his byrnie. I want to thrust enough linens through it that it will act as a makeshift bandage as we mount up and ride for the River Thames.

Again, the linen is quickly sodden, and I drop it to the ground. Hastily, I replace it, and this time, aware that Oswy is urging me silently on, I poke the linen through the small gap in the byrnie. It's not enough, far from enough.

'We need to hurry.' Even Ælfstan urges me now.

'Fine, mount up but don't use your right arm. Try not to move it all. It's still bleeding heavily.' My words sound more confident than I'm feeling. Three dead men already, Lord Coenwulf still insensible, and now Ealdorman Ælfstan is badly wounded as well. None of this is going well.

I aid an unsteady Ælfstan into his saddle and quickly grip my sack and return to Brute. The others are already moving on through the narrow gap that trapped us in the field in the first place. I come last of all, stooping to yank a valuable-looking cross from around the neck of one of the dead Wessex men. I don't want the gold and silver for myself. I know that Wynflæd will put its hefty weight to good use.

Brute is eager to get away from the lifeless bodies, and he quickly picks up speed, as we chase down the rest of our men along a field boundary. Here the crops have yet to be harvested, and the stalks stretch high, making it difficult to see what happens in front or behind us. I try and keep an eye on Ælfstan, but he's at the centre of our small group, with Wulfgar and the train of riderless horses between us.

I'm pleased to see the river getting closer and closer the further down the slope we go. I'm re-minded then that I was told there would be a ship for Lord Coenwulf. I'm going to have to ensure the ealdorman gets in it as well. He won't be able to swim across. He'll be too weak from bleeding, and if he moves his arm as much as required to swim, he'll also dislodge any scab that tries to form. I only hope he'll listen to me.

I can see that many horses have passed this way before us; the ground churned up and heavy with the marks of those animals forced to wear horseshoes to protect their hooves. I don't know if that means just our warriors or more of the Wessex men. From ahead, a cry ripples through the air, and my hand reaches for my bloodied seax, yet it's not a cry of outrage but rather one of welcome.

I rein Brute in before we stumble onto the muddy banks of the river, mud flying backwards through the air. Wild eyes look around, and I see that there's been a bloody fight here. Brute's front hooves thunk into the chest of a dead man, and I spit cold blood from my mouth.

Ahead, some of the men are already making their way across the River Thames, and my heart sinks. The ship is there as well, almost halfway across, Brother Eadgar and the donkey inside it as well as Lord Coenwulf. How then am I to get the slumped ealdorman across the river?

Hastily, I dismount while, all around me, men call

one to another, Wulfgar keen to have the riderless horses ready for their swim. I can see he's determined not to leave them behind, as he hastens to remove saddles that will make it difficult for them to swim, although he keeps their reins on them. They'll be valuable.

I take a hasty count of the dead Wessex warriors, hoping not to see any of the Mercian men amongst their number, but my focus is really on Ealdorman Ælfstan, so much so that, while I look, I don't truly see. Ælfstan is entirely slumped in his saddle. I reach up and run my hand over his back which is drenched. I'd like to think it was merely sweat from our exertion, but I know it's not.

'How bad is it?' Wulfheard asks me. The ealdorman hardly seems aware of what's happening around him.

'Bad. I wanted him in the ship. He can't swim, that's for sure.'

'Are all the enemy dead?' Wulfheard calls to Uor, the only man not to have already begun to make his way across the river, as he struggles to remove his byrnie. His feet flashing palely on the slick mud.

'I think so,' Uor calls, his words filled with concern, his face almost as bleached as the ealdorman's.

'We have the time,' Wulfheard assures me. I look

at him, feeling hopeless. Whatever I do won't survive the water.

'We need the ship back.' I jut my chin out defiantly. I know I'm right. Ealdorman Ælfstan can't swim.

'But it's nearly in Mercia?' Wulfheard growls. But he knows I'm right. Once more, I reach for my sack of supplies and pull forth more of what I need.

'If we get him down, I can tend to him, but they'll be no point if he's going in the water.' I don't allow any doubt to enter my voice. 'So, tell me,' and I fix Wulfheard and Uor with a glower, 'what do you want me to do?' I hold my hands steady, close to the ealdorman. Wulfheard looks from me to the unresponsive ealdorman and then at the expanse of the river before us. The ship is still in sight, but it's nearly on the far bank. We can't shout for them to bring it back. If we want it, someone will have to go over there and get it back.

'Arse,' Wulfheard huffs, moving to the ealdorman. With more care than I expect, he pulls Ælfstan from the saddle and lies him away from any of the dead bodies. 'Do what you can, and I'll go and get the ship. Uor, you stay here, and you, Oswy. But the rest of you, you're coming with me. You can keep your horses,' he further determines. 'If you have to swim for it, then swim for it. If you have to leave the ealdorman, then leave him, but make sure the Wessex bastards know he's too valuable to be cut into pieces.'

I don't like the sound of that, but my focus is on the ealdorman. Hastily, I use my seax to cut through the thick material of his byrnie and expose his back, seeing the many scars of previous wounds. Not that they concern me. It's the small but deep wound that absorbs my attention.

I reach for more linens and also for a plug of moss. It's in such an awkward position. I wish I knew how he obtained such an injury. But that doesn't matter. I need to determine a way of stopping the bleeding. The wound weeps, although much less than it did before. There's a small scab forming over the bloody gash. It would be fine if I could rely on him lying here until it was healed. But we need to move him.

Biting my lip, I consider what I should do, and then, knowing Wulfheard will return much sooner than I think he will, I set to work. I disturb the scab, needle in hand, and knowing the pig's gut will be inflexible because it's not been heated, I start to pull the skin together. I do it quickly, not caring to make it neat and tidy. The work will have to be undone and redone soon enough, or the reddened skin will surely take the wound rot. I don't want to swill the River Thames water over the wound, and I have no ale or wine with me. Neither will the others. I have only so much vinegar left, and it's not enough. I use it all the same, the sharp smell assaulting my nostrils and stinging my hands.

Oswy and Uor stand a guard around me and the prone ealdorman. Neither of them talks. Neither do they offer me any thoughts about what I'm doing as I tie the wound shut, add the moss, with vinegar soaked into it, and then add yet more linens to cover it. I notice that Oswy has removed his boots, and pre-pared his horse for the river crossing. I need to do the same.

'Help me,' I eventually ask. The only way to keep the linens and moss in place is to tie a long bandage around Ealdorman Ælfstan's chest and back. It's an effort, but we finally have it done, and not a moment too soon. I hear the scraping of the ship over the mudbanks and look up. Wulfheard is there, along with Edwin, Landwine and Osmod. None of them looks happy.

'Hurry up,' Wulfheard calls, and between us, we bend to collect Ealdorman Ælfstan and take him to the ship. His still body is heavy and unresponsive, and it's an effort to slide him over the low sides of the ship, the bilge filled with filthy water, and something that I think must be donkey shit. Only with the aid of everyone do we get him aboard, and then, just as I think we can all breathe a little more freely, do I hear the thunder of yet more horses coming to investigate what's happening.

'Push us into the river,' Wulfheard grunts, Edwin and Landwine ready with oars for when they should be deep enough to use them.

'What about us?' I pant.

'You'll have to swim,' Wulfheard cautions. 'Get the horses and bloody swim,' he growls as the murky River Thames water covers my boots as the ship finally floats free. 'And I'd be bloody quick about it,' he adds, the roar of the Wessex warriors easy to hear as they sight their dead comrades.

'Bloody wonderful,' I puff, racing for Brute.

24

Glancing behind, I can see where mounted warriors rush towards us. I wish I'd not thought to look because there are too many of them. Brute is already knee-deep in the water, and I hasten to grab his reins and pull them over his saddle so that they won't tangle his legs in the water, even while I'm removing my byrnie. I don't want to swim in that. It'll be too heavy when it's saturated with water. And I can't remove Brute's saddle either, or I'll have to leave it, and everything tied to it, here.

One quick look towards the ship, and I see that they're already making good time. They're out of spear shot, but I'm not.

'Hurry up,' I urge myself again, walking into the

river so that it covers my waist. Only then do I begin to swim, Brute beside me. His eyes are focused only on where we're going. Oswy and Uor are already ahead. I hope the bloody Wessex warriors won't follow us. And if they do, that none of the buggers can swim.

Water swirls around me as I keep close to Brute. I feel the current trying to drag me towards where I know the open sea is, and my arms and hands already ache from trying to power through the water.

I hear cries of outrage and consider turning back if only to tell the Wessex raiders what I think of them, but I don't. This'll be hard enough as it is without fear that they're coming after me. A splash of something close by has me turning my head, but whatever it was has already sunk below the waterline. I can't imagine it was a spear. Maybe they're picking up stones or sticks. Quickly, I dismiss it. They're too far away to hit me, or so I hope.

Brute's head is far above the surface, whereas I wallow much closer to the top of the water. I'm so low down I can't truly see the ship any more, although I can hear splashing coming from my left. Uor or Oswy, I assume. I spare a thought for them. They're both big men, tall and with muscle and fat covering them. It'll be hard going in the water, even more so for Uor who I know is wounded. None of us trains for swimming. We only know how to kill and stay alive.

The sound of something coming from behind, and I understand that the Wessex warriors haven't given up quite as easily as I'd like them to have done. I try to hurry my strokes, and kick harder with my legs, but I'm exhausted. I hope they don't have a ship. Maybe they merely mean to chase us across the River Thames. Perhaps they think of taking the fight to Mercia's shore.

I kick again, only for a wave of grey-looking water to cover my head so that I see only darkness and not the brightness of the sunlight. I start to choke, for all I didn't realise I'd swallowed anything. Flailing, aware that Brute might carry on without me, I kick out and upwards, surfacing in a great gout of water, reaching for Brute. I need to take a breath in, but first, I need to hack up all the water I've swallowed.

My hand fumbles for Brute's comforting presence, even as I choke, somehow almost managing to descend below the waterline once more. I still can't take a decent breath. Panic grips me. I can't die here. I won't bloody drown. Only then, my hand finally grabs something, and I feel Brute's strength, as I pitch upwards once more. Gripping his side tightly, I manage to cough the water from my mouth and take in an unsteady breath. I hack again while his powerful legs carry me onwards. I try not to hold him too tightly. I don't want to plunge us both beneath the water, but I feel weak from my lack of air, and choking again, I risk a shaky breath.

Should the enemy come at me now, I wouldn't be able to fight them off. I can barely keep my head above the water, let alone fight for my life. Despite having removed my byrnie, the weight of my clothing pulls me down. My boots are filled with water, making my feet feel both too long, and too heavy.

This was such a terrible idea.

And still, I hear something behind me. Are the Wessex warriors chasing us down? I wish I knew. But instead, I release my grip on Brute, and resume my swimming, working harder to keep my head clear of the water. Ahead, I hear the slap of the oars and also the sound of others swimming. The water's bloody cold, and it stinks. I don't want to consider what I might have swallowed. I don't even want to think about what else swims past me because it's not just the odd branch.

Ahead, a raucous cry of ducks assures me that the ship has unsettled the creatures, and then I hear something else. It's voices. I strain to hear them. Is it my fellow warriors or the bloody Wessex warriors? Only, of course, it's none of those things.

'What are you doing?' A voice calls to me, the accent soft, and I look up into confused hazel eyes, squinting against the brightness of the day and the glare from the water.

'Swimming,' I counter, concentrating on where I'm going and not on stopping in the middle of the River Thames. All the same, I can sense the man's attention.

'Swimming where?' he calls to me from the safety of his boat, unease in his voice.

'To Mercia.'

'Then you're Wessex warriors?' His voice is fearful.

'No, Mercians.'

'Then you've been to Wessex?' he counters. I can imagine his perplexed expression although I can't see him. He's shadowed by the sun.

'Yes.'

'And now you return to Mercia?' Even though I'm still swimming, the voice follows me, and I assume he must have turned his boat in pursuit of me.

'Yes, is there anyone behind me?' I ask, realising he'll be able to see much better than I can because he's higher up.

'There's another boat,' he offers, his voice coming from further away so that I know he's turned to look back the way I've swum.

'Filled with warriors.'

'Perhaps, yes. Certainly, they have no nets.' I realise then that's what the man must be. A fisherman, out to collect his catch for the day.

'Then I would get out of the way.'

'Yes, I will. But would you like some assistance? You seem to be alone?'

'Isn't there another boat and more men swimming ahead with their horses?' I huff the words, trying to make sure no water enters my mouth. I didn't expect to be having a bloody conversation in the middle of the River Thames. Silence greets my words, and I assume the man's looking.

'No, you're quite alone. But I think, to the left, there are others standing on the shore. You've drifted a long way with the tide,' he adds conversationally.

'Arse,' I huff. 'Point me in the right direction,' I implore.

'I'll lead the way,' the man confirms. 'They look like warriors. I'd rather be where the warriors are.' He quickly counters, hurrying to get in front of me, as he turns me almost a quarter of the way around, his boat only just big enough for him. It's not at all a trading vessel or as large as one of the Viking raider ships. I grip Brute and redirect him as well, pulling him to follow the boat.

'You could have let me have a lift?' I shout, head high above the water, but either the man doesn't hear me, or he doesn't want to, as he continues to paddle just ahead. I redouble my efforts. My arms are so tired, my hands as well, and if I swallow any more water, I might not need to drink for a week.

Slowly, far too slowly for my liking, I follow the boat. It's harder now. I can feel the pull of the current again, and I realise that I must have been dragged by it when I went under the water. Perhaps we timed our journey wrong, after all, not that we had much choice. In the end.

When I'm just considering calling to the man and begging him to help me, I hear the raised voices of my fellow warriors, Wulfheard most prominent among them.

'Icel, hurry up. The ealdorman needs you,' he bellows. Beside me, Brute surges to his hooves, and I quickly follow on.

'My thanks,' I call to the fisherman. He doesn't stop his rowing, and I admire him being able to direct his boat against the current all alone.

'I didn't really want to catch a horse and a

drenched warrior today,' he calls to me, already moving away. I turn, and glower over the river, where I can't see the Wessex warriors on the far side of the River Thames, but I can imagine them well enough.

'We were followed,' I huff to Oswy, as he offers me his hand to escape the last muddy reaches of the riverbank because, otherwise, I'll be going backwards, into the river water. Even now, in sight of land, my exhaustion is impossible to counter.

'They've turned back,' Oswy informs me, his words slow, as though it's an effort to talk. His face is pale, and his lips a little blue. The wind is stronger than on the other bank. I can feel the chill starting to seep into me as I drip onto the mud, sucking in huge breaths now that I can be assured I won't swallow half the bloody River Thames.

'We need a fire,' I urge anyone who might be listening, taking in the state of the rest of the Mercians, but it seems someone has thought of that. As I finally crest the bank, I smell damp wood and hasten to it. I pass where the ship has been pulled clear from the water and wince at the bloody marks over its dripping sides. Brute is ahead of me as I hurry to the spluttering fire, my eyes taking in all around me. Lord Coenwulf is in one piece, moaning softly. He must be in pain after moving him. But it's Ealdorman

Ælfstan who concerns me. If I thought Oswy's face was pale and his lips were blue, then that's nothing compared to the ealdorman, and he wasn't even in the water.

His face lacks all colour, and although they've wrapped him in as many dry cloaks as they can find, he's still cold to the touch. They've laid him on his front, head turned towards the fire, no doubt so I can get to his wound without disturbing him further. Maneca is slumped beside him, and while the horses have taken themselves off out of the wind, the Mercians are too fatigued to do anything yet. Whoever made the fire has done better than the rest of them.

Hastily, I pull my boots from my feet, a great gout of water pooling onto the muddy ground, and then my trews and tunic as well, which are sopping and stink of river water. The burn marks on my left leg flash redly against my corpse-cold flesh. Most of the others have done the same, and then pulled their cloaks or whatever dry clothes they have around themselves. If we get attacked now, we'll all be dead, divested of our weapons and defences, but it's either that or we'll allow the chill into our bodies. We have some small protection against the wind from a collection of trees at our backs, which are no doubt responsible for the firewood as well, but it's far from the safety of a ditch and palisade. I just hope that the Wessex warriors have truly returned to their side of the River Thames, or we'll have made it home to Mercia only to die here.

'Here.' Landwine brings me the sack of supplies that I sent in the ship, his single word filled with fatigue, and I fumble to undo the cord that seals it. 'Let me.' He quickly takes it back and then returns it to me. I realise then that the fire's been started by Brother Eadgar. Having journeyed in the ship, he's cold from the wind, but not from the water. His donkey is safe as well. The knowledge brings a tired smile to my lips.

'Water's on the fire,' he offers, but I know it'll take time to warm, especially with the snap of the green wood, which is all that's available. Anything else will have been taken by the locals.

'We need hot food as well,' I advise him, raising my voice so that Brother Eadgar can hear. I'm aware that many of the men are beyond doing anything, unless they had the comfort of making the journey above the water. Wulfheard hasn't yet made his way to the fireside. He must be checking the men or assuring himself that the enemy isn't coming. I don't know, but with my cloak swirled around my shoulders, also dry from the ship, I make my way to the ealdorman's side.

I can hear soft words from his lips, and I bend close, eager to hear what he's saying. But the words are too quiet against the force of the wind. I busy myself, trying to determine what to do next. We've got him over the River Thames, but that was only half of the battle. Now I need to do what I can to seal the wound properly and safeguard it from the wound rot. And I need to ensure that Lord Coenwulf is well enough to travel as well.

I banish such thoughts from my mind. Concentrate only on what needs to be done as my fellow warriors make themselves busy drying off the horses, preparing food, and just trying to get warm again.

We've hardly bathed ourselves in great glory, but we are all, apart from three of my comrades, once more on Mercian soil. I peer over the water, looking at Wessex. The Viking raiders are welcome to it.

25

It's taken us a long time to get Lord Coenwulf home to Kingsholm. But, during that time, he's learned to get around much more easily, with a handy curved branch helping him as he hobbles when forced to walk anywhere. I hold out half a hope that he might be able to walk without a limp, although I keep that to myself. I think it's better if Coenwulf doesn't believe there's a possibility of that happening. Then, it will come as a surprise should it happen, as opposed to being expected.

Ealdorman Ælfstan has also recovered from his wound, although, on the banks of the River Thames, it was touch and go for a few days. While I vomited, no doubt thanks to whatever I swallowed from the river, Ælfstan too struggled, his skin sheeted in sweat while a fever shook his body and made him cough whenever he moved.

It was a miserable few days, only helped when our fire brought a contingent of King Wiglaf's warriors to our side, come to seek out the cause of the fire, and bringing with them good food and, eventually, a solid cart to transport the sick and wounded. I counted myself amongst that number, the cold having seeped into my body, leaving me shivering and coughing.

We were brought before the king at Londonia, and it was Wulfheard who had to speak for Ealdorman Ælfstan's actions. I'm not sure the king will forgive our abandonment of our post anytime soon, but it was Lord Coenwulf who aroused the most anger from the king. Again, the poor man could hardly argue for himself. I'm sure, when both men are fully healed, that the king will take action against them. For now, the fact we killed so many Viking raiders on the Isle of Sheppey, and Wessex warriors on the far shore of the River Thames, has won us the acclaim of the king. I harbour half a thought that Wiglaf might even have determined that if we could sneak into and out of Kent so easily, that it might just be possible to reclaim Kent from King Ecgberht's grasp as well.

My feeble requests for more honey at Londonia eventually brought some forth, and now I feel much better, once more riding on Brute's back, Wulfheard at my side, Oswy not far behind us. Ealdorman Ælfstan and Coenwulf are still in the cart, wrapped in cloaks, with Ælfstan querulous and foul-tempered. I'm not sure if he fears the king's wrath or whether it's just his weakness that makes him so grumpy. Word has been sent on to Lady Cynehild to assure her of our success in retrieving her husband. The lack of a response niggles at me, but I've not mentioned it to anyone else, not even Edwin.

Are we allies once more? Friends once more? I don't know. I don't hate him. For now, that will have to suffice, but that's perhaps only because I feel the hollow of Frithwine's loss keenly. Frithwine and Garwulf, both dead, both the same age as Edwin and me. Such thoughts plague my dreams, which have been fever-wracked and are now little better.

Added to which, I must also mourn the loss of Æthelmod and Berhthelm. I still hate myself for not realising that Berhthelm perished on the Isle of Sheppey. It seems that I was the only one not to notice. That burns deep inside me. I should be a better man. I call myself a healer, and yet it took me three days to realise one of our number were dead.

'Hail,' the voice calls to us from the open gateway into Kingsholm. I don't recognise the man, but then I'm aware that Lord Coenwulf's warriors were seized and killed by the Viking raiders when they captured Coenwulf. King Wiglaf had little to say of the Viking raiders in Mercia. Yes, they've made some attacks on Mercia during the summer, but it does seem that much of their anger has been directed towards Wessex. While we didn't talk about it, we all held our suspicions. Perhaps, after all, King Ecgberht had chosen an ally poorly, reneging on his promises to them and suffering the ultimate revenge on his kingdom. It would be good to know the truth of events in the kingdom of the East Angles two years ago, but I'm not sure we ever will. Not unless we find someone who survived the battle outside Peterborough, and I don't believe we will.

'Hail,' Wulfheard responds, the pace of Bada not altering at all.

'Who are you?' The next voice is Lord Coenwulf's, and I wince to hear the sharpness of his words from inside the cart. Brother Eadgar rides inside as well. His donkey follows on with the rest of the horses, but he's been spared having to carry the slight man.

'My Lord Coenwulf,' the man offers respectfully. 'My name's Cuthwahl. I'm now in your wife's service.' Lord Coenwulf makes no response, but I can tell, all the same, that he's deeply unhappy.

I also detect a flicker of uncertainty as the man speaks about Lady Cynehild. I grip my reins more tightly, suddenly fearful. Yet the man says nothing further as he opens the gates wide and allows us entry. He doesn't even question who Ealdorman Ælfstan is, and I take that to be a good sign until I hear the shriek of a labouring woman coming from not far away. I turn to the guard, and he shrugs his shoulders, indicating 'what can I do', before hurrying to close the gates once our sorrowful-looking procession is inside. The donkey brays in response to the shriek of the labouring woman, before allowing Brother Eadgar to tend to him after the long journey.

Lord Coenwulf's already trying to get off the cart, a look of fear and worry on his face, which I mirror. Glancing around the tidy estate I last visited with my uncle, I realise that not one single person has come to see their lord returned to them. The sound of monks praying reaches my ears, and I swallow heavily as I dismount and hasten to aid the struggling Coenwulf.

'Here, my lord,' I urge, giving him my shoulder, as he passes me the smooth branch he's been using to aid him in walking.

'Hurry, hurry,' Lord Coenwulf mutters, and I do the best I can. Not that it seems to be enough. At that moment, I hear a door opening and then the delighted cry of a small child. Turning, I catch sight of a tiny, blond-haired child running towards Coenwulf. Behind him comes a woman hurrying to catch the unsteady tottering of the boy. But I don't need to look at Coenwulf to know who it is. This, then, is Coenwulf and Lady Cynehild's firstborn son, confusingly sharing his father's name, Coenwulf.

Edwin has quickly dismounted too, and now he leads his horse and the animal he led, for we still have too many horses and too few men, towards the stable. It seems larger than the last time I was at Kingsholm. Perhaps it's been enlarged.

'Hello, my boy.' Lord Coenwulf's face breaks into a grin as the child wobbles to an unsteady stop in front of him. But if any of us think the boy's pleased to see his father, the child quickly ensures we know it's the horses that attract him. He reaches his small hand up towards Brute, and for a moment, I hold my breath, but Brute merely sniffs the little hand and turns aside. There's no carrot there to be enjoyed. 'How is my lady wife?' Coenwulf asks of the woman, trying to sweep his son into his arms but struggling with his stick. He's let go of me as well, and I worry he'll fall.

'The new child comes.' The woman dips a curtsey, showing no surprise to find her lord restored to her at the head of a host of warriors. It seems then that Lady Cynehild was aware of her husband's safe return from the clutches of the Viking raiders. I realise belatedly that this settlement has lost almost all its warrior men. There will be women and children here who mourn for their lost husbands and fathers. That, no doubt, accounts for the subdued atmosphere. 'Is Icel here?' she then asks, and I turn from tending to Brute in surprise. Perhaps she'd been told what I look like, for I find her staring at me. 'Theodore and Gaya have asked for you,' she continues by way of an explanation. 'They're in there.' She points back the way she's come, which I realise isn't actually the great hall. 'You should perhaps wipe the muck from your face,' she suggests as an afterthought, and I hear Oswy chuckle. Damn him.

'I'll take your horse,' Edwin quickly interjects, meeting my eyes as he takes Brute's reins, as well as the two animals he already controls. Worry tugs at me. Why do they ask for me? What's happening in the birthing room?

'My thanks,' I reply, striding towards one of the water barrels into which I dunk my head, only to shiver at the coldness of the water. I run my hand over my face and down my chin, but it's all too hairy and in need of some attention. I cough away the coldness of the water, and it sets off a long series of hacking. I should have given it more thought before I did so.

The news that I'll see Gaya and Theodore cheers me, and yet a tendril of fear shivers through me. My eye catches the pink healing mark along my arm. Just another reminder of how long it's taken us to get back from the River Thames. Lord Coenwulf has been missing from Kingsholm for months.

Opening the door into the smaller building, I'm forced to lower my head to not brush it against the door lintel. A woman stands to prevent my entry, only for Theodore's musical voice to call out.

'Icel, it is good to see you.' I meet his familiar green eyes and hope to find a sparkle of delight in them, but they're shadowed by worry. Ahead, a wicker screen blocks the view of the rest of the building, and so I hasten to Theodore's side, where he's using a table to cut and prepare herbs.

'It's good to see you.' I smile quickly. He nods, his long hair falling over one shoulder as he does so.

'It is, yes. But I fear you've come too late.'

'Too late?' I listen to the sounds of effort coming from behind the screen. 'This child is not born yet?' I ask, just to be sure.

'No, it's not. But the lady's been labouring for upwards of a day now. It's her second child. The birth should be easier. I am fearful.' At these words, an iron weight settles in my stomach. I retrieved Lord Coenwulf for Lady Cynehild. I did it more for her than for him. If he planned to forge an alliance with our enemy, then he should be damned, as I fear King Wiglaf might well do, in time. But I owed Lady Cynehild.

'Can nothing be done?' I ask hurriedly.

'We do all we can for her. The child is large, and she's been in much pain throughout her pregnancy. Gaya is not hopeful.'

'Not hopeful of what?' I demand to know, my eyes focused on Theodore's familiar eyes.

'On the survival of either of them,' Theodore mouths sadly. I look at what he's doing, look only at his busy hands, the green of the herbs bright against the black of his skin.

'Then I was too late.'

'No, it is the bastards who stole her husband. Along with it, they stole her hope and joy. Not even the news that he has been found could rouse her. It has been a long and difficult few months for her. She even finds little joy in young Coenwulf. She should, perhaps, not have been so keen to carry another child as quickly after the first.'

'We must do something,' I urge him, trying to think of ways I've seen Wynflæd assist the labouring women of Tamworth.

'We have been doing so, my friend, we have,' Theodore assures me. 'Sometimes, it is simply not enough.'

'I should inform Lord Coenwulf.' This will break him, I'm sure of it, in a way that the Viking raiders and their weapons never could.

'He will have a child to remember her by.' Theodore's words are perhaps meant kindly, but they make me shudder. 'Be quick. She wishes to speak with you,' Theodore urges me.

'With me? Not with her husband?'

'No, my young friend, with you.' I turn aside, almost falling over my feet in the darkness, and a feeble moan reaches my ears. Quickly, I yank open the doorway, stumbling into Coenwulf, where he stands. I imagine he waits for news of his wife.

'Icel, how is my lady wife? Might I go and see her?' His words are filled with adoration and worry mixed with contrition for being away for so long.

'I must speak with you first,' I advise him, and his joyful face, only just clear of all the bruises that once marked it, falls abruptly.

'What is it? Is she well? Is the child well?'

I don't want to have this conversation here, but Lord Coenwulf seems reluctant to move aside, and so I stop trying to take him elsewhere and face him. Behind us, the warriors and horses are quickly dispersing, most to the hall for food and drink. We deserve it after all this time on the road, but it seems my tasks aren't yet at an end.

'I've spoken with Theodore, the healer,' I begin reluctantly.

'Yes, yes, I know who he is.'

'He informs me that the child has been trying to make its way into this world for a very long time. It should have arrived by now. Lady Cynehild is weakening, and there's no sign of the child being born. Not yet.' His eyes flicker from my face to the closed doorway. I consider what he sees as he stares that way. Did he witness the birth of his first son? I don't know.

'Then it will be soon?' he asks, and I realise he doesn't understand.

'My lord, the second child should be quicker than the first, Theodore informs me. He's fearful that your wife, and your child, may not survive the ordeal.' It hurts to say those words. It hurts even more to see the confusion on Lord Coenwulf's face.

'I don't understand,' he counters, the words of denial almost too quick.

'I don't either, but Theodore bid me to speak with you, and I've done so.' I think he'll fall as he wavers on his crutch.

'I would see her.'

'Of course.' I open the door for him. The woman attendant stands but then bows her head sorrowfully and allows us both to enter. From behind the screens, I can hear Gaya's soft voice, although I can't decipher the words that are being spoken. It smells of blood and garlic in the room, and I grimace, even as Lord Coenwulf stops ahead of me. I almost collide with him.

'What are you doing?' he demands angrily as I put out my hand to steady him.

'Lady Cynehild wishes to speak with me,' I inform him, wincing at the fury in his eyes.

'Why you? What are you to my wife?'

'I...' I start, and then shake my head. 'I don't rightly know, my lord, but she bid me rescue you, and I did all I could to ensure that was done. Perhaps she merely wishes to express her thanks.'

'No,' Lord Coenwulf counters. 'She's not to be disturbed, and you won't speak to her.' I hear in his voice the stubbornness that categorised our first meeting before he apologised to me on the instructions of his sister. The thought of Lady Ælflæd fills me with longing, but she's another man's wife. It doesn't matter how much I might yearn for her. Nothing will ever happen.

'My lord.' Theodore is at my side so swiftly I'm unaware of him moving. 'Don't deny your lady wife what might well be her final wish.' The words are harsh, although they're spoken softly. For a moment, I think Coenwulf might slap Theodore aside, but instead, he bows his head and, shaking loose my hand that steadies him, indicates I should go ahead.

I walk around the wicker screen uneasily. I really don't need to see Lady Cynehild in such a state, but rather than seeing her all sweaty and labouring with the birthing pangs, she's almost still on the bed, her eyes lacking focus. Gaya watches my approach with a regretful face. I can see she's as exhausted as Lady Cynehild.

'Who is it?' Lady Cynehild's voice is less than a whisper. I take a shaky breath before replying.

'It's Icel, my lady,' Gaya responds for me.

'Then my husband is here?' This seems to spark a response from Cynehild, but although her hands move over her expanded belly, she doesn't raise her head from where it rests on a pile of pillows.

'He is, yes. Would you like to see him?' I interject quickly, thinking that perhaps, after all, it's Coenwulf that Cynehild wishes to be with her.

'In a moment, yes.' I hear those words more easily. 'First, Icel, I would speak to you. Come closer, please.' I do as she says, brushing past Gaya who reaches out and squeezes my arm, as though offering her support, although she chooses my wounded arm and I wince at the reminder. Lady Cynehild wears a thin dress, but her lower body has been covered by a linen. All the same, the scent of blood is ripe in the air. If I were a hound, I'd know that I'd found my wounded prey. I feel a tear trickle from the corner of my eye and hastily wipe it away.

Lady Cynehild offers me her hand, and I grip it loosely. I can feel the shuddering of her heart through her hand. Her dull eyes seek me out.

'You rescued him for me?'

'I did my lady, yes. Alas, he has a wounded leg, but I hope he'll have no limp in time.'

'Then you have my thanks, Icel.' A soft moan leaves her mouth, and I watch as her belly ripples with a birthing pang, but it's feeble, although I smell fresh blood. I look at Gaya, and she's busy, having pulled the sheet aside. I don't look more closely.

'Then you've fulfilled a bargain I made long ago with your uncle.'

'My lady?' The mention of my uncle perplexes me, although I do catch sight of the silver object, in the shape of an eagle, around her neck that my uncle bid me give her as he lay dying.

'Yes, Icel, I know this is confusing.' She winces again, and now Gaya speaks.

'My lady, I think the child is coming after all. Next time you feel it, push with all you have. Icel, hold her hand.' The robustness of Gaya's words have Cynehild and me sharing a mutual look of reproach.

'I'm too tired,' Lady Cynehild murmurs.

'No, you're not,' Gaya counters forcefully. 'If you are, take some of Icel's strength. Hold his hand and take it from him.' I've never heard of such an idea before, but perhaps this is what Cynehild needs to hear.

'Here, my lady, you can take all that I have.' A

sudden brightening of her eye assures me that she derives comfort from that. I think of Wynflæd's assertion that believing something can be more powerful than the potion offered.

'Get my husband,' Lady Cynehild urges, as she grips my hand so tightly I feel another tear trickle down my cheek. Cynehild strains, her body tense, and I feel her blood thrumming through her hand as she holds on to me as though her life depends on it. I watch her, not Gaya, and turn my thoughts to her, even offering a simple prayer to God that she'll survive this after all. Wynflæd isn't above asking God for assistance. With a wry smirk, she's often told me she'll do whatever she must.

And yet, Lady Cynehild once more deflates against her sheets, and my fear returns all over again. I turn to Gaya, but she's engrossed in what she's doing. I see Lord Coenwulf, with Theodore assisting him, standing to the other side of the bed.

'Once more, my lady,' she calls, and this time, Lady Cynehild sits almost upright, her face etched in pain, her mouth open in a gasp of agony and the grip on my hand is somehow even tighter. And then I hear a sound I didn't think to hear, the shrill cry of a newborn babe.

'The boy is here,' Gaya announces triumphantly.

Theodore has entered the secluded area of the room, and now he's busily assisting Gaya, but my eyes are on Lady Cynehild. She sags back against the pillows while Lord Coenwulf, his eyes shining with joy, reaches over to plant a kiss on her sweaty forehead. Quickly, he bustles after his newborn son, but I stay with Cynehild. She's done it, despite all the warnings to the contrary, and yet Gaya doesn't wear a look of joy, while Theodore and Coenwulf have disappeared. Perhaps Theodore has seen this before. Maybe he knows it's not a time of great joy. I think of my mother. I think of what she endured to bring me into this world.

Lady Cynehild's grip on my hand is much weaker now, almost a flutter of a butterfly. But I'm fearful, all the same.

'Icel.' Her words are little more than an exhalation.

'My lady,' I respond. I'm still unsure why she wants me at her side and not her husband. He should be the one with his wife, but no one says anything, and Gaya is too busy tending to Lady Cynehild to send me away.

'As I was saying, you've fulfilled a bargain I made long ago with your uncle.' Her words are forced through pale lips.

'What was the bargain?' I demand to know, my voice too loud, so that I lower it, my eyes on the chain at her neck.

'You must take it from me.' She smiles sadly. 'It is your birthright.'

'My lady?' I don't understand what she's saying to me. If it's my birthright, then why does she have it? Why did my uncle demand I give it to her and not simply tell me himself?

'But first, Icel, I must have your oath on my life that you'll care for my sons and ensure they're protected, always, from the kings of Mercia and from their father's fear of becoming who he should be.'

I shake my head. I don't understand any of this, and she's talking as though she's going to die.

'My lady. You'll be well now. The child is born.' I look to Gaya for confirmation, but all I see are bloody rags, and more, Lady Cynehild's belly heaves once more and is still, but Gaya is not. Worry touches her face, and she smiles sadly at me, catching my attention. 'My lady?' I begin, but Cynehild's grip is suddenly tight, too tight, an urgency in the rising and falling of her chest. Her words come quickly now.

'Icel, you're the son of King Beornwulf. You should be king, but you're not, and I must have your oath that you'll make my sons king one day. They must have their birthright restored to them. It's only right. You can tell no one who you are, but you must protect my sons, from this moment, until your death.'

I shake my head, unable to absorb all that she says. I can't be whom she says I am. I'm sure King Beornwulf would have claimed me as his son. I'm sure my uncle would have told me.

'Your oath, Icel, I would have it.' There's iron in Cynehild's voice, and a rich scent of metal in the air. She's bleeding to death, and yet she would sooner exact this oath from me than have her husband and son at her side. She's not even gazed upon the new child.

I shake my head. I want to deny it.

'The eagle, at my neck. It's yours, given to your mother. It proves who you are and what you are. Your uncle took it at her death.' A rictus grin touches her lips. 'And now I'll give it to you, on my death, and you'll give me your oath that you'll protect my sons. I've kept your secret, Icel. I've kept you safe, and now you must repay that.'

I don't know what to say. My head's spinning with the smell of blood and herbs, the scent of sweat and pain, and yet somehow, it all makes sense. I watch her, tears streaming down my face, as her other hand reaches up and fumbles with the thong around her neck. She can't retrieve it alone, so I reach over, scrabbling, and release the knot and place it into her hand. Her fingers curl around the emblem.

'Your oath, Icel.'

I bow my head. 'You have my oath that I'll protect your sons, Coenwulf and...' I realise the new babe has no name.

'Coelwulf, he's to be named Coelwulf,' Lady Cynehild provides. I understand then that she's named her sons after the kings who were Lord Coenwulf's forebears. She's given them the names of previous kings. She's serious in her demands that I make her sons king in the future. I swallow heavily.

'You have my oath that I'll protect your sons, Coenwulf and Coelwulf, with my life, until their death, or mine.'

'Thank you,' Lady Cynehild murmurs, dropping the solid object into my hands. Its weight is an unwelcome reminder of the loss of my uncle, but now it brings much, much more besides.

The cry of the new child seems to come from far away as a faint smile touches Lady Cynehild's lips. I sit beside her, wondering where her husband is and why only Gaya and I keep a guard over Cynehild as her chest slowly stills. In the distance, I hear the chanting of the monks, the sounds of men calling one to another, the cry of a child wailing from some fresh hurt, but inside the room, there's nothing but silence. Neither Gaya nor I move, and Cynehild is entirely still. The life has fled her, and tears stream unheeded down my dirty and grizzled cheeks.

She told me who I am and what I am, and yet, in almost the same breath, she took it all away from me as well.

'Come, Icel, you should leave.' Gaya's words break into my reverie.

'What?' I say, unaware I grip the eagle so tightly in my hand that my knuckles are white. I can feel it pressing into the scar I already own on my palm.

'You should leave,' she repeats. 'Lord Coenwulf will return shortly.' I nod again and stumble to my feet, but not before gazing down at Lady Cynehild once more.

She looks fragile, and I'm grateful that Gaya has covered her and as much of the blood as possible, but the smell is unmissable. At that moment, I appreciate, more than ever before in my life, that while men fight Mercia's enemies on the slaughter field, the women of Mercia have to fight an even more insidious threat, and they must do so in their own bedchambers.

26

Outside once more, I stumble into the daylight. Everything has changed, but equally, nothing has. I consider that I'm still the man who entered the birthing chamber, and yet I'm no longer sure that I am.

'Icel,' Edwin's voice calls to me, and I see him beckoning to me from the open doorway of the main hall. Laughter spills from inside, but I shake my head. I need to be alone. I can't be the one to carry the news of Lady Cynehild's death when I can hear Lord Coenwulf raising a toast to his safe return and new son. I spare a thought for him. When his father died, he was a sullen creature; quick to anger and quicker to make snap decisions. The death of his wife will surely make him the same.

Perhaps I should be the one to tell him. While he offers my fellow warriors ale and mead, his wife lies dead, his children motherless. Who, I consider, will feed the babe? Who will become this child's foster mother, just as Edwin's mother was to me?

Moodily, I stride towards the stable. These aren't my concerns. I have a heavier weight on my shoulder.

Lady Cynehild told me the truth of my birth which I've always longed to hear, but now I'm far from as sure I want to comprehend it. I can do nothing with the knowledge, and if others know of it, then I could be in danger. King Wiglaf won't take kindly to knowing that I have a claim to Mercia's kingship. Lord Wigmund will certainly refute it, as will his mother. And then I pause in my stride, and think of Lady Ælflæd.

I feel my forehead furrow and, for a moment, turn back, wanting to ask Lady Cynehild about a sudden suspicion. But of course, I can't ask her. She's beyond caring. I think back to that day in the churchyard at Budworth when Lady Ælflæd's eyes focused on my mother's grave. There was something there that made her want to leave my side immediately. Is there something there that points to my parentage?

Hastily, I resume my path to Brute's side. At least, I think he hasn't changed. He meets me with a kick of the stable door and a shake of his head. I reach over and run my hands over his long black and white nose.

'Hello boy,' I speak softly. He stills under my touch. I consider mounting up and riding from this place. But where would I go, and what would I do when I got there? If I headed for Tamworth, I'd have to tackle the king's wife and the king's son, while the king is in Londonia, knowing, as I do now, that I could be king in place of King Wiglaf. If I headed for Budworth, I'd have to face the knowledge that my uncle knew who I was and did nothing about it. What other unwelcome secrets might I learn if I spent more than a night in Budworth?

The secret of my father is revealed to me, and suddenly, I have to reorder all my thoughts about King Beornwulf once more. As a small child, I enjoyed his attention, not understanding what it was all about. I didn't enjoy the attention of his wife, and now I comprehend why. I was the child she couldn't give her husband, and yet proof that he was capable of fathering a son. No wonder she was so conflicted about me when she was queen and he was king.

But King Beornwulf made so many mistakes and

left Mercia weak. If that's my birthright, then I don't want it. King Wiglaf has done a great deal to make Mercia strong once more. My father, it seems, for all his pretensions, was a failure. I don't want to be associated with him or his disastrous reign.

But, I am his son. That knowledge weighs on me. The East Anglian warrior told me I should be the commander of King Wiglaf's household warriors, as my uncle was before me. I declined to become so. What would he do if he knew who I really was? Would he follow me? Would he demand to make me king? I'm no one. Just a warrior of Mercia, a lord of Mercia through my mother's family and the landholdings at Budworth. But I'm nothing else.

Slowly, I open my hands and stare down at the eagle etched in silver. It's a beautiful piece. I should have realised when my uncle gave it to me just how valuable it was. I should have asked him more questions, and Lady Cynehild, rather than be grateful just to fulfil my uncle's dying request and try to forget it.

My uncle knew who I was, I realise. Why didn't he pursue my claim to the kingship on the death of King Beornwulf, on the death of King Ludica? Why did he allow Wiglaf to become king?

And then I shudder. I don't want to be a king. I find it hard enough to give orders. I grieve the men who died on the Isle of Sheppey. I couldn't give the order to ride into battle against the men of Wessex or the Viking raiders. I don't want to be a king. My uncle had the right to it, after all. But why, then, did Lady Cynehild feel the urge to inform me as she lay dying? Why did she tell me something I could happily have never known?

The words of the oath she made me swear come back into my mind.

She understands that her sons should wear Mercia's warrior helm. She accepts they should be king in the future. And she knows that her husband will never make good on that claim. She also appreciates that the children of her sister by marriage – Lady Ælflæd, should she have children – will expect to be the next generation of æthelings; that the future of Mercia's kingship lies with her blood.

I shake my head again, one hand on Brute's nose, the other holding on to the charm.

Lady Cynehild has made sure of my loyalty, set me the task of countering the claim of Lady Ælflæd, and I could curse her for it. There was no need for me to know. Lady Cynehild could have exacted any oath she liked from me, and I'd have done as she asked. I went to Wessex in her name to retrieve her husband. This is cruelty, and if she wasn't already dead, I could kill her for doing this to me.

I grip the silver eagle in my hand. What should I do with it? It clearly means something to some people, but are those people now all dead? My mother, my father, my uncle and now Lady Cynehild? Or are there others who might yet know of its importance? Does Lady Ælflæd know what it signifies, or does she merely suspect from what she witnessed at my mother's gravesite? I grit my teeth. I'd thought to return to Kingsholm with Lord Coenwulf, and have only to think about my grief for the men who died retrieving him, but there's now much more to those feelings than just grief.

'Icel.' Hearing my name rouses me from my feelings of anger, and hastily, I thrust the silver eagle into the money pouch that hangs at my side, which more often has a wad of moss or something with healing properties than actual money in it. I turn to face Wulfheard. Sorrow touches his cheeks. The news of Lady Cynehild's death must be well known by now.

'Lord Coenwulf has bid everyone to attend prayers in the church, for the death of his wife.'

I nod and turn to follow him, but Wulfheard stops me, his hand on my arm.

'What did the lady want you for?' he asks and, my

thoughts scrambling, I try to think of something to say that isn't the truth.

'To thank us for returning her husband from the clutches of the Viking raiders on the Isle of Sheppey,' I offer, trying and failing to find a tight smile for my lips. He holds my gaze for a moment too long, and I consider if Wulfheard knows the truth of my parentage. Perhaps it's long been suspected, or maybe it hasn't.

'I assured Ealdorman Ælfstan that's all it would be,' Wulfheard nods, accepting my excuse easily. 'It's a sad day,' he continues. 'A birth and a death aren't the most auspicious,' he muses as we emerge into the daylight once more. I can see where the people of Kingsholm are making their way to the church, the door wide open as they stream inside, many wailing for the loss of their lady. I look towards the building in which Lady Cynehild's body must lie. There's little activity there. Perhaps Gaya works to prepare the body for burial. Maybe one of the monks keeps her company before she can be taken to the church and buried in the grounds of the building.

'It is, yes. I always thought the lady didn't like me, but I was wrong, it seems,' is all I can say. I could say much else besides, but I need to keep my true feelings locked up tight inside of me.

'Lady Ælflæd will mourn her sister,' Wulfheard says conversationally. 'Especially as we have news that she's with child as well.' I nod, unsure how to respond to any of his questions. Overhead, I hear the shriek of an eagle, and glimpse it as a thin line against the outline of the sun. I can't help but find significance in it, and I wish I didn't. The eagle charm, the knowledge as to who my father was, of who I am. I don't want it.

I'm grateful to enter the church and allow the silence to envelop me, and smother my thoughts.

At the front of the church, the monks have gathered, all six of them, although I notice that Brother Eadgar has joined them, while the priest is already beginning the words of the Mass. I catch sight of Lord Coenwulf being helped into a seat at the front of the church, Ealdorman Ælfstan at his side. There's no sign of either of his sons, Coenwulf or Coelwulf. I hope the babe will live. It would be a cruel irony if the mother died only to be followed by the son, but that's all the thought I give to the child I didn't even see when he came into the world, my focus too much on Lady Cynehild.

I allow the priest's words to distract me from my muddled thoughts, focusing only on the familiar rhythm of service, murmuring responses when I need to. We leave the church in a sullen group, my fellow warriors streaming back towards the main hall, but I don't. Instead, I take myself to the wooden steps that lead to the rampart that surrounds Kingsholm, eyes upwards, realising the eagle still hovers there, on the wind, as though witnessing the momentous changes taking place within Kingsholm. Lord Coenwulf's return from Wessex, the birth of Coelwulf, the death of Lady Cynehild, and, of course, the revelation as to my true identity.

This then is the home of a king of Mercia, the family home of both previous kings Coenwulf and Coelwulf, the first of their names. And now two small children sharing those names live behind its walls, and I'm oath-bound to protect them. The thought weighs on me. I'm a lord of Mercia, a warrior of Mercia. An eagle of Mercia. I'm not a father to Mercia's children, and perhaps now, I never want to be. The thought of killing a woman through the act of creating a child is a terrible tragedy. I slaughtered my mother, although Wynflæd would assure me it wasn't my fault. And now, small Coelwulf has done the same to his mother. It'll be a terrible burden for the child to carry when he's old enough to understand what it means.

For a moment, I realise how alike Coelwulf and I

might be. But he's a babe, and I'm a man, and before he can become a man, I must continue my fight for Mercia against her enemies, or else, regardless of any oath laid on me by Lady Cynehild, there might be no Mercia for either of her sons to rule, or indeed, for me not to rule.

HISTORICAL NOTES

Look at any non-fiction book for this period, and you might be surprised by the lack of information about events in Saxon England. The A and E recensions of the *Anglo-Saxon Chronicle* (ASC) inform us under 835 (although this date has been corrected by historians and manuscript historians from 833, and I've kept the original date) that, 'Here heathen men raided across Sheppey' – '*Her hepne men oferhergeadon Sceapige*'. The A version is taken to be the oldest version of the ASC that has survived, and possibly the 'original' version, although this is a complex subject to examine in a few words (please see Pauline Stafford's new book for a fascinating account of how the ASC was written,

and how it has survived). The E recension is very
much a copy of the A version.

Perhaps we shouldn't be surprised about the lack
of information. The ASC was conceived during the
reign of King Alfred, King Ecgberht of Wessex's
grandson, and so this entry is far from contemporary
(written forty or fifty years after the events). The lack
of information about anywhere else in Saxon England at this time should be taken to reveal the in-
herent Wessex bias in one of our most important
sources for the period. Equally, we should be mindful
that this period in the 800s falls in between two of
our most important sources, Bede's *Ecclesiastical His-
tory of the English People* written in the 730s, and the
ASC, begun at some point during Alfred's reign, and
normally determined to have at least been started by
890 at the latest.

We're not told of events in Mercia, East Anglia,
Northumbria or Kent, either in the ASC or elsewhere. There's one surviving Mercian charter from
833, which shows King Wiglaf confirming a grant of
privileges and land to the Bishop of Crowland, but
this is deemed to be suspect and may well be a later
forgery from after the Conquest of 1066, a time when
the great monasteries were desperate to prove their
claim to land following the upheaval of the Con-

quest, and were not above using forged documents to do so. Historians can often tell when charters are forged because of errors in the witness list, and often these forgeries are based on other charters, and the wording can be determined to be a copy.

This, then, isn't a great deal to go on. Events for later years in Wessex are better served. But that doesn't mean that nothing was happening during these years. Certainly, in the coming years, the Viking raiders would begin to become more problematic. And for now, we know that Wiglaf was Mercia's king, and Ecgberht was in Wessex, his son in Kent, and Athelstan was king of the East Angles. The rest is, of course, purely fiction.

While writing this book, I was lucky enough to read *Winters in the World*, a fabulous book about the Saxon calendar by Eleanor Parker. You may find old words used by the Saxons for the month of the year, as described by Bede and others throughout the text. Haligmonað means holy month, although Haefest-monað might also have been used – harvest month. October was named Winterfylleð, November Blot-monað and Geola might have been used for December and January, the month or festival around the winter solstice. Previously, I had understood that the Saxons only truly acknowledged summer and winter, but spring and autumn/fall were being adopted by the years that the *Eagle of Mercia Chronicles* takes place. Interestingly for those in the UK/US, fall is not an Amercianism but rather reflects the point at which much of North America was colonised by the British. While in Britain, the term autumn came to predominate, in the US, it was fall. Prior to that, both terms would have been used interchangeably in the UK, specifically in England.

The medical remedies are taken from *Anglo-Saxon Medicine* by M. L. Cameron, a fascinating look at the Saxon Leechbooks and how much of the medicine offered at this period (written in the medical texts) can be seen to have been far more effective than we might think. I have adopted the idea that there was a desire to collate this information in one place for my healers. At some point, this is how the Leechbooks came into being. Interestingly, there is a great deal of research being done on these Saxon remedies, and while they might once have been dismissed as little more than futile attempts to treat the wounded and sick, it is becoming increasingly evident that many of these treatments did indeed have sound logic and understanding behind them.

Icel will return, soon. Thank you for embracing my young healer/warrior.

ACKNOWLEDGMENTS

As ever, a huge thank you to my editor, Caroline, my proofreader, Shirley, and my copy editor, Ross, for catching all my pesky mistakes. And to the whole Boldwood Books team. It is amazing to watch the company go from strength to strength.

I'd also like to thank my 'usual' gang of supporters for keeping me sane while I bash away at the keyboard, EP, CS, ST, AM, JT, JS, JC and MC, as well as AP and MP.

Huge thanks to my readers for embracing young Icel, and taking the time to read and review the books. Please don't stop. Icel will return. Soon.

MORE FROM MJ PORTER

We hope you enjoyed reading *Eagle of Mercia*. If you did, please leave a review.

If you'd like to gift a copy, this book is also available as an ebook, hardback, paperback, digital audio download and audiobook CD.

Sign up to MJ Porter's mailing list for news, competitions and updates on future books.

https://bit.ly/MJPorterNews

Explore the rest of the action-packed **Eagle of Mercia Chronicles** series from MJ Porter...

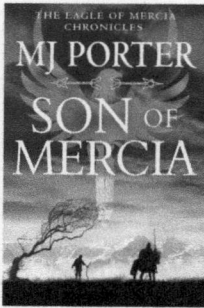

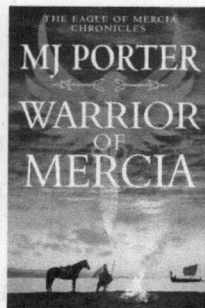

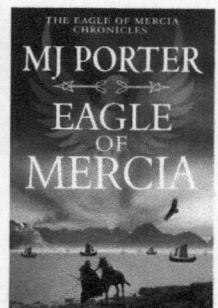

ABOUT THE AUTHOR

MJ Porter is the author of many historical novels set predominantly in Seventh to Eleventh-Century England, and in Viking Age Denmark. Raised in the shadow of a building that was believed to house the bones of long-dead Kings of Mercia, meant that the author's writing destiny was set.

Visit MJ's website: www.mjporterauthor.com

Follow MJ on social media:

twitter.com/coloursofunison
instagram.com/m_j_porter
bookbub.com/authors/mj-porter

Boldwood

Boldwood Books is an award-winning fiction publishing company seeking out the best stories from around the world.

Find out more at www.boldwoodbooks.com

Join our reader community for brilliant books, competitions and offers!

Follow us
@BoldwoodBooks
@BookandTonic

Sign up to our weekly deals newsletter

https://bit.ly/BoldwoodBNewsletter

Ingram Content Group UK Ltd.
Milton Keynes UK
UKHW041315010623
422719UK00002B/50

9 781802 807837